RUNNING TO FALL

Also by Kalisha Buckhanon

Speaking of Summer
Solemn
Conception
Upstate

RUNNING TO FALL

A NOVEL

KALISHA BUCKHANON

aalbc.com
AALBC Aspire
An Imprint of AALBC Publishing

Praise for *Speaking of Summer*

"The lives and loves left behind by the women whose names we don't say are shown in this novel."

-*Essence Magazine*

"A riveting read from a young woman who has become a major American storyteller."

-Sapphire, bestselling author of *Push* adapted to the Academy Award-winning film *Precious*

"Lyrical and luscious, *Speaking of Summer* is a literary gift."

-Bernice L. McFadden, NAACP Image Award-winning author of *Book of Harlan* and *Praise Song for the Butterflies*

"A powerful song about what it means to survive as a woman in America."

-Jesmyn Ward, *New York Times* bestselling author of *Salvage the Bones* and *Sing, Unburied, Sing*

"Fiercely astute."

-Tayari Jones, author of Women's Prize for Fiction award-winning *American Marriage* and *Silver Sparrow*

"A culturally crucial literary novel that contains the raw, beating heart of a thriller."

-Jenny Milchman, *USA Today* bestselling author of *The Second Mother* and Mary Higgins Clark Award-winning *Cover of Snow*

"*Speaking of Summer* has everything: beauty, bite, raw truth, nail-biting urgency, and a central mystery that's both timely and timeless."

-Abby Geni, Barnes & Noble Discover Award-winning author of *The Lightkeepers* and *The Wildlands*

"This is a New York story for the ages, the country, the world."

-Colin Channer, Silver Musgrave Medal in Literature Award-winning author of *Passing Through* and *Waiting in Vain*

"A mysterious and haunting tale about the powerlessness of women of color."

-Connie Briscoe, *New York Times* bestselling author of *P.G. County* and *Sisters and Lovers*

"*Speaking of Summer* endures the devastation of loss and embraces the power of love."

-Sandra Jackson-Opuku, author of *The River Where Blood Was Born* and *Hot Johnny and The Women Who Loved Him*

"Buckhanon has written an emotionally packed tale that reveals the fragility of the human experience for a Black woman in urban New York."

-Dr. Brenda Greene for *AALBC*

"Buckhanon unravels a powerful story that examines violence, race and grief."

-*TIME*

"The emotional excavation and centering of Autumn's experience is as crucial to the story as revealing the mystery."
-Publisher's Weekly

"This mysterious novel is well worth the wait."
-O: The Oprah Magazine

"Readers looking for contemporary suspense with a social justice twist will appreciate the storytelling."
-Library Journal

"Buckhanon captures Autumn's frustration at the undervaluing of Black women."
-Booklist

"A powerful story of discovery."
-Buzzfeed

Praise for *Solemn*

"Kalisha Buckhanon has no trouble taking readers into the lives of those we often pass by."
-Patrik Henry Bass for *Essence Magazine*

"Kalisha Buckhanon is a writer of great imagination and boundless empathy... *Solemn* is a haunting story that keeps pages turning until the end."
-Jonathan Odell, critically-acclaimed author of *The Healing*

"Reading this story, I found it difficult (though ridiculously unfair) not to think of Toni Morrison's first novel, *The Bluest Eye*."
-Kim McClarin for *The Washington Post*

"This standout novel is anchored by its vulnerable and brave heroine."
-Tara Betts for *Publisher's Weekly*

"Top-notch literary fiction sending a message about African-American struggles in the 21 st century."
-Library Journal

"Buckhanon crafts a hypnotic tale."
-Kirkus Reviews

"In this lyrical, haunting coming-of-age story, *Solemn* struggles to find identity and a way forward in the face of poverty and disenfranchisement."
-University of Chicago Magazine

"A wise beyond-her-years Mississippi girl's search for self and truth."
-Hello Beautiful

"*Solemn* is a beautifully written, poetic novel."
-Pride Magazine UK

Cover design © 2022 by Kalisha Buckhanon
Inside design: Natalie Stokes-Peters
(On Point Book Design; www.onpointbookdesign.com)

Hardcover: 978-0-9796374-2-1
Paperback: 978-0-9796374-0-7
eBook: 978-0-9796374-1-4
Audiobook: 978-1-7050-8193-8

LCCN: 2022917313
AALBC.com LLC
17401 Commerce Park Blvd
Suite 103-1998
Tampa, FL 33647
(347) 692-2522

Printed in the United States of America
10 9 8 7 6 5 4 3 2 1

This novel is for all the black women presently missing in America. I pray the families, children and friends of my missing sisters find peace, rest and answers one day soon.

Part 1: Denial

FREEZING

We all have times when life freezes us but we don't fall to pieces, when life heats us to the boiling point but we got ice stored in our bones. We can't break or melt. When it's all over, no matter how long since, we flip out these stories of what almost broke us. Sometimes we just let the fine details slip. Other times, we spill the full stories. They are a part of us. Features. No different than hair type and eye color. I've certainly had such times. Many. If I could take just one back, I would freeze in every one of them all over again.

Night. Fall time. High school.

I was in a blackout sleep. I woke up in my room, its pink walls bleeding. A heat glowed under my door—to yank me from my covers, devour me whole, and carry me off into the night. Maybe I watched Poltergeist too many times, so it was all coming true for me now.

Where my walls used to be, something like waterfalls came — blinding bright, ticklish. Smoky wisps curled up near the old black ceiling fan. That ugly, crickety thing always scared me. Only wiry threads had kept it up anyway. The fan started melting away.

It was all coming true.

Smoke circles blew to carousel shapes: the rocking horses, rabbits, bow-tied foxes I had called friends just a few grades and inches back. Beady eyes stared above their zigzag mouths and changing shapes. It looked like all could crash on me, light as a feather or heavy like a long semi. I never felt hot. I remember the cold. It was chilly that night.

Maples and oaks enveloped our whole quiet block, our just average house. Classic and normal Midwest style, reassuring and rich with cool breezes. I braced myself. A tree was supposed to hurl through glass and the plastic we covered windows in for winter. Its branches would come for my neck. That's what the movie showed. I was frozen. A brick in my stomach. My legs concrete. My eyes fixed on my low slanted ceiling. That was the best room ever, a corner one, top of the house, where the roof sloped down.

Blackness returned. I felt a tremble, vibrations from where I couldn't reach or name. I opened my eyes. A gang of fiery dolls ran to me, their arms open wide. These thoughts didn't feel like facts. But they still meant business. All the things I did and wanted to do, everybody and everything in between. I tried to hit one thing to fix my mind onto — so I could unfreeze, then rise.

Maybe the sun would come on, quickly. I'd be in the bathroom to outline my hair, makeup and mood for the day. McDonald's breakfasts would be on the kitchen table, like on my mother's days off, her treat for days not having to go to the cereal plant or housekeeper job or telemarketing office. She had so many jobs…

Maybe I'd be grownup already, and a famous writer, telling this story.

I heard my little brother crying, a light whine. He was two or three then.

Where was my mother? Her voice should've been mixed with her girlfriends, plump warm bodies, with greasepaint faces and cigarette cases they passed us kids dollars from, dollars to go to the store for them with. Gran's room was downstairs. I heard her, I thought. A drumline crashed down the hallway and stairs. Footsteps. Screams too, but more awful than that.

Where was my dog? He should've been coming in or going out the pockmarked chain link fence, wires snagging his tries. He would always make it back in, wait for us under a crooked swing and broken teeter-totter, run through our sheets and dresses on the line, muddying them, turning over the weekend work. But that early October night, I forgot to bring him back in the house. That mutt was always lucky, ever since he rolled up to our yard a half-dead pup and met friendly people.

My mind arose. I can't tell you how it came to me that all this wasn't harmless.

The house was on fire.

It was a Saturday night.

I was fifteen.

By Sunday morning, they got the fire out.

It was supposed to be my birthday. I didn't have birthday presents, a cake, a family, or any recollection of how I saved my life.

But I turned sixteen.

ONE

MARCH 2021

Right around time things started reopening, the late March thaw brought a lifeless girl up to the tail end of the Grayson River, in sight of a younger girl on a bike, after the living girl's Doberman pup raced to the smell of spring rabbits being born. The dead girl delivered a shade to the river and question to the air: "How did a young woman not from around here, headed off to the rest of her life, never show up there or anywhere — but wind up here with us, like this?"

She came the same time the usual spell of sparrows shifted senses and norms, subtracting and adding to the birds. The forensics of bitter cold, marsh plains beat out summer's damaging behavior with the dead. The water took her wig and her nails, but its thirty degrees slowed other thefts. The challenging Midwest winter preserved her brown skin body to grave wax, so it talked more than it would have been able to in other seasons or regions. Answers compiled soon. The later answers were what folks came to tony Grayson, Illinois — population 3,279 — to avoid.

When the text beeped in, Tragedy Powell wasn't really working on the book about her life. She was just keeping the habit, really. She was stuck, sitting in her spare and minimal office, listening to the silence. Scrolling Pinterest home décor one moment, checking for the latest celeb gossip and racial injustice the next. After all, she'd told so many people she was writing a book of her life, so it was mandatory to try. She stared at the last of the words it had taken months to get out of her mind and soul and into what she could finally call a first chapter:

"The house was on fire.

It was a Saturday night.

I was fifteen.

By Sunday morning, they got the fire out.

It was supposed to be my birthday. I didn't have birthday presents, a cake, a family, or any recollection of how I saved my life.

But I turned sixteen."

And that was all she could write before the past became too much to remember, even if she thought her life story would be empowering and inspiring for many other women from harsh backgrounds. After all, she had survived. She could look out to her big yard, circle drive and secluded neighbors across the way or far down a road to know: Her childhood didn't kill her.

She found writing to be lonely and scary so she craved interruption, though she didn't know it. The soft text alert was grace. Her husband's scruffier face, not his public clean-shaven look, was a bubble above a message: *Babe, they found Raven McCoy. End of the river.*

Another text from him jingled soon: *Road's blocked off. Stay in. I'm coming home.*

Tragedy smacked her laptop shut and started a dash down the stairs. Soon, anxiety caught her, so she slowed down. She knew one more careless step could be a broken neck to start a sad final chapter to her young life's story — like a Monday morning heart attack, a shoelace sucked into a treadmill conveyor belt, a choking fit. Her ginger tea with two protein bars breakfast wasn't enough, but she ignored her stomach. She was going to the river now to see for herself.

Victor Powell was on the run, as usual. Tragedy was supposed to be his manager. He was connected to people and things in the know of what everyone else still had to find out. This scoop was more personal. A mere cadaver washed up in such a place where this never happened before. Female. No age, no race, no story. One name came to the local people's minds for it.

Like many, the Powells were accustomed to mentions and impressions of a missing woman. It all began the day before Christmas Eve, when a nineteen-year-old African American female from Wells, Illinois, ceased answering her phone. She stopped turning up at home or in class. But along with season binges and video calls, the seriousness of this withered to the quotidian. The local law officers experienced a devastation of clues to her: a community under house arrest, witnesses in pandemic lockdowns, the ubiquity of face masks making them all suspicious. No one knew what the three months after her last sighting alive consisted of. Where she was, who was with her.

A search and rescue attempt had considered the river. But by the time Raven McCoy was a case, the river was a winter body of water. Sharp as nails in some spots, mean as wild mothers in others, cold enough to slow a corpse from floating, icy enough to keep walkers from its edges a corpse could collide with. Fairly shallow for just fifty feet at its widest channel, short on miles compared to notable Illinois River tributaries whole towns got named for. Hard enough to skate by January, when a crayon box of snowsuits and boots rushed atop it after long isolations. The river was a heartbeat feature of their place, not where the unimaginable struck.

The early tip: Raven was spotted at the edge of town, leaving a spa. Land was a start. State water patrol bowed out. The search stuck to Grayson's barren cornfields, mushy forests and snowed-in back roads. The Grayson Police Chief thought it rude to knock on the doors of these kinds of homes back then (it was still kind of Christmastime). The new year deserved peace and quiet after all everybody went through in the last. They couldn't go digging on a subject like that. Soon, snowplows crawled the lands of patient people who could afford to be snowed in for days or a week in some memorable storms. Some halfway expected a find. It didn't come.

Now, the vernal river had surprised them all.

Tragedy's ten-speed waited to unlatch from a back wall of the shed for abandoned projects, lawn stuff, and a wooden swing her husband gave her. She never rode it, but this seemed an occasion to stay inconspicuous and nimble. The day couldn't have been clearer, one people live to wake up to before weddings and funerals. She zipped a heather grey hoodie and perched her sunglasses. She started in the direction of the short bridge to landmark the way in or out of Grayson Glens, the hidden village she was one of about a thousand people lucky to afford to buy a way into. In five minutes, she just missed her husband turn his Jag onto Calliope Lane, their street in this sprinkle of widespread homes past a dash of security gates. In fifteen minutes, with only a few drivers who could have spotted her on the way, she was near to the end of the river.

Tragedy braked when a scene focused. She stalled at the edge of the empty road. She saw enough far back. Disappointing really, from a distance. Orange cones, yellow tape, black and beige cars, blue uniforms, mostly men and a few women, some white coats. She couldn't make out conversations. One car — a hybrid Volvo — came up on the back side of the scene. Its driver could crawl through. She hid herself uphill, into spruce and oak trunks, against pointy branches.

She beat the documentarians. Only so much time before specks would descend at the tree line to beam the moment into their phones, adorn it with stickers and post emotional remarks. This situation identified their small place to the world. Grayson, Illinois, was always mentioned in the case of #RavenMcCoy: that over-posed selfie face, with her elaborate microbraids updo and downcast eyes. Hundreds — maybe thousands — of flyers subdued her to a black and white complexion, obscured her rich nutty brown one. "Last seen in GRAYSON, IL," it announced.

Tragedy was overcome to make her hands less pointless with a flower, candle, cross or stuffed animal. She was alone and first to a vigil that was to come later, for the girl and all the women the world let get lost, pained survivors now reminded how helpless it is to hold on.

But she had nothing reverent, only her bike and her body and her clothes. Not even a water bottle. She made the sign of the cross, from her third eye to her womb and then across her heart. The young woman's people would assign new zeniths of course. Survivors would tribute memories of her high points and good sides. For now, she was the missing dead girl headed to become ashes and dust down in Wells, her native factory and farm town not too far away.

Tragedy knew where Raven came from. She was born some-where like it. Foster care is swift tides. For Tragedy: from a house with her family, to state care, to group homes. She crash landed to Chicago at twenty-one. She was no Lot's wife. She didn't look back so she could make it somewhere higher. Now, a helpless young woman she didn't know called her back to recall her past. All those small homes and new neighborhoods… all those girls like she was once.

She saw a bubble with her husband's face. She watched him putter off to missed calls. She stayed with the body she couldn't detect in the slight commotion. Finally, she typed: *Needed a ride and fresh air. See you soon.* She turned her back on the sadness, over the bridge in the direction of home, until the unexpected scene's vanishing point. She pedaled fast in irrational worries now: a candle or iron left to flame, a burning house, a birthday she may not live to see.

*

Depending on the house, the river girl's discovery was something big or nothing at all. If the house had young women, the drowned girl was worth sanctions. If the house was near the river, the news was a reminder to fortify weather-worn guard rails and shaky piers and weak harbors. If the house was next door to neighbors who talked to neighbors, it was like a pregnancy announcement or business introduction when a neighbor suggests having coffee, firing up the grill and chilling drinks. Or it was small talk in huge yards and at the ends of driveways. If it was one of the tiny houses people paid regular house prices for, just to be off the grid and feel better than everybody else, it was a consequence of modern society's greed and desire for excess.

So many of them haunted by the death. Nobody said so, though. They were too embarrassed. After all, the woman —19, black, no children, not married— wasn't one of them.

This population didn't watch her progression from wholesome and all-American to naughty and burlesque. That Raven McCoy audience had only come recently, and fast. She'd been an online grid of eyes peeking from behind colored contacts and filters, between fringed bangs of lace fronts and weaves. With a wardrobe and filters, she transformed from bunnies to smoldering bedroom looks to office bosses in suits, her clicks and likes multiplying. She *determined, manifested, visualized.* With her thick legs on display, she was always going out or coming in. She batted lashes like swords. She ignored, or didn't know, online reputation management cautions about great companies who checked social media history. She never heard of those companies anyway. They didn't come to her parts of the world to recruit, like farmers needing hands and pyramid schemes whose leaders set up posts out of her town' storefronts.

Yet still, something on faces like hers whispered a young age — sharp chins, linear jawlines, wide eyes, chubby cheeks. These girls even laughed young. They didn't need gel for their baby hairs to curl. They didn't kiss back as much. Men certainly knew they were babies.

All these girls still looked like they were somebody's little girl long before they became some man's baby. Everybody has childhood. They used to color silly pictures to give their mothers. They worked for gold stars from teachers. They wrapped Christmas presents for their siblings. They ran from worms after hard rains, begged for kittens and puppies and goldfish. They took a pet seriously if it came. But by late teens and young adulthood, they all seemed to become accounts online, and ones who never posted on family. In real life, they hardly spoke of family. Out of curiosity, real adults who paid attention asked often: "Where's your father?"

Tragedy recognized the type immediately in Raven. She knew that same multitalented bunch her life had fringed before she could hashtag her photos with #dreamlife.

The spa worker. Massage worker. Date. Film star. Escort. Model.

All "AFs."

Hot as fuck, horny as fuck, high as fuck...

They have faces beat, lashes done, brows on fleek, red bottoms, fishnets, stockings. The works. Many depend on blunts at glossy, plumped lips. All depend on designer logos and girl gang shots. As side hustles, they're apt sellers of anything. The next big energy drink, cryptocurrency, weight loss miracles, money flowers, weed, online followers, natural hair care products, Noni Juice. They never planned to work, to get laid off, phased out or retired to old homes and studios in senior buildings. This is what they saw happen to elders who raised them.

About a hundred people had shown up for Raven's first search party. January was the uniform. Bearskin hats, thermal underwear, spiked boots. Leather gloves and double mittens clutched free coffee, hard donuts, donated sandwiches. Commenters tapped condolences and emojis on (the) #RavenMcCoy scenes people shared. Following her name, #Grayson trended locally at first, then nationwide. Her name. Finally popular, famous now. But Raven couldn't even see it.

As the missing girl doused their conversations and thoughts, society bet without money. A suicide. A man or boyfriend most likely. The locals pontificated theories she was a mistress of a Grayson Glens man. The rendezvous went wrong. The wife came home early. He would never talk about it to anyone but a priest and his friend who was like a brother. They skimmed *The Grayson Herald*'s periodic requests for information, saw a number to the police station they moved there not to need. They entertained a serial killer among them. Not for long or for much. They were too sophisticated for such nonsense. Why complicate matters? They could incinerate corpses in plain sight just like dead leaves, sensitive papers and the refuse everyone stands out to burn. No one stands out for doing it. They didn't have to dump bodies in rivers.

14

And the discovery didn't fit the profile of their kinds of girls. No, it wasn't one of them.

When she was a girl missing, #RavenMcCoy was intrigue, community conversation, a cause. When she was a young woman found dead, she was to be forgotten.

The body in the river was the fault of different people, in a different place, with different lives. The people of Grayson and its Glens closed ranks against a specter among them.

TWO

This was over two years after the Powells first moved to Grayson Glens and a white woman drowned. The white woman was one of them, a Glenner behind gates. Her death didn't disorient Grayson. It was only a tragedy, not a mystery. That woman was a teacher in town. Kindergarten. Older than the girl who just drowned. Or, maybe this girl hadn't drowned. "Drowned" was the nicest thing anybody could say until somebody said different.

Catastrophes in country sprawl gave residents an opposite posture to those in news-riddled Chicago. They didn't stop over nor cruise up to offer help. They never heard emergency vehicles screech around bends and curves. They all lived too far apart to hear first responders beat their ways in. They only knew, for sure, if people behind nearby doors weren't white. After that, they maybe knew approximate ages, if they vacationed often and if they were such terrible people their kids threw fits at the farmers markets. Truth was they all peered off balconies and out of peepholes binoculars or camera phones zoomed in. Stiff drinks in hand. They deduced from what was new and odd, like if moving trucks showed up, how soon moving trucks took off, who showed up suddenly. The best neighbors never knew anything until they came into closed circles of a few Glenners they ate with and extended invites to.

But the Powells didn't have those people yet. At that time, they were only four months into unpacking, nowhere near ready for an unveiling, long before settling on furniture, and before the old owner's wine cellar was converted to their home studio. And they were just two of not many Black people. They were pioneers to dream houses in rural backwoods. They had to be cautious.

They only came across the drowned woman scandal because a Chicago comedienne friend had a condo-warming party that night. They went, happily. Chicago remained a welcome throwback from the Grayson Glens culture shock. At the party, so many colorful faces in one room relieved them not to be "minorities" for a change. They danced and drank instead of played diplomats on subjects they weren't interested in. They never said aloud they were relieved to abandon the inner city. You can never say that. They kept it inside. Grayson Glens was an escape hatch. They'd had enough of the city. It was time. They sank into fried catfish and perch dinners, a neo soul DJ and a tipsy Cha Cha Slide line on their way out.

It was a good night.

"We crept past the time we should've left and the limit we should have drunk," Victor quipped to his wife. She gave him a head toss laugh they wished would never get old. They stopped at 7-Eleven to get Victor coffee. They drove home to Sade songs, anticipating sex.

But a fire truck blocked a road, a half-mile from their turn to their Calliope Lane. Tragedy didn't smell smoke.

Her "Honey, don't…" came too late. Victor would help, certainly. He always did.

Victor chit-chatted with a senior volunteer fireman who came to clear the truck for them. The fireman apologized for the obvious: The company didn't expect passersby so late. The Powells were too new to get it yet. Quiet meant *quiet* here. Also, the fireman told, a boy called 911 to report: "Mommy's not moving in the pool." The boy was the kind who sleeps like old men. So much time passed, his call started a body recovery instead of CPR.

Victor remembered that boy from Mommy's house. How his teeth were coming in and out, and he sold lemonade in that summer. Victor had bought a few dollar cups when they first got there and Tragedy still didn't go past the yard, so thrilled to be arranging her own universe.

The truck cleared so Tragedy and Victor could get to their destination through the darkness: a bright, well-lit, two-story, pink brick house like Tragedy always wanted. Maybe not that exact house, but all it represented — 4,500 square feet and three floors of rooms of her own behind the most glass bitter winters would allow. Many exits, windows and doors. Nowhere to get trapped or feel cramped inside it. That home came with the price of marrying a workaholic who put paying for it ahead of her. Everything she knew she was lucky to have came with that.

After they made it past the highway and roads and fire trucks and Mommy's house, to their curated home, they sank into a poster bed. They had sex like they'd silently planned to along the way home. A déjà vu of times before and what they knew both would be happy with.

The August after Mommy's obituary printed in *The Grayson Herald*, it was a yard sale at that house. Mommy's sister came to put the house back into the family collection. Tragedy stood at the books table debating if she should keep up a losing battle to finish her Danielle Steeles before more arrived. A few women at the adjacent glassware table discussed a package deal offer for the wine goblets and some crystal. These kinds of people loved a deal. They debated if the bone china and broaches in the pictures were worth crossing the lawn to ask for a look, like the sign instructed. Eventually, the group bobbed to the mink and other fur scraps.

"Bad luck. Drunk herself to death outta one of these glasses," one of them said.

Tragedy recognized that one as the florist who kept odd hours. Another woman piped up.

"Tacky. Family should be ashamed to make money off it. Drunk might still be here now."

"It was an accident!" Tragedy roared in her mind. "Mommy wasn't moving in the pool."

Aneurisms. Strokes. Allergic reactions. Falls. Head injuries. Home invaders. Prison escapees. Crashes through windows to flee serial killers…. Many reasons explained how, for women, a few inches go fast from solid ground to ten feet below, no chance for a deep breath first and no time to fly. Still, gossipers had points. A vodka bottle in the pool and a floating glass spoke. Women drunks made real but not sexy. Nobody believes in them. Only perverts like drunk girls. Children don't like drunk women. You had to be rich and famous to look sexy at it.

So that first woman's drowning stayed a Grayson Glens secret. Mommy's accident was too simple to be newsworthy. It wasn't an anonymous millionaire strangled his wife. It wasn't a dangerous Black man scaling the gates. New homebuyers wouldn't learn about that stalwart kindergarten teacher drowning in her pool. They wouldn't visualize such an unimaginable befalling their kid or parent on a walker. No — here was ultra-safe, desirable.

It was rare for a Grayson Glens starter home to be the buyer's start. With so many farms out of business, or sold by new generations, or defeated by too much sand to plant upon, the Glens turned into a trend of affordable mansions, estates and fixer-uppers. All in seclusion, so worth ten times more in the long run. Next came adorable tiny homes speckling the acres with chicken coops, gardens and stone showers.

Joyrides through its approximately four-square miles were a fun pastime for nearby crowds who knew about the Glens. They just had to breach the North-South-East-West gatekeepers, more decorative than punitive. All black men, suited, accessorized in smiles. Half the time, gatemen didn't even work the night. Outsiders would creep through dense trees and gravel roads, assembling vision board dreams for homes like they see in movies. Most popular were the three- and four-story brick cottages with coach houses. Then, far back to the preserved woodlands were more distant properties. Along the way were restored antiques, weathered pickups and kid bikes next to luxury vehicles. Outdoor Jacuzzis, harbor homes, bathhouses and RVs dotted the pauses between some lands off 20-mile per hour roads at the busiest deer trails. Finally there were short creeks and a necessary bridge, mostly for the East and West sides, with a river in between.

Two decades back, a town council had seen the Glens as just a little subdivision. The main Grayson townsfolk didn't pay attention to it. It was where locally famous name families had turned over the same twenty or thirty acres for generations. Nobody wanted farms. Young ones started springing off into new lives past Grayson. Yet before long, optimistic transplants chasing triple the house for a third the money took over family homes and lands. Enough of them came to turn it into a village on its own.

Tragedy and Victor took up arms with tens of thousands of other African Americans to flee Chicago's inner city. A reverse Great Migration. They'd had enough. It was time.

The Powellcast, Victor's popular one-man internet show of trends and guests, changed everything. Big sponsors and ad revenue from high views helped pay a high mortgage.

For Tragedy, the Grayson Glens house was a no-brainer. With Victor's platform elevated, small city digs simply wouldn't do. City living was too compact for a home studio to produce so many more shows easily. They had no room to leave cameras and tripods out or set great shots. Audiences liked to see influencers live in largesse. The best lakefront or downtown Chicago condos didn't show the owners' worth. Each inch functioned to maximize urban domestic life. She knew what they needed. But the first time the realtor sent them a Grayson Glens listing, they squinted and huffed. "Where is Grayson Glens?" "Never heard of it." "How far from Chicago?"

The realtor had expected these responses. And winter heating would be hell on Earth, all agreed, with featured picture windows and many transoms and all glass for much of the front of the house. Otherwise, with design and space and privacy, it was what people work for all their lives. They didn't need the modern wine cellar the first owner created. They weren't investing in wine, just fans and attention. They needed an in-home studio. Now Victor filmed *The Powellcast* at double the pace, right at home in the old cellar, converted to a studio with his recording videos and soundboard. He didn't have to schedule studio time at the university's audiovisual facilities anymore. He became free to drop from professor blows to visiting professor prestige. They kept glitzy Chicago in their backyard. Their viewers expanded past colors, ages and lifestyles.

The come up wasn't cheap.

The annual Grayson Arts Center Gala brought home the price of hunkering down with folks who live in rifle-rife woods, far from CCTV and streetlights. Six months after the Powells moved in, they were good Glenners to buy their $2000 per couple ticket for the town's big party. They joined a cotillion of debutantes slowing down in number these days, as homes sold out.

The redwood Grayson Arts Center building overlooked the river. The Grayson debutantes to the fundraiser were supposed to fall in line with the veterans. Most would come to this lawn in summer for the family movie nights. Persistent towners insured all new debutantes left the gala pulled into some local group — a book club, small time betting scheme, bridge nights and so on.

Tragedy and Victor arrived an hour past the seven o'clock reception with passed hors d'oeuvres. They took a corner table next to a glum teenage couple into themselves. The center's ballroom opened to a dance floor with a swing band. At ten o'clock, a pianist came for standards, a tip jar on the grand. The bar was open all the while. So was a line for raffles: rounds on the Grayson Greens and passes to its "Pool Hall" substitution for a beach. Apparently, all this and an art auction going on upstairs sustained big grants to local artists and much for budding youth artists to do. The Powells counted nine other black faces and three were in the swing band.

Tragedy wore Gucci and Victor Ralph Lauren. Her wedding ring, her showy jewelry and his Rolex were their only seamless blends into a mostly white crowd. They whispered guesses as to sparse others: Asian? South Asian? Latin American? They were used to this, the whole globe spinning around them as if they weren't part of it. The chandeliers and candle lights and monotonous old-fashioned music dizzied them. A Gershwin song serenaded them to dance in public. Soon, they'd have to start talking to others or...? A trip to the ladies' room left Victor at the bar with the Grayson High principal and a few men who owned businesses around.

"Wild coyotes and skunks are a humorous Grayson myth," the principal said. Rarely seen, occasionally blamed for missing small pets and stench, Victor should know.

He should also know these men's businesses — from pest control to car detailing to construction to waste management. Grayson people kept each other's pockets padded. One man owned the limo and valet service assisting so many stumbling guests back to their homes without a single crash that night. So many clearly over their limits, taking seats and cooling off.

Tragedy's lengthy stay in the ladies' room line got her noticed again by women who had already noticed her darkness cloaked in violent under dim lights. A black-suited brown woman, senior and congenial, attended the bright yellow and flowered bathroom. Tragedy had left her champagne with Victor. She had no clue a woman of color like her would hold it on a silver tray and pass her a towel. She focused on other women's brilliances, latched to ears and fingers, their elaborate clutch bags. She smiled at "Excuse mes" and "Pardons" when scratchy sequins or shimmery fabrics scraped her bare arms. Escaping the city left her much to say to those approaching for introductions and small talk.

"We just lost those three a.m. train wakeup calls and six a.m. construction roars when we least expected it," she joked.

The attendant laughed, "I grew up with those."

"Oh no," deep-voiced a Glenner who had also said she ran the farmer's market. "Out here, we wake up to morning bird sounds and smart home alarms. Keep 'em on classical."

While Tragedy complimented their much longer and dressier gowns compared to her basic sheath, she mentally noted to find digital clocks with "beach wave" or "Beethoven" tones. She and Victor were still sitting up to cell phone alarms and radio alarm clocks from the past life.

"We escaped the beehives where people can just see you sleeping, or not, in your own bed," another woman laughed.

She passed a card where she titled herself "Food Blogger" and ordered people to subscribe. "Goodbye to frosted glass shower windows that tell everybody in the city if you shave your armpits, *really* wash your ass and can do it standing up."

"Now you can do it with wraparound windows and even easier eyewitness views," the farmer's market boss teased, for agreement from the others who didn't spill wine or step on any toes.

Tragedy tried to imagine herself calling these women for lunch or fun. They all seemed like they knew each other so well that they acted alike. The cologne, perfume, breath mints and booze aromas intoxicated her on the way back to find Victor through the crowd. It wasn't thinning with time. This was the power show of the year and some would hang on for dear life, several until dawn. The same aura came into these events everywhere, city or country. The grazing table, exploited caviar, shrimp and nearly raw head-on fish to pick at. Pungent cheeses and dips. Tragedy stuck to champagne grapes or pastries and men noticed.

"Into sweets, huh?" a senior one of them was bold enough to ask. Dark hair. A tuxedo. Martini. The start to a sweaty face and damp comb over that comes with having too many drinks.

"I am," Tragedy smiled. She saw the men watching her. She's always crossed lines of race when it came to men and how they stared, wondering. But this was a married people place.

The man who stuck out a brown hand she didn't see coming was "Mr. Christian Pitts" and his wife "Right behind you, is Mrs. Jasmine Pitts." The very light woman was statuesque under a Diana Ross level wig sparing no expense. She smelled like an Avon standard, Tragedy felt. A handshake wasn't sufficient. Mrs. Pitts was a hugger. The oldest of few black couples, Glenners for a decade, Tragedy learned. By the time Victor walked up, she had traded enough niceties to introduce their new paternal and maternal guides to the Glens: "These are the Pitts. Retired architects. They designed and built a solar-powered home on the East side to retire to."

"Good to see you out here, son," Mr. Pitts said. He leaned in for what Victor had heard so many times, in so many contexts: "You won't even notice it's none of us after a while."

The men chuckled and the women knew what it was about.

"That color is so beautiful with your skin," Mrs. Pitts gushed. "Children at home?"

Tragedy swiveled her champagne. "We're just enjoying life now. He has a daughter."

Mrs. Pitts leaned in herself and her grandiose matching emerald jewelry.

"How nice. But get one of your own, soon. Then, get them gone and go live your life."

The women chuckled and the men knew the territory of what it was about. The Powells landed in their first club: Mr. Pitts had a summer party every year, "For *our kind*." They were on the invite list now. They also had a phone number and promise to dinner when they all got past the upcoming winter. Mrs. Pitts signaled their own Glenner duty was done, so the Pitts left the Powells to drift to a small pocket of younger couples like themselves. Victor had a knack for sniffing out where he fit. The couple stood together and beamed out laser whitened smiles to join a conversation of ex-city folk praising their carriage drives or three and four car garages now.

"You're out of the city parking demolition derbies now, buddy," a tall and robust man roared. Anywhere else, he may have been distinct. He was but he wasn't here in a ballroom of other white men with well-dressed wives and dates. The Powells were relieved to hear some were just cops or accountants, their women corporate slaves to big names. Strivers, still. After all, they were unsure how this great big idea would work out. They had no Plan B.

The small crowd turned memories of city parking to a game of the dozens. "I lost my Escalade to a million tows and tickets in that 'First Come, First Serve' bullshit!" "It's just a 'Step right up!' circus for poor souls hunting a street space after you work your ass off all day." "I was mugged walking from a parking space three blocks from my condo. That was it for us."

See, Tragedy thought, *street parking hates us all. Beyond color, we're all human.*

She recalled how she and Victor once paid a $500 a month garage fee for two cars. Now, to prepare for a first Grayson winter, she'd put that $6000 on treats like better sheets and shoes.

It took a wife of one of the men to bring up the real jackpot: "I have *closets* now."

Tragedy would never share how foster care downsized her to drawers and trash bags. Once she was grown and fled to Chicago, she was like most urban folk: whisked from dorm rooms to clever squishing with roommates, to backpacks in hostels, to small but grownup rentals, to tight condos. "Walk-in closet" always a prime amenity in listings. Grayson Glens expanded an ex-urbanite's typical standing man closets to dressing rooms. More closet space made it easy to buy more things. Amazon trucks appeared on their roads all times of day and night, seven days a week. Smart home systems monitored deliveries. They were all guilty shopaholics. They knew it.

Yet it was no shame in Tragedy wandering up marble stairs to the auction room, finding a paddle in her hand, forgetting her husband. Maybe he was debating sports or bragging on his *The Powellcast.* With her paddle, "Number 74" she became in the small auditorium. Onstage, a lovely, fully gray-haired woman wore pearls and a shimmery floor-length turquoise gown. She swayed out paintings, from powerful to mediocre. A room of women like her, knowing they could spend what they wanted. One piece was just a small thing that reminded Tragedy of sunrise just right. "Number 74 down there!" bellowed from the stage. All eyes turned to her: a brown loveliness outlined in deep purple. The crowd's claps and excitement overwhelmed her.

She felt Victor's hands on her shoulders at the moment bidding closed on what she won for them to donate $5000 for. He walked her onstage. The audience saw a beautiful black couple diversifying them all. That diversity ended their night on the long patio overlooking the Grayson River, where fireworks still sprayed. Tragedy leaned into her husband and told him, "This is really becoming perfect." His eyes flashed the lights of ambition and he kissed her.

But when they got home, Tragedy kicked off pointy black stilettos at the door. She massaged her feet and she felt it — that edge and a chill living with her now.

One topic no one at the Gala had brought up? Crime. Nope, wasn't in Grayson. And they all kept an emergency generator, security cameras and alarm(s) rigged to police a few miles away.

"We can get a dog," Victor suggested once.

They'd put the thought in the box with the baby. A complication. "Keep up the pace," his brand manager told him. Tragedy had struggled in life and wanted to enjoy it, for a change.

City living was a box of walls in the sky. Only one way in or out. Check closets and under the bed for the monsters who thrive on fear and destruction. Close fire escape gates. Lock them. Grayson Glens demanded a new protocol. It was no insulation from the monsters, the nightmares, the anxieties, and bad memories. Here was see-through living now, multiple doors meeting the ground, windows floor-to-ceiling, acres as yards that could mute agony.

Here was the blackness.

So black it carried its weight and power into the house wherever walls stopped to bleed to glass. Even with Victor in the house, with the woman they hired to help as well, Tragedy checked closets and under beds. She re-latched windows. She crossed a flashlight over the yards, all of them: front, back and two on the sides. But no one could check the whole dark.

THREE

Ha! I never found those wine bottles. But the first night Raven McCoy found me, right around the spring in that year, all those bottles tinkered and shook behind my driver's seat.

Coming home behind the wheel like I was a superstar, selfies taken and posted already, I was dressed as a vamp, down to my shiny black leather gloves and a bustier. I removed the fangs for the drive home, to breathe right again. All for my first "Reopening Celebration." This one was for a beer and burger bar at the edge of Chicago. It survived on a year of takeout only. It was nothing close to what I'd hoped for after a quarantine of no partying, drinking and hanging on Victor in bars. The costume party twist solved the mask problem. I knew I went overboard.

A superstore liquor depot sat across the streetlights from the bar. Hey, I had no clue when I'd get back that way. It was impossible to find decent wine in my boonies. We didn't even have a chain supermarket. A Target, fairly new, was five interstate stops from mine. Nice, but the same cheap brands all the time. A shame to come so close to better only to go back to box wine and college brands. I did have a few hundred in cash left on me. Anyway, the depot's owners were so happy for the sale. They carried both crates to the back of the Jeep, fit them not to spill and gave me free lottery tickets. A dozen reds and a dozen whites in four cardboard crates, snug in separate sinkholes. Supposedly. Just one slam on the brakes and there goes that.

I saw red and blues behind my truck. I eased to a hedge of cornstalks. Judging by the pace and rhythm of the pea gravel's grumbling, I put on a decent show. The dashcam video centered the otherworldly darkness. My fangs were on the dashboard. A dry flask was hidden in the glove compartment. Everybody gets the party started before they get there, right?

The flashlight struck through my back window. Its reflection in my rearview mirror blinded me. I put up my forearm, tinkling with copper bracelets.

"Good evening, ma'am."

"Hello, officer," I replied.

I couldn't bring myself to add "Sir." He looked like he could be one of Victor's little students. He smelled sour, like a few beers he could just dip into a friend's house for. Bloodshot eyes, too. Of course, he drives by a high school or family friend's spot and drops in for a little weed, then goes back to patrolling nothing much. Our kind of place had fender benders, not fatal accidents. Noise complaints, not domestic violence. Roadkill, not gang warfare. Young people just having fun, not children who get tried as adults and locked up their whole lives.

"I just need to see your license, insurance and registration," the officer said.

He had out that little yellow pad, as if it was something certain to write. I needed to know what he was thinking and if we were thinking the same thing.

"Sure," I said. "Why am I being stopped?"

"You seemed lost," he replied.

All my leather and chrome looked sterile, ready for a heart surgery or baby delivery. He glanced at my dashcam a few times.

I could only stand so much surveillance. We didn't use the audio. He wouldn't know that. One of the flying monster insects around here came for my brights. It smashed into the windshield. I turned on the wipers. I couldn't help myself.

"Excuse me, officer," I said.

"No worries."

The wipers scraped as much slime as they could. I handed him my state ID, insurance policy and registration in the passenger side visor's tight band, in a long and thin leather wallet.

"Tragedy Powell, Calliope Lane…" he started.

This is the part when I'm supposed to say he walked to his cop car, took time to return, left me growing scared and thinking about that warrant out for my arrest. Then he came back and called for backup, surrounded me with SWAT, ordered me out of my vehicle, got angry when I stayed put, scared me out of my mind, saw me grab my cell phone, yelled "Gun!" and saw me wriggle out the passenger side to run off into the corn. He'd say that's why he shot so many rounds of ammo into the stalks, hit me somewhere fatal, and wrote a police report saying I threatened him and reached for a gun.

But it seemed too much trouble for him. He gave the papers a shuffle and handed the clutch back.

"So you're right around here," he grinned. "Almost home. I never saw this truck out here. I'm on this beat every night."

"It's barely six months old," I told him.

I squinted my 20/20 contacts to read a name off is badge.

"And Officer Castle," so he knew I was paying attention, "we usually take the sedan."

"Makes sense now. You know, just this week—"

"They found a girl in the river," I finished.

"Of course…" He stuttered on to a speech about heightened precautions in the area.

Before "just this week," nineteen-year-old Raven McCoy was, apparently, last seen when she was just eighteen. Grayson is where investigators discovered her phone last pinged. Then, a last reported sighting here. Chatter somewhere and everywhere about this. Others searching, scouring, praying, posting, blasting and supplicating on her behalf. Raven's stricken family pleaded in a few news conferences. Her mother, aunts, siblings and friends were interviewed.

We were all forced onto the search team. Everybody crossed paths with her face in the beelines for essentials — at gas stations, little food markets. I even saw flyers for her at Costco, Walmart and Target in a bigger anchor town nearby. How could anyone avoid not noticing every least little thing? For all of us in the pandemic, time slowed. Focus clarified. Senses heightened. Edges sharpened. Brains crammed. The perfect storm of isolation, nakedness and ennui made all the "Have You Seen Raven McCoy?" flyers earn easy keep in our waned, numbed minds.

I felt bad to cut off Mr. Castle's speech on the girl. *I'm a woman alone, I should be careful, he's just looking out... blah blah.*

"Think I saw you on that news conference for it," I smiled.

"No," he laughed.

I remembered my costume. The police officer didn't indicate it any way. He tapped the top edge of my halfway-cracked driver's side window.

"Well, you just get home safe," Officer Castle told me.

"Got it," I smiled. "Thanks so much."

Eventually, the police car's headlights turned off in another direction, back over to a one lane bridge and railroad tracks to the Grayson "downtown."

I continued in unforgiving darkness. I may as well have moved to the seabed. Twisted figures emerged in black ether, hulking. It took a year of nights for me to know in advance these were scarecrows and deformed trees. The scarecrows remained even when people down the roads pulled their life-size Werewolf Man, witches and scary clowns out for Halloween. I still wasn't used to it. I rarely drove alone at night without my husband's bad jokes, or his recaps of the personalities and food we just endured, his style wavering from Chris Rock to Fred Sanford. He was good company in the dark.

"Raise volume," I commanded the force of alternate dimensions.

Green levers rose on the dash. But the car rattled in a scream, primitive and near beastly. I covered my ears to the angry howl and roar. Whether just screams or words I couldn't tell. The noises were all there was in the world at the moment. The noises were female…

My pores were basted in sweat and stress. My Jeep stopped. My heart out there somewhere. My knuckles locked and taunt on the wheel. Darkness lengthened further than I could sense distance, around me and above. A sandy whorl in front of the headlights fell like light snow, evidence of how fast and far I must have skidded. "Help!" Maybe I heard "No." I heard licks like fire crackling. I saw Raven in the windshield. No, not her. A movie of her, swirling and reeling in front of me. I didn't know what was happening.

Then, it just stopped. I couldn't take my hands off my ears.

"I did hear something," I said to myself.

An old, known dancehall song came into focus. It had been playing all along.

"What's wrong with you, girl?" I said out loud. "Jesus."

I released my foot and rolled forward into a four-way inter-section with stop signs on all sides. I reversed back onto the road. I was past the bridge, the river, the slight downtown. I could've been home already. Keen onyx eyes on a strong old deer I hadn't noticed, maybe avoided hitting, stared through my windshield and watched me breathe deeply back on my way.

*

A few more hazy signposts and one Jodeci song later, I had circled my drive and parked in front of my door. I didn't have the energy to jiggle a formidable truck around my trusty middle-aged Chrysler, Victor's Jaguar and *The Powellcast* marketing banners and stands we kept in the garage. Nor did I have the energy to tussle four crates of wine. I gripped a cap and came up with a Spanish Grenache, not a bad spin of the wheel. I tucked it under my arm to walk around ceramic flowers and other decoratives, an unspoken competition these homes were in.

Oh — the flask.

Skip back, into the passenger side, fingers through the glove compartment, the Sir Jack's classic in my hands, then put into my tote bag. It was Victor's flask, really. My wedding gift.

Our door opened easily. Unlocked. We did that out here. I stumbled into one of those corny Sybaris scenes: Rose petals trailed up the staircase and cream carpet, the surround sound playlist pumped that soft sax music. LED candles gleamed everywhere. I was dressed for it.

"Honey?" I called. Twice. Nothing back.

We loved the peekaboo glass ceiling the first owner chose for the wine cellar, now Victor's studio. He was too used to it now for me to startle him like I used to, blowing kisses or stripping atop it for him to see. Never when he was recording or going live, of course. The studio was empty and dark now. The house was so new, still. The realtor's regular polish to all the marble and wood wasn't worn. It wasn't our huge responsibility to upkeep yet. New sponsorships filled our bank accounts fast. I was a boss in my husband's crowd, not arm candy. I had a title in our businesses together and that business was known, now. I wasn't prowling with a MAC counter on my face and Victoria's Secret store slathered from my butt to toe cracks, to hunt for successful men. I wasn't those men's girlfriends and wives. Those women went here to there with their men, all the time, just to guard their males from other females. They knew about affairs. It was only so many times I could get a thrill from spotting celebrities and personalities. Except for big galas and events, I stopped going with him. I changed my power.

I would *trust*. I wouldn't chase. I would be his every delight waiting when he got home, I had thought. Well now we weren't even waiting up for each other. This was the second year a housewarming party was supposed to come on my birthday, a wide guest list and group rates booked. With six months out and money to make up, I couldn't prioritize making a guest list.

Victor was in bed with a drink holder, a bag of popcorn and a *Sports Illustrated*. I slid under covers. I pressed into his warmth, wondering if I should find that extra push to wake him. He pushed out a fart. He ate well. His farts smelled like avocado nothing most times, sometimes near to basil and turmeric. We united in the magic and disgust that was the human body together or alone. I flowed away from memories of the figure imagined in my windshield. The dead girl.

But, I had pulled it off. I wouldn't mention the police stop to Victor.

I was glad Officer Castle had stopped me. Now, he knew more black folks around here, and our Jeep. Maybe he'd spread the word. Now Grayson's little, simple police force wouldn't pull that obvious, implicitly biased thing. They couldn't take a look and assume I wasn't one of the dozen or so black folks coming to or going from a legal address past a Grayson Glens gate.

Now, Victor was less likely to be harassed on account of my close call.

I got away with it.

That officer met the steely veneer I perfected early. He second-guessed himself. Let's be honest: a racism lawsuit and charge would be inescapable for him. Grayson-born or settled people never move anywhere. They live and die 30 minutes or miles from their births. That cop wouldn't be able to live a scandal, lawsuit, hashtag mess down. He'd always be *that one.*

So if he suspected it, he erred on the side of caution. He knew it was more than a confused driver to stop. He knew it's no reason for drivers to wiggle these simple roads. He knew all the cars go slow around here, but not as slow as I was going.

He might have been young, but he wasn't that dumb.

I might have been black, a woman. He might have been white, a man. No matter.

He knew.

I was drunk.

FOUR

Tragedy could almost smell the cedar wood paneling and taste cold, sharp lemon water in "Clean Me" offices. On a video projected from Tragedy's smart TV rolled down over the split-room fireplace, a slender brunette in a daisy yellow print dress waltzed through the Clean Me offices. The facility's square or rectangular minimalist decor was Tragedy's style. Only dainty succulents as shelf and table accents, sky-blue trimming along whisper gray walls. Screens in the office showed water waves, lilac fields and brooks. The video was expertly produced and shot.

The woman's hypnotic drone sank into Tragedy's head, especially as she wore her new high fidelity Bluetooth earphones, delivered the day before. She thought to set her main TV or devices on ambient sounds, so she could move around but stay focused on tasks. The world Victor made his name and face in was moving back into real life; they had a whole year of income and visibility to make up. Tragedy was "work from home" forever. His *manager*. She was the one who pushed the other and bigger managers to bring them deals. It was officially spring — time to get busy. This Saturday was supposed to be a great kick-off. And, as usual, she was supposed to carve out time to work on her memoirs. Her book was always waiting for her.

Yet she was on the couch in the near dark with no energy, just a massive hangover.

Last night, finishing a bottle of Grenache alone felt sexier than following Victor's lead on his plans for them. She could have summoned energy to awaken him by what she learned, as a method, was a few moments of sucking his Adam's apple. At the same time, she would rub his crotch. It woke him up to be ready, not astonished. Then she would bend forward and lunge him inside her. In these spontaneous times, unlike their anticipated and even planned lovemaking, Victor never needed breaks to be ready for her again. Tragedy never stopped coming. Sleep was a rude interruption. They'd lull off, tangled in the same position for hours. One would awaken first, start the touching and gripping and fondling, to continue the night as if one slipstream.

But the idea of winding on her husband wasn't as appealing as winding the corkscrew into a bottle. She had unrolled from their slate sheets in the middle of the night. She'd floated to the kitchen, opened a cabinet, set aside a waffle maker they never touched. It's where she hid the mechanical wine opener. *Shit — not charged.* Her eyes shifted and came to the snake pit of cords on the built-in appliance counter. She borrowed a similar AC/DC from a can opener. *Voila!*

Two hours and an empty bottle later, Tragedy took her last pee. She stumbled back to the couch. The sun came up but she was behind it, lost in dreams. One had something to do with meeting up with an old boyfriend. He brought his baby who looked like her replacement, a woman who looked like her. The dreams were all she had from recent hours. She missed the details of how she got on the couch. With blinds and drapes closed in full or in part in some places, the open floor plan wrapped her in an azure cocoon. She noticed Victor had gathered the rose petals. Maybe they were in the garbage or scattered to the yard now. The candles were blown out and re-boxed. Her wine glass was rolled under the branch sculpture coffee table, speckles of resin at the stem's start. The bottle was in the beige couch folds behind Tragedy, leaked to a small burgundy stain like blood.

From where she was, Tragedy could see the Jeep was gone from the circle drive. Victor was probably out running or biking or shopping near Chicago for gadgets he would have her write off for business. He could have gone to the trailhead to run. The Grayson wilds shut down for a few days of small-town police evidence gathering. A press conference was up online. The materials of the vigil were cleared and driven down to Raven McCoy's family one hour away. The "missing" flyers started to come unstuck from public business windows and street signs.

It had been just gospel and golf zones on Live TV, so Tragedy had fled to the interest streams to find just what she wanted. On a whim, she'd spoken "Stop drinking" into a YouTube search bar. A carousel of doctors, wellness gurus, yogis, authors and TedX talkers tripped her into a video from the cutting-edge Clean Me Sobriety Centers. She scrolled their hypnotic and packed channel. She didn't subscribe. She and Victor shared house accounts and passwords.

After an hour, Tragedy had CM's nearly 3-minute channel intro memorized. She was the one in three people the branding consultants and marketing experts obsessed over day and night. It worked. Their video had hit all the right notes to catch her attention. Then, to keep her wandering mindlessly through its playlists, returning to the channel main to restart the welcome.

She was stuck to the couch with no sustenance. All in reach was an empty filter pitcher and smashed bag of what used to be farm cherries, now just hard pits. The fruit was mushy, not what she'd wanted. She wanted a cast iron skillet egg frittata loaded with — maybe her body was crying to replace minerals — spinach, broccoli, and kale. She wanted coffee, some Colombian beans ground and French-pressed, with cinnamon and vanilla-flavored almond cashew milk.

But it was Ifa's day off. She was calling their trusty, versatile House Manager more and more at the last minute. Ifa had come to know why.

"You want me back again tomorrow, Missus Powell?" she heard often in Ifa's Ethiopian accent. Or "I'll be back to help you again tomorrow, Missus Powell."

Her drinking secret was safe with Ifa. Ifa was a young fifty-something grandmother, nearer to Victor's age. Still more of Tragedy's ally. She was a pretty and stalwart Earth Mother kind, not the either too shy or too overbearing kind of assistance other women complained about. Victor noticed — socialization decreased, but charges for Ifa's service had increased. They weren't having anyone over. Their schedules had slowed down. Victor didn't get it.

Sometimes Tragedy turned to Victor's bar for a plop of this or that, mostly strong cognac but occasionally rum, into her tea and coffee. She preferred her own things. She chose low platform beds in all three sleeping rooms, for style mostly. This meant she couldn't hide anything underneath beds. She buried wine bottles and drink cans in the dressing room, the join between the master bedroom and bath. Ifa helped her keep those so neat she could barely spot a nook or cranny to jam anything into anymore. She found new purpose to her pastime ordering curve-friendly maxi dresses. Her color wheel-organized collection was a main hideaway. She stuffed her secrets under the ovals of their hems down to the floor. She also rolled the wine bottles up into sweater bundles.

Tragedy sometimes outdid herself with these hiding places. She couldn't remember where she put it all or perceive what she'd hidden. Snack size bottles sank so conveniently into her bag collection. She risked satin and silk linings of her purses and clutches. She was negligent there once. What came to two dollars' worth of Merlot in a ten dollar 4-pack wound up staining a $2000 Balmain. No hope. So if she had to hide the bottle, she had to finish the booze. Sometimes she sat in the closet and chugged, swimming pools of drink, to never make that mistake again.

About every month, she gathered empty bottles into a nice tote and put the tote into the trunk of one of the rides. She disposed of the tell-tale bottles on her errands, like she was a murder with a body to hide. Only small store and grocery clerks on smoke breaks spotted her. Even then, she looked like an average Glenner who gave their cars regular TLC of junk removal.

Victor suspected but kept his peace. Everybody went through changes. Isolations and lockdowns disoriented them all. It wasn't worth troubling his wife for allowing a trusty confidante and staff into their bubble. They both knew Ifa had two children off in universities, one in medical school on the west coast. Ifa relished in sending supports and reinforcements to their campuses. Her husband owned a corner store with an attached juice and coffee bar, deemed essential therefore still open. The Powells paid honestly and substantially. Family, they all were.

Tragedy ruled out calling Ifa to an emergency day for her hangover. She decided on only a few more moments of auditioning for *The Walking Dead*. She had to get her shit together. She was lucky to spot a pouch of roasted cashews stuck between black photography books on the coffee table, both Victor's doing.

She crunched the nuts and rolled back CM's welcome video again. The medical doctor continued her vigorous welcome and online tour, a siren for her many nationwide state of the art centers. The pitch was a sermon beamed to Tragedy like a late-night preacher's, finessed to get credit card numbers ready to call centers in the middle of nights.

"Maybe your dreams are still here, but not how you had hoped. Trust me, I hear you! My dreams to become a family medicine physician came true. But they became aggressive billing, big pharma marketing and fast-food patient care. It was a race to see patients, go over charts, direct staff, handle digital overloads. I was creating a false sense of wellness and health…"

Clean Me's founder floated through a sample office's front doors to an expansive lobby. Then through a clear door, on to discreet side consultation rooms with buttercream hallways, the doorframes melted magically into long walls. Tragedy saw herself here.

"Here at Clean Me, we don't want anyone to feel they're entering treatment or just a number. No — we want you to feel you're entering an exciting evolution, a joyous adventure, and a sensuous new chapter."

Excitement? Joy? Sensuousness? Where had those gone? Tragedy thought. *Keep talking.*

All were how her marriage started out. How the turn of her life towards Grayson Glens came to be. How seven years took her above paycheck to paycheck and into the American elite.

Not bad for an orphan.

The more Tragedy went along in a few foster care years, the more distant family memories became. But the Victor Powell wedding made online mag and website mentions. Relatives wriggled out of woodworks to "reconnect" after that. Victor had a secretary as a perk of staying on faculty. She took time from juggling his affairs with students to address his wife's relatives: "The Powells thank you." She had a secretary to get rid of pesky people, now? Not bad for a statistic, she thought she was. All people are some statistics. She fell on the smaller sides of statistics about people, kids, blacks, women, orphans, children, etc... like her. She wasn't the most or least of anything wrong. She was regular on some hands, an anomaly on others.

"Here, we have no set number of steps," her new YouTube friend continued. "You take as many as you need. We have no required support groups. We match you with a tribe or you come in with one. We never tell you to never take another drink. We aren't tyrants. And we know that doesn't work for a lot of people. Great moments in life have alcohol. We want to teach you how to enjoy the moments — not the alcohol. We don't outline 30 or 60 or 90 day plans. Once you're with us, you're with us. Some of our clients have been with us for years..."

This was bound to be pricey. How would she run it through QuickBooks? No, this can't be a power couple moment or team effort. No #goals posts for this one. Victor wouldn't know.

Tragedy's location finder put the nearest Clean Me center way up by O'Hare in Chicago. She had friends that way, on the hazy level. Otherwise, she never drove that far. What would be her excuse?

Who'd be the one person she would talk about this place with? Such a big thing was bound to create a little voice inside her, eager to converse and emote about it all. She had some friends. They knew she drank. Well, they all drank.

"It's like a food delivery service to eat healthy," she'd say, "except to drink healthfully."

Clean Me offered a minimum $500 per month membership for an app to chart drinking (preferably none), one telehealth visit a month, weekly nutrition plans, blood work and a personal "Clean Coach." Bonuses at higher levels included a personal trainer (which she already had, only online now) and a regional wilderness wellness retreat with other Clean Me folks. Tragedy had her own checking account and cards. She wasn't a princess locked in a tower.

Still Tragedy thought, *Nah, too pricey.* And, *I'm not an alcoholic.*

She paused the Clean Me video into silence.

She estimated at least a few hours to sober up. Victor was prone to texting his eta, sometimes shifting in updates every few minutes. He wasn't pinging her phone to notifications. Not a good or bad sign. Sunshine beckoned. She grabbed a corded gray sweater from the mudroom. She tied its string belt. It was finally unfrozen enough to sit still outdoors.

Tragedy's body ordered her to give herself a workday out on the swing. Vitamin D and breezes… But first, to the metal shed for birdfeed (a bird feeder was Grayson custom, the trade for the image-conscious or professionals who ruled out damage and cleaning from house pets).

Unexpectedly, brass bells vibrated.

Tragedy regretted her loud, pretentious choice of door chimes instead of trendy volume-adjustable ones. The doomful gong sent her head spinning. She knew it wasn't Victor. He never rang. No one else visited without an invitation. She passed a bell camera and saw the tops of two heads. A male and female. Too old for the cookies and candies the kids sold. Not likely lost.

Tragedy invested a minute into the water closet mirror before she put on her mask to greet whoever was at the door. She would have bumbled to the door in her head scarf otherwise. She hung the fuchsia scarf around the pipe underneath the reclaimed sink. Then she ran a few cold splashes over her face and pumped lemon verbena lotion into her hands. She rubbed her hands together, next her palms from her neck to forehead as she shuffled to her door. A lovely scent and enlivened complexion at once. Because, after three years, the Powells still had no *"Hi, just passing by"* friends in Grayson Glens. She knew first impressions counted here.

FIVE

The first time the cops came knocking about Raven McCoy, the two people at the door didn't seem shocked I was black. Even with white face masks on, they didn't give me that funny look to tell me what they saw that I already knew: I was black. This happened with delivery and repair people. Their features morphed. Most people wouldn't notice. But it's impossible to miss when you've seen it so much. It's a common sight "The Only Ones" take note of and understand.

The white and maroon Grayson Police car sat politely at the back of the drive, some context to the visitors. Reflections of the recent past rushed forward. Yes, I'd just crossed paths with the cops. Now here stood a grayed white man in no uniform, and a maybe Mexican woman much younger. He was dressed neatly, blue pants and blazer, smart black tie. She wore black pants and an elegant, brown, button-down silk blouse. Low chunky black heels.

The policeman last night was white, young, I thought. *And in real uniform. This must be more serious.*

"How can I help you?" I asked.

"Good afternoon," the woman said. "I'm Grayson's lead

detective Giselle Wise and this is Grayson's police chief, Ron Loveless. We're hoping to speak with the resident or owner."

They showed badges. I stepped to the chilly threshold to examine the metal and wording. My emergence into sharp light had the effect of a cold shower on my hangover.

"That's me," I said.

And then — *Wait, no texts pinging. The missing Jeep. Victor.* I gasped.

"Is it my husband?" I asked.

Many widows started when police walked to their porches on gorgeous days.

"No, no," Det. Wise replied. "Not at all. I'm sorry to scare you."

"We're investigating the disappearance and discovery of Raven McCoy," the chief said.

"Oh," I sighed.

We didn't know the girl.

We didn't know anyone in the area. We barely knew people in the area code. Our residency in Grayson Glens came down to a real estate agent's shark instinct, high reviews online, bad ass sandstone marble floors and a spiral staircase that seemed a steal. An image we needed for ourselves in our environment, not people we wanted to get to know or live around. We didn't have children the victim's age — only Victor's teenaged daughter with his ex-wife. They were both in Chicago. She stayed some weekends, holidays.

"We didn't know the victim," I told the officers.

"Yes," Wise said. "Customary questions for all residents. Grayson's such a small place."

"We're getting to the whole junior high and high school, all two hundred kids, in case," Chief Loveless said. "We're trying to get to students in her classes at a community college."

"I even interviewed our chief here," Wise grinned. "Happy to say I eliminated a suspect."

"Suspects, for a drowning?" I asked.

That was the latest. Raven McCoy drowned. *Water in the lungs, no signs of rape…* It's what I thought I gathered somewhere out and around, on screens and in social media feeds. Now, as usual, real life was a different story.

"Yes," the detective said. "Still covering some bases, if you're comfortable with visitors."

Behind the strangers, the slim road and a few properties in the distance created a peaceable still life. Spring buds and leaf sprouts on ornamentals fringed the gates and shades. Summer tints and breezes readied to burst for lush thunderstorm days, freeing mosquitoes and fireflies. Leaves of our own dogwood and elms would block views to our windows soon. Who knew what suspects were behind barriers, fences, shutters, and high-climbing vines? In contrasts to city living, the innards of life stayed sewn up here. Never any girl gangs, boy packs, skateboarders, jump ropers. Lawn parties were rigid and planned. These affairs seemed to have the sound off. This folded up all noisy, ugly, and disruptive. But still, the devil could make light work of peace.

A dog came up to the curb. An awkward and swirly mutt, average, not a breed, so out of place around here. It trotted away.

"Come in," I relented.

I led them to the left side of the foyer into the mudroom and past our solarium of garden windows. White pillows and herbs on the ledges blurred the unreality of larger artificial foliage. The law's heels and soles made a show of strong strides. I pulled out two chairs to the breakfast nook we used for breakfast, lunch and dinners that weren't special. I kept up a big clear bowl of fruit.

Ifa caught on it was just to be cute. I was grateful to see she'd just cleared shrunken apples, sunken peaches, dotted bananas. A hung African Mudcloth and two floor vases of curly willow carried the space to earthiness. Police were our first guests besides Ifa for months and months.

"Coffee or tea?" I asked.

"Please," Wise nodded.

"Which?" I smiled.

"Coffee," she laughed.

"I'll have what she's having," the police chief said.

"Ok, lady and gentleman," I said.

Damn Ifa for having a day off! And damn Victor for sailing away to run, hike, bike, fish, jerk off in the Jeep… whatever men do when they leave home and it's not for work.

"Excuse me while I get my phone," I said. "I want to text my husband to hurry back."

"Yes," said Wise. "We do have to limit how many visits we make for safety reasons. It would be nice to talk to him"

I couldn't remember how or where I'd last seen my phone, purse or wallet. So much of the night before blurred. It only came into focus in random spurts. I needed some recognizable sequence of events from it. I gave up texting Victor to call him. I knew his cell number by heart, two digits at the end off from my own. I walked upstairs to my plain little office, a nursery's size, to the desk phone installed there. My husband's smooth jazz ringtone came quickly.

"You have reached *the* Victor Powell," he announced in a near new anchors' voice.

"*The* Victor Powell, it's your wife. You're wanted at basecamp. Cops here about this mystery in our heavenly neighborhood. Call the house please…"

I came down to find one fresh-brewed cup ready for Detective Wise. I began the next for Chief Loveless. I was going to need my own, soon.

Yes, the party… I recalled, silently to myself. Just last night — not days ago, as it felt. *Victor had a Zoom thing and couldn't join me there. Lucky him… Masks required at the party, so I made that fun. I came as a vamp. Costume theme. A policeman stopped me for… Not sure.*

The amnesia was so stunning I missed half my visitors' opening statements.

"Mother had no clue she had friends anywhere near Grayson. No serious boyfriend they knew of…"

"Forensics is determining how far the body may have travelled, slow currents… lack of depth in the river… mild freeze most of winter… She couldn't have come from too far…"

"She was frozen in time really… Witnesses place her in Grayson as the last known whereabouts anyone will talk about…"

"The spa … The owner and a staff remember our victim as an appointment…"

"Are you familiar with that spa, Mrs. Powell? Er, Mrs. Powell?"

"I'm sorry," I said, blinking fast. "What?"

I should have ignored the doorbell. This kind of house made it easy to appear not home.

"Mrs. Powell, right?" Wise asked.

"Yes, how did you —?"

"We have profiles on all the residences and residents in a radius of where the victim was found," Loveless said.

The second coffee finished. It took strength for me not to take it. One gulp, scalding and straight, to bolt sanity to my brain. I remembered my manners.

"Victim? Of what?" I asked.

"We don't know," the man told me. "We'd call it a simple drowning, maybe suicide or accident, if we understood what the young lady was doing here with no connections to the area."

"We're trying to find that answer for her family," the woman said. "To give them peace."

Wise set aside her coffee. She wore a thin gold band and circled it with her thumb. A simple wedding ring. I'm sure, in some situations, big stones got in the way of her job. Her perfume was gardenia or another strong flower. Creamy peach lipstick and small gold stud earrings full of taste. I wondered of children, if she had any. What they think of Mommy out here asking folks about dead girls in rivers and having to tell the girls' mommies the answers. Her bun was strict and tight. I could feel the hair pinch at her temples, making her eyes slant up wide. She could've been older than this made me think. She seemed more like a social worker than a cop, a prober of heinous things. Perhaps social work is all law enforcement did anyway.

"We assumed locals with something to offer the case would've come forward by now," Loveless said. "But we can't be sure everyone even knows about it."

I laughed out loud. The missing girl had escaped no one here. It wasn't possible. All we had to do the past year was know about things. Rules and mandates flipping and flopping at breakneck speeds. We knew about everything. We knew too much.

"How long have you lived in Grayson?" Wise asked.

"Coming on three years now," I said. I sat down with my cup, sipping all I could take through the heat. "My husband changed some things up and put more into his own businesses."

"This population lived in bubbles here long before the pandemic," Wise said. "They didn't need a virus to come to a remote place to shut down. People here are on seclusion levels you and your husband may be too young and active yet to know."

"Or, too poor," I smirked. "We have a future to fund. We can't afford to rest in bubbles."

"I'd hardly call anyone in the village of Grayson Glens poor," the police chief said.

"Oh, so no belly-up businessmen have killed their families for life insurance yet?"

He knocked on the wood table.

"Insofar as communities go, Grayson's still new," Wise said. "Anything is possible. But speaking of your husband, did you two speak about the missing person case?"

Soon as I answered "Yes," Loveless asked "Did you join the search party? Did he? You go together or separately?"

"When do you remember first learning Raven McCoy was missing?" Wise added.

"Was it the radio, a flyer, the news?" Loveless shot.

"Social media," I interrupted.

They stopped. Their eyebrows stood up like caterpillars uncovered under garden pots.

"Like most," Loveless said.

From somewhere, the detective produced a small black notebook with an attached pen. Her pocket, maybe? This was a day to accept I would miss my own name if called. She wasn't pointing a gun, yet it felt an assault to have my words and thoughts written.

"I follow the Grayson Arts Center," I continued. "Or, my husband does. He promoted the Center's fundraiser a few years ago. It was the first neighborhoody thing we did here. They asked followers if we'd seen Raven McCoy. It linked to a news story about a hair salon or—"

"A spa," Wise said. "She went to the spa here the last day she's accounted for."

"Right," I said. "The spa. An appointment there. Not seen since."

It was a standout year overall. A stiff cocktail of strangeness mixed with fear and overexposures. We all stayed inebriated from boredom or overwhelm, no respite in mediums. The unusualness of situations we found ourselves in, and watched others go through, muted our responses so we could take it all in. After a while, I sorted the missing young woman in the same part of my brain where gory or graphic sex art films I regretted go to die.

"I received contact about it," I told the officers. "From friends concerned for me. This is really far out from where we know people."

They couldn't understand me to mean both familiar faces and black people in general, even if the black people were strangers. It wasn't that others were mean or that no one was nice. It was simply an eerie isolation, a tradeoff in exchange for how great our life was out here.

"We hardly know our neighbors across or down the road," I continued. "We kept up with the stories. We certainly had to. She was a young black woman and, well, we're black too."

"Where's your black Jeep?" Out of the blue the detective asked me this.

"Pardon?"

My thoughts whiplashed to the content loaded to the television, mounted just feet away, around the room divider, for all to see. The whole recent search history revolved around drinking too much. Could this be about last night? But I was stopped for drunk driving so close to home it wasn't worth giving Grayson, Illinois, a lever up on the crime rate. Surely, they couldn't want to pursue that. No matter what, with the Clean Me videos up I was just a few back tabs from having my life and mind read. No good deed goes unpunished. I had to clear that up before they asked to take a look around, since that line always came in these scenarios.

But the front door popped like a snapping branch.

Six

Coming into the room, Victor looked like a chill Saturday morning. I smelled his usual coconut and oils scent. His hands held a gray mush: long fish bodies and downturned faces in clear plastic tied at their fanned tails. A sprinkle of pink perspired at the bottom of the bag. In his right hand, he had the mail. I relieved him of all this. The officers rose to introduce themselves.

My short journey to the kitchen gifted me a slip past the living room. I used the remote, not voice control, to get the big screen to black. Then I rolled it back up behind a wood panel, no sign it and what had been on it was ever there. I heard a soliloquy like Victor talked for a living.

"I see my own daughter in Raven McCoy," he said. "I've worried for her since this situation has hovered over us all. It's sad. Her loved ones have my sympathy."

"Yes, we see your blog wrote kind things about her discovery," Detective Wise noted.

Victor looked puzzled, then not.

"Oh right," he nodded to me. I, not he, had written our kind things about her.

"I'm sorry," he said. "My wife handles most of our communications."

So they had really looked into all residents. Victor had kept a pragmatic approach. He had wanted to refrain from associating us with it so much. "It's not many blacks out here," he had kept reminding me.

However, as a woman myself — and a black woman — I'd felt we needed to be active in this from the start. So I'd tied *The Powellcast* sympathy blog into words of caution for all parents, but especially of girls. A homage to community bonding and unity despite isolation. I made sure to highlight the link where we had donated to the McCoy family.

I tossed the mail on the island near oils, vinegars, and cooking wines. The fish was wrapped familiarly. From a Chicago River market on our ways in and out of the city. Just Victor's short weekend drive to free up from working, to flee temptations to stay always involved with people and his audience online, to wrestle his mind from the trending news cycles. I set the fish in the sink. I washed my hands under a low stream. The water released the pent-up tension of my sudden testifying. I went through a small orange Gatorade in six or seven swallows. My eyes fell on a manila envelope in the mail bundle, fat and square instead of thin and rectangular.

I pat my hands on oven mitts to dry them. The manila envelope had no postage. It had handwriting, not keyboard labels, and the script felt familiar. It was just something with Victor's name. Victor Powell, simple with no description or explanation, written out in a black sharpie.

Others were in the house. The rest of the pile was standard statements and bills — nothing Victor would look for or miss or ask about later. I stuffed it all in the cubby for print magazines, with the envelope with his name. He'd ask me where it was. Then, I'd ask about it.

I walked back to the others. Victor didn't do too much coffee, probably had green tea already. He carried a BPA-free water bottle out the house just for health nut show. He would be de-hydrated by now, I knew. I filled him a coffee mug of water and stood behind his chair. He started the table onto dark chocolate after-drink mints. I reached over his shoulder to select one.

"They were just telling me it seems to be little reason the young lady was last seen at a Grayson spa," Victor said. "You know, the one I gave you a gift certificate to last fall?"

I only nodded. I felt my face was tight. My throat was too. The envelope was in my mind.

"You were a patron there, too, Mrs. Powell?" Wise asked.

"Once," I thought out loud. "Maybe twice."

"She has her faves in the city," Victor said. "Most of our friends are in Chicago."

Magnificent Mile, Gold Coast and Streeterville skyscrapers remained my go-to for essentials. Mario Tricoci salons for my hair, to my shoulders for hundreds of dollars a month in blow-outs and deep treatments. I resorted to sloppy braids, split ends and grays with them closed.

Wise spoke through her melting chocolate, dead serious and deadpan.

"We have reasons to believe she was picked up at the spa by someone who lived in Grayson Glens and that person is the key to understanding what happened to her. No CCTV camera in that area. But the last time her phone pinged was a time we know she was at the spa."

"I had a pedicure, massage, some waxing there," I recalled. "I met the owner at the Arts Center Gala, so I got a discount.

I wouldn't be able to help figure out who was there recently."

"This was about four months ago," Wise continued. "End of December."

"That's more recent than the last time I was in that spa," I replied.

"You were at the local body shop recently," Loveless said. "Or excuse me, months ago?"

"No, I wasn't —"

I felt Victor's shoulders harden under my fingers. He waved his hand to quiet me.

"Yes, I had some work done there," he said.

Wise went back into her notebook.

"You, or your wife?" she asked.

"The Jeep belongs to both of us," my husband said.

"Some exterior damage repair and full detailing for a new 2020 Jeep Grand Cherokee, black, plate number ILBD..." Wise read. From notes.

"Yes," Victor said. "I met the owner at the Arts Center Gala and checked the dude out."

"Why?" Wise asked.

"What does what we do with our vehicles have to do with Raven McCoy?"

"We're curious about area vehicles that got body work or detailing around last time Raven McCoy was seen," the detective said. "A brand-new vehicle needed that much?"

"It did."

"And so urgently you dropped it off on Christmas Eve? For what, a holiday road trip?"

"Am I being accused of something?"

Victor's code switched up a notch. I'd seen him turn on a dime.

"Not at all, Mr. Powell."

"What's next? You wanna take this cup out of my house to get my DNA?"

"Victor—" I began. Too late.

"Sir, we're taking a real close look at men in the area and possible connections to a very attractive young woman, whose family or friends know no reason she was running around in this area. Or how she was financially taken care of. Where were you last December 23rd?"

"A Wednesday," Wise said. "Day before Christmas Eve, when you took in the Jeep."

"I don't know," Victor said. "Definitely wasn't getting ready to host a family gathering or go to church. We were getting arrested for that, remember? So, guess I was home with my wife."

"And we could verify all that?"

"You mean that Wednesday or Christmas Eve? I'd have to look at my books for the time. Let's see. For holidays we had Facetimes, Zooms, Facebook? I took in the truck, but…"

Victor was angry and he stood, a suspect of what we didn't even know.

"You seem to be looking for more than if I got work done on my truck. And you're planting some strange ideas about me in front of my wife."

"We're questioning all men in the area," Loveless stressed. "You're a man in the area."

"Yes, including young men and even boys," Wise agreed. "An age range."

"Like, a profile?" I questioned.

"Yeah," Victor answered. "A profile. Does this profile have a race?"

"Mr. Powell, be sure that has nothing to do with it," Wise insisted.

"Well, you can't get too far if your suspect's a white male. That's all there is here."

Victor started to the door. The police stood their ground.

Finally, Victor said "From now, my attorney can address anything to do with my profile."

"I don't think that'll be necessary," the chief said. "But if that's your choice."

I followed them out. The law's heels and soles played a different melody now. I imagined they were looking around. But I could've been imagining everything. The odd night, restless morning, hangover, strange envelope vibrating in a kitchen cupboard. All a fugue.

"Good day," Victor smiled from beside our front door.

We had come all the way to high price point boondocks in belief price tags meant something. That zip codes were bulletproof to the same old offenses. Now this.

After her backup was gone, Detective Wise turned back. I soaked up my husband's *get the fuck outta here* rage decades of professionalism had taught him to tame.

"Where does your name, Tragedy, come from?" she asked.

"It's a long story," I told her.

She smiled, nodded, and caught up to her boss.

I knew it took all Victor had to hold the door to its close instead of slam it. He turned, speechless. I went to wipe away signs of the intrusion. Neither officer touched their drinks. But of course. Everybody everywhere must offer them a caffeine jolt. Water, surely. It's just prudent custom for them to accept something. Empty chocolate wrappers, though.

I could see Victor wanted to speak. But the speech would go on all night. It would run over everything in its path. We would turn into people we didn't want to be. We would lose our humanity and just become profiles: black people in America, same shit, a different day.

I wanted to tell him to dig up the number to the grandparents we met at the Arts Center Gala. The Pitts were black people like us. Nothing like the squad of color we would have had with people our own ages. We hardly saw them but in town or at their annual shindig for all their black friends and family to descend on the Glens, camp out the weekend and drink copiously. It would be racial if Christian Pitts were a suspect — my God, he and Mrs. Pitts were more likely to have wanted to adopt Raven McCoy than carry out some affair or worse with the girl.

"I left some watermelon in the truck," I heard.

In solitude finally, I remembered something from last night. Something I'd left in the truck. Surely where Victor could see. Oops.

The crates of wine.

Seven

When Victor retreated to a room to collect himself, Tragedy snuck out to check the Jeep. It was like new, as usual. Victor's idea of stress release was scooting the auto vac around his old black Jeep and now their new black Jeep, Tragedy's trusty silver Chrysler, and his white hybrid Jag. He washed and waxed them, too. Tragedy didn't know if he poured out or hid her crates of wine bottles. Or if she never bought them. *I gotta calm down*, she thought.

Weather change, mass reopening and a river body was a confluence to mayhem. It wasn't just her. Babies were showing out in streets and stores. "A streetlight shorted and it was a wreck on Marigold," Victor recapped. Recently, *The Grayson Herald* reported a maid died of a broken neck; her step stool snapped in two. A coyote was sighted. Since Raven's discovery, the former homeowner's mail was showing up. Tragedy's mind and mood matched the area climate.

Victor spent the afternoon fashioning a smoke rub for the Wisconsin trout. He carried the few pounds of fish, a wood cutting board and two butcher knives with him to the veranda. Soon, nearby neighbors smelled their pit's hickory and Palo Santo wafting. Some maybe heard hacks and strikes, the offenses of the day transferred to watermelon and scales. He was trying to disconnect suspicion of him for a local incident from his race and put it onto his sex. He couldn't. Other men police questioned wouldn't know the feeling of being accused so much for less. But for the urgency to tend a freshwater catch, he would've been on his bench to press out his weight in the frustration.

I did all the right things… he lamented. *My people did me a disservice. They let me think I was good enough. They didn't tell me I would never be good enough. I wrestled away from bad paths the world pictured me stuck on. I gave my elders respect. I married black women like they told me to. I modeled a kind of black boy and man these motherfuckers don't want to admit.*

And yet a perfectly good Saturday is fucked up anyway…

Tragedy saw her phone glow under the boot bench in the mudroom — maybe it slipped when she wobbled out of stilettos. Some missed calls and texts. The treadmill was on her mind. Of course, her laptop and more chapters of her life awaited to be tapped out. However, a quick bath was more necessary. She body-brushed her way to better circulation. She stared into white Carrara tiles to conjure a clean slate. She slipped into a wide-legged gray jumpsuit tied in the middle, loose and detached from her skin, nice while the prickly hangover fever cooled down.

Then she came down to wash and chop cauliflower, broccoli, and carrots. Better weather was giving her new recipes to feel excited about. Tempting flavors rolled out: lime juice, chili powder, grated orange, red pepper flakes, extra garlic. She considered Victor's bar. A Puerto Rican rum to pour over the mixture. Just a splash for the meal. She pulled husks off roadside sweet corn to wrap any leftover fish in later.

By deciding not to think about it, she only thought about the manila envelope. More, the name on top and what was inside. She checked the magazine cubby. She didn't have much time to look. They had so much stuff there. And, she didn't snoop on her husband.

Now, through the kitchen glass, she saw Victor wrist deep in fish heads and split guts over a white bucket. He'd spill it all down into a nearby creek. He was consumed. She could get to it. She saw her reflection in glass and stone backsplash. Her father stayed a shadow in her face, seen in her tough grade of hair and owl eyes. Tragedy had her hand on the envelope. She held it out, thought of opening it. She perceived it to be floating, back where it came from.

Then, the kitchen's steel, marble and wood textures all sank behind a pellucid sheet of sheer moving images — of the missing girl, again. In front of her seemed a screen of Raven McCoy clips that replayed in news or online in recent days. This clip was the girl's high school graduation, snug tightly inside a crowd of friends. They beamed and yelled "Bye high school!"

Tragedy toppled behind herself. She hit her back on the edge of the counter and yelled. The room was just fine. She didn't know she went into a state. The tray of vegetables scattered from a perfect Pinterest pin for one of her online food boards into something to start over. The pitcher of iced tea smashed to a tearful brown mess at her feet.

"Honey?" Victor was in the room with her.

She broke down in his arms. He assumed he knew what it was about.

"Let's leave that shit behind," he told her. "It's over now."

Tragedy only nodded.

"And make sure you let me know what we're posting," Victor said, stern. "It was your idea to capitalize on us living in Grayson to get into Raven. No more. It's drawing attention."

Tragedy let it pass. The police chief and detective caught him off guard. It wasn't every day the law trolled them. More important than a blog and the cops, she was stunned at how her past life could cyclone to her door to make her disbelieve, momentarily, her own ears and eyes. She was scared. Victor watched her put his envelope back where she often put all the mail.

*

Only Victor's closest family and longest friends knew his wife's tough life and foster care past. However, he was a right circles kid. A child star really. Basketball scholarship shoe-in, from the St. Joseph's High School that manufactured them. Off to good schools. No NBA recruitment, but a stint overseas playing for Australia. His main family — not the do littles and ne'er do wells at its fringes— didn't believe in debt. He had college and a first big wedding paid for. Family help to deposits on a home with his ex-wife, then a condo for himself. He bought cars with bonuses. He didn't know ditches. He only worked to rise to profit, not wade or get by.

His people knew people who knew people. One of those people had gotten him interned at ESPN, into an accidental TV and media career. This was on top of the academic career that made him a professor. So he was just born to the kind who inherit lucky break after lucky break until it's no longer luck. It's just par for the course.

Tragedy didn't decode her new beau as a VIP for a while after they met. She was handcuffed to a shift job, in service. Sometimes she could barely get her lunch, let alone a look at semi-famous faces. She didn't know he covered black sports, entertainment scandals and race. Or he ghostwrote hagiographies a few stars called him "Friend" for writing. Or he was a Black Studies prof writing opinions for CNN and *The Root*. Or, he was angry that his life of so much work was less important than what rappers and housewives posted on social media. His college sweetheart wife got content and possessive. He had friends and supporters, sure. A great team, yes. But he didn't have that one super partner invested in everything else he saw was possible.

He was thinking he needed a sidekick long before Tragedy popped out in the distance.

His ex-wife had a big accounting career she wasn't giving up. But, Tragedy's $50,000 a year job was expendable. From the start, this photogenic woman loved his ideas and was happy to work on them. *The Powellcast* came to cause all the stress on him. But Tragedy jumped in and took care of followers, pitches and emails. Oh, the emails. The Powell Group became a stash of authors, poets and activists Tragedy turned into their image management clients. Victor took 20 percent for every situation or gig he booked for one of them. That was Tragedy's idea.

After they prequalified for Grayson Glens, Tragedy knew she made it. *"Crushed it!"* was her two-word caption to posts when they closed. Unapologetically juvenile. She knew it. But she had defied her name. She'd spent five years working one of Chicago's finest hotels and those who travelled into it. She had to watch their conference ballroom entrances, advise them on how to dry clean or launder name brand clothes. She saw people always get a little more help and go on to greater times for the money they could wield. She ate the pricey leftovers of their affairs. She picked over the lost and founds they didn't rush back to claim. Now, she was one of them.

Yet Tragedy often caught a glimpse of her orphaned self in mirrors and glass. Or she stared at her reflection in luxurious bathrooms. Fear stared back. She didn't doubt her intelligence or worth. Still often, she froze up. This self-image was a painless migraine, blinding at times. The detectives scared her and she felt the freeze again. Their interests in the Jeep and that late

December night returned her to a pit of the marriage. Tragedy didn't know she was turning the cold faucet on and off. On and off. Victor's fire outside, running water inside.

Her mind wandered to the day before last Christmas Eve.

It was just supposed to be exercise for her inner shopaholic. A "workout" — in credit or debit taps, chips and swipes at all the rock bottom sales, clearances and last-minute gift promotions. Tragedy saw this as excusable. A good deed, even. Retailers were rabid for customers after a year that lockdowns shuttered business. Storefronts broken, stores wrecked in racial injustice protests, lootings morning to night. People were primed to shop stress away.

Yet she'd crawled up the circle drive that early Christmas Eve morning, hours after she should have. Like this morning. No bearings to her phone. Victor was beside himself. A riot of damage to the brand-new Jeep. Profound scars. Bags and boxes scattered. And his flask, *his* flask she gave him for their wedding day ("How dare you?") — empty in the passenger side foot well.

She had slept at the wheel, in damp pants. How embarrassing she could have pissed herself. Victor carried her in. By late afternoon, when she had slept it off, Victor had cleared the car and Ubered from the body shop with a $2500 estimate.

Then, they had a serious conversation.

EIGHT

"Sure honey, spring break with us is fine..."

Tragedy winced at Victor's words. His daughter Joy was in some teen girl contention with her mother. Victor was the middleman. Joy's aloof father and his relatable wife had new appeal for her. Tragedy tuned them out while she dimmed the lights and wiped the main dining room table for dinner. Victor would set the fireplace. They normally ate in the breakfast nook. The lights were off there. Dark energy of the afternoon's guests and Raven McCoy's name clouded its air.

"I'm happy to pick you up. It's up to your mother if she wants to drive you or not," she heard Victor say. She rushed before him. "God, no," Tragedy mouthed to her husband.

The girl's mother always forced Tragedy into extended relating and niceties, like a fake *Modern Family* dress rehearsal. Tragedy never understood why she couldn't leave her cookies or brownies, or whatever she sent Joy with, and just get out. The woman had a boyfriend, finally. Part of why her daughter started preferring their home. Tragedy gathered the ex-wife's first post-divorce boyfriend wasn't exactly with a winner. Something to do with a little past alcoholism, maybe coke and weed, making middle age a do-over. Or that's what Joy had suggested.

She braced to think she'd have to deal with them again soon. She was at least satisfied to know she was eased into one of those couples who read each other's minds. Victor reported — and this was all they'd say about this shit again — that he did indeed dig up the number to the Pitts, a first contact between their households since elaborate holiday cards.

"Yeah, they got at us too," Mr. Pitts shared. "Just be cool, son."

He regretted to tell them his annual party was delayed again due to their ages and the pandemic. And that was that.

It was such a weird day for them both. Time to be easy with each other. Put themselves back to the heights of their minds before outsiders shaved them down. They had two helpings of perfect fish. They spoke of everything but Raven McCoy and police and isolation. They had the usual unavoidable business meeting on the calls, priorities and deliverables. She, still parched from the prior night, sipped iced tea she found a new pitcher for. He kept it to a beer.

Once Joy arrived, urges would go to quickies in the master bath and maybe the bed, never for long. So they started on sex like they knew in-house company was about to descend. First at the table — her ankles a clasp at his neck, his face in her breasts. In front of picture windows at the side of the house, others' picture windows in distance, an unblocked view from an open road through their section. *We should be careful…* She went to uncaring soon. She perched her feet on the table and dismissed her failures: getting drunk (again), feeling lousy, whatever was in an envelope that was probably just real business. He rushed them into the living room. Tonight, he had aggression Tragedy had preferred him for not having. His age made him stand out from younger guys who treated her like batting practice.

What's happening? Tragedy thought the more she tried to control him and couldn't.

Today wasn't the first day she entertained the possibility that Victor snuck in other delights to think about when he was with her. He didn't exactly keep banker's hours. Nor have one set workplace or one set crew of coworkers. He was at the perfect middle age to win over young, impressionable female admirers without trying and also to fall into much more experienced women's charms. Whenever he went back to teach his few courses in the classroom instead of online, his students would be twice as young as she. Some the same age as Raven McCoy, the girl who walked out of a tiny spa in Grayson to get into a car no one saw the driver of. And it could have been driven by a successful, wealthy and bored man who was her neighbor.

Or her husband.

Victor called her name and mumbled "I love you." She kissed him back but didn't say it this time. She let him continue, played along, chalked up this wild version of Victor to stress of being interrogated on short notice. And his daughter's impending visit, never without its pressures and guilt for him not being there full-time. They disentangled.

"Can I get you anything?" he asked.

He always did. Tragedy remembered the fruit salad chilled for dessert. The watermelon and cherries she pitted herself. She'd marinated it all in a little rum.

"And just a flavored water," she called as he walked away. He gave her a thumbs up.

She watched him go, admiring his form he worked hard at. An ex-athlete. Gray hairs his only changes. Other women she knew, many younger, made do without what had turned them on about their men. Long hours, material acquisitions, hectic travel, getting in time with the kids.

Back when they had a Lake Michigan view but just 1,500 square feet of city condo, she caught Victor speaking in hushed tones when she walked in a few times. Or in an awkward dance with his cell phone, if she turned out to be nearby and he didn't know it. He was no longer just a sporadic face or voice in the media, but not yet front and center either. Black cars came for Victor's more frequent trips —many first class now— with argument-sparking frequency.

After the shouting matches came days of the silent treatment. She piled department store boxes in the condo building's recycle room as her retail revenge. "I can't turn down these jobs," he would explain. Police showed up for this once. They lived on the Gold Coast, so the paper-thin walls were an inhumanity owners were supposed to pretend wasn't there. But everyone knew what new appliances husbands gave their wives and when the few resident infants were teething. A husband and wife arguing over other females calling and emailing was a lullaby.

After that, Victor increased the number of his calls, texts and Facetimes from his hotel suites. She came along more, stood by to make him look good. She never brought herself to hidden cameras or cell phone spyware. That's crazed killer stalker wife. Still every month he was in some new place, more cultural events and premieres and prime seats to athletes' finest hours.

She was lying about her drinking. Why wouldn't he be lying about other women?

Victor returned. He served them fruit on a restored settee his family passed down through generations. Tragedy's body was all his for the night, her lust echoing through the house and out open windows, dying down and rising up again. In between making love and coming back to their senses, Tragedy stared at the ceiling in a first-floor guest room they retired to. This was the bedroom she liked most for the ease to the kitchen and no treetops blocking a view, but she'd wanted the biggest one for herself. They didn't need this much house. But a Grayson Glens property was Victor's peace offering, proof of his intentions for the long haul. And the house always gave them impressive images and scenery online, in all seasons. They didn't have to parade Airbnb or Vrbo rentals as their own, like so many others who needed internet images.

Around midnight, Tragedy disentangled from Victor to wrap in a blanket, close windows and lock doors. She snipped and snapped the awnings, slid blinds up or across, double checked the sliding doors. It was a thorough night watchman's job with a motive.

She was looking for the crates of wines.

She walked through largesse as a symbol of what she always knew hard work would bring her one day. The space, view, aesthetics. The whole life — all spectacular. She had to work hard to see into homes nearby. Upstairs, out the veranda, through the gates and fences and trees.

"Seven years," Tragedy said aloud, struck by her own voice in the silence.

Seven years ago, she was in her first post-associate degree in a hospitality job. Standing, mostly, at an outskirts hotel's front desk. Overnight. Staring at tiny print on screens, handing out midnight snacks and towels, plunging toilets, jousting key cards with disoriented or drunk travelers, battling guest sex invitations. She stayed smiling so much she formed premature nasolabial folds. Crow's feet too, from lifting her eyes up to fake cheerfulness. She had to act like her view was the Pacific Ocean or Maui. She was really looking at a Bob Evans restaurant and blank trucks carrying livestock to slaughter. That scene wasn't inside any hospitality career websites and certificate brochures. Student debt for promises: *Adventure! Luxury! Excitement!*

She borrowed on credit cards to pay a resume service and joined TheLadders.com. It was a shot in the dark. She wasn't educated enough for that platform. *Nothing to lose,* was her mindset and truth. Soon she had a "No" to her application for Assistant Hotel Manager of a 5-star downtown Chicago hotel. But — she also had an invite to apply for its bell staff. She replied "Yes" to that offer and the slow coming employment offer from it.

For her last night in the boring place on the highway, and on account of her never missing a day, her Polish manager stayed over with his wife's homemade Bismarcks. The Jamaican head of maids left behind her favorite rum. A night cook, a maintenance worker and her replacement (on a second day) all toasted: "To way better views!" And, "To concierge in five years!"

She walked out the next morning with something to shoot for and dream of, tipsy off more than rum. Potential was the elixir. At first, the upgrade satisfied her just for a better salary and commute — only two buses to downtown Chicago. No more solo, long drives. It turned out to be better everything: views, uniforms, lunch options, luggage, perfumes, colognes, guests...

NINE

In my old life, I was an adult day carer. In hotel lobbies with rooms, instead of day care centers with nap cots and the ABCs pasted on a classroom wall. Some guests didn't know our alphabet — many tourists didn't speak English. I was more lost with them than with toddlers.

The last hotel I worked at was a winner: Mag Mile location, lobby coffee service, two hotel bars with top shelves, penthouse suites, foreign dignitaries and occasional celebs. It wasn't so brand name anyone came looking for them. I marveled at how quietly faces I maybe knew came or went. No drinking on the job for me. Only after work. Alcohol wasn't a problem then.

No way could I have handled working the luxury hotel industry in Chicago if I was hung over. The hours were punctual and long. Every minute, every second, a rushed and flurried guest came into focus. Travel and hotels are everybody's alternate dimension. An expert Los Angeles team of hoteliers helped train me. They flew in to teach trainees to see hotel guests differently than they would look in the regular world.

"The rudest and most demanding are always just the most stressed and needing of our care. If they're calm enough to be nice to you, then you really weren't hired for them!"

That was enough to carry me through my first year. I was black, a woman, baby-faced at not even 30, with rich or white or foreign or whatever people just viewing me as "the help." All shapes and sizes, all colors and kinds, all molds and breeds. Always, my natural black hair was conservative, my brown suit was neat, my gold buttons were tight, and my face was fixed.

So, I heard this one "Umm…miss?" and I replied, "How can I help you?" robotically.

"Well, I'm sorry to impose," the guest continued.

"Did you leave something? Lost and found is downstairs, in packages and deliveries."

"Not quite. I'm sorry. I wasn't a guest."

He didn't play sheepish well. Enchanting cockiness, not arrogance.

"I just finished the conference," this guest continued. "But I saw you here yesterday about this time and… If I remembered when you worked and came back later, I'd be kind of crazy right?"

I picked up a pen at the bell stand and scratched on a hotel pad. Nothing. Just marks.

"Well, I'm not a doctor," I told him. "I'm only hotel staff."

When a woman works in these kinds of environments, it's nothing to gaze at Adonises of all colors and kinds all day and night. They carry Louis Vuitton luggage, in hands with no wedding rings. They have rooms just a few floors away. Perfect for trysts. Afterward, they have secretaries to relegate a woman's calls until she gets the message he's nothing but a memory to block. So many men hinted propositions my way. I was a young woman with no wedding ring. Some stereotyped I was only there to be a call girl on the side. Here's where my fellow staff came in handy. Especially the older men who immigrated to America for this work or passed the career path through the generations. They protected me. I was *Mija*, *Córa* and *mia figlia* for them.

But all my male allies were rushing cabs, guiding ways and juggling suitcases at the instant I met Victor Powell. Later, I figured out he was a Renaissance man and hood brother in one: He bought oils from West Side vendors to mix his own formulas in plain unscented lotions. His scent was a shot to my brain. Not to slight myself, I knew I was especially resplendent that day. Just back from a long weekend off.

"Well, hostess," he said, "can I take you to dinner?"

The scene behind him disintegrated to busy mini-spotlights and crowds in slow motion. The Chicago behind me and the diverse, bustling hotel planet in front of me misplaced their sound.

It was supposed to be one first and last date. I was only 28. He was nearly 40. The restaurant showed his age: Michelin-starred, a Peruvian food world of metal and dark rectangles and squares for seats and decor, hundreds of dollars for our small plates and glasses. I fit in easily. What my paycheck could afford didn't matter. Luxury was my work world and language.

But we talked up a second date: a rom-com bomb with two stars we both loved but had stopped seeing much. It was so boring. We felt sorry for having to watch the stars fall off into a movie all teenagers slipped out of and no single people cared to come see it alone. A bad movie and that G-rated night alone in an empty theater morphed to this private joke we had.

Meanwhile, I checked dude out online. No average trick. Men tell women anything and everything. Truth as a process of elimination. But Victor's whole life burst forth just from Googling his name. I could've almost told him who he was. His education, Amazon books, bios, website, YouTube videos, a TedX Talk, a Northwestern faculty page.

Beyond checking him, I checked myself. I rented a little one-bedroom condo for a fair price. It was white room torture. Dull, quiet, decorated in a grayish Macy's clearance rack motif. Other people kept up family and relationship collages on the wall, spirits and souls besides theirs in rooms. I didn't. My few boyfriends had used me, I deduced. No man's face set my nightstand. My neighborhood was off a Lake Michigan beach, yet at a neglected end of Chicago. No El or subway. Icy gales whipped my butt on bus stops and train platforms. Gangs ran the streets.

I followed the crowd. My face was regular for boys in tight white shirts and corner doorways, dealing nickel and dime bags. At first, they read my neat clothes and glasses, nice speech. "You a cop?" they accused. Then I showed up enough the corners trusted me. I picked up overtime, never called off, came to all employee stuff. I wanted to move up. My work schedule slowed down parties. How much I picked up bottles on the corners stayed the same.

I was drinking and getting high alone. Or, I did it with two-bit men I circled. I lie stoned under their reasons to not want a girlfriend or not want to get married. I never met the men's kids by women they weren't with or women saying they had kids the men said they didn't.

Of course, I knew this man had a child. *"I'm divorced, a little daughter"* immediately —first phone call. Victor explained the last-minute switch for her summer vacation with him, from Mexico to Puerto Rico: His "ex-wife" Gloria haggled him on permissions to take the child out of the States. His location whisked him out of cell phone range. For days. He hadn't broken my social world online yet. I sent him an email. He didn't respond. I used the energy wisely. I said I wouldn't. People do it anyway: deep dive spy in the social media pits. It's just too easy not to.

One woman's post caught my eye. The caption to her picture was a typical rundown of fab women at a bar, why they're so fabulous. *Dr. This. Esq. That. PhD Whatever.* But also, the caption was "Divorce Dream Team! Anyone's who's gone through negotiations knows it's never easy. These ladies are reminding me women always fight for our worth. Cheers!"

The reality of this perfect older man? He was kinda sorta still married to a Gloria Powell.

I felt like a fool. Sick. Disgusted. I could've been left alone, at peace on my own. I knew how to do that. When I woke up on the couch late for work, my place was dry. Not even something white in the freezer, on ice like always. Not one wine bottle. I'd drunk it all. All over a man. *"Oh, hell no"* was my drumbeat from the shower, to the cab downtown, to my bell post.

I blocked this guest. All pathways online and phone. I left instructions with my building security. I counted the number of people I'd told about Victor on two hands. Not many, so easy to put him in past tense. A co-worker told me the married man pulled up at the hotel bell desk he first stepped to me in. Bronzed from Puerto Rican temperatures and the good life. Roses in hand. Looking for the "hostess," the one who made him rise to that "Umm… miss?" females reduce males to. That co-worker wasn't privy to my personal day but knew to play dumb. I'd taken off work to shore up to ghost Victor. Neighbors and the doorman stayed polite about what came next.

"What the fuck?" was my eventual response to him, off my fire-escape. He was below doing what a leading man would do in romantic comedies. "No, Victor. You're married, boo."

"I'm not!" he yelled from the sidewalk below my window. "Who told you that?"

"She's all over Facebook with it, sweetheart," I shouted down. "Tame your chick. Thanks for everything."

My slammed window chopped the volume of Victor's speech in two, once crystal clear but now drowned out. I could've let him in. I chose to be ornery. I agreed to come down, not do anything. Just to talk. He saw me, rose from the curb, and walked us to his truck.

But this guest was my friend now. His old Jeep was parked illegally near a fire hydrant. One kiss. The tinted windows weren't all that much. Still, he pushed back his driver seat and lifted me to straddle him. He manipulated my skirt and panties. He never revealed himself but let me know he was there. Meeting him felt natural. I was right at home, but off in an adventure. Drivers cruised past the busy drive. The spot was easy sidewalk and street appraisal from so many front-facing windows, any time of day or night. Police sirens whistled, customary for my side of town. Yet, Victor had pulled me into not caring to be careful. Or, simply, entitlement.

Drinking was always part of it.

We cut into a nearby wine bar at last call. Victor pulled out a black card and said "Tab." So the owner and staff didn't mind a giddy twosome staying while they cleaned up or relaxed through nightcaps. He earned time to make it sound good. He confessed to his sad divorce mess and custody fight. He pulled up documents on his iPad listing "irreconcilable differences," not adultery or abuse. I was into glass after glass of one bottle of the stacked Shirazes, Cabernets and Noirs standing in as art. The bar's piano jazz soundtrack made me feel like a P.I. standing in the rain, smoking cigarettes in a black fedora, a suspect at my mercy. On my own, I would've kept it to a glass or two. On this guy's dime, I smashed one bottle and took another to go.

My belief, and more wine, led me to less and less reason to take that frigid journey to work from another woman's condo I gave my paychecks out to rent. I could walk to work or just go a few bus stops from the condo Victor bought himself, downtown, post-divorce. Even when he was out of town, I wound up going to work from his place. He gave me keys.

Victor never really asked me to marry him. His proposal was one of the only times I recall him off game. He took a standard night of Thai food takeout into fumbling for a little blue box. He asked (or said), "Why don't you quit your job and come live with me, now?"

The wedding we could have had was traded to pay off his ex-wife and daughter's house. He drained his big, private, lifelong savings for that. Now, he hated Gloria Powell for it. But that was my smart strategy to cut the alimony, child support and reasons for Gloria to bicker. "We'll make more, now," I promised him. He made enough then for an elegant ceremony most dream of. A small chapel in the university where he taught. A nearby quaint hotel and DJ reception followed. I seemed loved by his senior parents, a brother and sister, close cousins. I had a few tables of my coworkers and old friends. I found my mother's long-lost sisters to invite.

It was easy not to get drunk. Me: Champagne-colored beaded column gown, Etsy-ordered lace cathedral veil and showcase bouquet. Him: basic black tux. His daughter, not born when her parents married, wanted her pink princess dress as a somewhat maid of honor. Victor's brother stood for him. I couldn't find my brother to walk me down. My old Polish boss from the sad highway hotel did it. Then, to a family style beef or vegan pasta dinner. Open bar until fireworks.

Wedding book pictures show I had two champagnes. One for our first toast, the next for a sweet photo op. I twirl in my dress with my hotel friends and co-workers and old neighbors and a few aunts clapping in a circle. My "Just Married!" Insta shot. Boom. The new Mrs. Victor Powell.

Victor didn't invite everyone he could have. Not everyone he invited came. A faction had to stay back to console his first wife. I was a foster kid. A faction of my life deserved to fuck off. My small tribe kept me from looking like a total Cinderella missing all my shoes, not just one glass slipper. Time taught me to ignore the same questions or to repeat the same vague answers.

"Where did you grow up?" one of Victor's frat boys small talked.

"What did you say you do again?" one of his distant but important aunts squinted out.

"And your parents, they are…?" the chaplain, trembling to his eighties, kept clarifying." An only child?" and "How do you live with no family?" and more from nosey others.

Their world bored Victor. They were *safe* people, happy to herd in corporations and schools up to the American Dream as examples of black achievement and success. They didn't even take risks in Las Vegas. He told me I excited him. I made him think about breaking rules.

Our honeymoon was a train ride down South, charming and chaste. Guest rooms at Big Mama's and Cousin Jean's house were our honeymoon suites. One of his uncles did have a ranch with a barn… I met rounds of people who extended the definition of family into reality, not fantasy. When my co-workers and old friends invited me out, I found myself out of town or doing something with Victor. I stayed chatty online, sharing ideas on things to do on imprecise dates that never came. I enrolled in a commuter college on Michigan Avenue to add to my associate's degree. By the time we left Chicago, I was officially in the college educated crowd.

Voila! It showed up: that amazing life of travel those hospitality industry job brochures promised me. Technically, I did get it through my job. I wouldn't have met Victor without it.

We jetted off to the Canada side of Niagara Falls, Lake Tahoe, the Caribbean, Italian Riviera. We defied a Mediterranean cruise captain's order in rocky weather to stay out alone — me at the bow watching the sea part, Victor behind giving me more entitlement to adventure. We rented a boat on Wisconsin Dells to recreate that one. We documented and recorded our love, building listeners and revenue. We were in the rooms when athletes and celebrities he featured played Chicago. *The Powellcast* exploded. Income and options with less to do for more money, at first. Then… well, more. He could teach or not. If he did, it was for more money and perks.

And for that I had five bedrooms and four bathrooms, staircases, a country kitchen and breakfast nook, butler's pantry, floating dining room to den, solarium, a finished basement for the man cave and she shed, a wine cellar for a studio and enough ground wrapped around I didn't have to talk to anybody but Alexa and Siri. I was uphill, against a cobblestone path to a brook. I added "Manager" beside my name on Victor's website and called it a day. "Producer" of *The Powellcast* as well. For responsibility, purpose and a resume without catty competitors and sexist bosses. Or male guests not as nice as Victor about wanting to get me into penthouse suite beds.

I also missed most of my life outside my husband's coming to a screeching halt.

Here I was snaking through my own house searching for where my husband hid a crate of wines. This was more important than sleep or making love to him or keeping a schedule. I gave up finding where Victor hid the crates. Hard liquor was never my cup of tea. Only in a pinch. I unscrewed a bourbon, poured a shot into a coffee cup. I couldn't believe I was doing this again.

No matter what Victor did, I couldn't leave this life behind. I had to work everything out with him, like a real marriage.

Otherwise, I'd go back to impressing bosses for good evaluations and promotions, crushed with people I barely liked for condo rental living. And dating. Men. Strangers. They would crush me, eat my heart and dump me in rivers. I couldn't leave.

And I couldn't choose the same bottle. People can measure liquor with their eyes.

Ten

Chile, find a fortress. Any locked door will do. Just hide and listen as best you can...

Sometimes Tragedy's grandmother assumed her inner voice as her spirit guide. Tragedy followed Gran's guidance when the sensors alerted her that Gloria Powell's Mercedes had reached the drive. Tragedy booked up the back stairs. The ex-wife insisted on driving her daughter down to spend the week. Victor always had business —shopping at the least— to justify the near hour drive and back to Chicago to get Joy. The last year, with all the protests and curfews, Victor was the only one who drove for Joy's drop-offs and pickups or Tragedy's city needs.

That was all passed. Gloria had no incentives in Grayson but to overstay her welcome.

Tragedy eavesdropped from just beyond view at the side of the balcony. Joy updated Victor on school and track. She asked, "Where's Tragedy?" Victor had thought ahead to the inevitable: "Let's move outside to slice this juicy watermelon before it goes sour, ladies." Tragedy wasn't above a total snub and full shade. She moved to spy from the back terrace just over the veranda. Joy's voice was still youthful and high-pitched. "You guys have a dog?" she asked. "No honey," Victor said. *"Oh, I saw..."* Gloria interrupted to lead them into talking about mask fights, how much traffic she endured, how online learning was stressful on parents at home.

Tragedy rolled into her closet. She switched out two-day old black leggings and a jersey knit top for a gray wrap dress, just her color and style, free of effort or suggestions.

All things considered, no drama foamed between the women or households. The ex-wife: an econ major, accountant, E & Y defector to PWC. Taciturn and observant. She initiated divorce from her big thinker husband, preceded by what he described as her against change and his skyrocketing career. Victor kept their conversations short. Once, one went long enough in hands-free mode Tragedy heard herself labeled "that uneducated thot." Victor saw she heard this.

The "thot" finally presented herself to serve a brunch she had created begrudgingly: some quinoa-kale-red cabbage detox confection for vegan Joy, grass-fed steaks and bland pastas for the parents. Gloria spited Tragedy and only picked at the salads, claiming "a diet."

Of course, thought Tragedy. *To fit in that tight chocolate body-adiyadi leather fishtail skirt* we *paid for...* She suspected they helped pay for the diamond drops and leather bag as well.

The drowned woman who put Grayson Glens in the news brought Tragedy face to face with the power children could have over a man. The news Raven McCoy was found had landed from house to house in soft order of Sunday morning papers tossed to porch steps. Long before it was really a death, Gloria used the missing girl case like she used everything in Victor's world. She called from her townhome Victor paid off in Chicago's historic Bronzeville neighborhood, to make deductions and continue negotiations. When the "Have You Seen Raven McCoy?" fog enveloped the Glens, the new condition was "Joy ain't coming out to them woods ever again!"

Who could blame her? The pandemic world caved in to such an eerie dome as it was.

When a new year came and the case was still cold, a fresh indictment arrived: "Is a dead daughter what we'll get for you chasing white folks to their spooky neighborhoods?"

That was a low blow. No comparable all-black communities of the South existed much in Midwest cities, which were historically segregated. Sure, homebuyers could find scenic blocks of black homeowners and condo developments. But a block or two within them came low incomes, high crime, and the epitomes of underserved. They considered L.A. or New York. But the amount of house for the money and an hour's reach to an airport was no match for Chicago.

Now, the missing girl was found there yet their daughter still wanted to head to the haunted Glens rather than spring break in violent Chicago. Gloria's spiel was: "You can move from the bangers in Chicago all you want. Nobody can predict where the white serial killers pop up."

Joy finished scarfing her rabbit food and went on to trace information.

"At the time she was last seen, McCoy was finishing her first semester at Prairie State College. She planned an Associate's in Fitness and Exercise, for a personal training career."

"Well, hope that explains all the thong shots," Gloria said. "Not sure how girls think they're gonna stay safe. The new wardrobe seems to be booty and more booty."

"Mom, wearing bikinis and modeling your healthy body doesn't mean much," Joy sighed. "We talked about this already."

"Oh, body positivity?" Gloria asked. "You can let it all hang out then expect men to read a dissertation on consent? Okay, Joy."

"Life doesn't work that way," Victor chimed in. "You never know who's watching. It's creeps everywhere."

"Creeps murder and rape total strangers all the time," Joy fought back. "They don't need to Instastalk for victims."

"But seeing average girls and women advertising themselves all the time doesn't help, honey," Victor pleaded. "Don't give the crazies anything to get started on."

"That's not what you said on the podcast," Joy snapped. "Oh Mr. Victor Powell, all about Me Too and Time's Up. Yeah, right."

"My job and my daughter are two different things," Victor explained. "And I don't want to sit up here talking about a dead girl. We don't know her. We're fine. Let's focus on that."

Tragedy refilled everyone's iced tea. She never knew how to fit into these family moments. She wasn't keen to be in the same position as the parents: an enemy Joy distrusted but needed, just a wallet with cash and resented otherwise. It took her all just to be cordial to the first love of Victor's life, a woman he made a baby with, a body who used to give him what she does.

"This isn't a hot topic or media talking point to make you look good Victor," that woman said. "This is really happening, you know."

"I'm sure they'll figure things out," Tragedy said. "They seem to have more than predictability to believe a man has something to do with it. They've questioned us already."

"Honey..." Victor's coffee complexion made him blush purple.

"What, Daddy?" Joy laughed into snorts. "God, my father's a killer now? You're going to seriously screw my life. *Please* don't get a mug shot on the internet."

"Are you a suspect, honey?" Gloria asked.

Tragedy's mouth and eyes flattened. Victor didn't catch Gloria boost the affection he'd just given his wife. Maybe he played it off. Joy was deep in fantasies of being part of the case. Her thumbs rushed to a flurry, ready to blast off texts of the *"You guys won't believe this"* sort.

"I'm not sure," Victor sighed.

"Of course he's not," Tragedy said. "But of course, men in the area will be of interest."

"Well, were you gonna tell us you were involved with police?" Gloria went up a notch.

"I am not *involved*," Victor sighed. "It's not our daughter. That's all that matters."

"Oooh, this is juicy," Joy wiggled with glee at her find: a true crime channel and its extended profile of the Raven McCoy case in Grayson Glens.

Joy slouched on her parents, setting her iPhone between them. Tragedy sized up the trio, Joy's pecan tone an even harmony of her parents' shades, angular features for all. She recalled a fuzzy picture in the office. A Father's Day. Joy was a toddler. At Promontory Point beach, Victor knee deep in shimmering lake water. He's about to dip his gleeful little girl. Victor respected to have no pictures of his ex-wife in the house. Still Gloria, behind the camera, always felt the strongest presence in this one. The image oozed what they had named their daughter. Victor's measure was Tragedy never had to ask him to nix photos of his ex-wife. Only Joy and the old Great Dane they once shared, Barney, lived as photos from his first marriage. The dog made himself known in junk drawers and closet corners and to-be-filed office piles, an eerie fidelity in pictures beside Victor, who was deliriously giddy and proud for being the man of a family.

Vegan cupcakes ordered just for Joy waited in the vacuum food saver. Tragedy excused herself for them. Mashing the food saver's button was effective stress relief. The lid untwisted. They held up enough to serve. Paper plates were too petty, perhaps.

And obvious. She settled for a neutral zone in basic eggshell white saucers. As she reached the breakfast nook with three servings balanced, a woman's pithy commentary over the video was into conspiracy theories bound to sprout. Young women. No — young *beautiful* women. It wasn't lost on Tragedy that Raven McCoy had a look that, alone, could have carried her far. This most certainly fueled interest and, morbidly, more flyers and tweets and soundbites.

"Her native Wells was a heartland factory hub. Now, employment stalwarts have closed or fled, leaving a population behind. Yet by her senior year of high school, Raven became known for flexing cash. Sources state she took friends and family on shopping sprees and spent big on credit cards. She explained the excess as being an Amazon affiliate and brand influencer online. But, a heartbroken community wonders if something more nefarious paid the prices."

Tragedy had enough.

"Joy, please," she said. "It's too insulting to her. And the town. Is she even buried yet?"

Victor tapped the video off.

"I'd imagine an autopsy or two first," he said. "Let's see the reports out of that."

"Dad, I just ate!" Joy yelled. "Don't make me url."

Dad tousled her hair. Tragedy and Gloria's eyes met but they darted quickly and cut cake. Gloria took two bites. "Would you like mine, honey?" she asked Joy, passing her plate.

"Were you in foster homes in Wells, where the girl was from?" she asked Tragedy.

"Maybe," Tragedy said. She glared at the woman. "I don't really remember foster homes. Why should I? Look at my adult home."

"Wonder what a girl like her would be doing, or headed to," Gloria said.

"I wouldn't know," Tragedy remarked.

"Is the pool open?" Joy exclaimed.

The Pool Hall was just one set for them to stage vacay shots without really going anywhere. A reminder the house was so much more than a home. It contained bigger plans—parties, retreats and conferences. They never saw spending a whole year paying for it but not being able to use it like they'd planned. For now, it was good enough to change the subject.

Gloria went on to a golfing retreat cancellation for her business professionals' group as a sign the pandemic still wasn't over. Victor explained the pandemic restrictions and its impact on the Pool Hall, someone's idea to give Grayson Glens a feeling like lakeside or beachside in the middle of corn. A unisex bathhouse indoors. Indoor pools, heated and not. Breakout whirlpools and Jacuzzis in separate halls. A water slide for kids. A café with snacks and adult beverages. A family friendly date spot. Off limits until a Glens council had a plan. The greens opened, though.

The brown circular mass on Tragedy's square white plate seemed to dot and swirl into an impression of a crude map. Or an aerial photo. Or an artist's rendering. By hand. In pencil or ink. The distortion demarcated roads, highway exit dots, corn and wheat fields, cemetery plots, dainty pretty churches and stooping clapboard ones, factory exhaust, a railroad yard, a big river.

In the center was a girl wearing a long white dress. Her toes peeked out from under it. Tragedy couldn't see her face. She sank tines into the world around the girl. She ripped off the fairgrounds and chewed them. Next, she sheared the state park, cut perfectly down the middle, then across. She was on the last crumb, or what she saw as the soybean field, when the whole map popped with a spark and became a puff of smoke. She was alone.

Then the vision was gone and it was just dessert on her plate. She was still alone. The group had walked outside. But when? She saw that woman give her husband's daughter a parting kiss and Victor a handshake. Perhaps she hadn't said "Goodbye" properly to Gloria. Oh well.

Tragedy scooped dishes up. Exhaled. The end of Jesus duty. Joy was now a junior at Illinois Math and Science Academy, far up west. The girl's ascension to high school was the turn of the screw. Gloria was no longer the package deal she used to be. Tragedy leveled up from scorned younger woman to adored bonus mom, relating to her stepchild in ways they chose to.

She turned from loading the dishwasher. Gloria stood behind her, startlingly so. Tragedy did her best not to react. A "How can I help you?" almost leaked out from her shuttered career.

"Did you leave something?" she asked.

"Keep your eyes out on her," Gloria had come to say. "She thinks she's so grown now."

Thot, huh? Tragedy thought.

Tragedy saw fragility in the other woman's eyes. How she gripped that lunch break gym workout like her life depended on it. With or without Victor's child support, she was that *type*. She put her financial services professional salary to only the best dermatologists, beauticians and makeup. A sheen quite close to her daughter's hinted at laser treatments, Botox, maybe more. All this on top of "black don't crack" gifts. Yet Tragedy sensed much was gone. It went to how a man she loved disappointed her closer to a grave. Or it passed on to the child they shared.

"Of course," Tragedy assured Gloria. She didn't tell her they didn't even know any men who lived short walks away from them, all the suspects around just a template of white men they smiled or waved at cordially. She told her: "Never any missing girls on my watch. I promise."

ELEVEN

"It's so dead in this country I can't stay awake," was Joy's excuse to turn in early.

When Gloria deprived them of her company, Tragedy was amped to go work on her big thing: her book. This left dinner father-daughter style. Victor and Joy shared club sandwiches (bacon for him and vegan ham for her), gluten-free chips Joy suggested, and guacamole.

By nine o'clock, Joy arrested a bathroom. She chose the secluded basement one to troll free samples, small bottles, perfume soap gifts, testers. The overflow of all Tragedy ran out of room for in her bathroom counter. She inflicted the underbelly of the house with citrus, neroli and mint scents. Damp in a beach towel, she glided up, weighted with a huge duffel.

Teen girls still carry enough for sleepovers to backpack overseas, Tragedy thought.

Tragedy came down just as Victor was blind, deaf, and dumb to his daughter now. He was working again— there, but only as if he wore virtual reality glasses. He had only a few Easter Sunday hours to connect with as many people as possible before phones and inboxes slept for the holiday week. Invitations and requests were slowed with The Powell Group. Race and racism were last year's topics. #MeToo and #TimesUp were also dated now. Tragedy took the hints. He would be in the house but not, separated in his well-lit man cave that was his office. There, he would face his microphone and advanced hybrid camera that filled the space where she used to be to help him with smaller equipment, when they had to squish in his city condo hustling to make it happen. And other faces would pop up on a big screen before him to talk about what everyone was talking about or should be talking about. If he wanted her part of it all, he would tell her.

Tragedy noticed Joy take up in the first-floor guest room instead of her usual one upstairs. The lower one was near the water closet. It required a trip up or down for a shower. Hardly decorated. Not outfitted with the "little things" Victor and Tragedy collected for her stays: house shoes, a giant lounging hoodie, drawer fragrance sachets, dorm snacks. They zipped her body pillow and weighted blanket to store in the closet. A clawfoot mirror from the local Davidson's Furniture Bonanza was a nice size for her to primp in. They stashed the bed by the solar sockets knowing her kind sleeps with machines. Her Christmas present sat on a lingerie chest Victor's mother gave as a wedding present: a beauty fridge to chill lotions, creams and makeup. Any guests who showed up could use it of course. But the spirit of it belonged to Joy.

Victor's tablet absorbed him and he hardly noticed his wife ask about his daughter. Tragedy found Joy sphinxed on the bed, her tablet on its kickstand. Drops from her wet hair dotted the bedspread. It was chilly with just a hung window lifted. But Joy was so involved, someone's presence in the doorway didn't register. She leaped when Tragedy swooshed shut the window. She giggled, a goofy huff she would grow out of. She was still connected to the former child whose body once didn't stretch the whole length of the bed as it did now.

"You're not sleeping upstairs?" Tragedy asked.

Joy shook her head.

"It's just easier if I get up early or in the middle of the night and eat something," she added. "Or warm something up. Don't wanna wake you guys."

"Oh," Tragedy nodded, still paused.

"My track coach says I need to eat more. Heats and meets are coming back now."

"Makes sense. Well, your father'll be in to say good night."

Joy meant it for Tragedy but spoke to the screen, focused on whoever wasn't with her and already blanking who was: "Okay. And thanks for the vegan food today."

"More tomorrow," Tragedy said. She paused again. Finally, she slid the wood door.

She wandered back to her husband and whispered, "I think your daughter hates us."

"If she's anything like her mother, you're probably correct," Victor whispered back.

"She's sleeping down here. It's not her room. Not normally, that is."

"It's a new normal, babe."

"She must've heard us having sex the last time," Tragedy guessed. "How embarrassing."

"You're being paranoid," Victor said.

"Maybe."

*

There was a method to Joy's madness. Trips to the kitchen for three sugar-free cherry popsicles in two hours and mock bathroom breaks finally yielded the result Joy waited for until midnight: The house was silent except for her father's snores.

Victor's spare laptop chimed out of sleep mode. Joy was a few thousand feet away from him, in a different end of the house, at a different corner. But paranoid. The master bedroom faced front and center at the top. Her smallest bedroom on the first floor faced the back and side.

Can you come now? She typed into a chat box.

She watched bubbles pulse into chat, then one word: *No.*

More bubbles came into the words. *Security patrolling. Had to drive around.*

Shit, she typed.

Soon, came back. *Don't worry. I'm coming. Look out.*

Ok.

Joy messed the bed into organized confusion. She retrieved her body pillow from her usual bedroom's closet and zipped it from its case. She fattened it under the covers where a body would center. Then she knelt at the window, one eye to the road and one to the chat box. Soon, a sphere of white. It could be one of the toy cops who rode around the Glens. It could be a resident. Or, it could be the main reason she had called her father to organize a stay with him.

Omar. The boy. No, the *man*. Almost twenty, he was.

Back in Chicago, Gloria had a slight hold on the situation. She could have helped Tragedy and Victor get ahead of Joy settling into the easiest room to sneak out of. But though it had been eight years, Gloria was still a bruised amateur in the ex-wife thing. She was stingy, holding pieces of her daughter's growing up and growing pains all for herself. So she didn't warn the Powells about impositions. All the spyware installed on Joy's phone. Hidden cameras — all entrances and exits, windows and doors especially. She put their townhome development neighbors on watch. She briefed the parents of Joy's best friends.

For Gloria, downtown Chicago's descent to a ghost town put all bean counters working from home. God's mysterious ways. In her first-floor home office, she posted up like a guard, aware of all ways in or out, rescuing her child from everything she worked hard for her not to be.

The boy — no, the man — lived with roommates in the town where Joy's academy was. There were no parents to call. He wasn't a fellow student at the exclusive school, where Victor and Gloria believed in the campus's strict dorm parents and guardian systems. No. He was just growing where planted, poised between music producing and Uber driving and selling weed.

Joy had crossed his path at one of the area's plentiful outlet malls. In the food court. On a joyride with upperclassmen who had cars and permissions. This guy offered to buy her table's tacos and drinks. She didn't understand why he came over. He was funny, but... "He's kinda old," she and her friends had howled about him later. Then they walked away from the situation where the boy got Joy Powell's number for fifty dollars in wispy paper wrapped taco dinners.

It was curiosity, revenge against boredom really, that fueled her text to him one time the senior she already liked didn't text back quickly. This newer boy was mature, by those standards. He wasn't so quick to jump around. He stayed available and Joy liked that. He had an emoji or GIF or thought for everything. She could pour out groans about teachers, her mother and her mother's boyfriend, girls she went from loving to not liking on pheromone whims.

One Saturday, Gloria's mother's wit acted on the signals. She had stayed quiet to hear hushed calls until wee hours. That morning, her daughter seemed too giddy to watch her leave. She skipped the beautician's deep conditioning that sucked up an extra hour and charge. She didn't text an eta from her usual hair appointment time. She parked down the block instead of in the garage. She came into the back door. In minutes, what looked like a grown man — husky and bearded — fluttered downstairs to the yard. Gloria tripped on shoes he left behind. Sprained her ankle, she did. And the mother shouted and the daughter cried. They agreed on one thing: Victor couldn't know. It had taken Gloria a lot to interdict favorable, advantageous custody.

Gloria hadn't healed to see her ex-husband as part of her tribe. He was still the primary reason for it. She hoped his status as Joy's father and Grayson Glens gates would be a deterrent.

She was wrong.

Joy knew the code to the usually unmanned gate of Grayson Glens. She helped Gloria, an accountant who left numbers at work, keep up with it when it was changed. That way, they were never locked out for trying to drive straight in rather than risk an overeager gateman. Joy gave the boy clear instructions on that gate and the code. The Powell alarm system was tight, state of the art. Joy had re-lifted the window Tragedy shut as soon as her father said "Good night." He never came back to question the sharp open window digital alert. Dads were always dumb, busy with work, shouting at sports, paying no mind. Joy was in the clear to keep it just wide enough for the boy to help her twist out. Next, she just had to sneak her father's laptop to chat with him.

Her alias account, just to send emails and chats to the boy's device, opened up.

Meanwhile, the boy — no, the man — stood by with cousins in the South Chicago suburbs, thirty minutes away. So many nosey old-timers on Joy's block of rowhouses, townhomes, duplexes and condo flats with close yards. So many people in her mother's post-divorce life — a coven of friends, clubs, church members, co-workers, relatives choking her life. Going off to school was all that freed Joy from the activities and chains of her mother's pain.

The boy managed to sneak in a few times when Gloria couldn't keep up the social straitjacket necessary to guard her child. Joy tried to use phones from her same age cousins or friends to Facetime and text him. When she could get with people her own age, that is. The boy gave her cash to buy disposable cameras to snap not so innocent pictures, to hand the past relics to her friends to mail to him, for him to pass for discreet developing to a "studio partner" who worked at CVS. Now, out in the open Grayson Glens, they'd found freedom.

The boy saw Joy hanging out a bottom window of the large house. He shot off bright lights he relied on to navigate the daunting curves, unmarked roads and a creative but confusing map Joy talked out. She waved excitedly. He parked the borrowed old Cadillac. He shimmied through tight hedges, up the lawn. His hands caught her. Her arms went around his waist to break her fall. She kissed his neck. They fell on the lawn in fits of energy and excitement, imaginations flashing. Bad Dad was on his way. A horrible *Final Destination* or Chucky doll was nearby.

"Shoosh," he finally said. "Let's get outta here before your pops peep me."

The boy had spent an hour circling the Glens, waiting for Joy. He was conscious he was out of Chicago or its South Suburbs, visibly ethnic in mostly white territory. No car-rattling hip hop tonight. He stayed parked at curbs more than moving. The practice runs gave him a good eye on a few good spots to park for an hour or two, out of the main homes area and on the dark river.

The boy already had her British favorite singers programmed to vibrate their pretty voices through the car. And bags of greasy rib tips and fries from the counter serve where some cousins lived. Joy tore into the meat, relieved of her vegan thing. She mostly used that to power trip over the adults and set herself apart as cool. He lit the rolled blunt when they were far from the Powell's section. He passed it to her. She wanted to refuse but she didn't. She managed its choking fit with the bottle of cranberry juice he emptied enough to fit a full fifth of vodka.

In twenty minutes, he had rolled the sedan into the tree line to the lowest it could go to still balance on the riverbank, over a shallow bed of detritus and burrows, scarce river view lights in the distance. He knew his twenty years, aimlessness and experience should have mattered. He had big dreams and visions, but no guts or balls to sacrifice what they took. He skipped out on falling in line with his family's local car dealership, to make a good living meant to pay for the college he dropped out of. His other girls and women were in the Midwest to stay.

Joy? She talked to him about leaving, immediately. A big city for college. Far from her parents. He guessed they were the kind who would set her up no matter where she was. All their conversations spoke of him following her to New York or Atlanta for college. The hip hop industries were ripe for him to make it in those places. They just had to be patient. And secret.

But they weren't there yet. They were only in an aging Cadillac an uncle let the boy borrow, a few miles from the luxury home that didn't know its teenaged occupant was missing.

They ate, smoke, drank and talked about everyone or everything to hate most recently.

Joy was no longer a virgin. That changed shortly after she met the boy. Then the missing girl case gave her mother excuse to ban her trips to her father's, an escape from punishing sanctions in the mother side of her life, even before her mother knew she had given it up.

Joy was nearly a pro at drinking and her parents had no clue. Her drinking started freshman year at the academy and progressed. All the kids did it. But adding weed made her delirious. She wasn't habitual like the boy. The high made her compliant, buzzing with sensation. In no time the boy convinced her to peel off her loose sweats and tee, climb to the back seat and join him in lust pent up for one full season. He released quickly from rubbing himself into her thigh, kissing her breasts. He was dreaming of them since they hatched the plan. He knew getting near to getting pregnant was her deal breaker. She interrupted his hold.

"The condoms?" she asked.

He fished in all his pockets to produce a few foil squares. She relaxed. He took his time, watching and hearing her respond to thrills he tried on her body, having her touch him.

Being out under moonlight untethered the caution they had held under ceilings, where her mother threatened and his or her roommates had lurked. They both paused whenever headlights manifested. Eventually, they caught on they were so far back from it all they had to be looked for to be seen. She knew her father and his wife. It would be morning before they were tea kettles and coffee bubbling, incense wafting from a yoga room, a treadmill's swoosh. The biggest hazard was dawn, when the car was visible. Until then, she wanted to stop and start, smoke and drink, stop and start. One or the other always had new energy for a new way to try things.

Shortly before 3 a.m., a male figure sulked onto a short pier on the riverbank, to smoke a cigarette and watch the night. Eyes roved down the water, far past the nearest yards, close to the riverbank's edge. It spotted a form blacker than darkness. The form was deciphered to be a sedan, a nothingness disguising itself much better than bright-colored, showy cars parked often in nooks, crannies and perimeters of the river. Amorous shrieks skipped across its still surface. This was nothing new. The distant river bends and swells were far from the oft-passed bridge and patrolled parks and trafficked trails. They were atop acres families left for the seasons and sometimes gave up on using at all. They were popular for the cheaters and high school kids.

The figure turned, then returned. A camera, for hunting, zoomed in. A window cracked just so. A young woman's long back, some guy beneath her, the back of his head bumping foggy glass, his hands rowing her waist. History assured they would be back. It was timing, luck, chance to know if Grayson Glens would be so generous to them next time.

PART 2: ADMISSIONS

HOPING

*O*n my sixteenth birthday, I was by myself, holding my brother, Merit. Just a kid.

The night before, when my mother figured out the fire, she got to his room across from hers. She stuffed him out his window, second floor. It was locked in new coats of paint and freezing winter temps. She couldn't fit through the few inches gap. God only knows how she fit him. His scraped skin, bruises and a soft dent in his head gave an idea how effortful this last effort of her life was.

"Will I get him back?" I asked a nice librarian-type lady about my mutt dog.

He never had sickness shots or vet visits for the "little things." I could handle him without a leash. Other people might not.

"Sure, honey," the nice librarian-type lady smiled.

I believed her. She'd come to the hospital with new clothes, underwear and McDonald's breakfasts. That's all I had the taste for in the months after it all burned down, from poor electric the landlord always patched but never truly fixed. I was in the hospital, sedated I later heard, my brother in pediatrics. Squealing and scratching non-stop. Like he's on fire, I heard a nurse say.

I knew the rest of us were gone.

I heard — from relatives who loved me not enough to over-fill full houses for me — what was found of Mom and Gran got cremated to fit into two small boxes. I didn't get one. Mom and Gran were the outliers, the black sheep, the castaways. Because Gran was gay after Grandpa died young and Mom was the only one to go off to college. My father was a man who had talked to me at family stuff, dropped off gifts when I was at school or put them on porches my mother ran him off of. One odd job and bright idea to the next. No occupation. Only "businesses." Mom said he was a gambler, cheat and soft crook cops could know all about but pay no mind.

"Hope" is the name they all called me. That syllable carried the echoes of memories everywhere I tried to step into the future. My body hung under that grim cloud. Small favor to be an older foster kid. Nobody wants those. Barely anyone wanted my little black boy brother.

"Hope" lived three years moving garbage bags. Underneath a different twin or bunk bed every few months, switching schools and addresses. About ten homes in three years. Relatives opened doors but never handed over keys. She starved, a growing girl taking what she was given. She tolerated mental cruelty; she was an older child, so she had uses, but they couldn't touch her without her telling on them. They wouldn't get jail. It was too many like her for the social workers to finish the whole investigation process. They would get their meal ticket cancelled. Hope had kind but overwhelmed teachers. They failed to reverse all the time lost in time to get her to college like her mother, an English and African American studies major, a Panther. Hope used to have her mother's exciting Black Movement meetings, Easter shoes and cinnamon peppermint Christmas mornings. She lost that to sleep outside ornery doors, run in one pair of shoes at a time and survive

winters when people's mouths moved but all the carols for Baby Jesus were silent.

I couldn't live a lie starting off with my name.

I wanted to name myself after that Dru Hill song "Beauty." Every girl wanted Beauty to be her name, like the song said. Mom made fun of the "young people's music," but she loved that one. Yet I would set myself up for disaster. My name would do the opposite of what I wanted it to from now on: tell the world where I came from, what made me, what lived under my skin.

One day, "Tragedy" came to me. It had a nice ring to it. Easy on the tongue. Pretty even. It elicited intrigue. Like a weapon on the table, it had power to stop people in their tracks. It could make them second-guess whatever they were thinking of thinking or doing. If it didn't always mean something sad for people to hush up, it sounded prettier than Geraldine.

It was far more honest than that one syllable — Hope. All its lame connotations. I filled out paperwork to become Tragedy for life. Tragedy grew up and moved on from where Hope was. I left that hopeless girl frozen back there.

And I learned women must add details to enchant this world to consider taking it easier on us. I never cared for being sexy or even wanted to be. But I knew I'd work to stay pretty. Few women can get somewhere without making that effort, every single day. She should get paid for it. Whether it's an odd scarf, apology jewels from the ex or the present man, a fortune spent on her hair and her face, a distinguishable perfume, neat nails, cute toes, eye-snatching heels.

I was a miracle far beyond a real home. I was about to be a whole house rebuilt. No longer Hope, no longer a ward of the state, no longer a child, no longer cared for. I was Tragedy Lawson now, a whole new person and name.

I was nineteen.

TWELVE

My memoir, *The Girl Who Didn't Burn: My Life in Foster Care,* was:
1) Three diaries I kept a lock on and for one I couldn't find the key anymore,
2) Two composition books I salvaged from high school, filled with questions and angst,
3) Two Dollar Tree photo albums with water and heat-damaged family photos to pick from, for those shiny pages of pics all autobiographies must have,
4) A crinkly folder of poetry and sketches my younger self dreamed would go somewhere,
5) A rubber-banded brick of index cards with a chronology of my life and facts of people in it,
6) A divider notebook where I outlined perfect chapters and parts,
7) Unfinished documents on two computers, mostly a desktop I didn't give internet connection powers, on advice from an online writing seminar to block distractions,

8) About 20 pages (mostly blank), typed on a vintage typewriter from an eBay whim.

It was "Tragedy's book" for Victor, for Victor's friends and family and business partners, for scarce women I called friends, for chicks I knew but not really, for old coworkers I kept in touch with and for old therapists who did their bests with me. Most importantly, for a big agent in New York City, Patricia Rogers. I guessed she signed me just off being Victor Powell's wife.

"The hotel is just my day job," I'd first lied to Victor, between my first (and last) bite of roast guinea pig on our first date out for Peruvian. "I'm really a writer."

"It's self-empowerment," I'd first promised the agent, "not trauma and poverty porn."

"Oh no," Patricia said. "Misery memoir is on the way out. People want to feel good, live large now. Survival. Beating the odds. Thriving. You're right on track!"

The agent was one of Victor's people who knew people, calling shortly after we moved to the Glens. Patricia Rogers Lit completely avoided serious fiction and made its killing off memoir, business books and true crime in audio or e-books. She was black but her client list was integrated enough to make you wonder, most with many branded titles and high followings online. She still emailed to ask if I had something for her. She also connected me to staff from an inspirational publisher and motivational speaker agency. They asked me to tell them more. I had no more, to say or show. I changed the recipients' names and addresses on the same letter I sent the agent. Victor never wasted an opportunity. I caved in to email him pages of my masterpiece sometimes. Always, he got LinkedIn influencers and mommy bloggers firing at me days later.

"Do you have an excerpt we can post?" "Can you guest blog?" "When is the pub date?"

"I'm not ready." "I'm not finished." "I'll call when we narrow down a deal."

My ambitious husband even came up with the title.

"The Girl Who Didn't Burn," he suggested one day over a lazy Omaha Steaks dinner, in Chicago, before the house and Grayson Glens and the in-home studio and a staff and… All of it.

"Same message, though. Hmmm…" I liked it.

Raven McCoy's pat biography and news popped up automatically on YouTube and in my feeds, whether I searched her or not. Even the cloud knew what I was obsessed with. It didn't know I knew Raven better than she was being shown and discussed. So stereotypical it was. Nice girl and good grades, but troubled childhood and problematic family, blah blah. The more her stricken mother and relatives gave the public favor of statements and appearances, the more the media picked them apart. The word salads about the perils of being black and poor were off base.

Would her own unique life story get any justice? Would a girl like Joy, with her parents and their net worth and zip codes, be spoken of in such limited terms? Was it race? Money? Color? Sex? In the McCoy family's tearful faces, I recognized the disposition and vernacular of my distant relatives. And even social workers who were nice to me, some foster people who were as well. Nice or not, they gave me a simplified profile, passed college applications right on by me, and limited my stories. Same thing they were doing to the new tragic African American hashtag. Even in death, it was a glass ceiling on the narrative for girls like us.

I, Hope Lawson was still here — free to tell the whole truth of myself. I was changing names of course, not that anyone was innocent or deserved protecting. I wasn't just Tragedy Powell and not Hope Lawson. Every time I encountered Raven, in the forms she made me think of her in, I felt my old name calling me back.

*

"This is gonna be so sick!" my stepdaughter yelled from the backyard hammock.

Joy's visit inspired her father to rescue fun stuff from the shed for the season. He finally fortified the wood swing, too. The weather was tipped to aloof, not hot but at least no longer frosty. Joy had begged me to see more of "Tragedy's book." I was set up on the veranda with a laptop. Sunhat and sunglasses of course, no matter the season. I was "Editing the book," I said.

"You still feel sick, hun?" Ifa asked. "More of the soup is inside, Miss Joy."

Ifa wiped her hands on her apron and started. I laughed. "No, Ifa. She means, I dunno. I only have to know the slang these days. Not explain it."

"Oh, okay," Ifa smiled, turning back to the vegetables, a wavy ponytail down her back. "My children's generation…" she sighed.

I respected Ifa to work in peace. I never wanted her to feel presided over. I knew that feeling from foster kid, group home days — always someone to make sure Little Orphan Annies functioned. We didn't have the heart to keep her away during the pandemic. And I needed her. Ifa was a do-over of the foster mothers. With her, I replayed those other women I lived with. "Sick" seemed an apt summary in context. Ifa showed me all I missed in mature, caring women.

The Kombucha tea hit. It was "alcoholic" non-alcoholic, only trace alcohol from fermenting. And healthy gut stuff. Joy loved it. We had a case delivered. I was supposed to be having fun. Today, I had tipped a little vodka into the tea.

I minimized my document window and tapped into the Clean Me website again. "Book an Appointment" was the site's pop-up button.

Not far away, Ifa turned portabella mushrooms, red peppers and corn cobs on the grill. I went vegan this week. Dieting and #bonusmom activities in one. We ladies fooled Victor, on camera, with Joy's version of spaghetti sauce. She tracked down something for the vegan "beef." She showed me how chopped walnuts could feel like meat, too. Dad was amazed. Followers were impressed with the food pictures, recipes and taste tests. Joy loved staring into the vacuum of her father's fans. I was happy to let her. She could fly out emojis and textlish beyond my comprehension. She joined my routines and habits, added flair, and created Instagram stories about them. We were #hydrated, #deepconditioned, #moisturized, #blessed and #highlyfavored.

The Powellcast subscribers and their likes eeked up every day Joy was on the case.

When Joy got up and running, that is. The girl had me scared she was pregnant. Her first week was a fever, poor appetite, late mornings. Ifa was worth her weight in gold. She had a red lentil soup solution. Berbere spice woke Joy up. Then our trio seeped into a normal mode. Victor became an open-door policy workaholic after he got in an activity for #girldad shots. So, his daughter and I together with Ifa were in the back holding it down. Victor's name and work went further than me working on them alone. Much of this work going to support a girl whose mother labeled me a thot, and that mother too.

A year after we married, we summered on Long Island to see if we liked New York. It was a peachy colonial. Short biking or driving distance to the Long Island Railroad. Joy, a big mature twelve, had to be there. I don't blame her. I never lived anywhere in my life but Illinois. I regretted it. It left nothing to say when Victor talked about college down south or playing ball in Australia, only a simple Midwest girl life when others spoke of their years abroad and East or West coast colleges. Gloria and Victor's fights over summer custody were vicious. Two against one, eventually. We owed the Grayson Glens house and everything to that one summer with Joy.

Victor wound up called to Manhattan and even Connecticut shows so often, he left me thinking Joy was my spouse and Joy thinking I was her biological parent. She was an energy boost and help before Victor and I could dream of affording anyone to work for us. I yearned to have a baby then. I was young, newlywed. That's what good women were supposed to do. I made way more money working for my husband than by just working. I was stable. He was the holdout. He had time yet, but he told me it wasn't the right time. He was right. The sponsorships, deals and commissions took us up to near half a million for the first time. Now? He was on the offensive. "Victor Jr. sounds nice," he hinted a lot. Picking genders was the thing. It was doable.

But I liked my life. My house was an island. I shared the end of my childhood with strange needy mouths, empty stomachs, and grubby hands. Foster kids aren't siblings. We were just litters thrown together. Now, I had a whole world all to myself. I kept up birth control.

Joy went on.

"You survived a fire! Whoa… You're gonna be on all the podcasts and the lives."

"I've told you that," I reminded her. "Why are you acting so surprised?"

"You never said it like this," she informed me. "You say it like nothing, really. Like it was a normal day. But here, whoah."

A normal day? Interesting my communication of it distilled it to what it wasn't.

"Hey — I wonder if you'll be on Joe Rogan or The Breakfast Club or Red Table Talk?"

"Now you're doing too much," I said.

Joy put down my pages to pick up my personal electrolysis tool, to advance the war against body hair to each follicle down to her calves.

She was a harmless audience to beta read my book. She devoured a lot, not the usual concrete blocks I saw for girls her age. She read James Baldwin, Audre Lorde and bell hooks. Anne Rice, Ntozake Shange and Sue Grafton. We'd all gone to Sunrise, a ten table and small counter Hail Mary breakfast place for truckers headed west to Iowa. Joy stuck to toast and fruit, hick diner canned stuff, but still better than our savaged flesh. I watched her head-to-head the manager on the origins of the eggs Victor and I ordered. "Are the eggs local, factory, farm, free range, Certified Humane?" she asked, anyway. She treated Ifa like her elder to respect, not a lower caste to bark orders at. This was many a Grayson nanny's or driver's fate from the kids, worse than their adult bosses who paid them. I saw them in the area. Interesting, I'd think.

In Grayson Glens, young people ignored me. It seemed they swarmed away from adults who gave them everything. Was a side effect of life's benevolence disdain taken out on no one in particular? How rich. These kids bunched up in the stores, arcade, diners, parking lots. The Pool Hall and Boat Club were full of them for the two and half months the Midwest climate allowed a short beach and boating season to make sense, maybe three if September was merciful. Fleshy girls in bikinis, burgeoning boys in trunks. Their jet speeds and toys, roaring laughs and music.

"Your dad's thinking about getting a real boat," I announced.

"What?" Joy exclaimed.

KALISHA BUCKHANON

Victor and I had fun with a rigid hull to be romantic and get great pics. Joy had been his only other passenger. They stayed close to land and tried fishing. But we drove past sailboats and a yacht parked at the Grayson Boat Club. Victor said it would be good to entertain on them. And photograph in them. It was a lot of money for something not to use that much, but it fit The Powellcast and all we could do. When things really were normal again, the look would be fire.

"Ok, so now I have to come live with you guys for the summer," Joy said.

I didn't mind. We had money to replace — Victor needed to start speeding to wherever and whatever he had to do to keep up with his audience, the causes, the people, the injustices. We had room. Five to be exact. Two were just offices, his and hers, like sinks. This left Joy two guest rooms to overtake. Sex would be complicated. He and I were far from newlyweds. We usually went a week or two with just the ho-hum before the fireworks. We'd manage.

Ifa finished making a vision of vegetables for us to fill up now and later. I snapped her perfect presentation to slot for the #MeatlessMonday show online. It was Tuesday. Gloria was supposed to come get her daughter Saturday. On Friday, I heard an argument.

"She's been cooped up in isolation for almost a year," Victor grumbled into his phone. "You're too hard on her, Glo."

So not just his "Gloria" tone of voice, but her nickname too?

Joy's second week in Grayson Glens turned into a third.

In three weeks, Joy and I ate a small garden between us. Ifa even made magic with silky green tomatoes from the garden of Mrs. Pitts, dropped off by Mr. Pitts, with a perfected recipe to fry them according to their Georgia-born relatives. Ifa convinced us it was legit. We went through my cryogenic and laser face and

116

neck tools. Manis and pedis out at the mall. We drove to the very edge of Chicago, the all-black suburbs, for even longer lashes. We binge-watched The Crown. We had little left to do for Week Three but shop. Online, bricking and mortaring.

"For my writer's office," I told Victor.

We hit the antiques store, flea market and suburban mall with a Macy's to take advantage of. It was nothing like Chicago's, but I adapted. Joy justified the price tags with eloquent sermons on "vibrations," "creative transfer" and "genius momentums." "Design life into existence," Joy smiled. Our haul was unexpected desk organizers, pen and pencil holders. Decorative carvings and plaques to make my gray neutral space "More creative," Joy said. All her friends were "creatives." She suckered me to their Etsy stores. Ifa got in on that action. We ordered necklaces from her friend who made waist bracelets and hemp jewelry.

I had mocked accordion lamps and a digital aquarium from Sharper Image's catalog. Silly, I thought. Joy told me to "Go for it!" I wound up with frayed hippie pillows from a farmhouse catalog this way. A body heat adaptable bean bag as well. "For your back and butt, or meditation between chapters," Joy assured me. She went for a special laser hairbrush to activate hair follicles, after ordering a tool to kill them elsewhere.

In one season's change, the "Have You Seen Raven McCoy?" flyers reached the end of their life cycle, dwindling from the environment. Like cicada broods simmering under the soil for nearly two decades, the flyers were subtle noise before ghostly remnants. Gummy taps of old tape on doors and windows where people posted notices. Stained corners of the flyer stuck up out of garbage cans. Other flyers trying to sell things pierced over to cover them. Each time I focused in on a sliver of the letters or picture, it was a second guess in my mind. Was it really there? Did I obsess over a missing woman? Did I obsess over her more because she was black?

Joy took special attention to one flyer in front of a printing shop, which made up all the stuff for the high school and local businesses. Other than The Grayson Herald printing line, this was the Grayson place Raven McCoy's face fluttered around the most in. Joy recorded a video in front. She hashtagged #RavenMcCoy and tagged Victor. She beat out her friends online that way, with her father's face that the young people knew from around the web getting more attention. He wanted us cooled and not exploiting it anymore. But hey, it wasn't me. It was his daughter.

I played along. Real always recognizes real. A single mother was raising her. One raised me. We had rights to dream and spend. Team Natural. Team Body. Team Booty. Team Shop Local. For the Culture. Joy had a slogan for everything. We read Victor's fan emails.

"My Man Victor Powell… you always go in!"

"Can you do a series on black women's mental health during the pandemic?"

"When are you and Tragedy gonna give us a little Powell baby to watch grow up?"

Joy emailed on, answering like she was Victor as I would normally do, while I set up each thing or nothing. Then she'd come snap a photo, tag where we bought it and rave over it in a video. She was the assistant I didn't know I needed. We transformed my workspace entirely.

After spending over a grand Joy clued me in on how to justify, I unveiled my new office to Ifa and Victor. Joy filmed the reveal. They walked into a funhouse of objects and shapes, a spectrum of colors. Shades of green, orange and purple. A revolving Himalayan salt lamp glowed. A mandala dominated a wall once a corkboard of bills, To-Do notes and snaky CVS receipts with expired coupons. The bookshelf came alive in crystals, stones and beads. Lovely fabric draped the picture window. And an altar of Grayson River rocks offset a Raven McCoy flyer, Joy's idea.

The spirits play mind games you can't play with them on, Gran used to say.

Victor was in shock. Since he'd known me, I was a fashion and décor square. No ice queen, just minimal. Everything had a shape, purpose and elegance. I wasn't a Devil may care artiste. Nowhere near bohemian style. I didn't even wear prints. Now, my office looked like a creative butterfly was on the loose.

"Like a whole different home it is," Ifa exclaimed. "My gosh. Joy here is talented."

"Thank you very much, thank you very much," Joy pantomimed.

The claps and cheers, oohs and aahs, went on until Joy yawned to signal she was off for one of her epic naps. I thought of the pressure she was under. Many blacks at her academy, but not many. Surely not enough. And in Chicago, for a black kid. For any kid. And, she was a woman.

Ifa waved goodbye for the weekend.

Victor took their exits as his chance to whisk me into the new space. A living, textured rainbow. It was a few weeks since we'd made love at length and not in spurts. In my remodeled retreat, we flew to a modern hotel room. He locked the door. We started on top of a tangerine orange area rug. Next on new mismatched pillows on the floor. Quickies are about pulling something down or up, not taking it all off. Yet our pants and shirts and more blended into shabby chic. We were playful, knowing it was only so far we could go and stay undetected. We sifted through pent-up things we meant to say but put off or didn't see as important at the times. "You're putting on weight, babe." "I'm gonna miss

you when travel picks up." "It's been good having Joy around."
"Gloria seems to be better with all this now." "We didn't make
a lot this year but we saved a lot." "God, I'm coming again..."
"Raven McCoy is haunting me."

"What?" Victor rolled from off me, sweaty and shocked.
"Raven McCoy? Haunting?"

"Yes," I sighed. "It's little things here and there."

"Honey, that situation's getting to you. All of us."

"I know. It's why I'm telling you."

"It's haunting everybody. She was found here. We've covered
it. It stays in the news..."

"No. I am seeing her. Not really her. Just impressions."

Victor put his head in his hands. He stood, paced, came
skin to skin again.

"We need to talk about something," he sighed. "When Joy
leaves, we've gotta —"

"I am not drinking too much and I am not drunk and I am
not crazy!" I yelled.

We dressed and came out. Joy was still in her daylight coffin. We wandered to the kitchen for whatever we could forage.
Leftover roast chicken Joy wasn't around to disapprove. Coleslaw
that smelled good enough. Clean and sober ginger beer. Victor
plated and waited.

"What was in that envelope you came in with, one day?" I
asked.

No reason. It just came to me to know.

"What envelope?"

If it wasn't there, he knew what I was talking about and then
he didn't want me to know. I emptied the cubby of magazines
where I'd sandwiched that envelope with only his name on it.
He'd picked it up from somewhere. It wasn't sent in the mail.
Subscription cards and perfume samples fluttered from pages.

I turned more over and shook them. The politics, sports, movie reviews, beauty tips, haute couture, miracle cures, cosmetic products, famous faces, car ads... a blur. Shiny covers landed to the floor in cracks and splats. Some landed on Victor.

We were arguing. He was walking away. Towards his daughter I didn't know was there.

"Dad," I heard Joy try to whisper, "what's wrong with Tragedy?"

THIRTEEN

Last spring before all this, Raven McCoy brought a gift certificate for a hot stone massage to Gracious Davidson's small day spa on Marigold Road at the edge of Grayson Glens, accessible to Grayson at large and elsewhere in the region. After the state ordered spas shut in March 2020, the spa still operated for a time, from a back door and a good set of drapes at front (Grayson was no place that talked). For higher prices, and on whispers. For local country and suburban women Gracious guerilla marketed to, Goodness Gracious Day Spa was the alternative to nixing the spa experience. Its clientele were women who didn't want to stay late in Chicago after work, or go to Chicago on weekends for a spa, or pay to fly to pricey West Coast retreats.

This fit. Thanks to Gracious, women found themselves only leaving the Glens for vacations and their maiden name families. Goodness Gracious was something to find in the Ozarks or at Lake Geneva or on Indiana Beach, but they had it just a half hour or less away. It was a relief when Gracious could let them back in under the new rules, one by one. Even on Sundays, if that's what they wanted and would pay for. Government holidays, too. Right on up to Christmas, even. And certainly for the houseguests let into their bubbles and wanting a little Christmas

Eve discount. Raven McCoy was one who bit on that sale. She had a gift certificate loaded. She set herself up for the works. She had called Gracious "So pretty for your age!"

But Gracious wouldn't have remembered the girl from that. So many people said that to her, Gracious was more likely to remember somebody who didn't. That "So pretty for your age" and its variations… She didn't overhear Raven say the same thing to the spa's teen receptionist. When Gracious emerged from the office to introduce herself, they walked the short store front to back, past the loose-leaf tea station and towel warmer, like old acquaintances who'd met before.

"I know my clients," Gracious said. "I don't think you're one I'm seeing often yet."

"I'm new around here," Raven told her.

The girl listed a far address. In Wells, an hour down. Another time — not this first time Gracious noticed Raven, but the last time she saw her — the tall, curvy brown woman left the spa with a ride from someone, presumably. She was only one of three clients that day, paying double. This was the only way the spa could open the door for such limited clientele. Raven didn't small talk. She checked out quietly and left. Neither Gracious nor her receptionist nor the masseuse saw the car she entered. Not its driver, or if any other passengers were there.

Gracious was so kind to offer her private lot to accommodate a nearby business — a little market that couldn't venture delivering to its customers — for going out of business. They let people in for a last day sale, then gave up to load remaining inventory into a 17 ft. white truck. The truck parked horizontally to the spa's open glass storefront. It eclipsed the outdoor security camera's range and the receptionist's last vision of Raven McCoy, walking to a vehicle behind it. It was nothing across Marigold Road but trees. They saw everything but her.

By the day after Christmas, the girl's mother and home-town people had gotten her picture to heat up online. Gracious checked the books and whispered, "Oh my God. That's her!"

She reported the visit. No one who knew Raven knew about her spa day. The woman, detective Wise, and Chief Loveless led a team of law officers through Goodness Gracious. Real fingerprinting and photographing. The ABC, NBC, CBS and more news trucks sped up in front.

"We at the spa and the whole Grayson community are just gonna keep praying for this young lady's family and friends to hear from her soon," Gracious said to many cameras.

The spa was on such limited operation all the publicity went to waste. The usual Tibetan bowls, chakra healing music and sound baths didn't blast from videos on mounted screens inside the spa. 1,800 empty square feet: the waiting room, three service rooms with client lockers, and a client bathroom. It was a back area for her office and a staff chill zone. She turned the back yard into an exclusive warm season treat, an outdoor spa for high-paying clients. It was all dead now.

Gracious rarely serviced clients anymore. She didn't need to. She retired from it when she made it past what people in newer lifetimes called 'The Recession,' but their older relatives called "What are you complaining about?" She didn't panic. She tricked the spa into a beacon of stress relief, with reason-able prices to start. It helped that she was married to one of Grayson's biggest businesses, Davidson's Furniture Bonanza. Her husband was a Davidson. Like his father before him, he bellowed on commercials in three states. His exaggerated pitch was famous. From average buyers to a high-price clientele. Her two sons handled sales. Her married son's wife maintained the commercials, the socials and customer support. Gracious selected the inventory.

When businesses had to be closed, Mr. Davidson capital-
ized on his famous TV commercial to drive new customers to
the website to buy. He smashed the competition for regional
outfits that couldn't stay open like the big box stores. Even with
Goodness Gracious going slow or not at all, the Davidson's got
richer as other people's worlds tumbled down.

Their money made up for reality that Gracious was the
only one of her family who'd been to college. She wished her
family was more proud and understood her better for it. But
it seemed college was out of style and it threw military service
the same way. No one expected people to want the job that
much or stay for longer than it took to find a new job. They
just wanted happy places to stretch out the time. So, Gracious
never had a right-hand woman. She was always it.

The Goodness Gracious building used to be the place she
rented a chair to do press-on nails and perms to pay her rent,
buy food and drive a used car. Back then, she was renting
a small blue ranch house in Grayson's first try at a housing
project. The hairstylist who owned the building retired. She
sold the nail and hair girls her building for not much. Only
Gracious stayed with it, the other girls selling out their portion
to her. She worked so hard she wrung out the money for the
lot next to it. She rented the lot, never a charge, to kids and
artists for big events.

She was a feminist among them, a rare woman respected
on her own. Into Grayson's most well-off circles, big just like
her husband. The couple moved to one of Grayson Glen's first
new timbre constructions to add to the original farmhouse on
the land. Davidson property was one all long-term Glenners
knew, a landmark nearly. For all the success, the part of her
that had wanted to be a news anchor refused to quiet. She
gave it up by age twenty-five. Burned out in the competition

and sexism, she met her husband about the time she changed tack. She was probably just two or three big breaks from never needing one more. *I'll never know*, she resigned.

Goodness Gracious was good enough, she decided. It proved her, gave the world evidence she had sharp talons. Her outdoor wooden bathhouse and showers were unlike anything other central Illinois establishments would dare. That novelty risk brought in the May to August bachelorette parties and more. The obscure spa getaway made her the go-to #BestLife spa party place in the region. Gracious and whoever worked for her at the time became pros at photographing. She loved to be on camera or behind one. Her online ads and clientele posts made her well-known online like her husband on TV. Gracious personally reached out to all disgruntled patrons. She always fluttered about the space, being the face of her own business.

Then, she would go into her windowless back office by the supplies closet, to sip the secret to her stubborn good mood and abilities: Grand Marnier.

Gracious was past the whiskey days. That's how she preferred to look at it. She was traumatized by short years in the boy's club of Chicago media, the big time. Whiskey shots were the ritual station heads and network bosses pushed women into at the Irish pubs, happy hours, holiday parties and celebrations for big stories or scoops. Unlike hot whiskies and rums, Grand Marnier's fruity scent added to the spa's overall ambience. The drink mixed nicely with coffee and tea, as she administered it in winter. Then, everyone kept a canister of hot liquid in hand with a tight cover until they drank. Unlike wine, it didn't require twenty unaccounted-for minutes to finish. Cognac was fast-acting and unnecessary to repeat much. Beer was out of the question; the calories would reverse the outcomes of her gym membership and Tai Chi classes.

Gracious never brought a bottle home. She took her time off from the spa as time off from drinking. She configured the empty bottles underneath or behind files in a locked cabinet of purchase orders, payroll sheets and tax materials she handed to a local management consultant to scan annually. Nobody else had a key. She waited until the night before trash day to release the bottles to random businesses' dumpsters left to alleys and curbs.

When summer days were longer than the spa's hours, she relied on black trash bags and her trunk to catch a day she could dump more bottles after dark. One of the strip malls or The Golden Age Movie Theater always had well-lit back lots for dumpsters. She did this the night Raven McCoy left Goodness Gracious. She wanted the books cleaned for New Year's Day, starting then. She blamed the pressure and stress for why she crept beyond her usual three shots of Grand Marnier up to four. Maybe five.

She reached the theater lot just when the last show was letting out. She wobbled to her trunk just a bit, at least to a song she did like. When she opened it, she momentarily thought the hunk of crinkled black plastic was a wrapped body she didn't remember putting there. It would have been slumped over, head cocked, legs askew. After this, she needed a rule: at least an hour to let the sipping settle before she'd get behind the wheel. She was known as a town leader, the one who helped fight for more school buses and a woman detective, the director of the Arts Center Gala and even its auctioneer for local artists' work.

But Raven McCoy gave her what she had wanted: her face on the news. Her phone and notifications caught fire after she was interviewed a few times on segments in three states:

Illinois, Indiana, and Michigan. It was just a 30-second flash piece on the days the story did make it. But sometimes, a couple of seconds included Gracious and the spa as last connection to her. Her college friends were seeing her even. They had kept on in the media game. They were all hounds for a story. Some told her they'd try to book her to talk for bigger things, if the story became bigger of course. Then, the websites and online news outlets came.

Her everyday comfortable, loose and almost French girl look felt stale in all the attention. She dug into her closets and zippered wardrobes to find the strong investments of her aspiring media days. The splurges she bought herself at small milestones: Prada blouses, Chanel blazers, Vanderbilt slacks. Crime and social justice vloggers kept her most busy. As months went by and the #RavenMcCoy hashtag expanded to national news, Gracious Zoomed her free time away. Someone had to speak for the wealthy Graysons and Glenners, the white America under siege to be accountable for its advantages and head starts. Somebody had to make them human, too.

"If I'd known something was going to happen to that young woman, I would've never let her leave my business," she told one of the most popular social justice channels. "Women are in this together. Beyond color, women owe it to other women so we all stay safe."

"Do you think her race may be a factor in not many people noticing her, that white women have more people looking out for their safety?" asked the channel's black woman host.

"I think the opposite," Gracious answered. "Grayson's a lot of things, but it's never been full of black people. If anything, Raven would've been noticed much more for that."

She was being honest. Gracious never figured all this just for calling to say "Hi, it's Gracious Davidson and I saw that girl who's missing." Her husband and sons were mad she didn't just stay out of it. Their days in the furniture enterprise went to strangers asking questions about her and the missing girl. When the body came up in the river, that shit started up again.

The police chief and detective kept prowling, wanting more and then more. She gave them a wealth. Even the spa day's intake form, where Raven had checked she wasn't pregnant. She'd circled the tenth circle with a smiley face for her mood that day. Detective Wise wasn't easy on any men. Gracious was helping, but Mr. Davidson was still treated as a suspect. So were her boys. She thought the Raven McCoy stuff would be a short story but it boiled to a mystery.

Then came hints people accused her of racism. She was horrified. Her name came up as not taking the protection of black women seriously. She wasn't living an alternative universe. Of course there was some racism in Grayson. Things people said. Jokes, slurs. References to niggers from the city. And, according to a longtime school board member, complaints from parents of the few black kids in schools about getting worse grades than they thought they should have.

Even without clients or a business she could open, Gracious owned her building and it was her sanctuary from isolating in a homestead for a home, with a man and his sons and dogs. She could go clear her mind. It was where she could transport her being and her thinking. She could have her own bubble. She could do bills or paperwork in peace, more efficiently.

And she could meet her lover, Officer Bobby Castle… just like she had the night Raven walked out her shop and she lingered for him to keep their plan.

Seeing lights on inside it and cars outside is what first made the new young police officer round the spa frequently. Officer Bobby Castle knocked on the window to catch Gracious tidying to close, or chatting with whichever receptionist, or to see a customer out.

Usually, after a few of her sips so she was relaxed. Where she came from, she was old enough to be his mother. They started the girls so young. Seemed women weren't human until they handed their soul over to a man. It was only so many compliments to her dress, outfit, perfume, etc…

No, this can't be right, she used to think of him.

Finally, she just asked the cop: "Are you coming 'round here for your job or me?"

"I'll wait for you to close," he smiled.

She had cheated on her husband before, twice with one man. Just an old boyfriend from where she was born across the border of Grayson. She was married with two rowdy boys and working two businesses to death. A lover eased the stress. Yet things were easy when she slipped with the cop. She knew what leisure meant. She was turning off the lights, her key out, when he buzzed. She only turned a knob and they were kissing. No, she wasn't that kind of woman. They both tried to forget that moment. Not too long after, she was in her office after hours cheating for the third time. She shocked herself. It hadn't been on her mind and yet here she was.

Castle had a girlfriend and things like that, nice and fun women to sleep with. Maybe the pull for him was thinking of when he could get around Gracious's complications. He stayed on the radio. Usually, the occasion was just a joke spread between a few other dead minds on the shift. He'd stop himself, chime in quickly. Other times, it was just a question of a non-emergency sort. "Do you want Italian or Mexican for the potluck?"

But sometimes, a couple had a dispute or a suspected car theft was in place. Once it was a real home invasion. Those came like eclipses. He flurried away. He left the gap to remind them they weren't supposed to be doing what they were doing. Gracious never took it personally. She wanted to hear details soon as it all died down. He couldn't call her cell overnight. But he always filled her in. He told her everything going on in Grayson that was never the story the news or the people told, not even her biggest gossips, like the farmer's market coordinator and local florist.

So Gracious knew the police and sheriff were investigating the body in the river as more than a drowning or body dump from a situation off afar. And she knew the reason was simple: Nobody understood how or why this young black woman was in Grayson to begin with.

Had she not called and identified Raven to authorities as her customer, it might have just been such an arbitrary dead body jinx that her body never even got identified.

In lockdown, Gracious was working from home while her husband could go show furniture. It was easy then. She and Bobby would sit and talk or dash to a next town for drinks or dinner. She could wash the guilt off. If her husband was home, she thought of something to need or want from the store or spa. She claimed she didn't sleep right and needed to use the salt bath.

Now she was back in business, rebuilding momentum, wanting whatever clients would venture treatments amidst the mass precautions. And the body was found. The story went back to the news and so did Gracious Davidson. It was reminding people of her when they had forgotten so much in the pandemic. The clients were back. Her building wasn't empty. At night, she went behind gates with her family, her husband and everybody who needed to see them all together.

A return to normalcy put her affair on ice. Gracious knew this was the right thing.

It was always in her to do what was right, how she stayed wrapped up in the town and playing the roles. She said a "higher power" moved her and then — "I don't even remember getting the idea" — she was looking at a flyer she had made.

It asked: "Have You Seen Raven McCoy?"

A headline in big bold font. Above the best pictures of Raven Gracious could download. She typed the police department's number on the bottom, large font. She covered her spa's glass front with two flyers. She carried a shiny folder of more home for her husband to post on his store.

At first and to start, she only printed a few hundred copies to leave with other businesses whose owners knew who she was. They all gladly did whatever Gracious Davidson said.

FOURTEEN

I was scaring my husband and his daughter and myself, so I
booked my first Clean Me appointment. Drinking was sexy.
Falling off the deep end wasn't. May fifth, Cinco de Mayo. It felt
appropriate. The date would remain an anniversary, year after
year, for change. Armored against cravings for wine, tequila,
margaritas, more. I just had to probe the site and fill out my
pre-visit questionnaire. I waited until Victor was taping downstairs and Joy was packing.

1) Come sober! We want to see you at your best and
brightest, get a baseline feel for your true aura and
essence.

2) Bring a list of medications and prescriptions. It's
important for our health team and nutritionists to
understand everything going into your body.

3) …

"I'm sorry for the drinking."

Joy was in the doorway behind me, her hand to her mouth,
like I was her dad she caught watching porn. I snapped the
laptop screen closed.

"I'm sorry? What?" I asked.

"Drinking," Joy sighed. "I took a bottle of Dad's... It was tequila, I think."

"Think?"

"Tesla?"

A housewarming gift from one of Victor's star athlete subjects. Two grand a bottle. The seal wasn't even broken. Victor adored the near sculpture the tequila swam in. This was on me, now. I knew what would come. I'd take the blame for this. It was far past just swiping his flask. Joy recited all the lines.

"Everybody drinks and vapes and smokes. You gotta do shots on Facetime and Zoom, you know, just because. And, honestly, I mostly poured it out..."

"I'm glad you told me," I interrupted, finally.

"You didn't know?"

"Joy, your father and I trust you to be responsible. We don't spy —"

"Oh, you've been looking up stop drinking stuff while I've been here. I saw it on your phone. Or your computer. Like now. I thought all that was for me."

But of course. Tap a few letters in a search bar from one device and get everything the other devices do. Our brains, habits and worse cloned to metal in a variety of shapes, sizes and colors. *Remember to clear histories,* I told myself. *And that young people's eyes are sharper.*

"Oh no," I said. "It's just, most people drink after work. Well sometimes with our lives, people drink *as* work. Since isolation, I'm making some changes. That's all."

I didn't have the heart to ruin our trip, a good memory of how April was spent.

"I won't tell your father. We all keep our secrets. But, that whole drinking crowd is just not where you belong. And —" I started.

I wanted to give her "The Talk." The one nobody was there to give me when I was sixteen like her. About how drinking makes you stupid and boys are after one thing, and sixteen is too young for a girl to handle feelings. Yet I wasn't her mother. It wasn't my place.

I was also no better. I saw myself tip-toe stairs, crouch in corners, look over my shoulder from closets where I hid bottles. I hurried to screw on caps from what I said I wouldn't drink. I snatched my husband's flask, a wedding gift, on my ways out — to fill with a little something something to sip on ways out. He never knew about that. He shouldn't know about Joy. I was a grown woman. Funny Joy didn't ask me not to tell her father. She must have guessed I wouldn't.

I was back alone in the interesting place she'd made my office now. So I changed one thing behind her back: I dismantled the Raven McCoy shrine.

I suppose this was today's response to the Grayson missing black girl situation she followed. I couldn't create my own haunting. This was Joy's home, too. But it was mine all the time. It wasn't remote. It wasn't collective. Whether deaths were about race or just death, I measured my compassion. I came to Grayson Glens to forget how hazardous life truly was. Raven McCoy was the ultimate reminder. My black mind needed a rest.

I opened *The Girl Who Didn't Burn* file. Given the commute and Victor's Chicago errands, I estimated an afternoon and early evening to work on it. If only the white lights of my accordion desk lamps were already a spotlight. I would just go pay to replace a $2000 bottle of tequila with my own money and name, not my allowance. Well, we called it my salary. Okay.

I rolled through the pages of my own work and invention, willing a good memory to start on. More than a fire, more than foster care, more than strange homes, more than loneliness. There were Thanksgivings, songs, dressing ups, backyard barbecues, trips to special places, birthday presents. And there was me, on my own, struggling to make it without wind in my sails from a family. It was tenacity, pride, self-reliance. I had to remember the empowerment part.

"…Starbucks is how I got out of the homes. My first big job — 30 hours a week. I could afford to rent a Chicago Heights room from the sister of this woman I worked with…"

It was sunset when the shrill cordless phone broke the trance I expected Victor's return to. No one called the house phone but the business leads and serious intimates, for serious things. I saved my document, a few pages longer now. I raced for the phone on the wall of the hallway.

"Hope?"

This was my old life's name.

"Who is this?" I asked.

But I knew who it was. I could describe the voice and identify it. I knew it before its depth and husk now. When it was just a clack and a caw and a coo. When it grunted and hacked for attention through conversations, music and shouting around it. When it gargled breast milk and drool. When it cried through old floorboards. When I was too frozen to come rescue it.

"This Merit," that voice said. "Sis?"

My brother held on to light sentence juvenile status like a hem in high wind. Then he got old enough to be tried as an adult. Most of his calls struck collect from jails so he could ask for bail money, or from big houses just to talk. Where I last knew he was, an Indiana iron city, it was near time for lights out — not phone calls. I lost track of his releases. He was an echo in my soul. He was a ghost in the family, the child who got away. He still circled through the cousins, aunts, and uncles from time to time, far more than I did without jail to stop me. He was back out.

Him: "You know I got me a shorty now, *Auntie*."

Me: "Oh? Didn't you just get—"

"Well you know now they made that law to get conjugal visits…"

"Got it. Congratulations, bro."

I'd been so engrossed in whatever "Tragedy's book" was I'd held hunger and thirst at bay. They both caught up with me. I found chips and popcorn, started tea. I spotted my phone's glow. It was Victor's new eta.

"You and old boy still going?" Merit asked.

"Still going."

"No shorties yet?"

"Not yet. Maybe soon."

"Saw him on the telly in rec, going in on those white dudes calling protestors violent."

"Yeah, he stayed busy on that last year."

"You know I would've been in the streets if I wasn't locked up. Tear all that shit down!"

"Not me. That's Victor's job. I stay out of it. Some of us have to live."

"Yeah, I see the crib — you know in the background. Damn, Tragedy. That's what's up."

"Thanks. Yay for the new workplace. The whole world just sees into your house."

"Those sorry lowlifes couldn't believe that was my damned big sister's house."

"Well, I am your sister. Miss you, kiddo."

"What's up with those crazy boonies? Y'all got black girls turning up dead out there?"

"I wouldn't say girls. Just one. We're doing way better than Chicago."

"One too many."

The tea kettle whistled. I poured boiling water over a scoop of loose mint leaves.

"Can't believe I'm talking to you lil bro," I smiled.

As the tea steeped, I walked past the empty wine chiller, to the dining room and the bar inside, to scan. No reason.

"I gotta come see y'all," he said. "And you come to the city whenever. I got my own spot."

"Anytime," I promised. And "I will."

Just a capful of rum into the teacup.

This would be our first long conversation in months. With his lifestyle, I took our talks as they came. This might be the last. We took from one another a backbone of identities and features. But our separate worlds contained nothing from each other to spend or touch. I judged Merit about as much as I mentioned him: never.

I still took his calls, so long as his name and face wasn't popped up in berserk murders. But Merit's deviance was never violent. He was young yet. This last time it was just stealing cars or breaking and entering, that brand of attention-seeking called petty crime. We didn't have what most petty criminals have: a family. In those, there's always a Big Mama, Nan or Gramps to go in that one hellmouth closet, where money's hidden somewhere other people can't find.

Our tale of two siblings had us together in only a few grainy pictures I could include in the book of my life. He was already in and out of jail by the time I was planning my wedding. After that, I met him once in the hood and once in the burbs. Both times, I gathered he kept up an equal opportunity crew of pink to white, caramel to chocolate faces leathered past their times. I ate chicken wings or filet mignon with their wives and girl-friends and baby mamas dressed to kill. I held their babies none the wiser Daddy (or Mommy) could disappear to jail any day.

It didn't take much to figure out Merit's crews didn't deal in corner store scores. The last time I saw him, a Greek man Merit called "my brother" invited us to a party. A smart home. North Chicago suburbs where I knew pro athletes and Mafia concentrated their homes. Once we got past a gate, a black car drove out to let us pass on to sensor fountains and high beam lights through a quarter mile drive. I enlightened to just how much more I had to dream of: a Calacatta marbled mansion, a half-floor kitchen, a totally blocked view through the front yard, an unblocked view to the sky from balconies, no litter or dumpsters. Merit sped me back to my condo in a black Range with a fake name on the registration and insurance ID. I know because I snuck a look while he dropped a package to a hoo-kah lounge along the way. After that night, Victor's downtown condo box I had loved felt like jail. And soon, Merit was back locked up.

An hour into catching up, into what happened to explain why he didn't marry a woman who followed him into prison and had his baby, a text from Victor. Simple: *Running behind xo*.

Joy's drop-offs were usually quick turnaround. Two hours without any Chicago errands. It was three hours after I had watched Joy wave away from the Jeep's passenger side. I put Merit's smoke-charred voice on speaker in order to text Victor back.

Where r u? xo

"You ever got any problems with anybody, you know I got you," Merit said.

I knew what he meant.

"Life is beautiful, bro," I said. "The house, the businesses. You into *The Powellcast*?"

"Yeah, from time to time. That man ain't got no hands on you, do he?"

I laughed.

"He's not that type, Merit."

"Don't underestimate. You out there alone with him now. Like I said — I got you."

My status as a grownup orphan occurred to me every day. I swirled in worlds of people with lineage, connections, relations. Nobody "got" me, in reality. It warmed me to hear at least one person did, however nefarious he meant. An AK47 at Victor's chest. A drive-by in Grayson Glens. Tarring and feathering my rapists behind trees, waiting to dump me in rivers.

Merit informed me of his plans — always back to school and staying out of trouble, now also being an example for his son. I listened, heard, responded and wondered.

"So how is Cousin Kenny?" I asked, while I multitasked on my screen.

Neither Joy nor Victor posted anything. I saw no silly singalong from the road, no greasy drive-through binge, no last stickered picture with "Glo" behind the camera. For all the times I self-tortured with ideas of Victor with other women I couldn't see to believe, he and another woman I saw didn't impress me.

"Remember the book I told you I'm writing about my life? *Our* lives? I've picked it up."

Four hours now. No Victor. My third hot totty.

"We gotta get together, sis. Whatcha doing for the Fourth of July?"

"Not getting in a mask fight on a plane, that's for sure."

"I'm coming to see you, kid."

Finally — an eta from Victor. An hour.

It was past ten o'clock by the time my brother's phone died and he faded back into the ether of not knowing. Shortly after, I heard an alert to the Jeep up the drive. I wasn't going to hide the rum bottle. Half was gone. An explanation could be a last dinner with Joy before he saw her again in a month. He knew I could easily text her to verify that. I was "friends" with his daughter now. But would she ever tell me anything if it meant crossing her parents?

Victor didn't grow up in a cyclone of shouting. His parents *talked*. If his principal mother and IT business father couldn't do that, they went behind separate closed doors or to a relative's house. They disagreed professionally. Rarely, since they were older now and being babied by American Dream children, one called Victor from where they were retired down South. It was to complain about the other, who'd come tell their side. Victor would suggest whatever people who love each other do, even if it's not right and doesn't make sense. He forced this love on me.

My brother emboldened me back to my roots. Back there, blows were low and cuts were deep. Volume was expected. Nobody born was any parent's dream come true, just hard facts to people who find out a baby is being born. This was known or felt, so nobody was being polite.

What took you so long? Was Gloria there? Would you tell me if she wants you back? Why are we giving her so much money?

"You're drunk Tragedy, again," was how he answered my pointed questions.

"You'd be drinking too if you were me!"

He started to do what his father does. I didn't have six inches of snow to fall back on like last time Victor wanted to run but he couldn't. Grayson only had three seasonal snow removal empires. The Glens were last on their lists, stained like our hearts and blood were alien, like higher rollers existed longer without clean streets for ambulances to come save our lives.

Victor bolted to the bedroom now to slip into comfortable clothes. He got to removing his shoes and shirt. I could ruin him. I didn't. He thought he birthed an angel, projected so in real life and online — *Check your bar. I didn't chug the tequila. Yeah, you and Glo created a drunk.*

"After all this time, after all we've built, and you still can't trust me?"

"It's not you I don't trust. And yeah, I'm drinking. Who do you think you are? My father? Throwing out my wine? I'm a grown woman."

I went to the bottle to pour it all straight into the sink.

"I'm not gonna argue when you're drunk. You're the one I can't trust. I'm out to a hotel."

"You are not! I'm not your mother."

"You aren't! My mother isn't an alcoholic wallowing and begging for drama."

"Your mama's boy ass wouldn't have lasted a second in dramas I survived."

"Oh really?"

"You're a baby. A bougie Negro baby, playing perfect black man for money. My brother? 'Lil Roughneck' you call him? He will kill you! Or send somebody to do it."

"And you're spoiled!"

"Spoiled? Do you even know how ridiculous you sound right now?"

"No. I don't. And I'm not doing this."

He sprinted. For me, that damned beautiful staircase took time. When I caught up, he was in his closet and shoes and shirt. It was his pattern. In the condo, a hotel was in the front or back yard. A few dozen in walking distance. We met in one. He didn't need to pack a bag. He took his keys, wallet and phone. He charged a change of clothes on State Street or the Mile at Nordstrom, Bloomingdale's or Saks. All right there. Not so here. Giving up was more complicated here.

"I gave up paying a production assistant so you could have Ifa!" he spat.

He sounded professional but this was a really low blow. Yes, I felt like a maid of our home slash business investment. And his secretary when I'd been working up to have my own. Everyone he paid for his PA gig came from the college he worked at or the circles he kept up with. They weren't doing much to really earn the job because they didn't have to.

"You can have your PA back," I told him. "I'll pay Ifa. I don't have to shop."

"Good! Then don't. You shop way too much."

"Oh and you don't? A boat? So, we'll be hashtag skippers now?"

He had collected a few things I knew he really used. His beard stuff. His oils. Our solar charger. I danced around his brown slippers.

"What next," I asked, "a zipline compilation down to the river where a black girl was found? Or, *The Powellcast* sex tape? How about a livestreamed marriage counseling session?"

"Maybe some time apart."

Victor wasn't asking me. He was telling me. This had happened before we moved. I unleashed. I ran to fight. My all went to see him tumble face forward. He was too strong. I fought for normalcy, for a past that didn't burn down, for more family than a brother in and out of lockup, for more friends than those who were the right type but they weren't friends that feel like family. For fear over how much I needed a man.

For how Raven McCoy wasn't following me and for how I was following her, just to have something all my own and not this man's, even if a ghost.

For how I knew some mutty dog I kept seeing and not seeing must just be imaginary.

For how dark and scary Grayson Glens was — like my brother's prison cells at lights out, like his heart over a childhood that wasn't right.

For even if I wanted to chase Victor's Jeep down our Calliope Lane he raced down now, away from me, I was simply too scared and also too drunk.

FIFTEEN

Raven McCoy was pregnant. The Medical Examiner declined to count the fetal matter inside her on its own. The mass was noted with the internal findings. Eleven or twelve weeks of it survived the cold waters, biding and bound to itself. The autopsy report included an opinion of suicide or homicide possible. The last Coroner answered the call to anchor the findings for this first human in their river, to play it safe and tell the truth, ruling cause of death "Indeterminable."

The sunken state had crimped her beyond recognition but her insides held tough. On the outside, her liquefied resting place had slipped the skin off her hands. Skeletal fingers without possibility for prints. All her teeth remained, as did a semblance of a face to identify her without them. No contact wounds. As the near black she was on top of the brown she'd been, external discolorations met with patterns of bruising. Something bruised part of her right chest, snapped the arm on the left, ripped her nylons still clinging. The river or a person or a deer could have done it. Scabs screeched across a few points her skin didn't hang loose, beholden to the bones.

Those who handled her remains were grateful to the climate. The winter freeze gave them so much more than other rising ghosts did, after shorter time. The presumption, not fact, was somebody or something got the girl into the river. Probably after she was unconscious, maybe high. They knew she would've passed out and died from alcohol poisoning before she could be so drunk as to fall in open water from it.

Even if she wanted to drown herself, she wouldn't have gone through with it. None do. They had rescues from those stunts all the time in the area, given the remoteness and the river. And she wasn't weighted. That's one way it works to say it was a killer. Water and currents scraped away signs of rape if it was one. She wasn't naked. Just barefoot since her feet floated away with the fibers, blood, and prints. The DNA of a father might come from the baby. It bordered on ungodly and went past pricey to try. It was no guarantee to match, if the male was never a suspect or prisoner to have it collected and he never did genealogy testing. Crime crept inside along with everything during lockdown. No reports of a couple fighting at a bar. Bars weren't open. No one came forward to say they saw a man and woman arguing on a road. Roads were emptier than before. No matter where it ended up, toxic love stuff all unfolded indoors now.

The sheriffs offered assistance to help the twenty men and women of Grayson's police force question as many as they could. The twenty included three secretaries, two detectives, the chief and a husband-wife cleaning team. Maybe the doomed effort was evidence. The sign to cast off the middle and look at places most likely or unlikely. If a young woman like Raven McCoy had become a Grayson regular, somebody would know when and why. But Grayson's population and potential witnesses drifted from anything useful to conversation on the sparrows, cardinals, corn growing, how useless swimming pools are in Illinois, yard sales, summer festivals, where to find the best tomatoes at what road, how much business the pandemic cost. Women protected the men. Men protected the women.

The FBI could stay updated, but there wasn't enough remains or evidence a criminal could be charged with. Girls run away. People take their lives. It wasn't enough to remain clickbait, a hot topic and a hashtag. It's likely they wouldn't have even known her identity soon or at all without somebody speaking up to say they saw her nearby the day she disappeared. Those at the top declared the identification of her body and return of some remains was the victory.

There were ways for her family to get more justice, but they couldn't afford them.

All this propelled Detective Giselle Wise down to where Raven floated up from and not where she was found. One hour down the interstate from Grayson to Wells, Illinois. Worlds apart. It was called "the country" by those with Chicago closer, not Wells townsfolk themselves.

Wise spent a lifetime in a place like where she was headed, to get into her second life now. Maybe third. About twenty minutes from her exit two counties down, urban radio scratched off. This was her youth in one of these places, not rural but not city and just not: her and her friends straining to trap radio waves in tin foil or hangers, their biggest dream to hear the same songs the whole world did. The more she outstretched from the city county and trendsetting locales, as windmills and cattails and cropland multiplied the milieu, the more her roots unfurled to well-drawn memories before she was Lead Detective in Grayson.

Her criminal justice degree at a state college was just supposed to get her jobs in the courts. Courts were always active in

Chicago. They paid well. She started with a transcription certificate. But she qualified for the student loans to get more, plus four years wasn't long. With the degree, she moved fast from the courts to the police force. She was a woman and Mexican, worth more than issuing tickets. Just like average Grayson women, too old to be born in young places, a man was responsible for her residency. Her husband became an administrator in the water works. She and one son came with him. They bought a modest house and had a daughter. They weren't the only interracial couple in Grayson. Other yellow, orange and brown hands held white ones around. Still, many stared at them. She tolerated it. Such a nice house for the money.

Wise found a league of women who supported one of their own not just joining the police force, but leading it. After only ten years. She had worked some murders. None in Grayson, but just around it. Breaking and entering things, career criminal captures, jilted lover results. Her candidacy started off as a joke after news printed a great age white male lead detective called in that he wasn't coming to work anymore. "A Wise Replacement!" the first sign read. But Grayson women, especially Glenners in the money part, loved good causes. Petitioning for her to replace him was enough for them, especially that one Gracious Davidson. They had influence and pull, to go along with the cars and homes they tried to prove they were so much more than. She was forty when she attained the position and went on the town website.

Those village women put faith in her to give them answers on Raven McCoy, the blemish to their picture-perfect real estate and successful self-images. The ghost. And Wise remembered rites of passage from her Michigan hometown, a much different sort of small town. No net worths. Penny candy homes for blocks. Boys and girls she grew up with were gone too soon and often. The crime rates grew up more than them all. The ways and rules of the different kind of people would come in handy when she touched down where Raven was born and raised.

Wise cruised off the exit. She faced a traffic light, wrought iron and headstones at one of the town's two cemeteries, waiting and patient. This one was for the people on Raven's side of town, the black and brown. She turned right onto the Wells Main Street, two traffic lights, then another right onto Chicago Avenue. Anything but. Raven's mother remained there in the house Raven was living in before she disappeared. Wise didn't go straight to it. She walked around first.

Old wood two stories with latticed foundations and sitting porches towered over siding ranches next to them. Doghouses were empty. Sidewalks and yards seemed to be what dogs preferred. Wise felt the animals were manageable unless she gave them reasons not to be. She strolled freely along, her Glock heavy beside her.

A few fellow Mexicans and couple of whites cruised through in American cars. Most faces behind the tinted windows, fences and screens were black people. White people were an unnoticed anomaly. Race mixing was no problem on the black and brown sides. The white sides, at the perimeter in farms and trailers or money neighborhoods, were prejudiced, Wise suspected. She comprehended unspoken segregation. It was the same where she was from, with all the colors of people. The working class who turned the town around at core, others circling. It was the same in Grayson, her white husband free while she sensed pause for her Chicana tongue.

She inhaled the air and found it to be different, sepia if air was a color scheme. Pollution had to be lesser here, yet she felt a clog. She wanted the case to take some breaths, to fill up the name, the story, the victim all over again. It was all dying. Raven

McCoy was old news. The fact a girl was missing had been news, for feelings — excitement, sorrow, worry. But her dead body wasn't feelings for anyone but those who knew her best.

The small olive-green house brought a lump to her throat. Its corner yard was cared for. Barn animals were a lawn decoration theme. A Rottweiler ran the backyard, a not too old orange Chevy backed up against the gate locking the dog in. A whitetail flashed past the skinny sidewalk to the stoop. The screen door was open. Wise had called first. She rang. A little girl met her. From the outside, the house seemed just one story. Once inside it became a split-level. Jumbo size living room and dining room furniture. The kitchen could be seen from a triangle of square mirrors someone pasted opposite its entrance. In a leather recliner next to the mirrors, a woman was asleep with a crossword puzzle book and an ashtray in her lap. She opened her eyes.

Raven's mother Marisa wasn't surprised she was pregnant. She was surprised the person at the door was the police coming to do something, not just the news coming to see something.

"I figured someone from up there would never come back to talk to me face to face," she said. "Like my daughter vanished all over again. It's been a month."

"My apologies, but please know we only held her body so long to do everything we can to understand what happened," Wise said. "She's been frozen and intact."

"Well, we have a funeral to plan," said her mother, smoking yellow into her teeth and partly gray hair. "I'm on midnights at the nursing home. People know this won't be an early morning thing."

Her complexion showed years of the shift, her dark skin the opposite of rich, with a pale base holding it up. She was small and sleek, none of her daughter's height and girth.

"Bring the detective a pop, baby," she told the little girl. "You like grape or orange?"

"Grape is fine. Thank you. So if Raven's car is here, how did she get up to Grayson?"

"I've no idea. I told police before, many times. I never knew about Grayson. I maybe heard of it, sometimes, with the weather report."

The little girl returned. She knew Marisa liked grape best, too. Their cans cracked and hissed open. High noon sun made Wise switch herself on the couch for a new view to sharpen Marisa, next to uninvited cigarette smoke. Virginia Slims.

"Raven had so many friends, always running around," said Marisa.

"Did they drive? Did she ever take the bus or train to the city?"

"Raven loved the bus. She'd hop on that Megabus and go anywhere. St. Louis, Nashville, Detroit."

"What was she going for?"

"Friends. And businesses she was involved in. You know, she was being grown."

Wise knew she was older than Marisa, but she'd never lost a child. And she'd left this kind of place that would have seen her start on to that possibility a lifetime before she did. She was nowhere near a mother to adults.

The little girl skipped through the kitchen, dripping pop like black inkspots on the linoleum floor. A thin door creaked open. Many voices squealing and a basketball hitting a backboard. Wise peered over Marisa's shoulders on the couch covered in plastic. A backyard of clotheslines and makeshift play sets, boards and bricks and buckets — the way she wished her kids would play. Along the end of the yards, cars swooshed down the same interstate highway Wise had just exited. It ran the length of the subdivision behind a ditch like a creek, lining the miles of fencing. She surveyed the room, its nicotine tint on knick knacks and glass tables. The walls archived a McCoy family chronology. Generations lived on in pictures charting growth spurts, sports teams, dances, graduations, new babies, a wedding or two. Four children from Marisa. Raven was second to oldest. The first one, a boy, left for the Army. His Army military headshot centered the living room. He never returned to Illinois, not even to look for his sister.

Wise ran her fingers along wallpaper — orange and white stripes, then flowers — to follow Marisa to a wing of bedrooms. It was skinny and claustrophobic. Just a long rectangular landing with doors opposing each other. She was expecting one door to belong to Raven's bedroom. Wells Police claimed they processed it in winter. Marisa corrected both assumptions.

"No, they didn't," she said. "And Raven was up here."

The women went just past a small bathroom with more linoleum tile and a dark wood cabinet sink. A slow drip faucet planted a rust trail like blood down the back of the sink bowl. A narrow floor to ceiling window covered with dusty slats pointed askew. A neat white flowered curtain blew in. Up two small steps was a carpet landing, then a keyhole door behind a curtain. *Not a linen closet*, Wise thought she would have mentally snapshot the door if she'd found it. And been so procedurally lazy for it. Or left a kid to get killed for it. Or cost seconds to stop the person from jumping for it. Or not covered a partner from the waiting gunman for it. Or…

Stop it, Wise thought, *Focus. On the second and what's in front of you.*

Marisa fiddled a key into the door and Wise realized it was an attic.

"Raven stayed up here," her mother said. "We fixed this up for her."

The house kept unveiling surprises. Nothing from the outside said an attic. The short stairwell up was brown carpeted. The carpet switched to neat parquet squares over all the insulation and wood boards of the ceiling. In the center, Wise could extend her neck to raise her head all the way. It would have been uncomfortable for a taller girl, a Raven, to manage life like this. Still, the room had a seductive and mystic attraction. A firm queen mattress set in a high frame, next to a sizeable circular window facing the back of the house. An ornate pillow-like headboard was drilled into wood with screws hooks, not actually part of the bed. It could serve as a background alone, without the bed's white duvet, cover and pillowcase.

The façade was genius. Wise recognized the life in Raven's videos, where she unboxed fancy stuff. Her camera propped higher so she could look up to it and no one would question the size of things all-around. A phone tripod and ring light were propped, tilted as if she'd just used them. A point and shoot camera hung from the wall. With just one round window, the sunlight looked ethereal. A joy to film in for sure. Dresses, skirts, blouses and pants hung on a line clipped to the rafters. Bright colors, shine, sequins, feathers. Shoes stacked up a wall high behind them. Equally elaborate. A low table mixed candles, stones and shells with mall bracelets, necklaces, earrings. The idea of art was a magazine cover display up to the point of the room, starting above the door — stacked women rappers and models, photogenic athletes. The white lamps — fluffy, furry shades — were elegant for a triangle at the top of a house.

Wise compared the scene to the crumbs of life left in posts. One would have never known Raven McCoy lived in an attic.

Bikini posing on BMWs and Porsches checkered the grids, too. What was that all about? The two-door Chevy in the yard was Raven's, Marisa had said.

"Mind if I take a look at her car?" Wise remembered to ask.

"Sure, but it can't leave the yard," Marisa replied.

"Oh no, just now. Maybe I might find something. Wells police didn't say she had a car."

"She was dead. Her car wasn't worth mentioning to 'em."

"So they didn't search it at all?"

"You won't find much I didn't clean up," Marisa sighed. "People were coming over to borrow that car the minute Raven wasn't here to drive it. Everybody was knocking and saying they'd put gas in it. They did. But now that they found Raven, I'm more possessive with it."

Wise tried to hide the frustration at all that could be lost. Sometimes a woman's car stopped moving from her home. Sometimes a woman disappeared with the car people found without her in it. Both times, the car told a story.

"Miss McCoy, did any evidence teams ever come out for the car or take it in?"

"Before, I said, 'Well, she'll come back to get her car.' Now I just want it all to rest. Raven paid for that car with her own money and she didn't even buy herself a new one when she could've. She bought me my car. A nice Impala. Used, but still…"

Wise was out of new ways to offer condolences. She nodded to show she understood. The things Marisa had left without the person's scent and sight and sound of them. She heard sprinkling of urine, a toilet flush, a faucet. The same child who was yet unexplained pulled herself up the attic steps. It was sunny, but too chilly for her sundress. She wanted to eat. Marisa muttered about hamburgers and excused herself with permission for Wise to "look around."

Wise figured it was stupid to have come alone. Someone needed to talk and ask while someone else watched and looked. But Raven McCoy was a privileged case. No ordinary cops could get on it. Grayson talked too much. Chief Loveless was tired of it. "First the pandemic and now this," he barked to his force. "The world is opening. People want Grayson back to normal."

Normal for Grayson and its centering Glens was elite and safe and white. Missing girls, dead girls, poor girls, black girls, "Not them" girls. Not a fit to the people's visions of dream life.

The detective got on her knees and turned her toes under to shimmy under the bed. Rubbermaid containers. She rolled in dust bunnies and fine grit. Soon, she understood the reason for the lock on the door. Small boxes of watches, bracelets and earrings in one. Diamonds, gold. Real things. Designer leather bags in another. She felt chinchilla and fur in one bin, then silk and satin. A McQueen skull print. Chiffon. These weren't knockoffs. Wise had worked those scores and seized counterfeits before. It was some money missing, trickled out of limp envelopes creased in the middle. One still held green. A few thousand dollars, hundred-dollar bills. Wise speculated the original amounts. Who'd found it? How much disappeared these last few months?

Marisa McCoy had to know this. Mothers let their sons work corners for the spoils. They all say they know nothing. Was this any different? Why wouldn't they let their daughters work men for the same? Why had this mother left a detective alone? Did Marisa want her to know?

"Shame," Wise said to powerful faces on the covers of popular magazines. All their lips shined outrageously but not one smiled.

Wise looked out the window at children playing like she wished hers did, smelled ground beef and onions simmering. She counted six other yards she could see into just by turning her head both ways. Marisa and her people were famous here, differently than they were in Grayson. Or on the internet. Even the country. Here, they were gossip. The reality of Raven's sugar baby image cut sympathy they received. It exposed a vapid truth and brought shame to her daughter.

Still, hassles of embarrassment aside, Marisa didn't want the conversation to end, Wise calculated. Her nonchalance was all an act. She wanted the devil to pay. She didn't want the matter closed. Wise continued to the things, photographing them on her phone.

Eventually, Wise did her best to reorganize the plastic treasure chests. She pushed them along the parquet. The ones she meant for the foot of the bed kept landing crooked. Something wouldn't let them flush straight with the wall. It was no bed frame. Just a construction of one. She walked to the back of the mattress and swung the box spring up a little for her to see the floor underneath. It was a small stack of big books she reached hard for.

All were on pregnancy.

Sixteen

With the mother pre-occupied to get one child's body and fix dinner for the rest, Wise moved on. Best to start back with best friends she spoke with on the phone. None of them posed anywhere or in any way with Raven online. These had been the hardy, fleshy friends of time. They came to the vigil at the river. It was too sensitive to drill them then. Now, Wise couldn't wait to talk in person. It was only so much to detect from a voice through a screen and the faces on the screen. As with Marisa, so much more information erupted from a warm body.

Wise estimated Raven was not involved with men where she came from. Since high school graduation, all she showed off online indicated big city tastes. Wells didn't even have a major luxury department store. Media was ever present and easy for all to see things on, but still. People tend to want to look and be like those around them. Raven was looking past Wells.

Wise took pictures of the books and notes on them, the ISBN numbers.

"Didn't she tell someone she wasn't pregnant?" Wise said out loud.

She thought and thought and thought. It would come to her.

She jotted to trace Amazon deliveries to the residence, starting from late last summer, when Raven would have conceived. Books especially. She could find the senders. The basic, *What to Expect When You're Expecting* was brand new. Surely a gift. A common one — standard fare in Grayson's rented Art Center rooms and its nicest restaurant's baby showers. There were also two books on diet, mindfulness, and exercise in pregnancy.

Then was the oddball *Birthing Justice: Black Women, Pregnancy and Childbirth*. Checked out from the library. The return receipt put it due at last holidays. This book seemed to be handled well, the spine broken and corners turned down to mark pages. She imagined dolled-up Raven engrossed in the book, against her makeshift bed, a moonlight or candlelight ambiance, in her private gift of an attic like Anne Frank or Emily Dickinson.

Wise had driven the streets just to get inside Raven's memory and bones. Past the parks and factories, railroad tracks and mechanics. In some parts, the homes were stately. Plantation like. So many vacant and boarded. Wise recognized the weathered couples settled in windows and doors to smoke, watch TV and open doors when people stopped by. She'd been to many weddings like theirs. Hall and church yards, food and beer for everybody. For older couples, the kids or lives they had before each other came to the point where people couldn't tell them apart. The men wore military caps so nobody forgot they served. The women wore hats and sunglasses so nobody forgot they had style. It wasn't possible for anything to be too out of order for too long in these couples. The place was too small and motions too set. The minute it was an error or change, it had to correct itself. Odds were Raven travelled for men not from around here.

"The spa," she said aloud.

She thought of it. The last place Raven was seen. The spa recorded evidence Raven was "not pregnant," according to what she wrote herself. The books proved she knew she was.

If she knew it, someone else knew it. No girl or woman keeps that entirely to herself.

Raven's impotent cell phone had come up in her pocket. Phone numbers showed up on records and off towers. Texts died with the phone. Burner phones had to be considered as well. The girls did this with paying men. Her known cell and number probably weren't used for that.

People's internet selves were harder to break into than their houses and money accounts. Social media outfits had departments to deal with crimes and law enforcements. Only, the young staffs didn't seem to get that these cases were real and serious. There wasn't much force after requests for Raven. A junior officer, Bobby Castle, had slow evening shifts. Wise thought she remembered he had tried to guess her passwords when the subpoena for them were slow, since courts were all adjusting to Zoom. When the apps did clear Wise to break in appropriately, Raven's DMs were all just girl talk and chatter. What was deleted?

Raven had quit one friend's job they shared at a big buffet. All girlfriends talk about men.

Something had to be said. Wise headed to eat lunch there.

She found the short, dawdling Dawn McDonald manning the desserts station, also doing hybrid community college from her phone. Wise fixed herself a colorful plate and waited for the friend to get a moment. The country music soundtrack was a familiar one. The time was early afternoon past lunch before dinner, so barely even any seniors and truckers, but all friendly faces. Besides her duty weapon, Wise looked like someone taking a break from the nearby office buildings or few standing factories on Route 50. She didn't feel on duty still in places like these, not at the ready for the astronomical odds of some mayhem among about 30,000 people in Wells.

Time passed. She set aside her salad plate to go back for rotisserie chicken and vegetable sides. A teenage Mexican waiter finally came up and asked her about drinks. They spoke Spanish about the weather and the town. Eventually, she said she was fine with water. Time passed. Dawn came over with a bowl of white ice cream with sprinkles and peanut chips.

"Is that all you're having for lunch?" Wise asked.

"I don't like the food here," Dawn groaned. "I normally drive to Taco Bell or Popeye's up Main. But today, I don't have time, since I gotta talk to you."

"You don't have to talk to me Dawn," Wise said. "Everything is voluntary. But you and other people who knew Raven are the best things we have to understand what happened here."

Dawn played with a cream fabric necklace holding multicolored beads, no other jewelry to be found, odd in a restaurant where the beads could slip into food trays. Her right hand came down from the necklace and folded with her left on her lap.

"Well, it's all outta hand because too many people who don't know her are spreading the story," Dawn signed. "None of you know. I sat by Raven all through school. McCoy, McDonald. That was us. It don't even matter what happened."

"Do you want what happened to your friend to happen to another girl?" Wise asked. "It wouldn't be your fault. But it is more likely if it's a man out there we need to be looking for."

Wise pretended to concentrate on forking green beans and melting a pat of butter into a dinner roll. Then her slippery cold water glass and the kind of cheap straw that always nicked her tongue. She understood a place like this, a circle of bonds.

160

"Raven didn't have time for a man," Dawn claimed. "She was about her business and school. She told dudes she was busy."

"She was pregnant," Wise revealed.

This wasn't in the news yet. Maybe it would get out. Maybe not.

"No, she wasn't," Dawn said.

"Yes, she was."

"Um, *nooo*. She was not."

"I have no reason to come all the way here to lie to anyone."

"All these rumors about somebody people don't even know. Raven was smart and running businesses and going to college. So now, she's gonna be pregnant by a pimp? That's the new story, right?"

"This isn't something being reported. But she definitely had a male in her life."

Wise remembered growing up like Dawn. Her skyline was factory smokestacks, a few prime buildings downtown, grassy hills that looked right next to her though they were miles away. Forty-hour work weeks sucked humor and patience from the adults. Work and come home was the cycle. Substance abuse took over. So did unplanned pregnancies. Most young men and women eventually made the rounds to tell everyone they had a baby on the way. Wise knew, like she guessed Raven and Dawn did, what it was to be more familiar with clerks in aide buildings and offices than with their fathers and his family. From a young age.

She had made do with having to try to remember a father her mother separated from —how he ate his eggs, whether he wrapped her gifts or gave them straight from the store, what his shoes were like. She broke the cycle. The children who needed helpful government workers grew up to be adults still needing them. These were part of life. Wise had considered becoming one of those government workers those children needed. She could help people too, patiently, through complicated paperwork the government required to pay their predicaments. She could've gently talked through all the words and blank spaces. She could've helped them talk out ideas to do better than this, as she was sure Raven tried to do.

Dawn carried on.

"This bitch came all the way here to get to lying…"

"I am not lying," Wise said. "A coroner's report is just facts."

"She's my best friend. She would've told me. Y'all must be dumb up in that Grayson."

Dawn finished her ice cream and went back to work.

Wise had last hopes. Raven's friend Sincere Brown. He drove Dawn to Grayson for a vigil at the river the night she was found. He also called the police force for an interview soon as information was sought. So, Wise knew him. He worked at a gentleman's store in the mall, on a strip of road where congested modern life came into focus and that life looked suburban. He looked like a clean-shaven model wearing neat eye makeup, track shorts and neon green trainers.

"I just wanted to believe she ran away from Wells without me," he said on a bench outside the store. He waved and slapped hands to a few who walked by. A track star, he had been, by her fast Googling and Facebook research. He didn't say what changed, why he wasn't burning up tracks on a campus somewhere or recruited, why he was in Wells running the mall.

"Raven was always thinking bigger than everybody."

"How do you explain what she was doing in Grayson?" Wise asked.

"That girl was into all kinds of businesses," he said.

"What kind of business?" Wise asked.

Sincere named the usual: diet pills and drinks, body scrubs and lotions, natural hair potions, bitcoin. Raven's social comments were pockmarked with codes for private business with men, "DM me" for a certain intonation in responses, one suggesting concrete details such as time and amounts. This was sparse, but clear. Gift hauls were enormous. Pampering days were plenty. Her last post was November 2020, more than six months ago. It was nearly three months ahead of the last time Raven was seen. That post mused about wanting a puppy. Then, nothing.

"Were drugs one of the businesses?" Wise asked.

Sincere smiled and pulled out a pocket mirror to inspect for streaks.

"Raven wasn't no hype," he said. "But weed, yeah. Gummies, lollipops…"

"She sold those?"

"Only edibles. We both did. My uncle was twenty one before us and knew a white guy who got that hemp license, so he did the ordering. First time we spent our whole checks ordering and it was all melted when we got it. We didn't pay for "cold shipping," some bitch on the phone told us. We knew better next time. We sold those at the high school. But nah, nothing hard."

"Just weed?" Wise confirmed. "And, what about sex?

Sincere's white male boss come to the opening of the store for no reason and went back.

"Raven wasn't a skid row hoe," said Sincere, standing. "She was gold."

"Yes, she was," Wise agreed.

Innocence was the most credible witness. Maybe these people had done nothing but believe whatever Raven told them. What bothered Wise so much is Raven had a chance. Clearly, she was willing to get herself out and beyond. But Wise knew the patterns she was up against.

Sixteen was state eligibility for a job. Raven's socials showed her last childhood hurrah was a sweet sixteen at the Pizza Hut one summer. She was popular. Many family and friends. She wore shorts and a PINK sweatshirt. Pictures showed she sucked air out of helium balloons to talk funny as she opened presents. Somebody set up purple balloons, plates and napkins instead of Pizza Hut stuff. It was a lot of bubbles. Clear soap circles floated above and around in all the videos and pictures. Her grandmother came out and a few other seniors sat around in blue jeans.

Up in Grayson, Wise was a feminine voice to explain to men what girls like Raven were up against. Childhoods cut short. Working women from the womb. They were stuck in a conundrum where everyone around them, bigger than them, could be broke or broken. But they were in a liminal space where their world called them "grown": cut off from expecting grownups to provide more than a home and roof, but ill-equipped to compete in the real world. No seed money, no favors, no rich uncles and aunts. Children, really, already on their own in life.

Detective Wise finished in the opposite direction where she initially drove off the interstate. Route 17 led to Raven's aunt's house in an adjacent township. The crickets blended together on the way. Lightening bugs came out. Aunt Bell's coffee breath was familiar. She was at the Grayson River vigil after Raven came up. Several times that winter, she had called the Grayson station. She ran an outskirts bowling alley with her boyfriend, a motorcycler. He brought in mounds of containers he had travelled "to town" for and then left without fanfare.

"Care for Chinese?" Aunt Bell asked, a cigarette dangling as she unwrapped it all.

"No thank you. I just interviewed Raven's friend Dawn at a buffet," Wise said.

"Oh, Miss Dawn." Bell moved around the small kitchen using her hips like hands to shut drawers and swing back chairs. "She tell you she can sing?"

"No."

"She's supposed to sing for the funeral. Whenever we get the body, that is."

"It should be soon. The medical examinations are complete."

"You can have the fortune cookies," Bell said. "I'm not superstitious."

Bell tossed two cookies across the neat table she pulled from a slot in the wall.

Bell's chopsticks roamed through broccoli and beef, chop suey and chicken fried rice while she clued Wise into things. Wise heard it all before — Raven was a cheerleader but a tomboy, a church girl when she was young, focused on her friends, no serious boyfriends. The women knew a man was at the heart of the matter. Or men. Someone had to drop the veil, admit Raven wasn't the Virgin Mary. Who was going to do it?

"We've had no luck tracking down any men she was involved in, strange for a girl her age," Wise shared. "Had to be some."

"Looking and acting sexy online is just what these girls do nowadays," Bell admitted. "Doesn't make them hoes."

"A victim is a victim," Wise said. "And I'm sorry about some of the stories out there."

"That's what black people get," Bell laughed. "We can never be just a victim. We gotta be the one with a prison record, drugs in the system. The prostitute. Get blamed for what other people do. Can you imagine? Getting blamed for things so much all your life you're gonna be dead and it's still all your fault?"

Raven would rest in a grave in the circle of bonds her homeland was. Her people would guard her in death, keep codes of silence to thwart stereotypes and stigmas from her name. Wise noticed Bell's face tighten and ready to tell a detail, then relax. It came back in another direction.

"Raven was her mother's favorite," Bell said. "Her mother let her father do whatever, so long as she was his main. It worked for them. They never got married so she still qualified for benefits. She still got Section 8 paying for that house on account of the kids."

"Ah," Wise said. She'd grown up where approval for subsidized housing was an achievement. Now she lived where people griped about having to pay taxes for others to have it.

"Before Marisa finished her nurse's aide license, you should've seen her at the annual certification time," Bell explained. "She'd quit tending bar a few nights for cash. Set her schoolbooks aside. She had to focus to be sure all her evidence got together. She dressed those kids up in whatever they got for their birthdays or Christmas the past year. So they could come to the office with her to influence the worker to overlook any mistakes."

"Did Raven help bring money in the house, the bills and things?"

"That's just what oldest girls do around here. Her father paid child support and that was gone when she turned eighteen. But Marisa makes more now. The little kids' fathers pay their part. Add in what she qualifies for as a single mother. Everybody does it."

"Does what?"

Aunt Bell laughed out loud.

"Everybody finds ways to work the systems. And men. Whatever Raven was doing online or Chicago or wherever, she was just following what her mother did. In her own way.

Everybody ain't cut out to work their lives away for a little pay-check. Some people want more. And trying to get it in this world right here, right now? Please. It's trying to kill us all."

"I understand," Wise smiled.

Wise knew the cycle. Kids learned it. A power to write "0" for income on a paper. Then the invisible gods come give their parents and caretakers food, housing and pocket change to pass along to them. It was no shame in it. It was almost shame in not doing it. It was a six pack of beer story as to how Raven went from the cheerleader pictures in her home to advertising herself, gently, on the web. It's unclear how far she went. Wise knew many online women of the night didn't have sex. But she was pregnant without a man or relationship anybody knew of.

Bell made Wise at least have the bathroom and read her fortune before she left.

"All of life is a dream walking, all of death is a going home," Wise read.

Bell set down her chopsticks and started to cry.

On the hourlong drive past phone poles and no rest stops, Wise worked in her head. She was relieved to see lights and flat buildings off the interstate in Chicagoland. The day down-state was good, productive. She knew the victim better now. It wouldn't take much to convince a young person here that things were easy. Space and leisure would make her trusting. Life narrows elsewhere. Raven would've been thrown to vicious wolves outside a familiar tiny place.

It could be worth a girl's trouble to hook the starter profes-sionals who bought condos outside Grayson Glens. Those men were recent graduates or stuck in thirtysomething bachelor life. Some older divorced men and widowers. Men who made money to spoil families and mistresses at once were in the Glens — the corporate titans, business owners and a few ex-athletes, remote workers. Not many men of color were among them.

That population was just as small as it was private. Money and reputations were on the line. A few used to be minor celebrities hid out there. They required and received discretion from their entourages, just in case they came back into style somehow. No one who knew of a sidepiece named Raven would say something. A wife in that world would be too humiliated to help law enforcement or a victim. Appearances.

The Powells still felt interesting.

Rare to find a childless couple their age in Grayson Glens. Victor was an attractive public figure. Wise could see a girl meeting him somewhere, falling in love, hanging on to him. Tragedy was an odd stay-at-home housewife in their kind of real estate, with her humble background and orphan past. Not a mother. Wise was familiar with this Grayson couple type. Either it was really true love or all just for show.

But Wise had to be careful she wasn't standing them out just because they were black. It was an unfair consequence of being in Grayson, speckled with color but dominated by whites. No reasonable connections existed. She would return to the evidence.

She stopped at a Grayson traffic light to write "Powells" in her handy black notebook. Right across the page she had free before. "Check Raven's car." And she hadn't even done it.

"Damn it."

She slapped the steering wheel. God only knew when she'd get back down there. She hadn't even known she would go down there today. She'd had to fight for the chance to do it.

She never sprang into her house from all this outside. It was always a transition. Lights beamed from an awning over the dining room window. Through it, a small chandelier by

Grayson standards. *Not bad*, she thought. Her husband was probably downstairs watching sports. Her children were in their bedrooms talking to friends or strangers remotely. Over in the Glens, the kids and husbands got wives, nannies and more to cook virtual restaurant meals homemade. Her career meant leftover delivery or boxes of cooled down food waiting for her.

She found the last fortune cookie and couldn't wait. Savoring its vanilla taste would ease her on from obsessing for another woman's child and comfort to that woman for the child. She would get the lives off her chest, move magically into her real self and her own children and life.

"Never forget a half truth is a whole lie," the fortune read.

SEVENTEEN

OMG, hun. U ok? We see that dead girl in Grayson everywhere now...

I saw the DM but didn't reply. I just closed the app. Over a month now, such notifications had slowed down. This alert included a share to the day's *Chicago Sun-Times* article on the case. I didn't read those. The picture attached to the story was one of Raven cheerleading.

The DM's sender was Gena, my old classmate. Back in the day, she gave me a tote bag as a gift filled with shea butter soaps, soy candles and Godiva treats in a bridesmaid proposal surprise. I'd told her "Yes." I started my hospitality career with her in a Customer Service Fundamentals class. By the time we got to Food Sanitation & Safety II, I knew she was funny with money. She even lived with me once before she met a gym teacher she would marry. I hadn't seen her in years. I had so many more friends where she came from, barely seen anymore, all just avatars and occasional beeps on my phone or laptop. I had stopped most cyber small talk.

"These ladies prove women can do everything men do and

they can do it in heels," I watched Victor say from the mounted screen. "It's time for our talented ladies to get paid like it."

From his frat brother's Chicago townhome Victor had left our home for, he travelled to O'Hare to LAX. His job this time was to interview a panel of cable actresses on pay inequities in Hollywood. The show would be live-streamed. We were talking again, a start.

"Come out here with me and we'll just chill," he'd said.

That meant going through airport and mask fight hell to stay in a hotel. Productions were in bubbles. Anyone who wasn't working couldn't break them. It seemed this was about to be the story for all appearances Victor made. Part of me felt left behind. More of me was relieved not to stand in the background while beautiful, rich women sat in a spotlight I never would.

"It was all stupid," I'd told him. "We'll make up when you get back. I'll be writing…"

These were weird date nights every time I was scheduled to watch him and Ifa was gone. I used to do watch parties with my coworkers and friends. However the more that came to watch, the less I watched with those people. Most of them had stopped contacting me every time they saw Victor online, in a trending story or on television.

Call time. I'm on in 30. Hope you're watching babe.

I am, my love. Make sure to ask them to position you on your left. You look better.

Of course. Any questions a smart pretty lady thinks I should ask these ladies?

Ask what their fight for equal pay means for black women who will follow them.

I settled under a cashmere throw. No wine tonight. Minutes wound down until all stores in driving distance closed. All the top shelf of our butterscotch-glazed bar was Victor's: throat-scorching cognacs, calf-colored whiskeys and specialty scotches, foreign vodkas, vermouths. Some was ours, Caribbean rums we hauled from our "reconnection" cruise. Plenty of beer in both fridges. But, nah. Beer was a staple smell in those foster homes, more popular than water with the men who came and went. I convinced myself I didn't have a taste for alcohol at all.

The Clean Me appointment was upcoming fast.

A trusty friend Face-timed. Faith Tucker was my lawyer but not really. I shared a legitimate lawyer with Victor, mostly for his business affairs and contracts. Faith stayed in my back pocket for myself. Just in case. We had a ritual of gabbing when Victor was out of town.

"Hello beautiful," she beamed. She tilted a frosty goblet of peach bubbly to her camera.

"Well, hello," I smiled back. "I see somebody's popping off tonight."

"Oh no," she laughed. "I'm in flavored water hell. The pandemic pounds gotta go, girl."

I thought if I should tell her about the Clean Me appointment.

"I'm taking it easy too. Could get pregnant any day now." It wasn't altogether a lie.

"Oh my gosh," Faith exclaimed. "You should be! I've been wondering when."

"Well, first he said it wasn't time. Then, I said it wasn't time and —"

"It's time! That'll halt the drinking for sure."

Faith's hair was a wavy blowout. She sat in her den against sliding glass doors out to their patio and pool, covered for the season. She radiated more than usual against her white cube LEDs, egg chairs and hallucinogenic faux foliage. It was backwards. She was so dowdy outside the house, simple buns and ponytails for the girl's night outs. She was a curvaceous brown woman with a flawless complexion. At home, she came out of her tight schoolteacher and courtroom self. Black women guarded against walking as catcall victims until we got onto canes.

Evidence of full house nesting littered her sectional: disheveled pillows, strewn hoodies tangled cords, abandoned devices. Men's size house slippers covered her feet. Beside her, prostrate, was a blue-eyed white Persian her family called Sunshine. She looked instead like a Gretchen or Louise, pinched and sad. Glimpses of her life made me see the future. When Victor was ready. When I was ready. When we had more than it all.

Faith showed the costs. She had two teen sons with her and her husband. They all drove sensible cars. She also did her own hair, even color. She baked her own Christmas and Halloween treats. She couldn't be lazy and order out like I did. She coaxed me into trading budget recipes to fill up big men. Some were comfort foods, out of style (tuna noodle casserole, succotash, fricassee, stew). Others were the rages (grain bowls, lettuce wraps, home-made pizza and sushi). She kept her postings to commentary on smart things, Supreme Court decisions and latest legislations. Besides drinking, her naughtiness was obsession with true crime TV, *Nightline* stories and nerdy details of killings played out on autopsy or detective shows.

Her take on Raven McCoy's case was the resounding one. A girl on the wrong grind. It was sad, but nothing anybody could do about it. Education and blah blah were the answers.

"I just read one of those juicy cheater and stalker true crimes," Faith said. "I saw the author's with that Patricia Rogers agent you won't work with."

"I *am* working with her," I said. "But I want my life story to have some purpose, at least."

"Long as it sells," Faith smiled. She finished off her fruity elixir. She poured more.

Victor would never have casual conversations with people from my life before him. He hardly knew them. I hardly knew them anymore. But what was looking more and more like my best friend these days came like everything else: from Victor's world.

Faith and I hit off our own friendship at the annual barbecue Christian and Jazz Pitts gave. When we'd met the Pitts at the first and only Arts Center Gala we could stand, we thought the senior couple's warmth was the beginning of something. Turned out Mr. Pitts just always had the party. We never saw the Pitts outside that invitation the next year.

Faith's husband retired early to start his own diversity firm. Faith left corporate litigation for nonprofits. They had free time they forgot what to do with. A black people party in white country sounded cool to them. At the Pitts' affair, with cots decked in the main and pool house, Victor and I were glad for the Tuckers' company. We expected maybe thirty people but walked into a family reunion. Mr. and Mrs. Pitts, dressed in clean cream linens, held court from a tented pavilion while about two hundred people sucked up the food and drink they left around it. An old soul dance floor and limbo corner stayed busy with throngs who were family or just in the loop. I barely knew the Tuckers, but I wouldn't have lasted more than an hour without Faith.

Eventually, the men separated to huddles revolved around how much they could jog and bench press. How much money they made and put out. This left their wives and partners stuck as strangers or fast friends, or squinting into a stranger's or fast friend's screen, or twirling our hair. I wandered to sit in a chaise lounge near citronella candles obviously not working. It's hard to stay flawless and survive height-of-summer mosquitoes. It's a personal failure not to have a good time in these circles. So I smiled and swat bugs, checked my phone and sipped my drink. The crowd and time were familiar except the Glens looked more like a party in Jamaica for it.

The men's good skunk weed, cigar smoke and sour alcohol odors contrasted our efforts at prim. Every sister not in a delicate way had a stiff drink in her hand. Gins and tonics, rums and cokes, wine coolers. I was tame: a Chardonnay. I knew manning up for the boys turned me into my hubby's designated driver. Our home wasn't far from this one, but I had to stay professional.

Faith was simple: a Corona.

"So, ladies… celery, scallions or green peppers for your potato salads?" she'd asked.

A sad, pale version of potato salad oozed onto most of our Fineline plates.

"Depends on if I'm doing it American or German style."

"Well, what kind of potatoes?"

"Celery, if it's organic. Otherwise it's too green or hard."

"I heard an enzyme in green peppers kills E. coli in case it's gonna be out in the sun."

"Oh dear! No, you have to keep salads inside."

Above the DJ's disco turn, I managed to squeak in: "I just use relish. The eggs and mayo of course. Maybe a little sugar."

"That must be sweet potato said," laughed one.

And for another laugh from a belly big with a baby: "There's no way I could have that."

"Green peppers give it all the color, so without that…?" questioned a woman who only called her potbellied husband "The Judge."

"That's what paprika on top is for," I said. "Anyway, it's just a quick easy thing. Potato salad was a regular at my house growing up. Nothing fancy. Just food."

"Actually," Faith said, "I think I'll swap out the spoonful of sugar I add to my potato salads for a spoonful of sweet relish instead. Maybe it's more nutritional value."

Then, we left the bitches and our sandals to go cheat on our diets at the Mexican station that was way better than the soul food one. Since then, she was the closest girlfriend I'd kept.

"The rivers not far from you," Faith reminded me. "And reports seem to be saying it was way more to that girl disappearing than just a drowning. You feeling okay there alone?"

"A creek is just down the hill in the back," I pointed. "Feels like the river sometimes."

"Too spooky," Faith teased. "My husband told your husband not to go anywhere the Metra doesn't. When you get out where they don't go to Chicago, it's drama like the hood."

"Oh, my husband," I groaned. "He left for his brother's. Hasn't done that in a while."

Her husband was one of Victor's best boys from college. She'd only been her husband's sweetheart in college. They were practically family. Still, she made me feel in the fold.

"Honey, got it," she sighed. "Being cramped up together has tested my limits with this married thing. One of the children, they are. You'll find out when you get busy on them soon. Get some of those toys and things. Handcuffs, whips. That'll smooth it over. And, you guys might actually need them out there. You got killers putting girls in rivers."

"You're being extreme," I laughed. "Everyone is. Things are fine out here, Faith."

I didn't say, "The corn seems like it's growing too fast and to get out the Glens to the rest of Grayson, to the world, I gotta drive through stalks taller than your teenagers now. I'm scared."

I didn't say, "The dust shapes form themselves to Raven McCoys in uncanny lights."

How could I tell her, or anyone, "The water faucets make the sound of Raven's name, like whispering in the swoosh."

I almost told her, "The candle lighter spell-cast me to stare into the flame and see Raven McCoy's face. Victor broke the spell. My hand and the flame were close to a pillow." Or, "That girl from the river keeps coming to me as water and fire and earth. She has her ways."

No. I just told Faith the normal thing.

"We should do brunch soon. How about Cinco de Mayo in a few days?"

Faith said yes. I went back to waiting for Victor to have a seat at some table, be a great mind and communicator, model great black men. I was supposed to like comments, reply and answer questions as he performed. I replaced some company charging him an arm and a leg to do this. This used to feel effortless in Chicago when I first started it. Since Grayson Glens, already so distant as it was, I couldn't stay too interested in people who weren't right around me.

But somehow, I tucked my wallet into a puffer vest. I stuffed my bare feet into wet black Stuart Weitzman leather combats, struggling the boots over jeggings. I swiped my keys off a hook. Our black truck better matched my mood shift, like I could head-to-head anything coming around a winding road, but my Chrysler would do. All this came on adrenaline for sneaking out of my own house. Just to get some drink. Drank. Juice. Sauce. Alk. Adult beverage. Cocktail. Hooch. Shine. As usual, one of the black gatemen were off or sleeping.

The Grayson Glens wind was good around the bends. An elusive point when living with the Great Lakes feels like the perfect idea, between soggy Mays and not yet scorching Junes. I lowered the windows and propped the phone up on the dash. The dashcam recorded darkness, cornstalks and endless trees in my lights.

Would Raven appear? If she came because I was thinking she would, and not on her own when I least expected it, was she still a ghost?

Eighteen

It was a syndrome in the Glens. It caught up to most of the women. Sometimes girls.

Dream homes started off as dreams come true. They were love at first sight, but in a short time they started to feel like haunted houses to worry inside of. The men were the first ghosts. After that, it was easy for the women to see what wasn't really there in everything.

Husbands, sons and fathers always had a reason or excuse so important, their calendars booked and their travels necessary. This wasn't a right of the women. The house was what they did now. When they weren't doing the house, they were doing the children. The wives knew what awaited their daughters and, in quiet prudence, pushed those girls to get away from Grayson. Go far for college. Then go study abroad. Go do that internship. Go for the trip to the jungle and the desert and mountains. Don't get married just yet. These were their small victories.

But a missing girl in the river infused the women with something they needed. Raven McCoy was a name, girl and situation uniting them all in their sorrows, different but still important. It was so new and fresh. They could be right to be so scared in this place their husbands had dragged them and their families out to. It sparked longer phone conversations and more dinners together. It excused private talks just between mothers and daughters. It banished men to knocking and asking to come in or talk. The trending Grayson mystery seeped down from the media into the general population, to make women and girls mysterious to men and boys again.

Many things still stood for Tragedy to discover about this place. She finally saw, doubtless over time, grown men felt absent from the women and youngsters. She rarely glimpsed couples in regular public life. Twosomes were stuffed away in restaurants and movie theaters and other "date night" places. That's it. In everyday shopping and streets and observations, it was usually groups of women with just themselves and children. Men alone and just with each other. Women and children congregated in the yards, for parties or play. Families together? Almost never. It was if men had permission to be invisible or gone in Grayson and especially the Glens. It wasn't just because of lockdowns. It was like that before. A place that first appeared so progressive was actually stuck back in time, only dressed in today's architecture and fashions.

Tragedy pulled up to the 24-hour station and its country music soundtrack of the region. Just as she parked, a pack of new driver's licenses rolled out the hotspot. Two cars. One girl among them was the color of chai tea. The pack kept their heads bent into a double life on phones. The exception was one tall male blonde. He was unthreading a thin lock from a cigarette pack. From the snippet Tragedy heard, chai tea girl spoke like a lost *Beverly Hotels 90201* audition tape, alerting the others she just shared what they had to go like. The dark girl brushed by Tragedy and never looked up or back to her.

The few black kids she encountered in the Grayson area didn't seem to care about being polite. Joy, a city kid, appeared lost among them as well. They sported flip flops in the freezing cold. They ran out with their hair soaking wet. They drove off in sound clouds of Katy Perry, Lady Gaga and The Jonas Brothers. These kids had no automatic pull or reaction to her. She was thirty-five, not fifteen or twenty-five. She wasn't expecting the boys to stare. She wasn't looking for females to extend an invite to the video shoot. She was maybe just expecting something like unity, solidarity, consciousness. In three years of living out here, it hadn't come.

White men broke from their semis and diesels outside. In the tight station's two booths, they fingered cups of what appeared to be tepid coffee. Shiny hot dogs set in white paper bowls or two fingers instead of two hands like everybody else. Flat sand-paper-colored buns of two-bite burgers spread on tinfoil papers. Crumbs of make-do beef swirled into abstracts of yellow mustard, red ketchup and maroon steak sauce. The men looked in the direction of Tragedy arriving, but not much. She wasn't the only black around. She was just unusual to see.

An older Mexican security guard could have been missed in a gray folding chair in the corner, newspaper outspread on his lap. He opened his eyes to look at her, nod and return to dozing. Wisdom told Tragedy to make it look good. She couldn't be coming out just for liquor. Once, she had found Mrs. Pitts at this gas station. The elusive woman looked ready to go onstage, makeup and hair done under a winter fur hat. "Mr. Pitts has the flu," she'd explained of her mortification to be the one to go get gas, soup, saltines and juice at midnight. Tragedy was stopping for the last time before a pending snowstorm that isolated her with Victor, exactly what she had wanted back then.

Now she faced cookies above moist fat cakes in shocking flavors and colors. She knew better. Almond and oat milks, hummus and decent cheeses awaited waist-conscious wives and a new generation. Tragedy decided on a spinach dip to join garlic hummus and pita chips on a side display with cylinders of mixed nuts — plain, spicy and sweet. She starred as the average Grayson wife picking up a little for a heated barn party, book club meeting or kitchen rehab unveiling. After all, people were free to gather and crowd a little outside again.

The male herd whooped from a joke Tragedy sort of overheard. It had to do with pussy and the pussies who don't know how to get it. She slid over piled cases of Old Style and Budweiser to the freezer's parade of lighter fare. A lot had stronger alcohol content. The selection as alluring as Crayola boxes and silly putty playsets for toddlers, all that cute stuff was initially marketed to young people headed to stadiums, their Snapple juices switched out. These kids thought this stuff made them better off than their daddies, granddaddies, stepdaddies, brothers and uncles. Those men had set off regular alarms with early and late morning stumbles over all the crunched beer cans they piled up overnight. These kids thought this new stuff wouldn't grieve their mothers, grandmothers, stepmothers, sisters or aunts. All the women getting the eggs and coffee ready to treat the men's tempers until night brought the next round.

This wasn't alcohol. It was just fun.

A frost coated the twist-off bottles and cans the freezer stocked. Tragedy chose a tropical wine cooler and bottle calling itself "Merlot" or "Chardonnay." Its real name, wine product, was stamped in small print at bottom edge of the label. Four bottles to hold her over until her appointment at Clean Me soon. She managed to get to the lottery machine at the register, up to Team D artillery: CBD drinks, THC gummies in tempting flavors, all-night energy tonics, stumpy bottles she couldn't define, discreet retractable whips, toy cuffs, lust pills for her, stamina pills for him, textured and flavored condoms for him/her/he/she/they/

them. Tragedy thought of the carnival it all used to be. Before it went down to photogenic fantasy recreations the more square footage one accumulated.

"Sometimes, you have to let an old phase die off, because that past is straining the present and blocking the future," the clerk was saying to the customer in front of her. "So, do not fear the Death card. You can embrace it."

Tragedy noticed the newsstand waiting for Sunday loads. A *Grayson Herald* was top shelf. The dead girl in a river was its front-page news. Tragedy swiped the last copy to skim over a heartbroken community, no answers and no leads, any information people can offer…

The clerk leaned around the sanitary safety plexiglass, speaking to a woman with a TV anchor bob of unusual volume and shine. Tragedy's wigdar was top-notch. This wasn't a wig.

"I feel great!" The perfect bob shook. "Last checkup came out in superior results."

Tragedy moved her wares closer in hopes of notice. Just a bum view of anime-style tarot cards sprawled next to a customer's Fendi tote and brown paper bags insulating what Tragedy guessed were the same bottles of wine product she had.

"So, okay. Now, we have the—"

The clerk was a young woman with face piercings and local inflection. She tapped a card, rolled her eyes and moaned. "This is the Ten of Swords. I'd be more concerned about this than the Death card. Usually means there's a surprise or shock coming."

"Like, I win the lottery?"

"Could be. Whatever it is, there'll be a dark aspect to it, some discomfort. I'd be real careful of new people and ventures, anything or anyone unfamiliar, now."

Johnny Cash inched past Waylon Jennings and the white male group stood to leave.

"Excuse me!" Tragedy called out.

"Oh, lemme check her out and we'll go back to it," the clerk said.

Tragedy moved close enough to see the clerk's name tag read "Charity."

"How was everything, miss?" Charity asked.

Tragedy attributed that recent "Miss" thing to some long gray strands. It made her bristle.

"Great, thanks so much," she nodded.

Before she could say more, the woman meeting death or swords or whatever noticed her.

"Oh my God, Tragedy!"

She was shook. The woman sounded like an ex-teacher, those who run into you when you're a foot or two taller but they still see you at their knees. The woman's blue baby doll top was dotted with flowers and her face mask matched to a tee, like she'd made it as a set.

"How are ya?" the woman bellowed.

Tragedy smelled a badass perfume, connected it to a cigarette smell on white church gloves. She assembled a memory of this woman's face but couldn't fit in a name. She was… a painting? Rectangular. Two by two at most. Small. Just outside the guest bedroom, so overnight guests would pass it before bed. A pastel abstract in specks and blobs of green, copper, peach…

"I'm great," Tragedy smiled. "What about you?"

She really wanted to fall back on "Tell me your name again?"

"Oh, I'm splendid!" the woman said. She turned to the Wicca trainee. "Charity, you just have to meet Mrs. Tragedy Powell."

That question Charity didn't get to finish: "That really your —?"

"Sure is," Tragedy nodded. "I really started the celebrity un-forgettable baby name trend."

Their intro facilitator laughed. Tragedy thought hard: *Where have I…?*

"Well, we were so lucky to get collectors like you and your husband at Grayson Arts," the woman went on. "My apologies I didn't follow up to bring more local artists your way."

Bingo.

This woman was the event host for the Arts Center gala and art auction Tragedy won a piece in. This woman was special: The person who last saw Raven McCoy at her spa in town.

And she had a "That really your name?" herself: Gracious.

"No apologies necessary," Tragedy said, relieved. "We've enjoyed the painting a lot."

"I was so grateful you got the Sage Wittington," Gracious whispered.

Tragedy had already learned Grayson women whispered often for no reason.

"I thought it wasn't gonna sell for much and you came along to see its worth. I tell you, that girl is really going to go places. She's headed to the Art Institute next. One to watch."

"Good for her," Tragedy said. "I'm proud to be part of her story."

"And an early collector," Gracious whispered. "We never know with these things."

This didn't happen to Tragedy in Grayson. She never felt prejudice or discrimination. The dividing line here wasn't color. It was money. Anyone near or past Glen gates had to have it or know someone who did. Same for those off Grayson's general exit. So there was always service with a smile for her. People surrounding her were polite. Still, she read hesitance or pauses behind the population. They did their bests, but Tragedy could still read her race in them.

"We've gotta get you more involved, Mrs. Powell," Gracious said. "Someone like you just can't sit in Grayson and become a pancake butt like everybody else."

Someone like me? Is she talking about my color or money to spend on art, or both?

9:17 — Victor was scheduled to be on in thirteen minutes.

"I'd love to get more involved," Tragedy said. "Do you have a card?"

"Why, I sure do."

Gracious set about unnesting the babushka doll that is every woman's big purse, where one opening just leads to another before there's nowhere else to go and a desired item surfaces.

"And I'm Charity."

"Yes, I saw the tag," Tragedy said.

"I don't live in Grayson, but I'm just down the interstate. In Irene, by the apple farm. I do tarot readings when I'm not at school. I do them here, too."

Tragedy stayed on her job to look at a digital total on a small screen with a short neck atop the cash register, pull one of the cards from her wallet and tap the chip to pay.

"I got my card too," Charity continued. "We can schedule a long reading when I'm off."

She disappeared behind a small door. This left Tragedy to bag her own stuff.

"Charity's one of our scholarship winners," Gracious beamed. "At a community college now and headed to ISU next year, we hope."

According to what Tragedy recalled Gracious saying at the art auction (it was coming back more now), she was a "lifelong Grayson gal." Funny. She seemed of a different time and place. Tragedy thought people only crept up dark stairwells or through grim doors on days they needed to talk for tarot readings. In mere moments, Gracious had changed her mind. She liked her.

Gracious handed Tragedy a card. The long header was "Community Activist," "Grayson Town Council Member" and

"Goodness Gracious Day Spa Owner." Charity reappeared with her phone's earpiece in. Tragedy heard a flirtatious "I gotta get back to work" somewhere in there.

"How's your book going?" Gracious smiled.

Tragedy blinked.

"Pardon?"

"You were writing a book," Gracious said. "You said, in your emails."

Tragedy had no idea what she was talking about. Well, she did. She knew she was thinking or trying to write a book. She just had no context to put Gracious into knowledge of it.

"Oh, right. It's going well. I have an agent now. Patricia Rogers Lit."

"That's just wonderful," Gracious said.

"My number's here and text is the best way to make an appointment," Charity said with the card.

"I see," said Tragedy. "'Charity's Fortunes.' PayPal, Venmo, Cash App, Patreon..."

"Well those are to make a payment, not an appointment," Charity corrected. "And Missus Davidson, I can finish you on the phone anytime."

"That would be so nice," Gracious said.

"Ok. Well, ladies," Tragedy smiled.

The Glenner women walked out to their cars. Gracious waved the keys to open her silver Velar and shouted, "We'll talk!" As their heels clicked to drivers' sides, Tragedy spotted a Grayson cop car lurking past the pumps, in the shadows against the tree line. The young officer waved. He was a relief. It made Charity seem less small in that store, all alone at night with a sleeping guard. This was just a few miles from the Cook County that was Chicagoland and all its scenes like those in apocalyptic Biblical pamphlets. This was walking distance to the river.

We don't have crime, Tragedy thought. *Not here.* Weed didn't count. Anti-depressants and pain meds were to be expected. But crack, meth, spice, heroin… all those things behind ladies getting knocked in their heads and immigrant shop owners held at gunpoint? That stuff was up there or back there or down there or anywhere but here. *Here* was alcohol.

Tragedy cracked open a cold tropical wine cooler. If she was lucky, Victor's program would upload highlights quickly. She could see the whole thing after the fact and call him like she was chained inside the house all night, waiting for him and on their grind.

She watched their notifications percolate. Her drink in the console. A hand free to scroll her mounted phone. The dashcam recorded roads back to the gates, moonlit and narrow, sidelined by tall and giant forms she was getting used to. She thought of the landscape turning up a surprise — a deer, monster or reflection of a dead girl. She was disappointed.

In that way, she had joined all the other women left alone in the enviable homes of Grayson Glens. The space and darkness made them friends with fears they invented and kept in mind to think about at times. Then, the obvious of their lives and homes wouldn't scare them.

PART 3: AMENDS

Drinking

My first drink?
    High school was an epic fail. I never took things out on other people, only myself. I was a zombie stare and self-starving girl. I packed some hips and a little chest back on. But after the fire, I was held back. This made me an older sophomore when school started. I graduated late.

My father? Out-of-state. California this time. They said he lived on the beach, selling weed. Finally, a counselor asked why I had on the same clothes days in a row. "My aunt I live with doesn't like me to use her washer." The counselor called children's services. It was a "check-in" from a social worker to my aunt's house. That was a big one. My relatives didn't want to risk the schemes if government workers started knocking, asking and accounting. My aunt was using my social security number to put her heating bill in my name. Stuff like that. I aged out of being useful or worth the troubles without much money for it.

The benefit of being older in the system was no "parents" cared about me past the check. Older foster kids could help them manage younger ones, for more money. That story of the Christian couple with the heart of gold, adopting teenagers to change their lives? Please.

My main torture in the homes, six or seven before it was all over, was as a Cinderella in the broom closet: a maid, servant, day carer and babysitter for all the rest. I was there to scrape scorched oatmeal and eggs, empty diaper bins, mix powdered milk and formula, clean fish tanks and dog pens and litter boxes. To be a woman too soon, earning my keep. I usually bunked or made do on one twin bed, with another girl or two in the rooms.

Social workers knew better than to put me in homes where young or old men were. But still, so many men came around the homes. They scattered when the various checkers, balancers and child protective servicers pulled quick random stops. Liquor was just around, nothing special. Same for the hash swiped from cigar blunts and instruments I could identify as for cooking or smoking crack. Cigarettes, packs and cartons, were more common than fruits and vegetables. Capsules of all kinds as well. I gotta say: being shell-shocked was a blessing.

I was seventeen when I came to a woman named Violet. Violet was a chain-smoking character who stayed under stiff wigs and the influence of food. She had custody of her grandkids with her husband. Her husband was diabetic, quiet and weak. He smoked and Violet ate. Looking back, she was a misery hustler, collecting case after case of person the government should pay, a good heart behind all this in her own mind. She was tolerable.

"Give shorty some of that Hen rock, son," was what got me.

Violet's young nephew was recently out of jail. He showed up and found a recliner to sleep in. The nephew and his boys knew the law: "Don't touch them kids!" Violet told all the residents that.

One night, the nephew and his friends were drinking in the living room. The nephew and his day ones brought a female with them. She was nice — silk wraps, lace front, mink lashes, a knock-off LV bag full of shadows and body sprays she let me sample. She wore clear heels, doorknockers gone green, army fatigue sweats *and a denim jacket. A bra, no shirt.*

While the couple and kids slept, we girls were like the restaurant hostesses for the party. I helped her fry hot dogs flat for white bread with mayonnaise. Sour cream and onion chips on the side. We mixed ice and whatever alcohol we had into red Solo cups. I was having fun. A golden swirl in a coffee-stained, stoneware teacup came to me. It was Hennessy cognac.

"I'm supposed to put it in here?" I reached for my cup of Sprite. They laughed at me.

"You don't mix good Henny," the girl said. "Pass it to me."

She took it straight from the cup. She poured more in for me. I followed suit, the teacup gone in a gulp. The 80-proof set a fire in me. I caught my breath. I didn't show how rough it was. Actually, I held the teacup out for more. The room stared, amused and shocked.

"Oh, you a real one, you a real one..." The nephew's snickers echoed.

They couldn't turn me into a joke after that. The drinks were a magic trick. I felt big in life. I was something more interesting than homeless, motherless, just less. I was having fun. I had four shots of the Hennessey that night, each one winding down in difficulty. Everybody faded out, sloppy and then sloppier. The CD reached its last notes and everyone faded out.

I sprawled in front of the couch, the girl's shoeless feet hanging over it, my arms for my pillow. I didn't know she was so drunk, she could roll over and crash on my back. When she did, I came to in sparkly dots. She rolled off my back to the floor in front of me, on all fours, cat-cowing to throw up. I ran away. I left her there, coughing and sputtering. I nearly broke my neck up the bunk bed ladder. My first night drunk was so hot and sweaty. I came awake several times. I tangled the covers enough to look like others were sharing the bed. It was a bacon smell, screaming, shouting and cussing that woke me up. The kindergarten girl was already gone.

I heard Violet cussing out the truth: The girl who was there was a prostitute. I thought she was their friend. The nephew let Violet throw her out on the street and no one even walked her home.

I didn't drink much after that. Just at times it was good not to stand out for not drinking. Always, with a drink, a few sips of something erased all commotion inside me.

I graduated foster care for group homes. We drank like fish in our rooms. We smoked. We screwed. We lied about who we were and where we were going. I told the housemates all about the night I woke up in a fire. I made plenty of friends but no one ever said goodbye.

Starbucks got me out of the homes. My first big job — 30 hours a week. After a few months there, I went to rent a Chicago Heights room from the sister of this woman I worked with. The woman was in the dark: Her sister's husband drank and they fought around their two kids. One night, things went to the left. The wife ran upstairs. I could hear the fight, the bumping and thuds. Then, it was a crash — and nothing. Twenty minutes later, the ambulance came up. I was all by myself, with these kids. That was my place, always, anyway. The husband told me: "I'll kill you bitch, if you say something!" When the paramedics came, the woman limped down and said she fell. Me and the kids? "No officer, I didn't see anything," I said for us all.

I waited until the couple went to sleep. I counted my money, saved up to $354. I snuck out their house to walk three miles to the Amtrak stop with a heavy duffel and purse weighing me down. The train took me just up to the Chicago Loop.

I never went back to the Starbucks or downstate Illinois until Grayson Glens.

I turned twenty-one.

Nineteen

We spent his first night back in bed, Victor intent to prove his devotion. He went on a mission to give attention to every piece of me. His fingers parted my hair and found the crown of my head. He massaged me and expected no return. He found the pieces I knew he would and loved him to. Still, I couldn't make love or sound. I only thought of a word: home. The childhood loss was everything he couldn't replace — not his stable roots, not his family, not his success, not our money I helped him make. I couldn't deny this anymore.

Weather horns sounded, a micromanagement we ignored. Our only tornadoes were the news showing them elsewhere. I smelled the rain travelling.

"We don't have to," he said.

"I want to," I said.

We continued. I flashed a thought of Faith and her man with whips and handcuffs. Victor was just the everyday world I lived in. In my mind, my husband turned into another man. This man was not significant, only different. His looks could change, too. He was a collection of men I had wanted in some ways at other times. He knew a place, by the brook I once walked to often before I got used to things, a short way down the back hill, where generations of trees gave rise to the Glens. I agreed to it.

A loose heather grey dress came onto me. The man slipped into Victor's closet. He returned in cream canvas pants. We walked downstairs, through the kitchen and out the back door, barefoot and embraced, to lightning sending birds and ruminants to shelters. We landed at one of the weeping willows, rounding to the back of the trunk to block long views to us.

The thunder cracked open a light spray. He circled slowly against me, let me find the way to begin. I wanted to bite, claw and pinch. He sensed I was outraged. And humiliated. And disappointed in myself. He tackled my fists, pulled me in to cry. The spray became a downpour.

I wanted to begin again. I tipped down my spaghetti straps and raised the hem past my thighs. He pulled my dress down to useless fabric in puddles at our feet. Soon came his pants. The crooks of his elbows became levers behind my knees. His neck was a lift and assist to meet him. Flashes of lightning glowed our faces. Sideways sheets and drops broke visibility more than the darkness already. The downpour became a torrent, willows thrashing above us.

We became one heaving form camouflaged with the trees. We drank the rain. The electricity was no threat. I searched for and found what I felt before wounds multiplied and divided me. I came on fire, leaping for relief, weightless without identity. He drilled his palms into smooth bark to anchor us. I swung forward, satisfying myself. We fell into slick mud. The rain went back to a spray, then a mist.

I untwined and rolled onto my stomach. He covered all of me, my fingers dug into the ground. We stopped gradually, cold and tired, bruised and depleted. We walked hand in hand across grass, drenched and dirty and not dressed. We didn't mind being seen. But he departed and I was alone naked in my bed with my husband, both of us tired and whispery, listening to rain on all the glass, soon snoring until Ifa rang in the morning.

The next day, Victor and I went into the motions. He was outside washing the cars, in his office scrolling a topic or guest, absorbed in books and videos about sports and racism, glued to the phone with our team. I was managing the people all around him while no one was there but me. I was chit-chatting online, peeking at the culture and trends, figuring out the next Insta meal or look, keeping the emails behaved, running down the wrong charges and oddities on the bank statements. That night, we were eating, laughing, playing games, talking about people we knew.

A Mexican brunch in the suburbs with Faith, no alcohol, was my Cinco de Mayo alibi for my Clean Me secret. Victor gave his thumbs up. "Have fun, babe! Tell the Tuckers I said hello."

I dressed casually in a light denim jumpsuit and jeweled sandals. I filled a slouchy tote for the day, a toothbrush and head scarf and change of underwear in case I found myself marooned with Faith overnight. I grabbed one of Victor's Stetsons for shade. And emergency use. It was hot. Humidity shriveled my twist-outs to afros with snags. I set out in the Chrysler at 10 a.m. I drove sixty miles from Grayson Glens to north of Chicago, past the airport, for the nearest Clean Me branch. By noon, I landed at the address's thirty floor office building.

My hospitality industry eyes told me the franchise could've converted this location from a boutique hotel. It appeared to be an old concierge stand and lobby bar. At the concierge stand, I checked myself in on a self-serving screen. "Welcome Tragedy Powell!" said bright yellow letters. A tag printed for me. The bar's shelves filled with empty glasses and decanters. Self-serve water, coffee, iced tea and lemonade mimicked booze. I poured tea. A simple system of yellow squares in prohibited chairs distanced everyone waiting. I chose a seat in the corner.

Apparently, a lot of drinkers wanted to get clean. A dozen or so masked people came and went through the lobby. My familiar Clean Me welcome video played over and over on a mounted screen. The brunette doctor and her speech I knew so well comforted me. Some visitors were waiting to go back. Others, who seemed pros, stood to receive a printout of their visit. These clients came in variety of ages, shades, and kinds. A salt and pepper-haired couple brought in a teen boy, silent and biting his nails through a face mask. A Goth husband and wife waited together. A senior man stared ahead. A shuffling receptionist distributed arrival clip boards or parting gifts — a stiff bag I saw others pull branded fridge magnets, water bottles, snacks and more from. She kept shouting out the company's socials and "Go ahead and like us now!" Everyone's eyes stayed dim over their face masks even if their thumbs complied with her orders.

I wasn't at the Clean Me to broadcast to the world I was trying to stop drinking. That wasn't normal, like announcing going on a diet or having plastic surgery.

I waited fifteen minutes before I heard my name called to the back. I met a long-haired young woman, pregnant, at mouth of the labyrinth of smooth walls I only assumed had doors. She walked me to a door I could barely see but she found easily. She took my vitals and blood.

"First time here?" she smiled, a statement more than a question.

"Yes, I'm just checking it out," I told her.

"You're gonna love your Clean Coach," she assured. "And the app is so easy to use."

She left and I stayed in the same stark white room. A knock. The black man who entered was so young. *An intern?* I wondered. No, just a younger millennial. He gave me a cup for urine and directions to a bathroom. I felt I was heeding a diagnosis, not a consultation. "How are you liking it here so far?" he asked. Wasn't much to go on yet. The bathroom was a colorful, gaudy departure from the rest of the space. A romantic Italian motif, rose and bergamot scented lotion and soap, light pink flowers patterned toilet paper. I went back to the white room. I sat wringing my hands, wondering what Victor was doing without me, and what Faith was doing while waiting for me. What both of them, and anyone, would think about Tragedy Powell at a Gen Z Alcoholics Anonymous. Victor wasn't so known that this would be big news about his wife. I wouldn't be splashed in *The Daily Mail.* Though I could think of a few websites and blogs… Still, I was curious. Across from me was a sign, centered in a lotus flower opening up on a pond: "You are always right where you are supposed to be. We are happy you are here, now."

My Clean Coach, Jonah, finally entered. He was white, bearded and in my age range. Handsome, tall, limbs long and balanced like a swimmer's. He was supposed to be a doctor, according to criteria I read about the Clean Coaches. Psychologists and MDs, on paths away from the Western medicine industrial complex. Introductions were brief. A "lie back" command and assistance. He applied a cold alcohol rub at my temple and fastened a round black node there. It was a cloth with green dots beaming from it. He continued the niceties the young man started. He was "Sooo excited" for me to be here and "Sooo honored" to be part of my "new path." He picked up my wrist and started on another node. I pulled my wrist away.

"What are those?" I asked him.

"These are just stress and emotional gauges," he smiled and held a node mid-air. "I'm so sorry. You didn't do the pre-appointment intake?"

"I received a folder after I checked in."

"Oh! Then you must have done all your info and consents prior to your visit, online."

"Yes," I said. "When I made the appointment."

Jonah was at a console and screen behind me. He was tapping, pausing, tapping more.

"Well, these should've been explained to you under consents. You had to read it and sign, or the document wouldn't have generated a tag and number for you. It just says that, since the subject of drinking can be emotional for people, we like to assess stress levels on the way."

I vaguely recalled something about it in webpages. Along with fine print I skimmed, privacy notices, data selling disclaimers. Did I just consent to be somebody's freaky research?

"I'm sure it's fine," I agreed.

"And before I go any further, drumroll... You're okay turning off your phone? We want all your attention on getting clean. We can review all your data with you from the app."

"I'm all in," I laughed. I shook up my bag until my white tiger print phone case rose to the top. I was happy to shut it down. I was the first time in months I'd powered it off totally.

Now, I was at the mercy of a Clean Me Sobriety Center. Jonah worked through smart screens I didn't even catch. I assumed it only a wall. However, at least three parts of one wall lit up after he touched them in the corners: Tragedy Powell, 35, Grayson, Illinois, my Clean Me profile picture I had uploaded; my vitals and overall health stats; my eating and lifestyle profile I filled out in advance; colors and levers he talked to without me.

"Blood alcohol level is zero today. That's wonderful. You're way ahead of most of our new clients on that one."

Oh my, I thought, *how could people arrive here drunk? Now that's a real alcoholic...*

"Overall eating patterns are good. Healthy weight. Great blood pressure. Very nice."

The space was soundproof and silent, only Jonah's voice. No sounds of nature the Glens made normal for me, rain and birds and breezes. I was back in the city, a din of millions of lives and all those lives required, melted to an ongoing rumble that melted to its own unnoticed quiet.

"Social drinking seems to be lower than most clients. Private, at home drinking is high. And you don't drink alone?"

"No," I said.

The green dot on the black node on my wrist flashed faster. I added "Just a lot with my husband. And our neighbors."

"Ok," Jonah smiled. "Well, for most, alcohol is something to do alone to fill the voids."

Jonah continued to read me to myself and ask questions I thought webpages answered. I was drowsy, no transition. So many questions. Such silence. Such calm. Here I saw the cost of my veneer. The drinker in me was a dead weight, a full body armor my real person hid inside. At Clean Me, that armor was removed, a rolled head and crooked limbs in a corner. In no time I was remembering how it all started.

"My first drink? High school? Epic fail... I was one of those zombie stare and self-starving girls. I never took things out on other people...

That story of the Christian couple with the heart of gold, adopting and fostering teenagers to change their lives? Please... Adults getting drunk and high was the norm...

Four shots of the Hennessey... I didn't drink much, still. Just at times it was good not to stand out. We all lied about who we were and where we were going... I counted my money. $354. Train station. Chicago Loop..."

"Just fascinating," I heard.

My Clean Coach, Jonah, sat in a chair with his legs crossed, in an office made spacious by sparseness, showing me wall-to-wall fresh cedar wood just like Clean Me videos had shown. Yes, that's where I was. I orientated out of the fog. I had black nodes stuck on me. What?

Something had happened to me. I'd drifted into a telling a total stranger what I'd just written in *The Girl Who Didn't Burn*, what I was only writing and not telling, hiding it for now.

"We find all our clients have different stories," he continued, "but they all lead to the same place. Drinking and alcohol are like tents they put over ugly and disappointing scenes in their lives. And even when those scenes finished or became nonexistent, the tent is still there."

"Right," I nodded. "Can I...?"

My body was stiff. My smartwatch indicated an hour passed from when I was a bundle of nerves in the lobby. I wound up in this room giving blood and somewhere else giving urine.

"Oh, sure," Jonah said. "Pardon me."

Soon, the doctor slash coach adjusted me upright. Feet on the floor. Cool. Alert.

"I'm so sorry for all that... drivel," I apologized.

"Not at all," assured my Clean Coach. "That drivel is exactly what we need to hear. You see, the nodes you asked about recorded your moments of most tension and stress. When you started drinking was a big one. You were homeless, depending on the state and foster parents. Also, when you left the couple's home. You seemed to go to nowhere. So, home is big for you."

Wasn't it for everybody? Didn't everybody have to wonder, think and imagine where they were going to live next? Or, if they would live where they were forever? I felt baited into hocus pocus. At least the consultation was free. Unlike those chiropractic specials that solicit at festivals and fairs. I was taken in twice to go pay the thirty-dollar special. I went in walking straight, I thought. I came out convinced I was lopsided, crooked, bent and barely alive.

"So, what are you doing with all this information you have on me?" I asked, unsure of all I had told this man. Which parts were just thoughts and which parts were actual speech.

"We have a baseline of your personal story, your drinking personality and your triggers. Foster care is over for you, but the sensors show that time is still alive and active in your body."

Foster care? My God. It was a low for me to drone on to that point. I needed my phone. I'm sure Faith was calling, texting, wondering. We had a good time waiting, budgets to spend, glorious homes. I reached into my bag, found its fashionable case and powered my phone.

"We're pretty finished here and I think you'll love our system," I heard. "You seem coachable and adaptable."

Victor's face was a bubble. Something about Gloria, Joy staying for the summer.

Faith's face was a few bubbles in notifications. I took time to read the last one.

T- where are you? Victor says you left hours ago.

"I'm sorry," I apologized. "I know rules, but I don't want anyone to worry."

I flew out a text: *Fine. Stopped on the Mile. Traffic. An hour?*
I assumed the jingle was a thumbs up.

"So," I said. "I haven't felt anything but a chance to grow. How do I start?"

"You already started," Jonah smile. "Once you pay the initiation and membership fee, we get your app activated. Think of it as a digital personal assistant to help you manage your alcohol use, which we know doesn't mean non-alcohol use for everyone."

"Jonah," I said, "I can be alcohol free any-time. I just run in certain circles where drinking is part of the crowd. Even part of the job. Things can get out of hand, that's all."

"We're not here to judge. We're here to assist. Your profile indicates bouts of heavy drinking. That's been a big side effect of lockdowns, for the isolation. We've seen a spike in people coming in concerned. You're not alone there. Bigger concerns would be things like... Have you ever passed out from drinking, to the point you forget things?"

"Would I remember if I passed out from drinking if I forget everything?" I asked.

"Actually, maybe you could later," Jonah smiled. "It's great you have a sense of humor about all this, Mrs. Powell. It predicts success."

I considered a lanyard at my neck or a wrist band to attach to my "clean device." An extra strong sensor I could barely see acted like a breathalyzer, any time of day or night. It was meant to be a deterrent from drinking, as Jonah explained clean sobriety readings were addictive. I could press buttons when I felt the need to drink. My Clean Coach's voice could come pre-recorded to motivate me out of it until he called. All this information would help us talk out my progress and plans when we met via video link for my monthly appointment.

My ultimate goal?

"I'd love to only drink on special occasions, not just in regular life," I admitted.

"Consider it done!" Jonah advised.

We walked out together. Jonah about-faced through quiet, seamless doors. A manicured hand held out a gift bag. I rode an elevator mostly by myself down thirty floors. Two times it opened but no one stepped in. I walked half a block, to the Chrysler parked in the garage. The older attendant was napping on the job. He made me think how my late father might look now. I honked my horn and smiled. He awoke and pressed a button. The gate lifted. I fingered the strange new thing hanging between my breasts. I rolled it off, into a compartment. I opted to skip the Clean Assistant's in-office help to program it perfectly. I'd do it imperfectly at home later. Faith had texted the Mexican restaurant she booked — known for its bottomless margaritas.

TWENTY

JUNE 2021

G rayson and the Glens met the mild summer blooming with force. The grim winter and spring passed on, compounded in troubles, natural and unnatural — a whole year of such. The end of June was hallelujah. Snarls and anxieties dropped. Vacations resumed. The outdoors spoke up. The ice cream truck raised its volume. The river got busy on its boats, swimmers and birds to become a surface of playful splashes instead of gossip and fright. Fishing was up. The little downtown, few shops and resumed farmers market filled sidewalks the prior summer didn't. People abandoned strolling for hurrying. Everybody had something they missed or skipped, both sellers and buyers. Everybody pivoted towards something new. Strange tropisms twisted them to feel like recent introductions to each other, exciting acquaintances. Anything that could blossom did so aggressively — trees, gardens, ideas, habits, promises, love, friendships.

A month since Tragedy had her last drink, oversleeping and difficulty concentrating were side effects she didn't expect. And migraines. And coffee addiction. The coffee didn't keep her up, necessarily. She'd didn't even love it that much. It was just a new drink to think about. Her book, her bike, her treadmill, her yoga mat, the inboxes. All dormant. Pounds and bloat crept up.

"I'm inflamed," Tragedy groaned when the ginger tea wasn't enough.

"It's the coffee," Ifa sighed. She ground, brewed, French pressed or went for it anyway.

From May until the start of summer, Tragedy succeeded in digging up her secret alcohol use. Clear bottles blended into carpet and clothes. Colorful drink cans at the back of shelves and corners of table legs, a little swoosh left inside. It was like finding children's toys for kids who grew up, superheroes stuck in their old shoes, torn paper dolls in books. The unwitting scavenger hunt showed Tragedy her drinking was never hidden at all. It was always hiding in plain sight.

It was why Victor never asked about the tequila Joy copped to smashing. He just assumed Tragedy did it. It was why he did something with the crates of wine he didn't ask permission for — probably hidden to use for gifts later. He knew Tragedy would just go buy more anyway.

Why Ifa brought wine bottles with groceries even without Tragedy placing them on a list.

Why they started paying for Ifa in the first place. Tragedy loved having space, but she did everything in it with a drink in hand. And, in time, she left everything half-done.

Why they hired a digital content creators outfit for *The Powellcast*. Victor's idea. It was pricey. But they had to do something. Tragedy wasn't staying up to speed. The only reason they floated the year was the world moved online. They had always been doing what everybody else had to start doing last minute, in a fluster and hurry. However, they were way ahead of that game. They were already in a workflow with contractors to un-snag their technical difficulties and push out promotions to get people stuck at home tuned into Victor and his content. They would have lost it all, otherwise. Tragedy, his "Manager," could supervise people Victor learned he could count on to deliver no matter what. She couldn't be counted on to deliver for herself.

The Clean Me app and Clean Coach padded her efforts. Soon it was impossible not to turn to what she paid to be a member of. Clean Me's website and YouTube channel soothed her. She buried in testimonials. Camaraderie. The Clean Me device be-came essential.

When Victor asked about it, she smiled. "It's just something new to track my diet."

He bought it. Her Clean App breathalyzer reads stayed at zero. She was proud of herself. She could tap for automated support from the Clean Coach, a recorded but motivating voice. "A glass of water always does the body good." Or, "Think of a great friend you can call to talk to now." And, "Alcohol isn't your friend."

She went into the nutrition and exercise logs with an A+ mindset. Every day she clicked boxes and checked squares, watched the color graphs form. They showed her the times she was most likely seeking comfort. Patterns emerged to find the triggers. This was exciting — at first.

Soon it became as tedious as monitoring ad revenue totals or scrutinizing deliverables from the content creators. Not drinking was exhausting her more than drinking had, it felt.

"Shouldn't I have more energy, instead of less?" she asked in a Clean Coaching.

"Even with light drinkers, there's withdrawal," Jonah assured.

"Withdrawal?" Tragedy laughed. "I'm not an alcoholic."

"I didn't say you were. I'm saying anyone who does substances on any level will find some discomforts when they stop. Initially."

"Even if they only had too many drinks every now and again?"

"Yep. The body's smart. It senses the slightest changes. Just be patient with yourself."

Tragedy could have paid for an extra coaching session that month but she refrained.

Victor never asked about the tequila Joy swiped. She let the wines go.

She expected her sex drive to go up without alcohol. It tanked. She wanted to be alone.

They had the structure to go days without seeing each other, like duplex mates. He was raised by a woman. He had a sister. He was married before, with a daughter. He knew the drill. The pace was picking up anyway. He scored a regular spot on an ABC affiliate channel show highlighting black businesses in Chicago; he joined the rotation of hosts to visit the venues and feature the owners. He doubled the opportunity by making the business owners guests of *The Powellcast*. More new "friends" to support. He was fretting over a birthday, steadying for middle age to be official. His daughter wanted to come live with him and her mother hated him for it.

He motioned Tragedy to the basement floor one day Ifa was in his office making calls. It was two weeks that she hadn't given him any indications. He turned her around against the sound board in his small, tight studio with the ceiling's peekaboo glass exposing them above. She didn't resist. She enjoyed it. He left town the next day.

The day after that, Gracious Davidson caught Tragedy at her

front door in her same top and skirt from the day before. No bra. Near to dinnertime. Her helmet hair puffed the satin scarf she wore to bed and hadn't done better than. Her mind raced to how much Pellegrino she had chilled to offer. Her memory jammed to where finger foods in the pantry were. Both women were embarrassed. Gracious for feeling she'd imposed, Tragedy for feeling off her game face.

"Oh, is this not a good time anymore?"

"Oh, no, come right on," Tragedy said anyway.

Yes, she recalled. Hearts, smiley faces and thumbs ups emojis were exchanged recently.

So impressed with your husband and all you guys are doing!

Thank you... happy to reconnect and maybe collab on the art center.

When?

Well now that things are opening, anytime.

When's a good time for us to pow wow? We have to plan. 2moro?

Pause.

Free 2moro if you are.

Lovely! 5 okay? Happy hour, you know lol...

See you then!

Can't wait!

So that is how Gracious was already up and at it by happy hour in Grayson Glens, greeting a startled and disheveled Tragedy Powell. No makeup. No coffee made. No deodorant on. No teeth sparkling along with the water a proper host would have ready. She sat Gracious in the living room, on the settee to face an astounding wildflower arrangement, grateful her new fresh delivery subscription started this week. She excused herself to do that flip women do to make themselves look all new without changing much. Just a little water on her hair flattened it. Water and a pea size of toothpaste freshened her mouth. A fat scoop of moisturizer plumped her neck, face and hands. A tinted balm swipe onto her eyelids and lips took her down a few years. No perfume. Moisturizer and great hand lotion gave enough scent for her to smell like something other than yesterday. Last thing? She slipped the Clean Me device off her neck.

Tragedy returned to find Gracious brought Lambrusco, dried figs, cauliflower crackers and Brie. Grand Marnier as a gift to the house. She walked them to the kitchen to arrange things.

"This is one of the most spectacular new properties I've seen," Gracious said.

"A long way from our little Chicago condo," Tragedy laughed.

"You must have a wine cellar, too."

"We turned it into a soundproof studio, for the podcast."

"What's the lovely music?"

"That was Noname and this is H.E.R."

Gracious didn't understand but Tragedy was in charge, now.

"Lemme help you." "Oh no, please, relax. I'm so happy you're here."

The Lambrusco was already chilled. Tragedy placed it in the empty wine cooler anyway. It would be impolite not to drink, right? She just needed time to fathom a decent excuse. Trying for a baby was always a good one. Medication too, but then she'd have to make up the illness to go with it. That would leave a lie out to remember or back up again. As her taste for the wine swelled, her walls faded. She saw herself slipping through all the glass.

"Let's enjoy the evening outside," she told Gracious.

Midwest summer is different from eastern, southern, and western. It'll promise but not predict. People trust daily life climbs out of an Arctic brace and its fashions out of the igloo lane. No one dares ask for more. Victor kept torches and tikis mounted year-round. Now, they came in for the saves. Tragedy offered Gracious a throw for twilight. They sat on the veranda cast far into the yard, to look down to the brook, as this is what people who lived here did in summer even if it was still cold. They got lucky for it: robins and a woodpecker to the bird feeder.

Maybe they would have done this long ago if the world hadn't gone so complicated. How many more women were out there to do the same things with? They marveled at the coincidence of their meeting, apologized for not keeping in touch, made sure the other guessed their financial lives weren't in peril.

"My old receptionist quit and I've just hired that young lady from the gas station to work in my spa," Gracious confided. "Tarot readings on the side. She's really good."

"I might try a reading," Tragedy smiled. She took for granted she had lived more lives than most people of any age. It was all a hocus pocus, a fun exercise. Fun seemed a good word.

"I was so happy to offer her the job because, you know with the Raven McCoy situation, we just can't have our young girls out here alone at night."

"That's true," Tragedy agreed. "We have enough women and girls alone all day."

"I'm in with police pretty good. They still aren't close to figuring out what happened."

"Shame. I don't see how we're supposed to feel until they do."

Gracious's eyes flared up at the hint. *So… This one too?* Of course.

Tragedy was fairly new, but still. It caught up with all. Back where she came from, Gracious learned not to let a man take the reins, confine her to a monstrosity, slip her quietly into the same class as his children, isolate her to fight for his attention. She was a veteran of the place. She knew the syndrome. The

regulars of Goodness Gracious, the ones who made her who
she was today, all had it. They forgot how to fill their days after
a while. They micromanaged the young children, overboarded
the older ones and threw themselves at mercy of the house when
nothing worked. Meanwhile, men stayed up and off in their
battles, wars and quests for more. More money to buy more
things. More things. More things. Everything got larger after
long: diamonds, furniture, cars, bikes, boats, RVs. People could
hardly see through to each other.

"Where's your husband? I'd love to say hi."

"He travels a lot, to Chicago mostly, sometimes elsewhere."

"And no children or family around? You must get lonely."

"I do. I have Ifa. Not our housekeeper. She's our house manager. His daughter Joy comes out a lot. Friends in the city. And
the digital assistant and partners and whatever. Remotely."

"Don't you want your own bundle of joy?"

"One day. Soon. When it calms down. Things were picking
up for him when we met, and we had to take the opportunities
when they came. I don't want to be a married single mom."

"Smart. Boy, we got a lot of those around here."

Tragedy shocked herself with the honesty. But the visitor
today was as incongruent with daily life as her frank remark. It
was all going hand in hand, a quick new world shifting her into
a new person. Ifa was a friend by now, but still an employee. It
was a line. And she was Victor's, too. Faith was far away, and
also Victor's. Merit was Merit. Mrs. Pitts hadn't lived up to her
promises, maybe sensing Tragedy's needs and backing away.
How nice a nearby girlfriend could become.

"No matter where you live and what you can afford, it's always gonna be the same when you're the woman," Gracious
said. "I stay active with women in this place. Some of them are
downright nuts. But we have to bond, girl. Leave it to men and

we'd stay in bed or chains."

She knows, Tragedy thought. *But how?* How could another — different age and race and everything — sense how she felt so quickly?

"And they don't do it on purpose. It's just in them," Gracious continued. "They think girls and women are so easy and simple. I mean, they get taught a little rose can get them any woman they want. Imagine? Something we can pick up ourselves, with thorns at that, makes them think they are so special. But my husband works so hard. He loves his family."

"Real talk. I never want to sound ungrateful. My husband does a lot. We're a team. We had big plans out here with this house. Guess we never planned to make sure it was a home."

It struck Tragedy Gracious was the first person she wasn't blowing Victor and their life together up to. Besides Ifa (who saw it and knew who they were for real). Lockdown was a curveball that cut the extraneous to hide behind. They probably shouldn't have survived it.

"You're so young and you're still really newlywed," Gracious smiled. "So, what you must do is just manage what the dark and quiet does to you. Otherwise, order and perfection feel worse than stress and chaos. Or, they become them."

"Yes, the city had lights, especially downtown where we lived. Here, it's like the moon."

"People with means like to feel they live on their own moons."

"We really are still just starting out, compared to—"

"No one just starts out here. We all left something behind."

Tragedy thought about confessing to her. She stayed on the honesty roll. And there was the Lambrusco, just twisted apart and cooling them now. They were tipsy in the dark.

"I think Raven McCoy left a part of her soul behind in my

spa. It's made me think I was seeing cartoons in the air," Gracious confessed. "One time, I thought the whirlpool bath was tinged pink. I was so scared I cancelled appointments for that next day."

Tragedy was relieved to hear she wasn't the only one, but also sorry. Raven's ghost wasn't hers alone. Was anything in the world just hers? Even the bank still owned the house.

Gracious went on in her status as the infamous last person to see Raven McCoy alive. About her insomnia starting the day the missing case story broke. Two weeks of it. And her worry over a child that wasn't hers and was a person she didn't even know, and how the wraith upped her game: "I assumed, with ghosts, you were protected around other living souls."

"So, you only feel it when you're alone too?" Tragedy asked.

"Well, this one time, I saw something dart from behind our privacy hedges. A figure. It twisted between the clothesline, all the sheets I had hung up. Drying linens in a machine is a sin for me. I'm sorry — I don't judge. From the window, looked like she dirtied them. I spilled my coffee right where I stood. My husband was fit to be tied. He didn't see it. And, we went out but the sheets were still white as baby cotton."

"It was strange for me at the tomatoes in the farmers' market once," Tragedy confessed back. "Thought a girl was there and then she wasn't but she'd just been. I squeezed the Roma in my hand into a juice bomb mess. I dropped my basket and took off."

"Oh my gosh," Gracious gasped. "Were people staring at you?"

"People always stare at me here. I'm always the only black person."

"Well, you never have to worry about me asking to touch your hair."

"Thank you."

"You think Raven is really her name? Or just what she put

up to be exciting?"

"It could be. That name's pretty popular now. Common even. Sad. It's too pretty for that."

Even with hot flames above them, bugs came. Gracious was ever ready with scented repellant lotion. Tragedy went in to put away their plates. She felt better than in recent days. Victor wasn't there and this was good. Amen — some company besides him. He didn't even know about it. Tragedy thought of the last time she'd attempted Grand Marnier. She stepped on the lever to raise the trash can lid. Underneath was a family of turtles, piled and misshapen. She netted the scream. Still, without it, the creatures should have moved to the light. They didn't. More thought revealed Ifa forgot to say she had butchered pineapple on sale, to store and freeze. The fruit's rough, carved skins took shape. Well, she was sober for over a month and in just a few hours she was at a drop, then a trickle, then…. oh well. Tragedy found equal portions of pineapple chunks neatly in Mason jars in the fridge. She took one and sparkling waters outside.

Gracious admired the lovely woman. Like a model, she was. She was trying hard not to, but she couldn't help but make her neighbor and new friend more interesting because she was black. She had black friends in her life — from college, online, clients, in business. Not many. And not close. It was a good thing to have different people in the Glens. Folks were complacent.

But it wasn't just race. Tragedy explained her husband was off guesting or hosting or whatever for an ABC affiliate, in Chicago overnight. A man after her own heart. More in common with this young black couple than the socialites of Grayson, the church clubs, the town leaders she called friends, the same drama queens turning up year after year after year.

"I used to work in news," she told her new friend. "I stopped.

It's easier on the men."

"I used to work in hotels," her new friend told her. "I stopped. It was easier with a man."

Working girls they were, really. The old-fashioned way. Not much honest work to do from home back when they started. They had to hit the streets. Long days and nights. Downtown ladies. Professionals. They were so much deeper than the domes of privilege and ease they were suspected of. They deserved to rest, now. So many others were born with silver spoons and handed silver platters. Why not them?

"I should join you and start writing a book about my life," Gracious laughed.

"I haven't been doing much writing on that."

"I'm sure it's wonderful. Women are really coming out with their stories now. We could do a big gala for it at the Arts Center. You'd be a great guest speaker."

"You're so great at speaking. It was so nice to hear you emcee the fundraiser. How did you get interested in news?"

Gracious was so happy Tragedy remembered. It was like Raven calling her "So pretty for your age." She always talked about the spa, the furniture, her husband, his commercial, the kids. All of those involved others. She wanted to let who she was on her own out. Tragedy likewise.

"Well, I'm no stranger to these things in small places," Gracious said. "When I was young, a man killed his wife and their daughters on a farm. They were being evicted, but the sheriffs knew the man's daddy so they came late. If they'd been earlier, who knows?"

"Oh my goodness. I'm so sorry."

"Oh, I didn't know the people. The farm was out past where any of us ever went. And my men were decent. But, news came to town. From Chicago. Maybe Indianapolis. Michigan too. First time I saw a TV news truck off TV was at the main gas station lot. Not Grayson, but across it. We weren't money folks. But it had the nachos and chili cheese fries, so my mother went there. This girl walked in the station with a maroon coat on. Plain cream, maybe yellow, not canary. Everybody else wears gray and blue and brown coats there. And patterns on their scarves. I watched her and realized she wasn't a girl. She was a woman. Her lipstick was too thick but perfect in the lines. She got peanuts and a Diet Coke. I left my sisters and kept behind her. She had a card to pay with. Well, we were scrounging for change and bills. Her coat sleeve came down to a big city watch. Her perfume was something like pears and lake water and a clean house. And my mother honked the horn, so I had to go get my sisters. By time we got to the car, the lady had gone off. That night, I pointed at the TV when she came on it. She was the lady anchor the news kept showing all that night. Everybody was watching the same thing: our town on TV. Now, I learned later she was just a little nobody at the station if they sent her all the way out to talk to us about dead kids on a broke farm. But she was the first person I saw in real life on the television. So nobody could ever tell me what I saw on television wasn't real."

Tragedy knew the story. Always, even next to her mother, she saw the women in the world who were watched while no one ever looked at her.

"My mother taught me zip code matters," she shared. "She was the first one in her family to go to college and they never forgave her for it. The problem was never having my father. She was back and forth with him for years, until he quit on her after my brother. That was it. One time, she told me she saw how men without fathers grow up to be ones who'd kill her daughter. So, we had to pantry in our town. Ridiculous, it was. White cans with black letters, government cheese, powdered milk, concrete for peanut butter. But my mother had connections. Her college roommate lived up North in Chicago. The roommate told my mother that seniors or people with government checks up there didn't need anything. Still, they went to the area food pantries. They just claimed a small income. Meanwhile, they lived in Lakefront condos and shopped the Magnificent Mile. So, Mom used the woman's address to go to pantries up there. It was like she went to the back of gourmet restaurants to shop. A full upgrade, for just ten bucks in gas and an afternoon in time. My grandmother bought us a freezer for it all. We never stood in line with food stamps or put stuff back. My school lunches were smoking. Yep, all for a right zip code."

They laughed to this, as Tragedy suggested tea with Grand Marnier. This suited Gracious perfectly. The women sipped and talked all night, curious who or what or why this new person was. Soon, both women forgot Tragedy's power-charged tea kettle. It was ready to boil at one light tap, but it cooled as they drank alcohol and peeled back more neglected layers of themselves to each other. When that little mutt figure came up to the yard, Tragedy ignored it.

TWENTY-ONE

JULY 2021

It took Gloria a whole Saturday night and Sunday to notify us she hadn't heard from Joy. The girl went to see a movie with friends who lost track of her. No phone ring, just straight to voicemail. No tracking apps past the theater. Spyware documented the camera's covering up. In a nearby trash can outside the theater, Gloria found it. This is what killers demand of girls they snatch, how rapists isolate victims. How pimps take power from virgins they traffic. "I knew you'd blame me," was Gloria's pathetic excuse. Victor did. I stayed clear of a kind of wrath nothing with me had ever conjured. Perhaps nothing with any woman. This was his daughter.

I eased around Victor and veins in his neck I'd never met, rushed to pack both our bags. Overnight duffel? Carry-on? Full-size rolling suitcase? We didn't know. We spiraled to depths of imagining and uselessness we never had to feel when a missing black woman's story was in our air. We were only theorizing, empathizing. Maybe just pontificating. This was real. Did we grab a stranger's sad situation for attention? Was this karma to see how it feels in real life?

I wanted to drink, to sling my fingers on the stem of a glass of something red. Or to pop a cork, invite something cold and peppery to my tongue. Or to be discreet with Victor's bar. I was in my closet's wrinkle-free section, once the scene of the secret drinking crimes. I rolled up leggings and tops in case of no chance to iron on the way to finding Joy in some river. Possibly. No, never. But I still spoke into the Clean Me device: "Stressed… I'd love a drink right now."

I learned all its responses, though. Jonah claimed Clean Me was rolling out more soon. One came back I knew. His voice advised: "Pause. Take deep breaths. Stressful things always have solutions. Imagine yourself in the solution, not in the problem. Have a walk or a jog."

"Whatever, Jonah," I muttered.

I slipped the device lanyard behind my shirt. Gracious Davidson's gift of cognac appeared on a shelf of heels. Behind some red slingbacks. Not as much left as I thought. I'd been tame with sips here and there. I reached behind the shoes. I finished it off and got back to work.

I knew my husband well enough to know how he'd wish to look to police, lawyers and Gloria's people angry with him for choking an educated black woman in America into a single mother statistic. She'd filed against him, but never mind. Couldn't dream of not ironing what I had to choose in that regard. No hoodies. No jeans. Nothing relaxed. A silk tie. No, three. The better watch. They'd all have to know this black man had money and what came with that in order to take his child's black life seriously. I'd be no slouch. I packed my hair stuff, make-up, fragrances. I zippered my diamond earrings and pendants in the safe combination compartments.

Faith called me back.

"First of all, calm down. Teenagers do this kind of stuff. I have them. I know."

"It's been two days, Faith," I groaned. "I get it, but two days? She's not that kind of girl."

"Has Victor spoken to the police yet?"

"Not much. Cops haven't even passed it to a detective yet. Matter of fact, cop asked Victor if she was still in school. You know, like, maybe Joy was a dropout."

"Dear Lord. Well now's not the time, but I'm interested in seeing their custody agreement, if this girl can disappear in the care of one parent who doesn't call the other."

"You think I wouldn't stop working for my child? Are you serious?" said the howling below. "You know, you've taken this workaholic shit to the bank for years, Glo! For years…"

"I'll call you from Chicago, lady," I smiled.

Victor hauled what could be life in a Chicago hotel room for long to the Jag, not the Jeep or Chrysler. We thought alike. This is where police shot black and brown kids in the back or sixteen times with their hands up or in back yards of decent black neighborhoods for running from a stolen car. We were somebodies in the zip code we escaped to. But, we were last on the list in that urban sprawl relegating people like us to neglected or terrorized zip codes. Or else.

In those few minutes hubby arranged things in the trunk, I somehow glided to his gold-plated flask, my wedding gift, shiny at his bar. I thought how to fill it. He wouldn't miss a grocery vodka, half the 750 ml now in my possession. Just a sip now. Not much. Refill what I lost. To the mudroom for a jacket. It was the Windy City after all. Put the Clean Me device in another jacket. Safe for now. Our child as a missing black girl was an exception to new rules.

Then I drove because Victor needed his hands for his devices. It takes one mid-afternoon radio show for Illinois pastoral plains to dress down heading up to Chicago. From all-American tourist brochure to gray, rumbling, chaotic interstate madness. I listened in as best I could in my own clouded anxiety and wild imagination. *Joy in a river. Joy in a dumpster. Joy in a ditch.*

Victor said "Lemme call you back" to a frat brother, a resident in the town of Joy's school. The friend would do what he could. Victor switched his tone to one I recognized as reserved for Gloria: a businessman hoping a banker will approve a loan. I seethed. I never budgeted it into the adventures and the travelling and the dinners and the sex and the "I dos."

"Don't matter if I'm the one who wanted her off to school," he went on. "I'm not the one who's there and responsible to know where she is at all times she's not with me."

Gloria's hysterics seeped into the car. A trucker on mental auto pilot waited forever to signal a lane change. A red Kia clipped in front of the hood. I mashed the brakes. I just missed an accident. Victor gripped the dashboard where the airbag could have burst out.

"What are you — ?"

"Just talk to her," I snapped. It was only one sip of vodka, for heaven's sake.

Their conversation went on into apologies Gloria tended to elicit. Apologies for letting her down with a delayed visit or money transfer. Apologies for missing some shindig her family or friends wanted him at. Apologies for some bitter memory or minutiae of their past together.

This wasn't an occasion for me to drop him off and check into our hotel downtown. We booked a room in the university neighborhood Gloria's young townhome development fringed.

It was a carefully choreographed treatment to come soak up the bio mother's pain. Gloria's nearest woman neighbor and older sister buffered the display. Gloria was wan, unmade up and helpless. Victor came to rest at her feet. I felt a chill, but I froze into a supportive pose. She hugged my husband and they cried. All his anger and fury evaporated to tears they wept together.

"I'm sorry," I heard from the woman for the first time since I'd known her.

Soon, the senior neighbor had coffee and crumb cake on the dining room table. The sister smoked and no one complained. Detectives wouldn't return our calls until morning, if that. No sense in invading the station Gloria reported it to. If nothing came tonight, we had to go higher than that. We waited without a word from Joy or words no one wants to hear from others.

At the hotel, out the shower and finding Victor conked out, I met my husband truly exhausted. Not outdone with deadlines and appearances. Not after moving us in or out of American dreams. Not after the personal trainer whipped his butt. Not in jetlag across time zones. His whole skin and all his edges softened. He was still in shoes. You can't rest that way. I removed them. He stirred, took my nudge for his legs on the bed. I unbelted and unzipped him.

"Thank you," he said, half-asleep. "Thank you for everything. Not just today."

I clicked off the ESPN channel that was his normal at this time. And the headboard lights. I found the basic hotel bathroom predictably uncomfortable to sit in. A towel on the floor and my back against the wall would do. I clutched the flask. It was no reason.

I did everything the Clean Me system told me not to. I didn't tell anyone what I was doing, for more support. Victor offered to clear the booze. I had tricks to make that seem unnecessary. Five minutes I could've helped my husband, checked windows and alarms, made sure I packed our vitamins… Anything, *anything* other than focusing on a flask and vodka.

Drinks with Gracious were always nice. My new friend told me her husband thought she didn't drink. Ha! June was a song of fast friendship. Kindred spirits we were. Victor didn't center my thoughts. I had plans and pep to meet up, talk about art, hear about women in town, walk into a spa. I wanted to shoot her a text, about Joy. No. Gracious was a self-starter. She'd have flyers up all over Chicago by tomorrow. Followers would trend us for a black hole, not a star turn. Nope. I'd wait to tell my friend. "My friend Gracious" was staggeringly satisfying to say to Victor. Just the other day: "Where are you going?" His long nude body was no deterrent.

"Out with Gracious…" I admitted, halfway out the door already, abandoning our business of his fans and his socials and blog and his… Everything.

"I've gotta treat you to a nightcap," Gracious had said after we saw a movie at The Golden Age Theater, open only for special groups. Gracious's new local women's movie club counted. Any woman she called "friend" was a group member and got to go back to the theater.

What an estate she had. Everybody came to know the property. The stone and stucco mansion didn't retreat off into invisibility. It stood out close to a main road, a high black gate guarding several acres for a yard, a tiny part of gate open to a paved runway I'd tailed Gracious's lights to drive down. The rainy night was too black for her intended impact of pretty landscaping, a verdant daylight scene down to odd diagrams and shapes, a fountained and lanterned path to an elevated gazebo sculpting a night sketch. We chatted onto an impeccable wood floor entrance. An umbrella and coat stand awaited, rows of blooming flowers in bronze altar vases before me.

Once inside, I saw how Gracious had subdued the embarrassment of riches from outright to subtle. Soft lightening, stained woodwork and framed portraits conjured an amber sensation. Gaudy candleholders and pioneer length candlesticks warmed the air. A cream baby grand anchored a living area ahead. Wide, arched window ways feminized an otherwise stark glassy view. Beady chandeliers glowed, but didn't sparkle on low wattage bulbs. Ivory and occasionally soft mauve paint for trim was all matte, no sheen. My heels tapping wood sounded lighter here.

Mr. Davidson was a shock. The chipper guy from the TV furniture commercials proved to be so unlike Victor. The persona he put out there wasn't anywhere near to himself. A peck to Gracious's cheek. An apology for having work to do and not much time to talk. Sweet ice breakers — "Hope the Glens have treated you well" and "I think I've seen your husband at Grayson Greens or in town" — then fluttered off to his den with two black Labs.

When the rain ended, Gracious and I fluttered off to her back meadow to the farmhouse. She refused to Airbnb it, against Glenner rules. But she knew "Some break it. You know the pandemic was hard." I could have miniaturized it to a dollhouse I would have loved as a girl.

"We could do your whole Grayson Book Club meeting here…"

Such a beautiful thought. Soon we stood in the gourmet kitchen, circling relaxed with our backs and butts against pristine hickory cabinetry. We clinked our glasses of Grand Marnier on the rocks.

"You know my sons were prime suspects in the Raven investigation?" Gracious said.

It seemed so unlikely. Victor and I just had to get to Davidson's Furniture Bonanza the moment we came to Grayson. How could we not? We saw the commercial if we snuck off into guilty pleasure court TV shows and live paternity test results fodder. We heard or saw Gracious's name before she had auctioned me to a painting or I'd walked into Goodness Gracious.

"Oh, of course," she said. "My single boy. I've been trying to push him to some nice young women, but… Some people in this town have had it out for me for years. Gossip about what we do out here on the land. Secret girlfriends and drug parties in my farmhouse."

We roared in solidarity at carving out a piece of heaven just to become suspects there.

Now, Victor snored in the other room, his phone at attention on the nightstand. I scrolled Joy's socials and friends connected to her. I sipped more from the flask. I'd chosen well. Vodka has no smell. The familiar sink into concentration and happier thoughts was its gift to me.

My drinking buddy Gracious was the only one I'd talked about my Clean Me effort with.

"I'm trying to manage things better," it had come out over wine at Corky's Bar. "It's something like a healthy meal delivery service or weight watching thing, I guess."

"I completely understand," Gracious said. "We have to know our limits."

"I'm getting older," I laughed. "And hey, the hubby freaked out over some binges."

"Bottles or cans or glasses blended into the scenery where I'm from," Gracious said.

"I know that well," I signed.

"Kids never minded going to the store for it 'cause we could get something too. Back then they didn't mind selling to kids. You just had to give them a name of who it was really for."

"You'll enjoy my book," I laughed, and I was talking about it with someone interested.

The wine was thick and generic but nice that day at the little game room bar we snuck off to when she closed her spa. Off in the near and common commercial suburb with the strip of malls, car dealerships, family chain restaurants and superstores. But it wasn't just men. Long before them, we were both prepared and ready for chances. We knew we could never wing it.

I imagined what Gracious would say to it all if we were at Corky's, or on my veranda, or in her farmhouse with pastries and cognac. Such a support I was to all today. I deserved it.

My new conversations lightened my plights. With a woman same as me, just different. Caught in the middles, neither here nor there, sliced in fractions in the gristle through to better worlds. Gracious had no short answers as to how she got to Grayson. Or to anything really. She slipped and snort-laughed the admission her family still didn't know her mother did drugs.

I sipped more vodka and went into Joy's feeds, silenced after the #girlgang shot on the way into a movie. Could that be it? The finishing act of a life is a post.

Maybe Joy was kidnapped. But things like that only happened to girls like her in movies. She was lucky. Hard to believe if sixteen was having all Joy did, a girl could run away from it. I was on a floor losing the plot that it was all about her, now. Was I anxious to return to my delicious life far past all I had to run away from at her age? I was still drinking my way past it or out of it, I realized. So I willed myself to fall into a hotel bed drunk instead of letting Victor find me drunk on the bathroom floor of a hotel. After all, I'd been his love at first sight working for one.

TWENTY-TWO

Grayson law officers were like all. They met up slightly out of town or districts, away from those who knew them and could wonder how many drinks. Chief Loveless was on tap and Detective Wise had quit long ago. They were at Corky's Bar on the near commercial suburb's strip, where chances people knew them dropped. Next steps after today were critical.

It was hard to get the Chief's attention or favor and he wasn't used to much like this in Grayson. Wise had begged. They should've both been off in family dinners, TV and maybe bed with their spouses. But things had changed drastically.

"A Glenner man is pimping out of town girls for sex and promising them college for it?" Loveless couldn't believe.

"Yes," Wise said. "And preying on girls like Raven to help him do it. For money. Lots of it, in her world at least. Things, gifts, the usual."

"Jesus."

*

It wasn't the mother or the aunt because maybe they didn't know it all or never cared to ask. Maybe they suspected but thought they couldn't offer Raven more. It was the friend, Dawn.

On a whim, Wise had thought it worth it to go back to Wells to check out Raven's car.

Can't hurt. You never know. It could...

The curiosity took the better part of her day off. The midday. It cost her a bad mood from her husband, which he got over, as he had to when she put her career ahead of their plans for life outside it. The mother Marisa was cool with it. The little girl at the McCoy house before looked like a different one. Raven's ten-year-old car was clean like new inside, dull outside from pollen or old snow, the battery dead from not moving still a month after her long funeral. Trunk was cleaned. The glove compartment hid no smoking gun. Just oil change slips, a registration to Aunt Bell, insurance papers, car wash coupons, makeup, hand sanitizer and face masks. No well-off raised print business cards, no picture of a man, no phone number taken with lipstick. Just a car.

Dawn walked up on Wise's feet stuck out from the passenger side because she was on her stomach across the seats to feel and see under them without doing it on her knees outside the car.

"You're back?"

Wise thought the question sounded like she was remembered but not. Dawn had left her at the restaurant in a huff. Insulted and hurt. Now Dawn sounded happy to see her. The song she sang at Raven's funeral wasn't in her mind. She was bringing Marisa plates from the buffet. She certainly did a new number on her hair. To her, Wise was now just that police officer who was just around and in it with them all now.

"Yes," Wise said. She rolled out of the predicament to stand.

"What you looking in Raven's car for?"

"Evidence," Wise told her.

"Of what?"

"I don't know. I just have to see it."

"You're not gonna find anything in there," Dawn laughed. "Raven only drove it around Wells. Marisa told me I could have her car, but it's too much for me to have two. I wish she'd give it to somebody else. I know she won't."

Wise left her card again and this time the Wells area code came to her cell phone not even a half-hour to home. Wise turned on Bluetooth straight to the car and looked for a shoulder to pull off on. She activated police lights. The black notebook in her console. A pen should've been ready. Wise had to listen while she battled her purse for something to write what she heard.

"I told Raven not to do it. She wasn't nothing all the stories said she was. Everything in socials is all talk. I mean, she had dudes. But, nah, she was just fronting. These girls just want the attention. Dudes just talk shit. None of 'em do anything. But this one was different. Raven met him our senior year, when we came up to get the city lashes. We turned it up for Chicago and all, so I guess she just got noticed. All the dudes — black, white, Latino. She was always the one for that. This one was at a gas station. He was white. Old. Well, *older*. And yeah, we drinked and smoked on the way. That's what you do. So I guess she was feeling good. I was. *We*, were. At first it was just little parties. She drove the car up for it. Grayson. We didn't know it before. I came. He met us at the gas station and we followed him to his house. Off by itself in these woods. Other houses around, but not close. Strange. It was way too dark. The house was fire, though. A pool outside, two Jacuzzis. It looked like a porn movie house. But we just hung out with him, you know. Said he was married and all that. Wife outta town. I dunno. He would help us out. He paid for college for some girls. I mean, we ain't dumb. You know you gotta do something for that. I never went back. She told me he said he liked her the best anyway, so. She didn't like it. Then she said she kinda liked it more. And he was taking care of her.

He started sending these cars for her. Black trucks. Black cars. She didn't have to do nothing but be ready. And he wasn't even paying for college like he said. Just giving her money and stuff. It was other girls around. Other men. These… parties. And he said he liked to have more girls, so Raven just invited them. She got paid for it. She said she could get out of all that if she wanted to. So long as she had more girlfriends the cars could pick up. She asked me to go, but I don't know… I —"

Wise had a pen.

"What was his name?"

"I don't know. She called him Jay."

"Jay what?"

"Just Jay."

"In Grayson? Grayson Glens?"

"Grayson, I don't know. Maybe Glens. We went through gates that said something."

"You know any exact dates you went through gates with this man?"

"Not with him. First in Raven's car. Then he told her just to wait for his cars to get her in Wells. Uh, maybe some days I could tell you, if I think about it hard."

"Did you ride in these cars or see them?"

"Nah. One came to the buffet. Right before she quit. Just a big black truck. Tinted windows. Fabulous, but not all tricked out. Just plain."

"Who else knew about this? Anyone?"

"Well, I don't know. They'd have to speak for themselves. He never picked her up at her house. Or any house. Just out somewhere. Like she'd walk a little bit or wait out at the mall."

"How did he contact Raven?"

"Sometimes other guys and people contacted her for him.

Men, whatever. They passed her the deets. He gave her a phone.
A better one than she had normally. She called me on it sometimes. But mostly recorded her stuff on it. That's what happened
that night. The phone."

"What night?"

"Last time I talked to her. That night. You know that. You
asked me what we talked about before."

"That's all in her file," Wise said. "It's a lot of notes. Help me
remember. What did you two talk about?"

"Well, I lied. Whatever I told you. I'm so sorry. I didn't know
what to do. I think I said it was just normal. 'What you doing?
Whatever, whatever.' But it wasn't. And I was scared. I didn't
know if all this was a crime. And I didn't know his name or
where he was."

"What did you and Raven talk about that night?"

"She was pregnant."

"So, you knew?"

"I'd bought her some tests. She had all the signs."

"No boyfriend?"

"It was his. Jay's. Or one of them. I don't know. She said it
was different men, or some same. Just… parties. And sometimes
they didn't strap. But I don't think she was getting down with
anybody else. Just the main guy."

"Did he know? Did she want an abortion? To keep it?"

"She didn't want any abortion. And she didn't want to do all
that anymore. She was done with it. It wasn't worth it. I dunno.
My friend wasn't feeling or looking right anymore."

"What did she say that night?"

"She said she told him what she said she was gonna tell
him. And he took the phone he bought her and her bag and the
Blahniks and hit her. And he looked like he was gonna beat her

up or kill her. And he said he'd kill her and all the girls if they told. She said she was running."

"What was inside the house again? You said a pool, Jacuzzi?"

"Yeah, that. Nice furniture. I don't know. Not much to remember. It was hot but plain."

"What color was Jay's house?"

"It was too dark outside to tell."

"Did it seem like it could be white or gray? Or look like you couldn't see it at all?"

"I barely saw anything until we were right there. It was black like the real country."

"What was around the house? Was it trees, a dark gate, a white fence, a long driveway?"

"We passed by a river."

*

A bartender bounced down and Loveless went from the tap to the top shelf. Wise took a basket of fries in place of the dinner and movie at home. She saw the things she could do to her husband later to make this all go from a sore spot to history. They were pleasant and wanted.

"I'll get back down to the witness," Wise promised. "I can pull more details about the house. I'll narrow some faces down and bring her some pictures."

"No stab wounds or ligatures. No bullets. Could've been poison. But that's long gone."

"I already have a few properties in mind. I'll get the gate tapes."

"I'd bet my life all the partying stopped when that body came up," Loveless said. "And those black cars were a service. But get 'em on the DMV for the black cars and trucks anyway."

"Well, sounds like the Glens are Zone One and it's many dark houses out there," Wise said.

"But only so many pools. Glenners were always delusional there."

"Dark houses, pools and Jays."

"That's not the son of a bitch's real name."

In her mind, Wise flashed through reams of faces at the festivals, Boat Club, Pool Hall, Grayson Greens, Arts Center Gala. All those men who looked the same, barring age and hair type and weight. They all were the same profiles on paper (wife, kid, high net worth). All those men in their boy's club of wealth and privilege and great service from everybody. It would take a good Christian to be so honest as to turn in the truth. But Loveless and Wise knew God or church had nothing to do with what they always knew, on some level, was going on out in these parts.

Wise left craving a plan, a compartmentalizing and organizing of her mental until this was ended. Blackout dates and times on this madness to remember most people are normal and good, not taking the best of young women and leaving them to die in rivers. Otherwise, she'd lose her mind. Wise hated Dawn but she loved her. The girl gave her the relentless tension she knew well but disdained. It was a finish line now, yet the gun couldn't go off until she found something else. More. Always more. And always other cases and work. All serious. A victim was a victim.

But this was the one.

People, or things, or men like these always stepped back and laid low then started over. It was a matter of time before the next poor girl looking for the unreal good life was running to fall.

Twenty-Three

"So, your baby was christened before she fell out the crib? Alright. The cards can read both dates. People didn't even have birth dates until like, two hundred years ago. Babies died so much. Mothers died having babies. Now add on old-time diseases, famine, war. So they got the babies christened almost the day they were born. In case they died. Thank you. Ok, both April and May. Hmm, that's ram, warrior energy right there. Then bull. Now let's ask: Will little Jamie come out the hospital well? Will little Jamie come out the hospital…?"

"Oh, thank you. I know this looks crazy but my husband and I can't sleep and I just saw your tarot sign and…" Sniffles and sobs, fluttering and flapping, pleadings and thanks.

Charity was a surprise eager beaver. Once she started, she left Gracious few choices with her lover Officer Bobby Castle. They had slipped into her office on his break, but it was uncomfortable and sleazy with people in the spa. His car had all the cameras he couldn't turn off long. Her car was better, but she was too scared. Bobby could leave one of his hairs or wallet for her husband to find. His work schedule and her changed situation turned it to a month since they could get alone together. He always came by the spa to check on her, be cordial and leave it to her to tell him when she had time. She thought she would have time, but Charity stayed on a roll.

"Wow, the Emperor card," Charity continued. "Perfect. Total control, ruler of all things."

The service station sure wasted this child, Gracious thought. She'd admit: Charity's help at Goodness Gracious, with the deal she could post a sign for tarot walk-ins and read cards, was profitable. A new energy arose. Teen daughters popped in with the mothers, a tarot reading the attraction more than mud scrubs. Charity's office assistance in between was stellar. They set a dinosaur file cabinet to the curb thanks to the girl's patience to digitally scan records, receipts and customer intakes up to something called Dropbox. And Charity wasn't on the streets late at night anymore. This is what Gracious loved to do in Grayson and the Glens: make differences.

She and Bobby had considered hotels. He was free to pay with no wife to see he did. But finding the girl in the river strained the force. His hours and days spanned nights. They couldn't have a gossipy Glenner see them where it wasn't quick to play it off like they were just friendly.

Now, her husband was home watching the Olympics with other out-of-shape men, consuming liquor and meat. Gracious and Bobby settled on the sauna this time. The back apparatuses all fenced in; even in Grayson, Gracious minded her business, guarding against cheap late night commandoes running up electric, water and heat bills.

So Gracious wriggled Bobby inside through the extra back door workers came in if they parked. Then, he went out the other door for the clients getting to the back yard. Charity's voice was a singsong to a walk-in customer: *"Pairs, clubs, aces, and wands..."* Gracious opened one door and Bobby slipped in. She walked part way up to the front. "Going to the gas station!" she yelled.

Then she went out the back door behind Bobby.

Moments later, Bobby's weapon was unholstered and so were his pants. No time to undress, only for her wrap dress to open down the middle and their underwear to fall. The sauna wasn't booked that day. No heat mist. Still, the hideaway was small. It held on to a whole day's sun. The light was too risky. They dealt with the dark humid stuffiness.

Bobby was always interested in her breasts, like sweet jellyfish to him. He had brought her to heights from those alone, in those days the spa had to be closed so they were alone in the building. He wanted to do that, but they were on the clock. Tonight was less methodical, more medicinal. What could help them concentrate and function over the next week or two. Maybe month; in summer, all the Grayson festivals and fairs gave him overtime. It was also the spa's high season. Free moments were hit or miss. They succumbed to a daze. The silence and rush. Suddenly the radio crackled next to the pistol. Grainy voices. Beeps. They were gasping and trickling, the wood structure creaking. They always thought about it. But they both knew it wasn't wise to say "I love you." Maybe not even true. The radio was on again. On again. On.

Gracious helped him climb over the fence, out of all their childish nonsense, to get through her spa in secret, to rush him on to the adventures men take when they want. Then, before she walked back into work, she cried for being in love with this to risk all she had.

*

Officer Castle raced up to find the girl inconsolable, shaking and guarded and mean. Barefoot. Wavy long hair wild. Thankfully, it was a woman who pulled over for the child. A baby in a car seat in the back of a Tesla. The baby was smiling one second and disgruntled the next. It had a bottle, so the problem must have been a wet pamper. But for the redhead driving, everything stopped and a running girl became the whole world and this world was fucked up.

"911, what's your emergency?" the voice had slurred.

"There's a girl out here on the roads in the dark and she doesn't know where she is or where she's going. She's upset and crying and really needs some help."

"What's your location?"

"Up near the west Glen gates. Uh, off road 82. If they come just past the bridge and follow the road, they'll see us. I have on my brights. I have her in my car. She's safe."

"How'd she get in your car?"

"She ran out in front of it and I almost hit her and she was asking for help. A man! He got her in the city and brought her down on the interstate and she jumped out at the Grayson exit."

"And what's the girl's name?"

"I don't know. I didn't ask her all that."

"Stay where you are. An officer's on the way." The girl wanted her daddy's house from the woman. The girl didn't know the address but she knew the way. Calliope Lane. Totally opposite side of the Glens, a wilderness of trees and gates and shotguns ready for suspicious bodies coming on the lawns in between. She wanted the woman to do it for her, snake her to the right house. Not the police. She had the story all ready.

Her father and his wife knew it well. They feared it and her mother warned them about it: She was kidnapped, almost raped, and a gang of boys were going to make her the next Raven McCoy. But she escaped. They all wore masks. It was so many like them. They were black boys. They wouldn't tell anybody. Just her mother. It would be embarrassing for her and today, with the internet, everybody would know. And then her mother would see chaining her up in the world and watching her every move wasn't going to work anyway. She'd let her free.

But the woman singing with the 80's station on the way from her sister's house was a grownup and right. This barefoot girl on the roads was a child. My God. Could have been her or any other woman — desperate, panting, waving, praying. *How dare that monster…?* Now, the police were on the scene and this was a real thing and the girl was a survivor of a violent crime.

"Joy Powell," said the girl. "My father is Victor Powell. Everybody knows him."

Officer Castle knew the Powells like he knew most in Grayson and the Glens, just faces to nod at and be friendly with until they needed him in moments he hoped to be a cat stuck in a chimney. He went on the radio to ask if he should take the girl to her daddy or to the station or to the emergency room. The supervisor on duty went for the daddy first, emergency room next. A traumatized witness was no witness at all. A mental patient loses credibility. They couldn't have evidence technicians in that quick for this. It wasn't that kind of force. It was to stay simple here.

A night of rest and then they go all in with interrogation. They get her clothes from the hospital. Check out the parents. Call the Chicago precinct. Pass it all back up to them. Black, female, young. In Grayson, again. Damn! This Raven McCoy shit ain't over yet?

Castle knew memories were short. The girl wasn't ready, but the ride still had to work.

"So, the lady back there said you said you were at the movies around your house in Chicago and a man…?"

"No. It was boys, not a man."

"In the parking lot or in the movie theater?"

"I went out to get a signal on my phone. I couldn't get it inside. I wanted to call my mom and ask her if I could stay at my friend's house. This boy asked me to use my phone and…"

"And what?"

"He took my phone. He threw it in the garbage and more of them came."

"How many boys?"

"I don't know. I didn't take time to count them. I was screaming and trying to get away."

"Was it a car or truck?"

"Just a car. An old car. Big and raggedy and loud."

"What color?"

"Maybe brown. Dark red. I was fighting, not looking at the kind of car somebody drives."

"What color were these boys?"

"Black."

"Dark black or light black?"

"They had on masks."

"But you knew they were young black men?"

"Yeah. A gang. You know, Chicago has gangs?"

"Would you know these boys if you saw them again?"

"Of course. I almost just died."

"So, you think you can do a picture of how they look without masks? Was it the face masks or killer masks?"

"No *real* masks, not what we wear. Maybe the voices I'd know. I'm not gonna forget killers."

"They tried to kill you?"

"What else were they going to do?"

"So, this was Saturday night?"

"Yes."

"Well, where you been since Monday?"

"I don't know. It was a dark house. In a room by myself. They just gave me sandwiches and water and wanted to drink. They wanted us to have sex but I'm on my period. Today they just took me out and didn't tell me anything. One said he was going to kill me somewhere and dump me in a river like Raven McCoy. You know that girl? The one who went missing here?"

"I know the case."

The pink sandstone brick looked all dark save for the yard lights set to sensors at the circle drive to the garage.

"I have my key," said the girl, brightening now. "Thank you."

"You kept on to your keys all this time?" Castle grinned. "Wow, you're good kiddo."

"They're in my pocket. My jeans are tight. That's why I jumped out their car for here."

Bobby kept the car doors locked and police lights on. He triggered his door to get out.

"Wait!" said the girl from a locked backseat, trapped, smashed hands on window glass.

No answer to the doorbell. For minutes he waited. No answer. Back on the radio.

"Calling about suspect, reported abduction near the Glens. I'm at the victim's father's house, on Calliope here, and no one's answering. Over."

"Bring her in," crackled back.

Castle could understand the victim's disbelief and anger to roll away from her father's house, the bed she planned to sleep in, protection she deserved, people who deserved to find her with the doors locked. She'd survived a nightmare. The minute she said "Chicago," he was prepared for something different than the usual. But all victims are the same. They're fragile. He thought of himself as one of the good cops who knew you can't take anything personally.

In ten short minutes, Castle just let his young black female victim from Chicago curse him out as he walked her into the pen-drop quiet and well-lit Grayson police precinct.

TWENTY-FOUR

Victor raced us through fog atop narrow gravel roads. Gloria followed us in our darkness. She wasn't used to it. We weren't. Everything was bigger and limper from August rains showing up early. Our world raced into a ravishing autumn, trying to keep up with its unleashed people.

Victor fidgeted with the wheel to act like he wasn't lost. The fog gripped us — sleepy, hungry and tired. Just one wrong turn had us wasting gas and time.

"We're definitely close to home when Kenny Chesney is all we got," I joked.

What hell a weekend became. Gloria looked like shit. So did I. Victor never did. It was a rare besting of men over women, to do little or nothing about their looks and still do it all.

Victor gave up and pulled over.

"We should be able to see the weeping willows somewhere," he said.

"Through the fog?" I asked.

"Maybe."

"Why are we stopping?" Gloria yelled through the dark.

Her cigarette smoke curled out the car and through the air to reach me. Victor left to rummage for a flashlight in the trunk.

No reason I couldn't empty the flask before Victor returned to driving. It took two fast sips. The vodka gave me a dry tongue, but I wouldn't drink water for the long ride, now longer, with no bathroom.

Joy was found, now. Waiting at the Grayson police station. Abducted. Leaped out the abductor's vehicle near Grayson, Illinois. Hungry, terrified, walking to her father's. The first ordeal was over. Our new ordeal would be lengthy. Maybe lifelong.

Victor could call plays or next moves in sports. He could sniff out the phony notable people he met. He could know when his irresponsible or distant relative calling to sound nice really wanted to borrow money. Yet, he didn't know his wife was drinking.

Put away or give away glasses and tools for alcohol: corkscrews, bottle openers, shakers, chillers… Tell people in your life of your new journey… Bring non-alcoholic beverages to gatherings... Or anything like that my Clean Coach had advised in our last remote meeting. Almost time for a new session, when Jonah and I would talk like I was doing great no matter what.

A flashlight beamed. Victor walked in search of a landmark. We never came around this part. The Pitts were a mile in an opposite direction, I guessed. The Davidsons were somewhere further than that. I knew a black family could be near. I only knew that because they had a rummage sale. We weren't going to be three black people knocking on nearby doors this late.

"Victor, hurry!" his ex-wife shouted.

Since I was already drinking, my craving for more grew. A frosty glass of Riesling on the hot tub's ledge. Without Clean Me and Victor's perfectionist nagging. Without adult work and a business to run to afford the best in life, my life would be a nice wine bottle on a peaceful island. Victor motioned Gloria to follow and drove us closer to a kid crisis none of us had experience in.

We found Joy waiting on a couch behind a windowed door at the small station I'd never been inside. She rushed to her father, totally blanked her mother behind them. I stood in the doorway. The officers gave us some time. The family reunion included me, for once. Joy a mess, no shoes and stuttering the story. 48 hours in the devil's hands and world. I knew the feeling.

Victor vanished to put his foot down to the young officer who got his daughter and the supervisor, any uniforms within shouting distance to hear: He wanted these motherfuckers caught. Joy's red and tired eyes narrowed onto her weak mother: "I want to live with Dad now." We had coffee and vending machine chips together at the station. Finally, the weakened mother who loved her child more than anything in the world gave her what she wanted now. That child wanted to wait until the morning for the hospital and get on to her bedroom at our house, now.

*

I lie in bed and informed Faith to expect my call tomorrow, after we sat with Joy in an official interrogation. "No, I'm calling off and coming down for it," she said. "Noon," I told her.

Then, I made a rude call to Ifa outside her work hours I never disrespected. It was an emergency. We would need her. *The Powellcast* had to go on. The Powell Group had to get busy again. I had to tend to the new requests and orders and opportunities for Victor's public image to go out. We needed the follows, views and money. Always, more money. Ifa would be the right hand to my left for the indeterminable time it was best for Joy to get out of Chicago. Gloria and Victor would talk out the particulars. No way could the girl just disappear from her mother. That's never the game I wanted to play. We were learning on the job to parent the generation who could do everything while sitting on screens looking like they were doing nothing. We were in a world of Raven McCoys. "I'm praying for you," Ifa said. She would be here for more hours.

Victor's knock interrupted our call.

"Hang up the phone," he told me. I did.

We talked long, while the baby was tucked in and put to bed with the security that her father was asleep on the couch, guarding all doors and glass on the ground. After she scarfed her favorite cauliflower crust pizza we had left from her last visit. After we all shared the whiskey shots Victor guessed would do her better than the expired painkillers I had left from dental work.

But I turned off the light above the bedpost aware Joy was far from just no average angel as I'd thought. She was the demon child I could never afford to be and was satisfied I didn't have.

She had a boyfriend. Or, a man friend, according to Gloria. Just now spilling this information, too. Joy's girlfriends had caved in after Gloria's frantic abduction news to their parents. Playing the roles took a lot out of them, I'm sure. Nope. All a plan, all along. What dastardly little witches.

All for "Omar" and Joy to have two days in a hotel doing God knows what and then a dump out near her father's house, because Dad didn't know. But, maybe it was all the sex or the booze or whatever and the kids couldn't get the route or story straight. Knowing men like I did, Omar probably left her wherever when he was through. Now, she was rescued by good white folks we had to come clean to.

I had no care to intervene in the commotion below, from this clever child my husband awakened in a rage. The rage kept storming into the phone at her mother and back out into our house at the child. It came up to something about bringing this shit out where we lived with all these white people now and black people having to always be better. Was he slapping her?

I fell asleep to the sounds of a young woman crying and remembered when it was a habit.

In the state of Illinois, the penalty for filing a false police report was one to three years in prison. Yet, this was Chicago and Grayson Glens. The Chicago Police extended sympathy to the mother. They cleared one more thing off their heavy plates for two hundred more by sunrise. The Grayson police had time. But it was Grayson. And, Victor was in the Glens. They prided in and depended on a low crime rate. Everybody's money was tied up in it, since that added to keep property value high. And, they had to treat him the way they would treat a white man there in the same situation, how they would handle it for his white daughter assumed to have a bright future not to mess up. The Grayson Police extended sympathy to the father and wiped their brows.

To our luck, Gloria hesitated to take her fuss higher; she knew it was most likely the boy behind all this. That boy was a ghost. Someone Gloria knew of and saw but Joy wouldn't give up. The lovers found out the father she was supposed to run to in peril wasn't even home. Their plan to relocate her was over. I guessed she told him her dad went out of town a lot. I guessed she said I was a stepmom she could run over. I guessed he told her he loved her. Then came another night. And this girl was gone from her people and police would be looking. The boy knew he'd take a hard fall if this girl didn't say the right things. That's why I guessed he dropped her off anywhere with no phone in the pitch black.

"Deuces," I guessed he said as he drove off in the warmth and safety and light.

If I had pulled this with relatives or in a foster home, I would've been sleeping on a park or bus bench. I learned homeless girls in the city slept on the train and buses. I didn't get up to Chicago for that option for awhile. I'd choose church steps. That was my girlhood fate for less. I was unwanted for less. I wouldn't be whisked to my father's huge home to, to… recover.

Joy was one of *them*, like her father. His biggest complaint about family was his mother hadn't wanted to go into real estate when his father did and this made his dad bitter. Or, his father two-timed his mother when they were young, with a woman named Patty who still comes to the high school reunions and funerals to flirt with his father after fifty years. A family crisis for the younger brood was when a kid tried to drop out of college and go pro. In his professionalized family, where they all *thought* and *talked*, Joy had run away and put adults through hell. But she got a vacation with her father, and his wife was supposed to understand.

We couldn't press on the boy. We had to be grateful it wasn't worse. And we had to coach this good kid out of this mess so she'd understand any more of it would ruin all we had to give her. The "Summer of Joy's Recovery" changed what I thought was going to be a new life for myself. The middle of summer, the time people and things looked normal again, and all the things Gracious had thought of me to do with other women around my new home.

Just like that, the house needed me.

PART 4: RECKONING

RUNNING

*W*omen are magicians with secrets. We juggle them with the facts of our lives, past and present. We hold them close to our vests and take them to our graves. We rock them to sleep. We visit them in dreams and put them on in the mornings. We hide them before we hide ourselves.

This keeps us the magicians of begging.

Women will beg for a half hour to take a hot bath. For a man to come or come back. For the latest try at a baby to hold. For that awful night or sex to end. For low bank accounts to make dinner, pampers and gifts near a birthday cake. For miracles to wrinkles, gray hairs and cellulite. For the people who know our secrets not to tell them. Seems no matter how careful we are with our secrets, our most prized possessions, we must beg others for them.

It worked in my favor that foster care gives its girls a life like assassins. We have a trail without an identity. There one day, gone the next. We don't have a style. We're dressed in what we're given. We don't have relationships to mine for clues about how we should be treated. Some understood the assignment. Nobody was coming for us. It was a way to level up. It had to involve sex and our bodies.

I got off the train in Chicago after I left the group homes and rented room with an abusive husband living around. I had hot dogs at a stand. I watched people go by, some watching me to know I had nowhere to go. Men. I told them, "I'm waiting for a ride." I knew a girl. I borrowed a cell phone from one of the men who wanted me to go with him or let him take me where I had to go. I called the girl — Destiny, she called herself.

"Hope?" she asked of my voice. Sure, for now.

I first met Destiny in a tiny foster home, a house full of foster sisters who liked to fight. I accustomed to hearing her mostly talk about herself. She had the men telling her she was thick and juicy. Like a steak? She had the small waist, wide hips and au naturel behind that turned her own body into her biggest threat to her safety. And this was before she wound up a ward at thirteen. I asked her where the wads came from. "How can you afford to give me money?" I wanted the younger girl to tell me. She laughed. After her, other girls I met had wads. And they had clothes and cash to take us all out. No complaints. They barely went to school and stayed in bed past noon. You can't make that much paper hugging a pillow all day. I finally caught on.

18, 19, maybe 20…? I'd find myself guessing ages in the group homes. Some girls were in school. Some had ornery or poor family around who just didn't put up with them, but they could still go to them. Some had jobs and identities in clubs where people did poetry and rapped. Some went out with no money. They knew boys or men would pay for us. Just a fun time, then back to donated beds. We claimed 25. Perfect — that age I learned men expect women to crystallize into for them.

Destiny and I lost touch because we aged out of high school, then foster care, then group homes. It's hard to think about being a bff when your whole life and days sink to "Now what?" We couldn't linger. Any young person who lingered, expecting adults to care *about or for them, got their feet tangled in the prison or psychiatric industrial complex. I put in an application to Starbucks. A job. It gave me house keys for a change and my first own bedroom since it had burned down. Too bad it was in a house with strangers who hated each other.*

I only had $354 I'd saved up. I knew it wouldn't even pay for a good hotel. I didn't know the sex work life was a real job. I thought it was just something on TV, or something really poor girls did, or something really fast and lost girls did — never thinking I was really poor, fast and lost. It wasn't going to be a career. It was just going to get me on my feet. It was settled quickly: Get a cab, go pay Destiny for a week, and then start making money.

"Hey, mama," the shadow in a slip in a doorway of a weed-smelling place said when I made it from the train station to the address she gave me not too far away.

Destiny took me to a couch on a second floor of a building with separate apartments but easy ways between them. She never called my old name again. All the girls there had new names.

Squads and roommates formed out of these set-ups, but it's a roller coaster of losing touch. Destiny was a constant. If one of us found a great guy, we would get a real place to stay for awhile. Always, the situation ended. Mostly, we shared a handful of apartments for young women like us. We kept bags of stuff there. We could bring men. Or, we could show up at night.

Then, I suddenly just stopped hearing from her. Everyone who knew her did.

"I'm 'bout to really get my bag," she bragged over sushi and sake the last time I saw her. It rained that night we left this one apartment building we crashed in with other young women like us. We found a trance playlist and Asian fusion in a place by a big downtown university our old group home had taken us to visit. Her eyes sparkled underneath glistening gold eye shadow and

precise cat eye. She tossed back thimbles of sake like sips of water.

We rode the Green Line train far away, just for a different scene for the night. People recognized us in our neighborhoods and ones we met men in. The pimps hung around and wanted us. Destiny had a few. I was always on my own, making just enough cash for my looks and my clothes, not much left for food but that was fine. Hunger kept my body stacked. I stayed off my knees in alleys and cars that way. A pretty young black escort won't stay unused for long. The inconvenience of not having a main man was I stayed guessing at the next home or hotel suite. When one wasn't there, I had to go to buildings where the work sounded day and night.

"I wanna go to hospitality school," Destiny had said. "You know, write papers and talk to professors. Corny smart kid stuff. Run these hotels men got us working them in."

She made sense. We were in hotels all the time. We'd certainly been forced to be more hospitable than most women have to be. While those women got fathers and husbands, we got the men's dark sides. We never got to talk. We could only listen. We were the ones who'd go to jail.

Downtown Chicago still had yellow cabs then. So that last time I saw Destiny, we got one back home. We paid in cash a man shot out of an ATM nowhere near where he'd met us. No tracking, record, or bank evidence any one was ever together. No trace anybody ever even knew each other. This was the world we lived in. Underground. No identities. Invisible.

So much time together — talking, partying, eating, drinking, laughing — and Destiny's people didn't know I was someone to tell of her funeral. I just heard about it from another girl like us. She wasn't on the news. Not in the papers. No news for Destiny: ex-foster kid working up in life, just a young black female dead in an empty upstairs apartment in Chicago.

Not too long after, I was down on Wabash one night. The guy in the nice car who stopped and asked questions was married and white. Irish, he said. Older, didn't do this much. Ok, I smiled. I never did cars. No shower or minibar to drain for it. It wasn't a home they wouldn't want me to leave until right when their wives were coming back. But I was tired. It was quick under the Cermak train tracks. He asked if he could call me to do it again. I saw his black hair was thick and full, maybe fake, or he had money not to stress into balding. And he had bumper stickers for animals and the environment. He was the one I tried to manage an escape on.

The third time he called and he had a hotel room now, I told him I was losing my apartment. He let me stay in the room until he took me to a North side studio apartment in a building at the beach. Lake Michigan and Chicago out front. One room, kitchen and living and bed all together. The place was already something before I arrived, borrowed from his friend who owned it. Over five months, I pinched six grand cash off him.

It was autumn when I put three months' rent on a South side apartment I called about from an online ad. I left the cell phone he paid for at the uptown studio. I left the bed. I left his things he left there — shaving cream, cologne, toothbrush, pants, ties and shirts. I put the things and stuff I liked in the cab — my succulents, tea kettle, yoga mat, two bags of food. I rode to the side of the city with other brown, black and yellow faces. I blended in. The new apartment was dusty, old, eerie and tight. But it had doors and locks to keep men out. I passed all the easy tests at the temping service. I waited for its calls in the mornings to do little security and secretarial jobs. I put the rest of the six grand I got out of the man into hospitality school, to start.

I was twenty-five.

TWENTY-FIVE

I had finally cracked open the depths of my life and wanted to write it all out now, then sort through what I wanted the world and my husband to know about me forever. Just having the story on the page freed me from the secret and I felt light. I password protected *The Girl Who Would Not Burn*. And, I fell back to drinking to stop the story from flooding my mind.

It didn't help two other women were in the house with me: the girl and her mother. Joy couldn't help mentioning Gloria, a fact of her life. I always listened, interested and polite. I never interrupted her or Victor's calls to the woman. If Victor sensed a toll on me, he didn't show it.

I rolled back to drinking wine in the open. Nightly at our family dinners, worked up by Ifa, while I worked on keeping numbers and money up with our emails and problems down. At times Victor and I would be eating with no reason not to have sex at seven o'clock instead of midnight. At times we would be talking about our business and interests, but Joy's interests and topics of discussion were our priority. Yes, we saw this or that she loved. Sure, we could think about this or that. Those things cost money. Of course, we'd help her.

I rolled back to drinking wine before bed. Every night now, the phone of the house rang and the caller was Gloria. "Gloria was at dinner with her boyfriend" or "Joy just finished shopping with her mom," Victor would tell me. Along with her daughter's, Gloria's life was fast presumed to be the storyline in my life. This worked both ways. Joy loved to beguile her mother with tales of our domestic goddess adventures, shopping and cooking. I was always agreeable to her ideas, she bragged somehow. I recognized the kind of friend Joy was being. They never lasted.

One day, Joy took a break from hybrid school we had made up a reason to put her online for. Past the normal, but the parents paid a lot of money to dictate the school. Soundlessly, she appeared at the doorway of my office. She hadn't spoken to me about the boy. I'd never asked.

"Spinach, arugula, cranberries, chickpeas, capers and broccoli sprouts," she smiled.

She held the latest salad recipe she took Ifa away from me to keep going for her high maintenance vegan mandate. Slicing, dicing, scraping, and dressing just for her for hours.

"Thank you," I said.

I was hungry. Ifa would ask what I wanted and I didn't have an answer until she left. Our content specialists were readying for the fall season. It would be hectic now that things were open after being shut. They were planning the themes, looks and high points for brands ahead of time. Victor gave me some idea of where to direct them, but not much. Joy was his priority. They had to *talk*, as his family loved to do. They had to go off on walks and meals together, to *bond*. I was left to think how *The Powellcast* and clients of The Powell Group could make their splashes.

"You took down the pictures and shrine to Raven," Joy noticed.

"Well, I figured it was over for us now," I lied. "Our part at least. Everybody hoped it would be different. That, maybe, a girl had just run off and she would show back up again. That's the best way for these stories to end, after people go through so much because of them."

"I told my dad and mom I was sorry, Tragedy," Joy said. "I'm sorry I never told you."

I wanted to be a caring parent. I wanted to be a grownup. I wanted to be the wise woman. No one could get by Hope — the girl Joy read a little about in the few pages I'd let her read. I wondered why I trusted her to read it. I thought of the point of letting others like her read it. It wasn't any use if they didn't see all they could have suffered and didn't. Patricia the literary agent had emailed again — *Tragedy, I was just seeing if you did more on the book. I have some high download memoirs now! I've still got what you sent me... Fantastic!* But I questioned if it was all going to just be entertainment, people like Joy engrossed in it but taking nothing real from it.

"You've read some of my story," I said. "I wish I had a life like yours when I was your age. I never had time for a boyfriend or falling in love. I never went to prom. Life was hard."

"That's what I feel like nobody understands. People think my life is perfect. It's not."

We were the same: stuck between her mother and her father, a consideration for us with no choice but to lose Victor.

"I wouldn't get too involved with men right now, if I were you," I told her. "They aren't always just about one thing. Some are better. But men are always going to do what they want and leave the women dealing with the outcomes of it."

"That's what my mom says about Dad," Joy told me.

*

Many weeks and salads later, four women sipped light mimosas on the outdoor patio of La Maison Jolie, the only restaurant allowed in largely commercial-free Glens. A small house converted to the restaurant. Tented nuptials readied across a lawn of flowers and statues peeing in a fountain, forty or so masked people in ribboned chairs and the charms of a lone violinist.

The reservation was my idea. A girl's club last hurrah before a race to survive creating memorable holidays for our homes, families and in-laws. Faith, Gracious and I knew the drills. Nothing would come before the dish bringing, the gifting and the chit chatting for the holiday partying. We'd dip into darker colors in our closets and get outtalked by all the old friends, mostly our husband's. Joy just came along because she was to be "supervised," no matter how.

It would have been five of us, but Mrs. Pitts was staying home still. "Precautions," was her excuse this time. I wasn't sipping with all the girls. I'd been in Clean Me red zones every day. This made more emails or notes from that Clean Coach Jonah, or his robotic doppelganger. Beyond that luxury, I was watching Joy watching me drink a lot.

Gracious had a daughter-in-law but no daughter, so Joy intrigued her. I felt good to offer an amusement. I was sure Gracious and Faith would get along. They did. Both "working girls," as Gracious called us. She meant real work. Hard work. Work we often weren't appreciated for out in these big bad streets and cities and towns.

"I'll drink to that," Faith said.

Faith was the one to go find a waiter to hurry the mimosas. Gracious was the one to make her rounds to the Glenners she knew, just two tables so they didn't say she didn't speak. Joy and I sat behind with our phones, feeling something end that she wanted to continue. How sad her father's bigger life without her mother made her mother's life look too shrunken for her. Still, I liked my big life. I didn't want to share space with someone who would take up so much.

"Everybody drinks mimosas," she told me. "They aren't even that much alcohol."

I let her drink. I could adapt. Joys and Ravens and more were new creations, evolution, and an alien species. They assumed powers my larger self didn't feel. She came around my chair and put her arm around my neck, her mimosa in hand, her chin in my hair, her phone on our slice of life. We became #girlpower, #sexy, #hotaf and more. She went into a new dimension against reality around her and into a world of fast finger taps that put our video up online.

Since her husband was working out instead of out drinking, Faith knew she had a designated driver. Noble Tucker came down after more than a year of not seeing Victor during the pandemic. They had ventured to a Grayson park to shoot hoops one-on-one. Victor always regretted these times of going back to his high school and college days. Tonight, I'd have a job: to get him through the hot baths, Epsom salts and massages until he wasn't stiff anymore.

Today, we girls all tried for summer dresses and made it. To many late couples who knew better anyway, outdoor wedding season finished. A chill in September. Still, for people like us, dining al fresco had to be done until the last possible second. We awaited local farm bacon, crepes, and more mimosas. Joy was already on her second drink and fruit instead of the meat.

By the third light mimosa pitcher, we were on the common subject. Gracious didn't know the occasion of Joy's sudden Grayson life. For a new friend not behind my veil: It was a mutual decision to expand a child's horizons, a delight for her to get to know the Grayson community, her last chance to do so before she's off to the solar system of being in college and going abroad.

"Sad no one knows how Raven McCoy left my spa and wound up in the Grayson River, still," Gracious responded. "You'd think somebody would tell something. Somebody, anybody."

"Unimaginable to be a mother with no closure," Faith said. "You should see some of those mothers talk about cold cases. Oh my goodness. You can see the life drained out of them."

"I'm not in the mother club yet," I said. "I know it must be unimaginable for most who know her as well. The friends, the other relatives."

"You're so right, Tragedy, but a mother just has a bond with her children," Gracious said. "I know many women who've gone through it. It changed them. They were never the same. Like ghosts, they were. That's the part these young girls don't think about when they just run out in this big bad world all for fun. One false move or catastrophe and another woman's soul just gets eaten alive for it."

Faith set her eyes on Joy and said, "I'll drink to that."

The wedding reminded us of itself. Purple forbs and lavender flowers gave accents to the ironic minimalism. It cost so much to rent the grounds. No one had reasons to be spare. Yet a bride walked somewhere out of the back of the restaurant in a fluorescent white gown, straight with a short veil and thin train and stumpy bouquet, in step with a father type and the violinist's song. She did what women do on that day — commanded all the attention, even from strangers. She gave a warm feeling, a hope now. The ugliness lifts for all to remember love.

Maybe I was sleep deprived. And, we had wandered off to that scary subject, *again.* The girls didn't act strange about it.

Their "Awws" and "Oohs" mixed with Gracious's identifications of this or that person turning to see the bride. Joy was sharing what she'd do differently to the dress. Faith was wondering who was paying for it, her side or his.

Yet I was seeing a scantily clad girl approach our table. She wore all-white, a half dress or dress bikini or whatever girls work a stroll in. Black. Not Raven. Not anyone. Just a figure.

The violinist finished the song and the bride was holding hands with the groom off in the distance. A lovely scene the handful of other diners quieted for. It was silence but for a happy reverend's jokes and forks on plates or icy water pouring over tall glasses.

But I couldn't hold on to my senses. The figure was next to me. She slid my wine over to a place suddenly made for her at our table. Mine was hers now. Just one gulp to finish it off.

"What are you doing?" I asked.

My companions turned from the show. They were squinting and whispering, then not.

"Why are you here?" I whispered. Then, I asked, loudly.

The figure was part of it all now. She watched the waiter gliding to us. She already tasted what I ordered. I knew she was going to take it. But I was confused because she should have been Raven McCoy. She wasn't. If this was happening to me, it should be precise and I should be the one controlling it. The power to think it was just dead girls and rivers and men was mine.

"Tragedy, who are you talking to?" Faith asked.

"You don't see her?" I shouted.

Gracious sprang into action. Faith stood to block other people's views. Joy faded into the background. Altogether they managed to get me to my feet, keep me in arms and pull me inside.

"It's okay." "She's fine" "No worries, everyone. It's all under control..."

They smiled and grinned to fidgeting diners. I saw inconvenienced wedding guests turn around. I glimpsed the curious bride and groom, a pair who looked serious about it. They turned to see like the others. I heard snickers indoors. I looked back and no one was following us.

After a nap, I left home without telling anyone. I stopped at a little market for wine.

Thanks to Gracious, I learned I was the "black woman" who was the talk of the town.

"That was a Cook County judge's daughter getting married," Gracious told me that night over the phone, calling to "check in" on me.

"No one knows my name, do they?" I cringed.

I hadn't foreshadowed the Google and social media age being one to appreciate a plain Jane name for. 'Tragedy Powell' in any search engine would be precise. I connected not only to Victor, but Grayson and Chicago and Raven McCoy. *The Powellcast* posts and pleas for notice fired more attention than Gracious's old-fashioned flyers before the TV news came along.

"Oh no," Gracious gasped. "And even if they did, it's not like they'd repeat it."

Someone had repeated something to Gracious or she wouldn't have known my little scene was the scene. But I was noticing: Anything goes with Gracious and all her little clubs of various reasons, which I was in now. A circular cult of stories, always evolving and correcting.

"Now's a time to keep a low profile in Grayson," Gracious warned. "Seems that missing girl case was the tip of the iceberg of what this place has seen. You poor thing… I know it's scary."

The "syndrome," it was called. That's what it was at the restaurant. Nothing new. This place made women have fits, turns, outbursts. Every day, another woman was storming out of restaurants and bars and yards. But Grayson didn't have paparazzi. We were all fairly anonymous even if public eyes could tap our whole lives up into screens. We were the new population and places where everybody could know where we lived but not how to get there.

"Just everything blows out of proportion after while, in the quiet and dark," Gracious elaborated. "No matter what's going on, good or bad. And, more bad's on the way."

"Oh?"

"Well, you know my little Grayson police force friend tells me it's more than just a little swinging and hanky panky going on in the Glens. I mean, people all know but don't say —"

"What's going on? A murderer? Rapist?"

"Seems the police are taking that sugar daddy idea seriously with the girl. FBI even."

"No! Finally?"

"Finally. All sorts of theories, and, guess that lady detective is determined to get to the bottom of everything that happened. A few Glenners might be getting some surprises this fall."

"I'll pray for her family," I said and then I got off to *rest*, as my syndrome required.

Of course. I knew from losing Destiny that Raven McCoy would not be forgotten. Their spirits were strong and I shared their pain. I had just escaped the life and they hadn't. Now, I had to get back on my habits and unwind myself from all this crap in the air that had nothing to do with me anymore. I had made it and moved on. It was time for the bike, treadmill and yoga mat. More work, less play, saving money. And, maybe I should burn *The Girl Who Would Not Burn*.

My big birthday slash housewarming party this fall? Would be a costly waste of time. Everything was still getting cancelled left and right. We would have had our first party flop in the storm of everything else trending nonstop, online carnivals of reopening around the world.

"This is not working," I told Jonah one random night, as I'd wanted to do for some time.

On the phone screen, my Clean Coach's eyes were bluer than I'd noticed in almost three months of working with him. He was clean-shaven and tanned, back from his vacation that he still kept our video appointments during. In Puerto Rico, open to Americans, a lucky break. "An alcohol-free resort!" he'd exclaimed on all his pictures posted to the Clean Me socials.

"We'll keep your information and everything stored for when you come back, Tragedy," he replied. "Many people stop and start with us. That's common. It's all about your pace."

"Well, I won't be back," I told him. "The situation's all under control."

"What situation?"

"My drinking. It's not the problem I thought. In fact, I rather like it. I think it helps me."

"Alcohol isn't bad. It actually can help. But it's very dangerous as a habit or pattern."

"The danger is hiding it and lying about it. Trying to pretend I don't love to drink when I do."

"Tragedy, I —"

No. I hung up. I had less on my mind when I drank. I just had to be more organized, not all over the place. Professional with it, like Victor's family. Was it any different from their little pills and prescriptions for diagnoses everyone sent them cards for? At the last Thanksgiving before the pandemic, I found out a depression card was in order for his aunt. Why should I be stigmatized? If being sober wasn't going to erase the pains, I could be drinking. Just the fact I could do Clean Me short-term proved I could manage it. I didn't somehow save my life from burning to bone only to kill myself as an alcoholic.

TWENTY-SIX

Gloria saw herself in the guest bedroom's clawfoot mirror, Victor behind her, her curved back leaned over his chest. His hand between her thighs. A single pulsation between them. Just to finally do this, she had arrived earlier than she needed to come get their daughter from him. So many years of really, truly knowing each other fortified hypocritical trust.

Those years gave them confidence the other wouldn't make any trouble. They both knew the stakes. Those stakes would stop their urges to text, call, pop up, otherwise become apparent or pressure things out of a clear, tight box. They would just borrow a place, an illusion of peace — not steal lewd moments in the meantime, before a war. They were professionals.

Tragedy and Joy were gone, at their Goodness Gracious spa day. Friends with the owner now, Tragedy was. It would be a long day of extra special service. Probably, they'd do a girl talk thing after. Victor had dinner reservations for seven o'clock. A surf and turf twenty minutes up the interstate near the city. About twenty minutes from "Glo's" place in Chicago. They had time.

In every second of the act, one or both wondered how and why it got to this point.

They'd felt it all month. This boy situation volted them into passion. Gloria was always willing. Victor was the one with every reason not to dream of it. He didn't. Now, it became up to one of them to say it. Once, Victor had to take Joy to Chicago to see "Glo" for family dinner. They had to have "The Talk" for this thing sometime. He sat through the stress, tension, and horror that his daughter could hate her mother. Glo didn't deserve that. She wasn't that kind of woman. They texted and talked more. Their laughter and jokes resurfaced.

"I need you," she started off one day when Tragedy and Joy were out to brunch with friends.

"We should just meet halfway, at a hotel, like our last time back then," Victor had suggested. He caught his face in the mirror and saw a monster. *Why am I…?* were his thoughts.

"I dunno, I should just come to the house," purred his "Glo." *Come to Grayson Glens. Show solidary with Joy's father and stepmother. Then, away we all go…* were her thoughts.

The plan was to just get it over with. Then, back into co-parenting reality. Respect his marriage. Be good friends. Never again. Tragedy deserved better. But the darkness was unkind. It got to him, too. The house was Tragedy's wish and idea. He was no longer a big man in the city due to her. Like the rest of the Glenner men, he kept his reasons to escape. Their life, fun, meals, sex, movies and dinners. He loved them. He loved her. But he was a city boy. Always.

No, don't blame her, he'd thought, pouring whiskey or tequila or something he knew his troubled and maddening wife never stopped pilfering no matter what she said. *This is on me.*

Soon as Tragedy and Joy left for Gracious's spa, he started drinking, ready to answer Glo's texts or calls if they came. His mind raced. He could reject Gloria. Turn the plan into a discussion instead. He could start it. "Glo, we've been through a lot this month. It's stress and things aren't paradise for me either and neither one of us is thinking straight and…"

No. He kept drinking and waited for Glo to show up.

She was on her way.

Gloria let mood music take her all the way to the Glens. She was careful — no emojis or constant etas. She didn't walk out in ridiculous mistress dress. She was bankerly, all-business. A maroon skirt suit. Her assured briefcase in her hand. Smart brown pumps to the door. She rang as if she was unexpected, maybe a saleswoman. Not that anyone in the Glens was surveillance, at least not for any confidentialities but their own. Victor had deactivated the doorbell video and outdoor motion cameras when the girls left for the spa. Not that his wife ever looked at it.

He was waiting.

We can still have the discussion, he was thinking right as his Glo sounded the bell.

There was talk. He offered Glo a loud drink on the rocks and she took it. They were talking about Joy. About that man. About them. About why. About how.

They sped into a little play in the kitchen, that gold medal kitchen Gloria hated Victor giving to another, younger woman. The touching and kissing felt silly and strange, but they were sexy people so it continued. *I can still have the discussion*, Victor was thinking. He was surprised he didn't feel worse. The girls wouldn't be gone all day. Somebody had to make up their minds. Gloria opened her eyes to mostly glass facing the back of the property on its acre. She saw space and leisure another woman got while she got a townhome in an urban development in the city and a poor excuse for a yard. No, she didn't feel bad at all.

Not in the Powell marriage bed, of course. In the first-floor guest bedroom. Joy had lived in the upstairs bedroom this time, wanting to stick close to her father. They'd make time to straighten the room instead of leaving it messy. Not like when they were married, when this was normal. As Victor sank down into losing worry he'd be caught, Gloria looked out into the mirror. This was a mirror documenting it really was herself with her ex-husband, while her daughter was out with his new wife. And they were supposed to be family. They *were* a family. She saw the digital weather station across the dim room. The time was later than she realized.

It was up to four o'clock, the time Gloria had to sacrifice her twenties and thirties and part of her forties to finally be able to leave early at. Then, she would sleepwalk to her commuter train from downtown to the South of Chicago, to their daughter or her friends or a meal alone if her daughter was off at school. Or she would sleepwalk through plans, dinner, chit chat and domesticating with the man she settled on to fill the void — one of the "Tryers": a man silencing mistakes to explain not matching her financially. Not today. Today, she was happy she'd set out from work before noon, when Victor's "girls" were going to a pink salt bath before a clay scrub, then facials, then outdoor showers and things — all she would have had with him.

It was a quarter past four o'clock.

Victor and Gloria knew their marriage had deflated to competition. It started back when Gloria felt sluggish and shaggy, committing to her final job she assumed. Her family of bankers were like this. Victor seemed energized in rapid fire opportunities coming his way. All their friends asking about just him. She wanted another baby fast; he did not. She wanted to live on the South Side near her family; he did not. She wanted them both on daytime work and not all over the place like those power couples with nannies feeding their children; he did not. She never changed in his eyes. She stayed interesting and bright. He never cheated on her, not for real at least. A handful of flirtations and games. He was the same with Tragedy, until now. Just a man.

They had that one long and funny talk about racism a few years ago. As "just friends," in his old condo's closet-size kitchen for Joy's thirteenth birthday. Tragedy was there, a fast take to Joy's friends. They were all the poster modern family, co-parents, exes, stepparents. Everything.

That day at the party, Victor had noticed Glo's plum-colored lips and milky eyes. They stood out more due to her round afro she briefly switched to after their divorce. He was holding a beer and his phone. That stopped him from reaching to sample his ex-wife's new hair. Then there were Joy's track meets. He never missed those, before his chronic apology tours for not having boring daytime hours Glo forced on him. And they drove together alone, twice, on visits to set Joy up at the academy. They were always appropriate. Tragedy always had his texts and eta.

Still, the natural sedative that was time sentenced the old lovers back to hints, then plans. Victor wasn't a hound like he knew other men he rolled with were. He had many chances with women all the time. Never. Yet still, they argued about it. At least this one wasn't a new flame.

It was half past four and that's when the guilt quieted down. It was just pure enjoyment.

Gloria was the woman so the wiser. She knew they had to hurry. Victor was too besotted with her plump curves and arcs, its variety from Tragedy. He was delaying the inevitable end to pleasing this woman he knew before his wife. He had to enjoy it. He couldn't do this again. He would never be the same man. What would happen next? If they kept going for a next time, maybe even just ran off like two crazy kids, he could look in the mirror. But he only cared about the moment. So many years had passed since the hundreds of times they'd done this. It was wondering what to do like when a lover is a stranger but remembering what to do at once.

"We have to stop," he heard. "I know," he whispered.

It was a quarter to five.

They would just act normal. They would fool everybody. They would be nicer to each other. People would notice that part and would be grateful for it. They would be, too.

Their words blurred with "We have to stop" to "I know" to "I can't." Finally, "I love you." The confession was powerful enough to create more time, in their minds. He would have to arrange a story for the state of the room or get it right quickly. They resumed in a frantic rhythm they knew, relieved they had finally done it.

*

Ifa was on time, as usual. Her husband needed help at their store after his usual worker called off. A switch to a rare evening shift was Mrs. Powell's compromise. It worked with Mr. Powell's surprise anyway: a spa day for her and Joy. Ifa knew Tragedy and her spa days. A clean eating kick was going to start. A promise not to drink. She'd work harder for awhile. Then they would be on the floor with piles of papers, bills and mail to do something with in a hurry.

Ifa regarded the Powells, at this point, like family. No others in her world were paid so well for days off, half days and even days just sitting with great people. Nothing like Ifa's free reign with the black cards and cash to roam the few stores. And their daughter Joy relished her traditional Ethiopian food, so spicy and vegetable-centered. Victor was grateful she steered him from the beef and pork, unlike most American's homes to work in. She was fortunate. Teased and mocked. Her family called her bosses "the rich Americans" and her "the Princess."

Now this had been an Olympic summer, when Ifa snaked through the job's bonus cable and smart TVs while she worked. Victor talked about the Games on his show and in his house with her. They rooted for the brilliant Ethiopian flag with the boring American one. They both agreed the athletes didn't get the cheers and credit they deserved in fan-free pandemic stadiums.

Her husband hated her driving those crafty roads in the dark, especially before harvest when corn was high. They were in a suburb. But she promised him to return by eight o'clock. Light chores to get ahead for: laundry, dishwasher rounds, closet straightening, surface cleaning. Food prep: the cutting and chopping and slicing for what Tragedy liked to toss in olive oil for quick salads or health smoothies. "Should I wear this one or that one?" and "Should he go serious or casual for this show?" were questions she hoped for. They made her workday go fast in the fun.

She parked her Toyota behind a visitor's Mercedes. She saw herself in through the breakfast nook sliding screen doors. As she set her keys inside a pocket, sounds came from down a hallway. Her feet stuck in place right under her. Her concern, a degree of fear, soon downgraded to surprise. The sounds were just clamor of a man and woman who forgot to shut their door.

She expected Mrs. Powell to be gone. She imagined the car meant Mr. Powell to be somewhere in his office or the living room with the driver. She planned to make tea or coffee for him and his guest, whatever they wanted for dinner. She misunderstood. Now, she was in a jam.

Something must have changed the schedule. She knew her bosses wouldn't expect her to come all that way and not work or get no pay. She only occasionally stumbled into tell-tale noises behind the closed master bedroom when she let herself in. She chuckled to think her boss's spa day had come with a bottle of wine for Mrs. Powell, a few daytime drinks for Mr. Powell. Wine and spirits often made people think they had time for those kinds of things, only to wind up taking way longer than they planned. She pretended she never heard a thing of their marital business — family and friend gossip, disagreements, shouting matches, crying fits, sex or anything in between. No good would come of stripping her bosses' veil of privacy.

"It is foolish to start a fire just to see the flames," the proverb was.

Ifa was certain laundry waited in the basement. Mrs. Powell had neuroses for crisp sheets and towels every week. Ifa took it as all the baggage she talked about from her foster kid days whenever she was tipsy. How beds were hand-me-down, grimy with other children's residues, sad spirits of loneliness and sometimes tampering. She could get to the washing room through the basement's alternate entrance outside. She often started this way before coming inside. This would make sense and make them think they'd been alone all the while. She wouldn't see flames of humiliation rush Mrs. Powell's cheeks. Outside, the couple's good time muffled underneath cardinals and sparrows, a little breeze, a lawn mower. She opened the entrance to walk down.

It was an old habit Ifa had. Since she was young, before America and marriage. She never loaded clothes into a dry washer tank. Others did, in a rush. But her patience got her proof a magic trick took place, all the suds and soap swirls she wanted to see to believe. So she was still just sorting through the usual — cotton, spandex and nylon from the workout clothes. Many new things, tags still latched — Mrs. Powell liked to run her lingerie and undergarments through a warm delicate cycle, to be sure. Same for bath and kitchen towels, throws, pillows and more.

If not for this habit, Ifa wouldn't have had an option to escape the fire or the flames. The clothes would have been ruined if she didn't stick around to dry them. The process would have taken an hour and a half. The lovers would have caught her, somehow.

However, her phone pinged. A beautiful, smiling face emerged from pixels. But Ifa checked that face and the name twice to be sure it went with the message. Yes, it was Tragedy.

Ifa, my apologies. Running late. Let yourself in. Thanx!

The large capacity top loader started a pending roar to a full tank. She didn't load anything. The wash cycle would finish and drain in thirty minutes. Odds were neither Mr. nor Mrs. Powell would slip to the basement before. After all, Mrs. Powell was not around and Mr. Powell was occupied. Ifa hurried up the carpeted stairs and locked the door behind her. Thoughts of it all gave way to the crackle of gravel up to her blue Toyota behind the other woman's car.

Ifa drove long past Calliope Lane, the bridge landmark and Grayson River. She stopped to reply to her boss. She pulled the phone out her purse and thought on what to say. Prayed on it.

She tapped each letter and word carefully.

I'm sorry Mrs. Powell, must cancel tonight. Will you need me tomorrow?

In twenty-five minutes, Mrs. Powell and Joy were up the driveway. Gloria was here with Victor. In the beginning, this was sometimes strange. Victor and Gloria alone. It didn't happen often enough to think about. And they both had other times and opportunity. If people like them wanted to cheat, they didn't have to do it in back alleys. They could fly somewhere to do it.

Joy readied to face the inevitable return to her mother. It was left to time to see how that would work out. Tragedy had to check on her solution to distance and tension with her husband, inevitable with all they'd gone through. They would be child-free again. She had bought all the beautiful new things. Only, Ifa canceled and now she had to wash the new lingerie herself.

A battering from the basement. A spin cycle, it was. *Victor must have washed*, she thought. She would have to wait for that to end in order to load the new things. It ended. She heard the voices going on above her and wasn't interested. She'd done her best. She was imagining the night, when she and Victor would be the only ones taking up space.

But nothing was in the washing machine, she saw. Only moisture and remnant suds. Life was always strange and she was never not haunted. But this was real. It wasn't visions of her past, lost and burning things, dead girls. She knew when she was almost just making things up.

She got started on the hour it would take to wash lingerie on the delicate cycle and dry it the same way. Victor was going to dinner with his daughter and her mother. She was opted out, by choice. When he returned, they would be the couple they were six months ago, before two seasons of the world shifting back to normal. They'd leave the human population's new normal of jockeying for position while howling at the moon. They'd be playful and lazy. Besides their phones, no screens the next day. And the rotation would go on to them fulfilling plans with the house, starting with the dinners and parties to get more people into it as "The spot" now.

Where are the things?

Tragedy had placed the lingerie in a silky gold bag they came in, on top of all else in the laundry bin. She dug and dug. Why were they mixed in the middle and underneath stuff now?

With the washing machine humming into a cycle behind her back, she walked up to meet the trio upstairs. Joy had bags at the door. Victor was ready to haul them. And her man and the woman were both heated up, and tired, it seemed to her. Or hyper acting. She didn't know. They weren't normal. Tragedy skipped greeting the woman.

"Victor, why'd you run the washer with nothing in it?" she asked.

"What?" he looked at her. It was a different look.

"The washer was going," Tragedy repeated. "But nothing was in it. Ifa already did the hard water and freshening tablets on it this month."

Victor knew his wife was batty. She had these… times. A wild imagination. Her past was hard and he grew to suspect it was harder than she would admit. She hated therapy. She called therapists "social workers." She drank. She worked hard when she didn't. He loved her anyway.

"We'll figure it out later," he nodded.

"How was the spa?" Gloria asked. "You look refreshed."

"Thank you," Tragedy said. "I surely needed it. You know, a lot going on this summer."

The women smiled and knew they would never talk about things alone, in private as friends, not even if Victor was dead. "Shall we, ladies?" he asked. He kissed Tragedy on the cheek, lips and forehead. But she thought he was just going to kiss her at the side of her mouth.

As the trio stepped out the door, and Tragedy wanted to switch all her plans for the night to go with them, she knew she was one of them now. Those beautiful and smart women populating Victor's world, classy and flashing the bling, scared to leave the man alone. At his hip at the parties, shows and stuff. They were aware of the reality and they weren't going to leave it.

Not that it was a thought to worry about and not to leave Victor alone for. Just a feeling.

TWENTY-SEVEN

SEPTEMBER 2021

Joy's departure and the pending autumn brought about no normal. Normal was a past thing. It wasn't a new normal. It wasn't something to get used to. It was learning all the changes, even in people. The night I planned to be a pinup wife, I fell asleep before my husband came home from dinner with his ex-wife. The show was over now. The ground rules returned. I couldn't imagine his child going this far again anytime soon. So, Joy wouldn't be back. It would be nice not to hear Gloria's name for a while. Maybe not even Joy's. Damn her. The first morning I woke up without Joy and her mother's spirit in my own house, I recalled my dream.

My body was in possession of higher authorities. I was sat in the back of a police car, my wrists clenched together behind me, silence from the stern men in front of me.

Husband or lawyer? Husband or lawyer? Husband or —

Victor can call a lawyer. He'd choose Faith for me. He can get to our tiny police station sooner than the lawyer, in twenty minutes or less. Or I assumed I'd go to our local tiny station, surely not getting locked up in real jail so soon. That can't be how this works in Grayson Glens.

But Faith could call Victor, and everybody else, to arrange bail fast. How long will that take? Will it mean a weekend in jail for me? What will I eat? Will they take my phone?

My lawyer can maintain composure, precision and calm. She can match wits. Yes— *she*. Of course, they'll be surprised she is a she. That would throw cops off.

Call the lawyer, I decided in the dream. And say nothing until then. *You didn't mean to*, repeated that deranged loop in my head. That little voice had burrowed deeply.

The dream was vivid and meant I was trapped. I would need a lawyer, soon. These were the hunches. I was still a married woman. I still loved the hubby. I was only thinking out loud.

The next morning, the quest began. If it wasn't Gloria, then it was a woman and I could find out. I had a feeling. When we had lived in the Chicago condo, the tower of lives as an adult dormitory, I didn't mind shouting. Sometimes, Victor needed a lot to understand my life didn't revolve around him. Here, I had no impulse. I was taking up enough space, as I always wanted. I didn't have to fight for it. It was mine. If Victor had other women, I'd join that club Gracious told me had their houses bought by their ex-husbands. Total douchebags. I would start over.

The ferocity of my disconnection from Victor scared me, but I'd been there before. I was a slave to short-term relationships. I had to put up with people's abuse and try not to run away. But here, now, I was a piece of the puzzle. I knew more about things than Victor. I was essential to his businesses, name and image. He needed me.

He felt like a different man, more genuine than genuine. He brought me a bottle of wine one night. Shiraz, the first I drank with him. I didn't even have to ask. There was dinner for it. He insisted Ifa had nothing at all to do with it. Roast chicken, fingerling potatoes, green beans.

It was no use to look at his phone. He was too smart. There was so much to monitor with a man today. Passwords and accounts floating in the air for any woman to grab your man out of the clouds. He was the same cool cat to all the associates we worked with. I wasn't so tuned in to them that they would know anything anyway. Or tell me. Whatever he has hiding would have any traces of it put in the studio I never went down to. I wasn't banned. It was just Victor's domain.

He had friends, golf and photo shoots. Business owners to interview. It wasn't even that hard for me to snoop. Ifa and I kept everything in order. No descents to cut-offs and late charges. No disgruntled digital assistants or editors or agents or mangers saying they didn't get what they needed from us. He was in that new paperless world while I still wanted my paper statements. His cards and accounts were ours to a point of one account he kept off for himself. I doubted he would entertain other women from that. It had been immune to everything since I'd known him.

Gracious and I discussed it. If you thought your husband cheated. What to do if he did.

"Honey, all men cheat," she said. "It just doesn't look like it. Or people don't say it."

It sounded so different from what would be said in the worlds we were from. They claimed this wasn't true of all men, when it really was if you looked at the situations.

Gracious probed me for the clues. I didn't have any. Victor was always on the loose. It's just the way things were. Gracious was careful to influence it either way. She suggested Charity.

So I came to the spa for my reading. Also, for the new hand

treatment and hand mask innovation Gracious spread the word about. It really was heavenly. I sat with my hands soaked in a warm plastic glove while a massaging chair kneaded my body. I wouldn't ask if my man was cheating. I asked if my marriage was going to be successful. Charity went about her rituals and mostly I got all good cards. I had some things to work on, too, of course.

"This is the Devil. The Devil card means there's something dark in your life. It doesn't have to be a person. It can be anything, like the dark web or a secret. But it can be a person."

All in all, we concluded, my marriage would be successful. I was just facing a transition and people always fear changes. I paid her in cash and went to Corky's Bar with Gracious.

That night Victor ran up to his brother, who happened to live in Chicago. That was closer to Gloria. I went into the studio. I had the keys, both a fob and manual. He didn't lock it because he didn't want me in there. He locked it because the equipment was so expensive. That's what we said to be polite. It was small and tight. I wondered how anyone could spend so much time in here. We had planned on in-studio guests, fun overnight visits and weekends hosting cool people. But the world changed. So this was just a solo domain, a room really cut down to size.

No space for storage beyond a dark solid wool chest with paperwork, mostly files of info stored on topics and guests. Old marketing pieces and bills. This is where I started. I wouldn't do much. Just a few things here and there. I wasn't obsessed, just curious. I didn't want all the time Victor was out of the house wasted on thinking about him. I'd go back to my own world.

One night, he was in the studio recording — still no traces of hiding a past life with Gloria or present life with any woman there. The house phone rang. This was an alert not allowed in his soundproof world. It was up in mine, even though it was more likely to be his people. His serious business associates or family. I braced for the next bomb from Joy.

"Whattup sis?"

Merit's voice sounded younger than the last time. He went into his new plans and job, as he always did. I went to fresh-squeezed orange juice from the very last local farmers market, ending its season just as hunting season was starting. A nice glass, ice. A tinkle of rum...

I avoided the bedroom. Victor would crawl up there. He would finish his business. He always acted like a big man about town whenever he recorded, not needing my help anymore. And then he would want to come to the woman he was fine to let slip off to being a stranger in exchange for strangers on screens. I stretched out on the guest bed in the first-floor bedroom.

"You gotta meet my shorty," he said.

"Yeah, sorry I dropped the ball on that. Summer's been wild. Where are you working?"

"I'm working with my guy. He has a few businesses. You know. I'm helping him out."

"Be careful, Merit," I said.

"I'm good sis."

I heard Victor pound upstairs from his work. I motioned "I'm on the phone" when he found my voice where he wasn't expecting it. "Tell my man I said what's up," Merit said. Victor told me to say "Tell him to set a date to come out." Then, I filed my nails and twisted my hair while I heard Merit's tales of life in these Chicago streets in between him choking on a blunt.

"My husband's daughter is messed up," I interrupted.

"What?"

"Yeah. Lemme tell what you this little child did. She got some guy up where she goes to school and —"

"He's getting it."

"Right. So, they decide he's going to come get her for a weekend and lie to say she was kidnapped from the movies in Chicago. And black guys in gangs in Chicago were going to rape her or kill her or I don't know. Then, she would come home and act like this didn't happen."

"What? Damn, it's like that?"

"Yeah."

"It was just black men in Chicago? No names, no faces? Not even hairstyles?"

"She just called out the profile."

Victor yelled out old hip hop rhymes when he wanted my attention. That was my cue. I was supposed to come out to joke he was blessed in sports and talking but leave the rest to the pros. I didn't. Then, he went to the kitchen to whip up a racket. He only usually made a grill cheese sandwich and protein drink. He bought the rest or waited for women like me and Ifa to feed him. I had just refilled my juice and rum. I wouldn't go near the kitchen again until he left. I lowered my voice.

"So all that time, y'all thought this girl was kidnapped and she was with some dude?"

"Yes. We were beside ourselves. Not sleeping. You know I had to get drunk."

"Yeah, who wouldn't?"

"And that's not the worst part. She actually got to come live with us anyway, just like she planned."

"So all that was for nothing?"

"It worked for her. In a roundabout. They're talking about what kind of car to get her."

"That's wild. But, you know how these ones big up. You got it, you flaunt it, right kid?"

"That's right."

Then, we drifted into fantasies of how to kill Gloria and Victor if necessary. How Merit knew people. They could navigate Grayson Glens in black cars in the night. They would bring guns and silencers. They would have me tell them how to make it look like an intruder. They would wait for the signals and come take him out. Gloria would be harder. She had the girl. They wouldn't want to get the kids in it. But, they could show them what a real kidnapping was like. Just the mother. And they would leave her somewhere in Chicago no one could trace to them.

Merit fell asleep on the phone, Victor was snoring and I was feeling nice from the rum. I lie back in the bed, tight and clean and not including Victor. I would rest here for the night, at the foot of the bed. I talked the lights off and listened to the central air. My eyes adjusted to the dark and I opened them to the clawfoot mirror. Nothing special. A Davidson Furniture Bonanza thing I bought before I knew Gracious.

It was moved. It should be near the head of the bed. That's where I thought it always was.

I waited for the moments and times he would go for his runs, hit the gym, meet a buddy and leave the house. Then, down to the studio and through his files. I ran back his tapes. I would scan his search history he didn't clear because he didn't know. Victor was a nerd so I never knew what could pop up. It was all more in the realm of that or work than anything I was looking for.

Until a manila envelope stuck out, at the start of the bottom drawer of the chest. It was right in reach of where Victor wouldn't have to move from his seat to turn around to grab it.

Nice penmanship had written "Victor Powell." A sharpie. He had carried it in this spring.

Victor was in Chicago. A yoga studio owner was his latest feature for the ABC affiliate. No hotel tonight, he said. But, he always cruised through old restaurants and more to make an odyssey out of getting home to me. I would hear him come in before he made his way to the back stairs, to look through the studio's peekaboo glass ceiling. I had time.

Inside the file were a few piles of papers stapled neatly together. Each paper had its own highlighter color and post-it note color. It was Victor's style, not mine or Ifa's. We were simpler.

A DVD in a thin white paper jacked slipped onto the floor, its silver refusing my reflection. The first pile of paper was early news on Raven McCoy, alerts to her disappearance and calls for help. The second was a detailed estimate, invoice and warranty. For the Jeep. Not his old one we fell in love in. The new one we leveled up to last year, without anyone going anywhere or driving much and when we had three working cars. It was from the time around last Christmas, when I took the Jeep for Chicago shopping but woke up in it in a stupor.

The last pile showed the next name to take me by surprise besides my own. It was "Faith Tucker." It was her email exchange and handle… No, wait. It was an email conversation printed out. This wasn't her job account. This was personal. I knew the address from confirmations or forwards on things we reserved and booked. "Havefaith" and something else at Gmail. And, this was all with Victor's personal email address I never checked for business.

I sat on the floor against the chest and scanned this. It was certainly Faith.

"Just stay calm and be cool," I read. Yes, this is what Faith would say.

Then I read from Victor's reply: "That's kinda hard. This girl my wife hit is becoming something in the news. They're going to be looking at this."

Nothing about their spouses. Nothing about the kids. Nothing about their clubs and networks. Nothing personal at all. Lawyer to client it was.

Faith, can't get you on the phone. You're still in meetings.

Victor, we'll have to delete these emails.

She was passed out! I don't know how she even drove home. Never done it up like this before. I looked at the cam video out of curiosity. I was gonna have to tell the body shop and mechanics something. Faith, she nearly hit a tree then she hit a girl.

Remove the dashcam's SD card and get a new one. Splice out video of the accident and copy them in a separate file or format.

Already done. I got the video editor and DVD burner down here in the studio.

"What?" I went back to make sure I read what I did. The email date leaped forward.

Meet at my office. It's privacy. No one there due to quarantine. Don't forget the video.

I'm shook. That girl was out of nowhere. Off the side. From the dark. Running. Right by the bridge we cross over the river. But the whole ride, Tragedy's dipping and diving. Could she really have been that messed up?

Victor, Tragedy's had a drinking problem for a while and it tends to get worse when people are in denial. Lucky she made it home. Don't email another word about the video.

I heard a door slam and pounding above. No! I was just thinking things. The only sound was the furnace already, warming time that tells me my fall birthday is coming and I shouldn't trust it. I was alone. I lowered inside my soul, my perspective and mind and bones all crashing down. The studio was so small. An old wine cellar tucked past a door I never passed, in a man's tunnel, a house on my back. I went over the past of the conversation and then I went forward.

Faith, I can't reach you. I can't wait on this. Getting rid of the files and DVD.

No. It's evidence. That can be turned in your favor. Keep it. But delete these emails.

Evidence my wife hit and run a girl who's missing now. Evidence of fleeing the scene of an accident. Evidence in a murder, possibly. This #RavenMcCoy situation is spreading. I cannot get mixed up in this. I've worked too hard. This woman is going to destroy everything.

If Tragedy left the girl dead on the road, somebody would have found her body where it was left by now. So it can't be homicide. Maybe she got up with internal injuries. Maybe she jumped in the river. Maybe she's off with a man and they don't even know anybody's looking for her. There is no body. It's just Tragedy clipping her on a road. It's no homicide.

They couldn't be talking about me. I trembled, scarcely able to read the words.

Getting rid of the video. We're not part of it. The story's set. It's done.

No! Don't expunge evidence. It was an accident. She was drunk. Calm down. Act concerned and act normal and don't say a word. It's all clean. Tragedy Lawson. Hope Lawson. I checked. You're good. No violence, no charges. Loitering at 23. Nothing. It's an historical item.

It's not history. This Raven girl is everywhere. And Tragedy's lost. She's nagging me to join search parties and post about the girl. She doesn't remember what she's done.

Good. Keep it that way. The less people know the truth, the better.

I was sober now. Not a drop all day. Or the day before, either. No urges, only waits for Victor to depart so I could look for what I felt. Now, I had a DVD I wanted to break in two.

But it's evidence, I thought, Faith's voice in my head.

So are the emails. Victor was always so paperless, but he printed these out. This is something he never wanted to risk the internet pulling a fast one on him with. Finally, lastly, one of Victor's emails dated in the spring. Near the time Raven McCoy was found, near the time he disappeared for a Saturday morning

I was hung over and wrangling cops alone, near the time he returned to rescue me from the intimidating officers and he carried this manila envelope in hand.

Faith: The girl's found now, dead. Coming to get your copy of the SD video file. You were right. We're gonna need evidence we didn't throw her in a river.

My computer with a DVD player was upstairs. I'd have to go upstairs to get my laptop and bring it down to watch the DVD or watch it upstairs and bring it back. But no, this was sick.

What a load of bullshit people these were. What wild imaginations they had. Almost a year came flooding back to me. If this was not a joke, Victor had been my best friend and worst enemy. They were probably cheating. All this time, I thought it was Gloria and it was the one pretending to be my friend. At the end of the day, Faith always came from Victor's world.

The explanation for this was in the files. I would find it. I was better than they said.

I vibrated and sweat, in this crypt built for men by men. Without air it felt I was trapped and left buried alive. I left the papers on the floor to run outside just to take in breaths. I would go to Gracious, her farmhouse, to hide. She was more likely than those Pitts. After two years without their party or any acceptance of our invites, I'd forgotten the way to their home. They would send out nice reminders of themselves in between. No, Gracious would understand.

I returned. It was a small chance to take. I replaced the papers, envelope and files in Victor's neat way I knew. I replicated it behind him often because it's what he expected. Except for the DVD. It was mine, now. I walked slowly through my house, no rush. Nothing to fear, here. To my office, for that laptop with the DVD player. Already powered up, as I told Victor I was writing tonight. I went into the master bathroom. I didn't lock the door. Victor would never.

The date on the record was late December. In the middle of the night. I saw nothing at first but all I knew: a maddening dark requiring nerves of steel to navigate to homes to brag on. From outside real view in real time, the landscape was more sinister and lonelier than I realized.

And Victor was right: The girl who tumbled out of it was the girl everyone looked for.

I knew signs of life. I thought I saw them in the body the video had no full frame on. She appeared in widths and fragments, not even identifiable but by the story of her. It was movement and breath. The body rolled. The arms moved. I thought I heard "Help." It was wishful thinking.

The person watching the video will hear her before they see her. The camera angles catch what's in front, not on side. No hint from the cornfields dragging to a sudden break. Certainly no hint from the dark. Just a fast flurry out of the trees and black images they make. Then, a cry. A soft collision without an echo. The person watching will hear or watch me wait, as the camera does not move. I am just waiting. No movement or breath. I am frozen. Then, they will see the camera view pull back away from how far ahead it went. Revealing a figure on the road in front of it. A body. Hard to tell. A girl. Black. A thick line in the road that sticks out because gravel is light. The line is her long brown arm. Then the camera freezes more. Then, the truck rolls on.

And the person watching the video will see the only part I knew was true, that I had proof and certainty in myself to be able to see in my own head, that I knew without remembering I did.

I drove away.

Twenty-Eight

An agent from the FBI took her lunch break with the file on a Raven McCoy from the Grayson, Illinois, police because she was going on maternity leave and wanted nothing on her desk to haunt her. This wasn't possible, she knew. But, the little things were doable and this was a little thing. This happened all the time, all over the country. No others like it within the same area. Not another like it since. It was a misfortune, not a series or federal matter. Still, that Detective Giselle Wise was insistent and a woman, so Agent Jenny Light understood.

Wise knew they were privileged simpletons. Their police force broke up kids who were skateboarding and smoking weed. Or drinking beer near private properties at two in the morning. Her detective work stayed a nice cool drink of stolen car reports, since Grayson had the best of them, popular with crooks into that sort of thing. She'd done a few banks that had to blow up employees with sticky fingers. It was never disappearances, dead girls in rivers or sex rings for a whole office of unspecialized people to be thrown into. It wasn't entry and exit wound analyses, much fingerprinting, DNA sampling, or autopsies beyond old age and what the doctor diagnosed.

Wise had begged for the FBI help.

Light was sending Wise documents en route via air mail. A magnified, blow-up of part of Raven McCoy's postmortem left arm, loose and missing skin. Diagrams and index to go with.

"Tire tracks," she told Wise, in her office before a report from a break-in to a Glens house, where all the statements hinted to an inside job by an employee or wayward child.

"Really?" Wise said, setting that file aside and running with her cell to her ear.

Raven McCoy's file was on her totally detached partner's desk and he was off on cancer treatment this week. She had to keep Light on the phone while she guessed which pile it was. She was fortunate Agent Light even took her call back. She had missed Light's call earlier. Now Light was watching the sun go down on her last day at work before six months of bottles, fairy blankets and ointments became her shields against the madness she worked.

"The coroner messed up a note on the body diagram," Light explained. "He correlated dents on the back left arm as scars. But those aren't scars. They're impressions from tire tracks."

"Who could miss that?"

Wise had photographs of what they found in the river, moved from bags to slabs to tables to a hearse to another slab and hearse, finally to a simple cream coffin. It was hard to follow.

"He shouldn't have. But I worked a murder before the pandemic where tire tracks came up in it. They're all just now getting into court. Maybe my mind was on it."

"So, the tracks would've been new, fresh?"

"At least recent. But, nah, you can't tell those things from this state of decomposition, from a picture. Just a naked eye look and magnifying glass told me the note didn't match. You got a little bit of two grooves to work with, opposite each other, across and down."

"Any idea if a truck or a car or —"

"I'm not a tire specialist."

"Can we pass her on to one?"

"Good luck. There's a heavy backlog for ours I know off top of my head. They're all just contractors. And so many people hurting for money after the pandemic. Accidents are up. We've gotten put down for the insurance companies. They pay more. But I could try. After the baby. Or leave it for agents covering me. They're further behind. Anyway, there's a cost."

"That's fine," Wise agreed. "So, you think the victim was hit by a truck or car or —"

"Again, I don't know tires," Light said. "Just something I noticed from looking at these things every day for a decade. I'll say it's not a semi."

"No, those can't get too far in Grayson. But she was found in the river, not on the road."

"Getting your arm run over won't kill you. It'll hurt like hell. Maybe it didn't even happen from who or what killed her. I'd go on a hunch to say the arm was run over."

"She could've been fleeing somebody, jumping from a car."

"Well once they got somebody run over, that's it if they wanna kill 'em. That knocks victims out pretty bad. But I'd see more tracks on the corpse. Killing would've had him run over the torso. I would've seen it on the flanks. It's none of that. The internal exam report didn't find any blunt force injuries or chest compressions. Hit and run, maybe."

"An accident, instead of a killing and dumping in a river?"

"Either one. Whether it's a helpless girl or a dog, people hit things that fall and they back up to see if they hit it. If they're gonna run, they pull off fast and don't care if they hit it again. Some of these other notes could relate to that. I don't know. You should take another look at it."

"Right," Wise agreed, writing notes for Loveless or the sergeant and lieutenant or anyone who called the info line to help. Take another look. Take a different look. They were fine saying the victim wasn't from there. Men in Grayson don't use young black girls for sex parties. They could be fine saying she wasn't run over either. Wise would add it up for them.

"And she wasn't weighted or bound?" Light asked, suddenly.

"No," Wise answered. "No. Not even her hands. Her mother said she could swim."

"And she was dressed, right?" Light asked.

Wise could hear the small ice chips tinkling and the straw agitating the ice inside.

"Yes, right."

"Killers will weight or bind or undress a body. Unless it's the first time they've done it. They're nervous then. So, it could've been homicide. A first one. Again, nobody dies from getting an arm run over. Could've been running from something or somebody. Got hit by a car. Victims get up and keep going if they can, we find. But, getting hit wears 'em out pretty bad."

"Yeah, have you disoriented and terrified and wandering to the edge of bridges or banks or..." Wise said.

"What was that?"

"Nothing. I just said it's dark and scary enough out near Grayson Glens without being a hit and run victim."

The women wrapped up with talk of a due date and birthing plan.

Wise had it down to eight houses and male heads of them in Grayson Glens. Wise knew it. For all the size, many homes in the area weren't full houses. Kids were grown. Off at schools. More likely to find the new babies and middle-aged kids bringing their children out, and not much in-between. Many of these couples were for show, distant. They left each other a lot. This gave a man time and opportunity to keep a rotation of girls coming through and men for them.

Loveless was right: "Jay" couldn't be his name. No "Jays" owned a Grayson Glen house. The Glenner men whose names started with "J," and there were many, had old marriages or light houses. None were bachelors. It wasn't a place for much of that because the homes were too large. You're not right if you're a man living all alone in your own palace. Yet, three bachelors were owners past the Glen gates, having to pass the river. One was never at the house. He had inherited it. Two were. One of their houses was brown. The other's was stark white.

And from there, it was enough for Wise to count on one hand and a few fingers to explore. The men to narrow it down to. The men to set up surveillance around. The men who should pay for luring girls from sixteen and the latest music and boyfriends to unrealistic dreams for sex. The men who would charge against her and Grayson for false, smearing accusations.

But Dawn was back to reasons she couldn't get off from the buffet or miss her classes.

"It would really help if you drove around here with me to try to remember a route or identify a house," Wise pleaded. The Wells Police had gotten her call and Dawn's story.

A black male officer grew up down in Wells. It was a few of them in the mix. He called Wise to tell her he believed her. No, this isn't normal. Yes, we should care. "I know that little girl Dawn, and her mother and father too," Officer Shakespeare Gold said. "I'll go talk to her."

But the best friend was disenchanted. She didn't want Raven's car. She didn't want to stay connected on socials in memoriam, the custom now. She didn't want to be a witness in courts. If Wise couldn't lock her into a statement and the DA had to subpoena her, Wise couldn't predict what Dawn would get up in front of jurors and say.

Wise received Light's copies and understood what she saw now. Tracks were clear once somebody pointed them out. She had a cousin who was a mechanic back in Michigan. She could get the evidence to the local tire shop and car dealerships. All of them she would cover, then she would get to narrowing the vehicles. "It is possible a Glenner would hit a girl and throw her in a river to hide it," she told her team. They had questioned as many as they could, the team told her. It wasn't a big force. "You gonna go 'round measuring tires?" one of them laughed.

In Raven's file Wise took home, because her husband was out that night, she went through to notes from the local car body shop. Due to the nature of what the missing person's report and Gracious Davidson's claim came to be, an abduction and murder in Grayson caught the force off guard at Christmas. They'd only expected a break-in or two for gifts.

Back in December, it was originally Wise's idea to check on car details in the area. Her male coworkers weren't thinking like her, as men didn't want other decent men bothered. They didn't see the people they protected and served as predators. So now, months later and with the force caring even less about Raven McCoy, Wise went back to Luxury Vehicle Works alone.

The owner wasn't there. The mechanic who ran things in his absence was. Wise remembered questioning the man there that week Gracious Davidson sighted Raven at Goodness Gracious Day Spa. Like all the men, he had an alibi. And he hadn't had many customers and cars to discuss. In the pandemic, people weren't going out enough to care if their cars gleamed and impressed. It was the regulars and seniors who just set the dates for detailing as something to do. It was the area's Uber drivers who used them as a hub, also slowed with little to travel riders to.

And it was a Jeep. Nothing special about that, Wise thought.

A black car was on her mind. The Jeep was black.

"What was the Jeep in for?" she asked.

"Body work to the front passenger bumper, some scrapes, interior and exterior detail…"

"Lemme see."

She saw the name and remembered somewhat. The Powells. Yes, a newer couple. It wasn't too many black people in Grayson Glens. She went to a square on the page for scribbling notes. She deciphered "Owner drop off" and "Hit a deer" and "J.N."

"What's J.N.?"

"That's me. We initial our work. So, I did that one."

J.N. gathered the papers from Wise as she put him in her mind as just a "Jay."

"Yeah, I came in to finish some stuff before Christmas and guy was shocked to find me on Christmas Eve. Lemme see. I remember this. Black guy. Really cool. But, the deer part. That's just what he said."

"What do you mean?"

"Well, he didn't hit no deer. Wasn't enough damage for it. Could've been. Not likely."

"How would you know?"

"I got people who hit deer come straight to me all the time. And I'm a hunter."

"Why would he lie?

"You'd have to ask him."

By late September near to October, Wise's husband was joking Raven McCoy was one of their children. She had moved into the house. She had dinner with them. She slept in the finished basement they used to have Super Bowl parties and great sex in. The eight "Jays" on her list were all their separate files. Each one had a reason not to be likely, according to her partner or boss. The Chief thought this was all a mistake. Nothing was proven.

"The proof is there if we find it," Wise said.

"We don't have the manpower and time," Loveless said.

Officer Bobby Castle was manpower with time to kill. But it wasn't that kind of force. It was just, now, he was re-examining things. No reason, only naturally. The woman he was cheating with had gotten complicated like the others without a man. He was noticing they had tit for tats. He was stuck at the same pay as he was two years ago. No incidents. Good record. Just stuck. More and more, Wise was there later as he was just getting started. She was a nice start to impressing somebody up to a promotion.

"This late, still?" he asked. "And for what now?"

"Nothing new. Just Raven McCoy."

"Still? I could've helped out with that."

Wise knew he could have. Her bosses and co-workers were family men. Dulled in routine, domesticity and time. Bobby Castle was close to the moment. He wasn't at privilege to know about possible Glenner sex rings yet. Orders were to keep it quiet. The news certainly couldn't hear a thing. Loveless told her it was because men like this were smart with money. They knew how to act. They could disappear. Wise knew the bigger part was a code in Grayson that had to do with money and white people and their lives. It only took more and more. No one could deny the evidence. Then she'd file her case and Grayson would deal with it. It was her job.

"You could've helped. In fact…"

She flipped through papers and pulled out a gruesome photo, invoice, and diagram.

"Well, I have tire sketches I think could match this couple's Jeep here. Original Firestones that come with the vehicle. It looks like this traction scheme matches up with these bruises on Raven's body. Somewhat. I can't tell. I'm not a tire specialist."

Castle came to see like he knew what he was looking at.

"Could be," he said. "Well, could be other pairs too. You need more to tell for sure."

"That's what I thought," Wise said. "Or a real tire specialist and resources and staff."

"I'm gonna put in for some things if they ever open up," Castle said.

Wise would speak up for him, if she liked him, he thought.

"Who owns the truck?" he asked her. He knew people, a little.

"Victor and Tragedy Powell. The Glens, Calliope Lane."

He felt he was just Gracious's plaything. She didn't love him. She used him for a real man, unlike that neglectful clown selling dining room tables and dressers on TV for thirty years. He cared for her, was in love with her once. He never thought about if or how it will end. He thought on how many times Gracious had mentioned Tragedy and said, "I know the couple."

Wise was itching to break the case to the whole force. The dozen or so beat cops, like Castle. They had drinks, dinners and days on boats with faces, names and personalities she didn't have to see until serious problems. "Not yet," Chief Loveless admonished. She followed orders. *Damn them*, she thought of the men outside the door, and the few women who just went along.

"What's that couple like?" she asked Officer Castle.

"I don't know them. They're the ones when that Chicago girl was supposed to be missing, but wasn't —"

"Oh right, the false report. Young black female running the roads in the dark one night."

They had never investigated that girl. They simply trusted the couple. But they didn't know the couple. They knew the address. Wise wrote a note: "Go back to kidnapping false report and get the girl's name."

"Wife's a lush," Castle quipped.

"Missus Powell?"

Wise recalled the woman she met, somewhat. Nothing seemed off until her husband showed up, defensive and guarding.

"Oh yeah. Big one. I stopped her once. Never seen her before. But I saw her a little more over the summer and remembered that's who it was. She was driving sloppy. I made sure she was alright. She was by home, so I let her go. I looped behind with my lights off to be sure."

More notes. Wise would have to check the route to that house. She thought Calliope Lane was over the bridge and off sections where the riverbank was in falling distance from the road.

"Did you do a DUI report?" she asked Castle.

Wise was his superior, but she knew the rules. Grayson was low crime. No, almost no crime. The call or problem or concern had to be super serious for them to document it. There were almost no drunks in Grayson. No thefts or robberies. No bruised women and children. No rape at all.

"I checked her license, registration and insurance," Castle said. "She was right by home."

Wise nodded. Castle was messing up. Now he had told her and she could tell somebody. He didn't sense that type, but a few on his beat had started asking him why he was so slow to the radio. He didn't know if he was being watched. That was the problem with Gracious. Her life — her business and her home and her man — kept him caught, compromising his job to find her.

"And she runs with Gracious," he said.

This was his job. But they weren't supposed to be on a first name basis.

"You know, Gracious Davidson?" he corrected. "I check her spa a lot when I'm on."

"Of course. Gracious is friends with Tragedy Powell now?"

"Yeah, they just got really close. And, well, Gracious just told me Tragedy Powell loves to get drunk. But hell, so does Gracious."

"Oh yes," Wise smiled. "Everybody knows Gracious Davidson loves to get drunk."

Castle turned to leave but Wise stopped him to ask pointed questions about the Powells and their sex life. Castle didn't know anything about that. He told Wise Gracious Davidson never said the wife said the husband was dealing with other women, certainly not young girls.

Agent Light's ideas came up in Wise's mind. What she said.

Whether it's a helpless girl or a dog, people hit things that fall and they back up to see if they hit it and if they're gonna run, they pull off fast without caring if they hit it again. Some of these other things could relate to that. I don't know. You all should take another look at it…

"But we need proof," Chief Loveless said.

A few days later, Wise felt silly with the real camera she bought out of town, where nobody knew her. She'd find proof, not bullshit detective work they counted on a phone now. She had the right thing. Spying and ruining her marriage. Working while virtual reality and food deliveries mothered her children. She didn't need the Nikon's long-range lens. Glenners stuck in their houses and didn't look past their yards, or pretended not to. Nobody noticed her beige Volvo, not the force's vehicle. She circled and circled Calliope Lane to think and watch.

The black woman was pretty and she looked young. Not like a drinker, at all. But black women had strong skin and more collagen to do them favors. Wise had gone back to Castle because she could tell he was itching for more to do.

"Nah, husband's too vain to get off into much drinking," he

said. "Least that's what Gracious said. Wife was in some rehab and didn't even tell the guy."

Wise sat and watched with the week's plan in her mind. The black officer in Wells had agreed to tag team Dawn with her. She was feeling more certain she'd get Dawn's statement.

Then, some husbands and bachelors in Grayson would get her knocks to their doors. Castle would go with her. He wasn't being used. After all, she'd argue, she's not just a detective under orders but a woman who needs protection in a place where women wind up in rivers.

When she slapped down shots of what was left of Raven post-mortem, it would be easy to judge her suspect's reactions. She would vex them with comparisons from a woman's real self they destroyed, peer at their shock and guilt. They would remember ramming her down with their vehicle, how she screamed and ran and tried to survive. Or they would recall finding her hit, maybe, and finishing her off. They had to react. Any one who disappears would be her man. His flight would be the kicker to get the F.B.I. to know real criminal charges were in pursuit, to hunt a wealthy white man wanted for questioning about a young black woman who disappeared.

The Powell's nice-sized house was a special and distinct color Wise would have chosen. But Wise didn't have that much choice given what she and her husband made to fit in with the Grayson population on. She watched the woman come home with groceries, another woman to help. A mother, maybe? Through all the picture windows, a glass house she couldn't afford, Wise saw the two women talk and live over two days. Yes, a wine glass in hand for the woman, the long lens showed. The husband never came to sight. That was the Grayson norm, though.

What came when Wise gave up on this was Gracious Davidson's Velar up Tragedy's circle drive, about the time that spa closed. Glenners didn't visit each other much. Otherwise, the place would be a high school and drive-in at once. The people only went out together, mostly.

So Bobby Castle had been right. Maybe the women really were friends and Gracious knew what she was talking about.

She called up the young officer.

"Castle, I think I can use your help on the McCoy case. Maybe we can start with checking out this Powell couple, as you were right about Gracious hanging with the wife."

He answered, "Just tell me what else you want me to find out," without any hesitation.

She could see inside the house to Gracious and Tragedy at a table, clinking glasses.

TWENTY-NINE

"Going out with Gracious!" I yelled to Victor, already out the doorway. "Get Merit's number if he calls."

My husband gave me a thumbs up. "I love you," he mouthed. I smiled back.

Two new engagements for clients. He was going to be a guest on a podcast himself, and it was a podcast giant. Just readying the soundproof domain he kept from me for his show time.

I saw my husband, but I barely looked at him anymore. I smelled like expected, all my perfumes and moods he'd learned so soon. I was everything he expected, as always. He expected I'd sail along in his life and never give him traction. He expected a faithful sidekick. I wore what he expected, sunglasses and a sweater and a light vest jacket as my wardrobe to warm up for winter reclusiveness. My late October birthday was always cold. Half the time I knew him, we made no big plans or any plans far from home for it. This year, since we were free now, it was big plans far from home: flying to somewhere he wouldn't tell me. I just had to wait and see. We would post my reaction in real-time and I'm sure was supposed to look surprised for the audience.

Nobody came to that part of the river I drove up to. I had recognized or found the setup of the trees, felt the low number of worrisome seconds past the bridge. I went back to an estimate of it. It took many views of the video to add it and remember it. I measured with my eyes. The boathouses across the river seemed like vacant forms to the landscape. Even the water was still, in autumn. I guessed Raven was strong. She wouldn't have rolled and wobbled and toppled into a cold river in the dark from here. Girls like us fought. I didn't hit her hard. Hardly a sound.

I hulked over the spot where I guessed we had been and her body had fallen. The distant cornfields were low and dead like I felt inside. I wriggled through shrubs almost as tall as my young self, swept back thick columbine and crushed Jacob's Ladder. I felt where her body may have rolled over. I ignored the owls who let me know I was watched. I shut out sounds of bats' wings, early because October was coming to a close and we had almost no daytime anymore.

Soon, it would be a year her mother and people were without her. They had to be used to it, more. It was no use begging the secret to be undone. It was only to keep it. #RavenMcCoy was no longer a trend. It was no longer a story. No one was looking for what happened.

I didn't catch myself tilting down the riverbank, the spikes on my boots keeping me upright. I was a monster. It was no excuse. I'd survived hell as a young woman I wanted to forget I'd been, only to send another one to hell. Down, down, down onto that riverbank dancing until she was clumsy and maybe I made her that. It was so easy to fall now and I was sober, not in any pain, running from nothing. It would've been easier for her to do that night, how I left her.

I was a monster who left her for dead or deader for someone else. Maybe just for dead.

Yes, I thought, water up to my knees, *the Grayson River's easy to fall into.*

In the center between opposite banks, I saw Raven. She held her head back and floated in peace. Her pink wig's hair flared around her and she floated easily. I was starting to her. We would go where the river took us together. But I heard a shout. A man's voice. That deep howl. The water up to my waist, a current. Scarier than the river was the man shouting and shouting at me. He was a figure across the river. Oh no, he'd have to fly or speedboat to get to me. Finally, a shotgun blast. Then another, a sky exploded to black birds, sending me back, away from her.

I looked up. I came to. I felt myself frozen with water up to my knees. Then, I heard another shot. *"Hey! Hey, stop... Stop!"* a voice called out across the water.

Raven McCoy's spirit was gone.

I was drenched and climbing the bank, racing to my car. From so far, the man with the gun couldn't see that I was black, or it was a Chrysler or anything to tell the authorities about a woman walking herself down into the Grayson River just past the bridge on way to the Glens.

I struggled fast inside the car and revved it up to 50 miles an hour in no time.

This was speeding, believe it or not.

"It's all wrong!" I screamed.

I'd never fit. I had never wanted this. I had only wanted out and into my own home.

I never wanted the isolation and estrangement, an entire solar system revolving around a marriage and a man. The baby was around the corner. I could feel the urges growing for a new life into this one based on him. What Gloria knew and had with him. An increase in ties and variety to care to make it with each other for. We put down so much on the house it was doable. A few years of going hard, then back to the cities. Maybe he'd get hired in L.A. Just not here.

I slowed down and should have known: No one was following me. I had probably only imagined being seen. I was no one worth paying attention to. For what?

I'd done nothing wrong.

Was this how guilt felt? If so, I wouldn't be able to take it much longer. The view to my eyes came in fine lines now, every part and sound. The guilt was even more multiplied in my home. For weeks, I had scripted what to tell my husband so he'd know we shared the secret, but I had yet to say the words. I was parked in front of the Pitts property. I was sober. Still, I forgot the whole drive there. I heard a leaf blower but I saw no one outside. I considered running to the doorbell. I wondered if the Missus would make tea and serve cake if I appeared at her door suddenly, to spill my story. Would I be welcomed into her bubble or put out?

The likely answer led me to Gracious's road in my aimless driving. I was careful not to stop or slow too much as I drove past. I could bash a paned window to her farmhouse, easily. We both confessed we hadn't upgraded our sensors and rarely updated security apps. She had brick cheeses, sweets and wine in the cabinets. Great towels ordered from the same place she ordered them for the spa. I'd leave off the lights or find angles not to be detected at. She only took people to the first floor, never the top or the cellar. If push came to shove, I could buy myself a few days here if I really had to.

These are things Merit would know how to handle, but I couldn't risk a word to him at all, and certainly not on the phone.

But no one knows you did anything, I reminded myself.

And I knew I did nothing. I did not kill anyone.

Gracious's road seemed so much shorter when I was stalking it. Since it wasn't nearly as long as I'd always thought, I left there as well. I'd have to pack a way better bag than the one I had with me if I was going on the run, to become a fugitive instead of stay silent and wait or confess and see what comes next. The guilt of the present was heavier than my whole past.

*

Once when I was just past the age Raven would have been, I stayed at this apartment in the Chicago neighborhood I would wind up renting for real later, before I had a legitimate job in hotels. Some relatives answered my calls back where I was from. None knew the extents. Most offered nothing. Sometimes, I'd get wired a hundred dollars or so. This one huge house was three separate apartments on each floor and girls could go to all three. Not women, just girls.

"None of them old hoes," the men who run it all said at the door. "Her again? Hell nah!" And always, "Bitch, don't bring your old ass back here." It wasn't a hoe house. It was just a home. The girls or women who always looked younger but older at the same time didn't bring men there. We were just for the men who might let us in the door.

My turn came up when one wanted a good time with me. He was an old G Rasta near my father's age. I was always sleepy. Heavy shoulder bags wore me down, especially in heels or summer. I would've done anything not to leave the apartment, with a bed I had in a room only other women slept in. This was the winter, now. The City and State had warming centers. They were crowded and worse than bus stations. People in blankets and stages of sleep everywhere, a disaster like the decks of shipwrecks. It felt easier to sit tight in warm places with the price of men taking advantage of me.

I don't know what I did with the man or for him. I went along with all the drinks he gave me, to fade to black and feel nothing. For the next two weeks, he never touched me again. He gave me money and I bought fresh clothes. He bought groceries for the house, so I cooked instead of ate on the run. The nutrition pepped me up and bought me some time. The men loved my cooking. Still, it was best never to overstay welcomes. I saw that was how to get put in the place of women they put out. I just dashed off to the next place or places, well-rested and stronger for it now. I looked at the time I don't recall as a reboot of my system. I never called it a blackout.

And, I had survived it. When it went black that first time, I was shocked to come back.

*

The Grayson Herald had reported news a man in the area may be linked to Raven McCoy. Not a Grayson man. Not a Glenner. Just an "area man." An investigation pending.

I would have my fun. I brought that day's paper to bed.

"*The* Victor Powell," I teased. "Are you the man they're linking her to?"

I let my husband squirm me into other another subject. We were waiting for my birthday, a show *The Powellcast* had to put out. This was the second year of no housewarming party for my birthday. We didn't want the criticism of gathering during a pandemic. But, we both knew parties were out and producing life online was in. It had all worked out.

We had my glitzy #bday video scheduled for real production, a Hail Mary to hold on to all the online views and follows and requests and gigs now that people were living offline again. The ad revenues and sponsorships depended on people being online. We were losing money.

But after I viewed the video, I spared no expenses. I decided on feasts instead of meals. I went into Joy's territory. Everything was "organic" or "free" of something. Ifa and I assaulted the counters and tables with our finds. "We're gonna be having parties," I told her. My phone beamed with notifications and calls. So unimportant now — especially Faith's, unanswered.

Then, I stopped drinking. No urge. No tricks or apps. Not even food.

"Just soup and tea again, Tragedy?" Ifa asked me some days.

"That's it," I'd smile.

The last day I saw Ifa, I gave her an envelope.

"It's just between us," I winked. "Early Christmas bonus."

"You're such a doll, Mrs. Powell," Ifa sang out, to give me the hug of real family on her way to discovering $10,000 from our combination safe Victor told me was for emergencies.

For the last quarter of the year, Victor always expected me to really be checking the money. I always managed the basics. The smaller accounts to cover all the automatic payments: our websites, subscriptions, donations and such. The account for all our payables: the contractors, the servicemen, Ifa. The agency and business accounts for receiving. Victor liked the bigger expenses paid off in cash and so we did not have those, except for the mortgage on the house. Still, for a year, their numbers had flirted together and now they were hand in hand. But Victor had more money. He was a careful, frugal man by nature. He lived well, but he misered the long-term stashes. It was our joint accounts I needed to start with. There was mine to squeeze out. My own protections no one could touch, what I would need to defend myself well.

Victor made it easy for me to focus on my escape from our bubble of lies. A couple just stops touching each other. I was off into my world and things. He was in his. He seemed relieved at my nonchalance for his ex-wife's sneaky little calls over nothing and her silly fake niceness.

I wanted to talk, operate like his family would. I wanted to tell him what I knew and how I felt. He took my ghost and my truth. I wanted to ask him how he took my power to choose. He wouldn't do it my way because I would tell the truth and fight if I had to do it.

So I made the call in the dark. Outside, when Victor was sleeping without me beside him, as our marriage had required. He was off to JFK in the early morning for a conference. I didn't have a flashlight. Maybe I was finally used to the dark.

"911. What is your emergency?"

"I'd like to report a hit and run," I said.

"What's your location?"

"Grayson Glens. Calliope Lane."

"Are you safe? Is anyone hurt?"

"I'm fine. And yes, people are hurt. Many people have been hurt."

"How many? Emergency medical services we have a…"

I could hang up. I would join the nutty women Gracious laughed about. She said they just did things like call 911 or go to hospitals with breakdowns because they get attention. Or, they stayed seeing things and people. She had a police officer friend who told her he responded to this all the time. Women in Grayson Glens and their loneliness or threats that weren't there.

"Don't worry. Help is on the way. Just stay where you are. Did you see the accident?"

"Yes."

"And the driver just hit a car, a person?"

"A person."

"A man, woman, child?"

"A child."

"Did you see the car? Get a plate?"

"Yes. I saw it all."

"What's your exact on Calliope? Gosh you can't see any numbers on houses out there…"

A day I returned from an errand, the bank for a reason, Victor said "Merit called." He handed me a notepad with ten digits scribbled in a hurry. I called Merit back. My digits were not scribbled. I was neat. "You've got to have it somewhere," I wound up whispering. I was talking about a bank statement or checkbook. Preferably a checkbook, with the routing and account number I needed to transfer money. I expected too much. Merit's was a world of cash. I didn't have time for that. I wouldn't feel safe carrying it in the city. Still, I had to do it somehow. "Give me your username and password to your online banking," I told him. I got the numbers that way. It took some days to get $100,000 of what I could get out of our accounts whisked into his.

"I'm in my own house," I continued to the 911 officer now. "I was the driver. I'm the one who hit someone and drove away."

"I'm sorry?"

"*I* am the one who hit someone. I drove away."

"Tonight? I'm sorry, ma'am. I'm not following. Where are you located on Calliope?"

"No, this happened last year. It should be over. It should have never started."

"So, *you* hit someone last year and you're just now calling to report this?"

"Yes."

"Sheesh. Well, who did you hit?"

Ifa would stay with Victor, for cheaper, I knew. And he had "friends." His people knew people. He probably wouldn't even lose the house. I didn't have to get him mixed up in it. He had lost the woman who made him who he was. I would tell the police that I'm the one who erased the dashcam and made the video of it. This was my evidence, Faith said. Yes, I hurt Raven McCoy. But I left her on the side of the road, alive. I had nothing more to do with their investigation to the area man who got her out in the dark or found her after I'd done my part.

"Raven McCoy."

"Raven McCoy? Raven… That missing girl? The one in the river?"

"Yes."

"But… How? Ok. What is your name ma'am?"

"My name is Tragedy Powell. And I'm an alcoholic."

By the moon it was on to the next day.

I turned 36.

THIRTY

The eight a.m. news anchors came up to inform me how many poor strangers died from gunshots that weekend in Chicago. I hit "Send" on an email, *The Girl Who Didn't Burn* manuscript attached, my full blessing for Patricia Rogers Lit to sell whatever I'd put down of my life. It wasn't the book I planned to write. That one to inspire and motivate. The TV was only on for the weather, to know what Victor was in the air flying through. "Stop" I told the screen. I missed ambient sounds I once committed to. I commanded the system to go into Zen mode.

Ginger tea was perfect. I'd given Ifa the day off. She would need it. Soon, she would be called to say what I'd said to police who came about that couple I lived with who hated each other, but the woman stayed for the children: "I didn't see anything." And Ifa would be honest.

I set a hissing tea kettle back onto the stove. I squeezed farmer's market honey into a Royal Albert teacup, a wedding gift from Faith. I blew ripples on the water, waited for a taste. I sipped and looked at my backyard. Already too chilly for gardens. The birdfeeder missing the sparrows. The dogwoods and elms shifted fast to colors, so they'd be bare soon. How little I used the wood swing I put up to meet reading goals on. I never slept in the hammock. I didn't finish writing my book on the veranda or in the backyard, writing "The End" from atop a blanket with a picnic basket, smoking a cigarette or drinking a glass of champagne to celebrate myself like famous writers do. I finished all I had to write at the dining room table when Victor was recording, the exhaustion of tears sending me to bed in pain and insomnia.

Suddenly, blue and red dots reflected off cabinets and back-splash I designed myself. Purposefully, to look like broken glass. Artsy but commonly so, seeing my face like a funhouse mirror in them. The driveway sensors did their job. An alert meant someone was coming.

I dropped the teacup. I slid across the kitchen's pecan floors. If we hadn't slacked on varnishing, I could have fallen. Broken neck. Bleeding on the brain. A jinx split-second end to life. The ultimate evasion. I walked to the front window seat to peek out of its lovely frosted decoratives and picturesque arches I customized myself. I was used to them so never saw them anymore. I was right: Police were here. I had called them to me, to us, to my wonderful life.

I ran.

I caught traction on hall corridor area rugs. The rugs covered my footfalls. The cops were already in the house. They must be. They would swarm — but nobody in eye's view knew us or talked to us anyway. We couldn't be embarrassed. The living plotted plants looked angry with me, frowned and bent, all of them tall from Ifa's watering and the sunlight through all the glass.

Life had capsized in two hours. I'd made love to my husband the first hour. Almost eight years after our first time, he still tangled me up by surprise. He could feel like a nuisance, even an assault. That morning was my turn. He knew it would happen. It was my birthday. We had tickets somewhere to really celebrate it when he returned from being more important. We were going to stretch out my holiday, lose our phones, and bond on a beach for all we survived — a year of isolation, lowered income, white people, Raven McCoy, Joy in love.

I wanted to tell him we'd have to leave the house, leave Grayson Glens, leave Illinois, leave Gloria and Joy, leave missing black women and secrets and lies and accidents, leave alcohol and followers and images. We couldn't leave each other. We only had so much time. His car was to arrive for the airport by seven a.m. on the dot. Off to his Superworld. Gone to be a star. Gone to do exactly what I dreamed he would and told him he could, my body feeling him when he's not there. I was a coward but maybe I had heart to leave him his ego for one last trip.

The tell-tale lights gave me a courteous head start. I tracked down the basic black tote I was using now. It set, like a black car waiting, in the bay window seats where I'd left it. I needed my cosmetic bag. I'd long outgrown those clear plastic envelopes, the glittery ones from Claire's and Forever 21 that junior high girls loved to unfurl from tissue paper in gift bags. Back in those days I overcame, I figured out those cheap clear things would just blend in with the whole house I needed my purses to be sometimes. I was a working girl. I had to stay ready for the gift of a meal and impressive bed for the night. I was a pro at making beauty my name, playing men to give me things, filling my body and mind with shames that drove me into the hotels the wrong way.

When I sophisticated on, to working a job and planning to fit normal women like no one had taught me, I grew into bright pouches with showy brand names stamped on. Department store "gifts" for us who spend more. I found a white patent leather rescue kit wedged into a corner of my tote. I trusted it to have something energizing in it. I found a strip of Juicy cologne torn from a *Vogue*. The rough strip scratched my neck. Tinted gloss on my fingertips, at the exact middle of my lips and apples of my cheeks. No mirror necessary. I tousled my curly twist out, fresh from my last Mario Tricoci salon visit. I smoothed down my long gray skirt and ivory t-shirt. Finally, to the shoe cubby. Black leather thongs waited bottom and center. I put them on.

I slid back the sheer lace panels at the blinds. Two male officers — one skinny and tall with dark hair, another his opposite — strode across my lawn, the white and maroon Grayson Police Department car at ease in my circle drive. More sirens or another siren. All the same now.

The cello music the digital system suggested was light as a feather, interesting and ironic.

Elusion was a possibility. At my best, when I wasn't drinking too much, I was a treadmill jogger and a biker. I did yoga and Spin. I slung my bag over my shoulder. I tackled the winding stairs. The banister stressed under my weight, helping me hurl to the top. I looked out the glass.

Here was that detective, a woman, who prowled with her questions. I thought I saw her, too. The backyard was where I would end up after I pushed out an upstairs window screen, rolled down the back roof slope, landed on the veranda roof and then its bottom. Then, limping or concussed, I'd crawl acres of Illinois woods stretched for many more acres, to the city interstate. I could hitch escape, follow the North Star to Canada as an American Dream refugee. I could be a nudist colony tent dweller who caught fish for food and made campfires with hippies.

The lower egress windows could save me a risky jump. But those sliding doors could…

I froze.

The nearly evening daylight fused with the elegant music and view across the street. Altogether, they showed me everything my drinking put at risk. Still, who were the neighbors in the sun-bleached or earth-colored houses we all looked at every day, with dainty window boxes emptied of summer flowers and autumn leaves their new ornaments? What were their names?

A soft spider presented itself. It arrested my planning and finalized my choice. I would stand in my house and watch a spider work its web between porch lights and window ledges.

My purse would have its contents seized with everything I thought I could depend on. *My wallet.* All the cards, of course, pictures of my Merit, mother and Gran. *Cash* — at least a grand or two at the ready. My whims and needs never down to the authority or permission of numbers, chips and clerks. *ID.* Always the same face, new names. Hope Lawson. Tragedy Lawson. Tragedy Powell. *House keys.* I could, maybe, return home after a little questioning. They could believe me and I could bail out. *Phone.* For my one call. Maybe it wouldn't be immediately confiscated. This was Grayson Glens. We had paid everything to be treated special. *Cosmetic bag.* To rescue my dignity with the same deft I'd just put it on with.

The DVD recording. I had my evidence. I was a drunk driver. I was certainly no killer. I might even become a moot point in their investigation to the white man who sent Raven McCoy running through our high-priced darkness, to escape men's sexual madness I knew the extents of.

One last thing. *That damned flask.* Victor's wedding gift. I ripped it out of my purse. I heard that once-soothing swoosh swish rock along inside. I rolled the flask into the cubby I retrieved the shoes from. Finally, I slipped off my wedding rings, clawed my fingers into the nearest potted plant, buried them for now. The soil's dregs speckled my feet.

Those cops were surprised when their suspect opened her door. My name moved — in an instant — from useless to a Grayson headline. A national one. Not super-duper news. Still, it was #RavenMcCoy. Hit and run. Leaving the scene of an accident. Something. And my husband tampered with evidence. Obstructed justice. It didn't matter I wouldn't tell the police his part. I was enough. Victor Powell's wife. Arrested. He was done, for now. His kind never stayed down.

My décolletage was misty. Fear and shame have their smells. At least a puff of good perfume arose from the handshake I offered.

"Hello — I'm Tragedy Powell. I'm the woman you're looking for."

I sailed alone in the back of a cop car, another behind it. I watched my lane in life go by. "Calliope Lane" it was called. The police cars passed our community's gate entrance. Bronzed maple leaves mutinied against it, where golden mums and their pearl-size buds were hanging in there. I saw the patina of fall the cities refuse to do justice. I learned the real personality of the seasons out here. The possibility of life with no flowers or greenery was a long, hard thought.

I turned my face away from the day's guard, a black man whose face and name I knew. It wasn't like Grayson Glens had that many of us. I'd been "professor's wife" one day and "that guy on TV's wife!" the next. But I never took time to know him closely. I turned my face and held my head down so this man who didn't know me at all wouldn't see me go out.

A siren's whirl is so much louder when you're captured than when you're free. I've seen and heard interviews with criminals whose names or sins I can't recall. Some of the ones who would say they really did it talked about relief when something they walked away from catches up. How they were almost happy it was over. How they were no longer scared. How they always knew they didn't get away with it. I took comfort in their confessions to sink into an undoing. It felt nothing like the frenzy I worked myself up to think it would be. It felt better.

The squad car rolled off the community's quiet and slow back roads. I watched Grayson Glens get smaller and less impressive the more distant it went, along with the shallow people in it and the person I became to become one of them.

ACKNOWLEDGEMENTS

Thank you to Kailey Brennan DelloRusso, founder of WriteorDieTribe.com, for organizing its pandemic quarantine novel writing group in late 2020. This online gathering renewed, restored and resurrected this novel before it passed as just another "Maybe one day..." file on my computer. The camaraderie and courage we writers displayed every two weeks over Zoom is an unforgettable part of my recent life. I owe all the writers who came into this group my love for their examples and feedback that kept me writing: Kristin Benoit, Nicole Borello, Diane Englert, Tamar Mekredijian, Rachel Prendergast, Narmin Shahid and Rishitha Shetty.

To special Chicago friends and neighbors Terry McAfee, Keren Joseph, Khalia Poole, Lori Miller Barrett and Tiffany Gholar for the dinners, pow-wows over the book and career push. Also to friend and New York state novelist Jenny Milchman and my Kansas City cousin Maria North-Morgan for loving my initial ideas to write about women, materialism and alcoholism.

To Jennifer Lyons and all at her Jennifer Lyons Agency for believing in my writing and loving this book when it was only excerpts about a girl in a fire. All your feedback, love and care made this book and more writings possible to sprout from me over the years.

To all the readers and fans who continue to read, buy and teach my works — I am always, always writing all by myself for all of you.

And finally, my gratitude and forever "Black Power" fist to great literary friend Troy Johnson and his legendary AALBC.com, which I dreamed of being listed on when I was just a college English major, for picking up this novel as one AALBC would take a chance to publish in America. Being the first black writer and novel African-American Literature Book Club publishes actively is an honor and highlight of my career I am filled with pride and joy for.